BY TOM COOPER

The Marauders
Florida Man

FLORIDA MAN

FLORIDA MAN

A Novel

Tom Cooper

RANDOM HOUSE

NEW YORK

Published in the United States by Random House,
an imprint and division of Penguin Random House LLC, New York.

RANDOM HOUSE and the HOUSE colophon are
registered trademarks of Penguin Random House LLC.

Hardback ISBN 9780593133316
Ebook ISBN 9780593133323

Grateful acknowledgment is made to Lee Ofman for permission to reprint
"Miami Dolphins No. 1" by Lee Ofman, copyright © 1972 by Lee Ofman.
Used by permission. All rights reserved.

Printed in the United States of America on acid-free paper

randomhousebooks.com

2 4 6 8 9 7 5 3 1

First Edition

Book design by Elizabeth A. D. Eno

To my brother, Michael Paul Cooper

Solastalgia: a longing for the world as it should be, for nature when there's no nature left.

—Robert Macfarlane, from *The Lost Words*

We are tied to the ocean. And when we go back to the sea whether it is to sail or to watch it we are going back from whence we came.

—President John F. Kennedy

We are the ageless, we are teenagers
We are the focused out of the hopeless
We are the last chance, we are the last dance
—Public Image Ltd., "One Drop"

Levels rising on the island / Shows no sign of soon subsiding.

—David Berman, as Purple Mountains,
"Snow Is Falling in Manhattan"

There is no time.

—Lou Reed, "There Is No Time"

Suspect every man. Ask no questions. Settle your own quarrels. Never steal from an Islander. Stick by him, even if you do not know him. Shoot quick, when your secret is in danger. Cover your kill.

—Old Conch saying

Miami has the Dolphins
The Greatest Football Team
We take the ball from goal to goal
Like no one's ever seen
We're in the air, we're on the ground
We're always in control
And when you say Miami
You're talking Super Bowl
'Cause we're the . . .
Miami Dolphins,
Miami Dolphins,
Miami Dolphins Number One.
Yes we're the . . .
Miami Dolphins,
Miami Dolphins,
Miami Dolphins Number One

—Lee Ofman,
"Miami Dolphins Fight Song," 1972

Contents

CATEGORY FIVE
APHRA
AKA
LANDFALL IMMINENT
(2008–2019)

Characters

MAIN PLAYERS

REED CROWE, proprietor of the Florida Man Mystery House and Emerald Island Inn

HENRY YAHCHILANE, ex-military, semi-retired, jack-of-all-trades

HEIDI KARAVAS, painter and art curator, ex-wife of Reed Crowe

WAYNE WADE (aka Cool Papa Lemon, aka Mr. Video), factotum, Reed Crowe's childhood friend

HECTOR MORALES (aka Catface), Mariel Boatlift survivor, assassin

EDDIE MALDONADO (aka the Coca-Cola Kid), ersatz boatswain, student

OTHER PLAYERS

ANDREW FREDERICK KRUMPP, proprietor of Red, White and Blue Liquor

BARRY BOONE, pyrotechnics expert, Big Gorilla Fireworks

CHARLEY ALEXOUPOBULOS, hardware store owner

CHILL NORTON, owner of The Pervy Mermaid

FONG, attraction owner

XVI CHARACTERS

GABBY VU, physician

JERRY VOGEL, yachtsman, playboy

LEON CAESAR ARANGO, Cuban refugee

LILY CROWE (aka Otter), Heidi Karavas and
Reed Crowe's daughter

MARIPOSA ARANGO, Cuban refugee

MARLON ARANGO, Cuban refugee

MOE REYNOLDS, ornithologist, Myrtle's girlfriend

MYRTLE BREEDLOVE, mailperson

NATASHA YAHCHILANE, Henry Yahchilane's daughter,
financier

NATE STERNBERG, deputy officer

NINA ARANGO, Cuban refugee

PETROWSKI, deputy officer

SEYMOUR YAHCHILANE, Henry Yahchilane's son,
professor of art therapy

SHELLY CROWE, ex–Weeki Wachee mermaid,
Reed Crowe's mother

ZIGGY SCHAFFER, sheriff of Emerald City

TROPICAL STORM

A Falling Meteorite of a Man

(1963)

THE BOY CAME INSIDE THE GIRL.

Reed Crowe rolled off Heidi Karavas with a final shudder and moan and lay next to her in the gunwale of the rocking aluminum skiff. Some wee morning hour, the August air sticky with heat. The planetarium of the Florida sky, a thousand score of stars strong, glimmered down. The vast Everglades was stretched in every direction around them, miles upon miles of black swamp and saw grass hammocks and mangrove thickets. And to the west on the distant shore, like votives arrayed along an altar, shined the lights of Emerald City, town of Crowe's birth, the beach houses and shanties and houseboats with windows aglow.

The boy and girl were still catching their breath when Crowe said, "Puerto Rico."

Heidi asked Crowe if he pulled out in time. He told her he did. The girl asked again. Crowe reassured her. And he was almost certain. Ninety-five percent certain. Still convincing himself, he said, "You hear me? Puerto Rico. How 'bout Puerto Rico?"

"You're drunk," Heidi said. She stood, hand on the gunwale, sweaty skin separating from the cold metal bottom of the boat with a tape-peeling sound. She picked up her mint-green panties. Slipped a thick shining thigh through a leghole, slipped the other leg through.

To the boy she was a vision. Her fulsome Greek figure, her wide hips. Her dark curly hair, sun-kissed from a summer almost past. Her blouse embroidered with little yellow and red flowers, the cotton startlingly white against her olive skin.

Crowe loved her.

She was seventeen, he on the cusp of eighteen.

In 1960 they'd met during Hurricane Donna, in Emerald City's hurricane shelter, a repurposed gymnasium. She was from south of Tarpon Springs, visiting her grandparents, a girl from a Greek sponging family, and right away Crowe knew he had to see her again. As soon as possible. And before Donna had scythed across the state, he asked her on a date.

Flaming Star with Elvis Presley.

Three years later here they were, Heidi asking what the hell was in Puerto Rico. She settled next to him, pillowed her sweaty cheek against his chest.

They smelled like each other. Briny animal teenage lust.

Crowe popped a match and lit a cigarette. In the brief flare of light his green eyes were smirking. "Pamphlet in the mail the other day. A sign. Selling nice little houses on the beach out there, for cheap. Little huts."

"You wanna live in a hut now," Heidi said.

"Nice huts. Place you could live like a king. Dollar a day."

"You'd die in two weeks."

They often played this game after lovemaking, talking about where they'd run away. Fantasies, pipe dreams.

He had no money. She had no money.

He had no plans except far-fetched.

In May, the destination was Rio de Janeiro. In June, Isla Margarita.

Somewhere far, far away from their warring families.

About this they agreed.

Heidi's clan, the Karavases, was leery of Crowe and his kin. Rightfully so. The history of the Crowes, among the first homesteaders in this outpost so far-flung in the jungly reaches of Florida, was long and sordid.

To the Karavas family, devout Catholics that they were, Crowe was guilty by association,

By blood, by birthright.

Wherever they ended up, the place had to be close to the water. They both loved the water.

And they both loved this place, Emerald Island. The only reason why they'd leave was their families.

Now Heidi asked Crowe, "You know one lick of Spanish?" Knowing damn well he didn't. Heidi, fluent in two languages, English and Greek. Three, counting the conversational Spanish she picked up from all the radio stations down south in Miami. When the weather was right and when the signal was strong, you could pick up the signals this far up along the Gulf Coast.

"Way you learn's living in the country," Crowe said, with as much authority as he could muster.

"I like how your voice sounds when I put my ear like this. The rumble."

Night creatures—insects and frogs and alligators—babbled around them.

A mosquito lit on Heidi's knee and she slapped it. She dipped her hand in the water, swished it, flicked off the drops. She wiped her fingers dry in Crowe's hair.

"Hey, goddamn it," he said. Kidding, leaning away. He smacked one of her fat brown ass cheeks. God, did he love her tan lines. Her ass.

She bit softly into his neck.

Crowe settled back and he went on. "Forcing yourself. Like throwing little kids in the water. Teaching them how to swim."

"You been throwing kids into pools?"

"Hola. Bueno. Coma estas." Crowe drew the last drag of his cigarette, put it out in an empty can of Hamm's beer. Little hiss.

"Nasty cigarette," Heidi said sleepily.

"I'll dive for sponges. Scrape barnacles off yachts. Empty slop buckets. Lots of possibilities."

Heidi cocked her head, held up a finger.

"Juggling," Crowe said.

"Shush," Heidi said. "You hear that?"

Crowe hushed.

They listened.

Now they both could hear it. The *put-put-put* of a small engine, a mile-high mechanical cough.

The *put-put-put* grew closer, louder.

And now they could see it, a small two-prop plane coming toward them, quickly shedding altitude. They could see the flashing beacon on the tail. The jerking navigation lights on the tips of the wings.

Then flames engulfed the fuselage. Metal shrieked and ripped.

A rudder broke free as the craft fell farther yet, closer yet.

A fulminating dragon in its death spiral.

Crowe saw something shear loose from the plane. Another part of the craft, he thought at first. But no, the flaming part was moving, screaming.

A man was dropping from the sky headfirst. Like a daredevil. His arms were pinwheeling, his legs scissoring, his body flailing like he was fending off a frenzy of hornets.

And then about a hundred yards away the falling man walloped the water, landing in the fringe of weeds circling a mangrove islet.

Still the plane spiraled, now so low and close Crowe could feel the heat on his face, the sting of fumes in his eyes.

Without thinking and without warning Crowe hooked his arm around Heidi's waist and he tossed them overboard. All he heard was her little crying yelp before they went under clinging to each other.

Then the water jolted massively as if meteor-struck.

A roar of sound. An underwater supernova of light.

Crowe and Heidi flailed against the undertow.

They surfaced, gagging and retching against smoke. The wreckage of the plane flamed around them. Gobs of fiberglass and plastic so hot the little fires sputtered green and purple and blue.

Several yards away their capsized boat bounced on the big black waves. They frog-paddled back to it. Crowe flipped the boat over and pulled himself in. He took Heidi's hands and hoisted her out of the water and they sat gasping for breath.

"I wanna go home," said Heidi Karavas. Her voice was pleading, her eyes pure devastation. Like Crowe she was shivering and soaked.

Crowe told Heidi, "We gotta go over there." He didn't like how his voice sounded. Scared, boyish.

"No, no, no." She was sobbing. She gripped Crowe's arm, her fingers digging. "Just let the police."

"People," Crowe told her. "Never find this place again."

"Don't be stupid. Don't be crazy."

"Oh man. People. They're people, look. No, don't. Don't look at them."

"Are they dead?"

Crowe didn't answer.

Heidi asked Crowe again.

"Yeah, yeah, they are."

It took him several minutes to oar the distance to the wreckage and he did it alone. Heidi would not look. Could not look. She had her knees drawn up and her arms circled around her legs, her head hung down.

When they drew closer he saw the bodies in the water. Three men, charred and smoking. Dead.

"What's that smell?" Heidi cried.

Crowe didn't answer.

The nearest man lay belly-up in a stand of cattails, half his face scalded off so his jawbone showed through. Two other men bobbed in the water near the plane, the flesh of the bodies still aflame, their limbs skewed in angles anatomically impossible. Rag dolls twisted amok.

A hot swell of nausea rose in Crowe's guts. He leaned over the gunwale and retched up a spate of Hamm's beer. He cupped a handful of water, splashed it over his mouth and face. He spat, but his mouth was dry.

He forced himself still. He stared into the dark and waited. When his eyes adjusted, he spotted them floating in the water. Five or six bale-sized packages, wrapped tight in plastic and burlap and twine.

Crowe took the oars and he shoved them closer. He grabbed one of the floating parcels and heaved it onto the boat. Maybe sixty-five pounds, maybe seventy, whatever it was.

Crowe had a good idea.

He was almost sure. The smell, pungent and sticky.

But he dug his keys out of his jeans pocket anyway. Tore into the package with a key and reached into the hole. Even before he pulled out the leaves the stink was unmistakable.

A bale of marijuana, dank Colombian.

What locals called a square grouper.

"Goddamn," Reed Crowe said. "Oh shit."

Heidi knew damn well what the smell was. She smelled it often enough on Crowe. Now she was telling him again that if he didn't take her home now, she was never talking to him again.

Crowe was all but deaf, he was so rattled and chock full of adrenaline.

A fresh shock went through him when he thought he saw one of the burned men watching him. The man closest, who lay burning in the cattails. A pain-crazed eye fixed on him and stayed riveted. His skin smoked and bubbled. The tatters of his clothes smoldered on his scorched body.

Reed Crowe stopped and waited. He stared into the dark. He called out.

"Hello?" Crowe said with his hands cupped around his mouth. "Mister, hey?"

"Who're you talkin' to?"

"Don't look."

She told Reed he was being an asshole. That he was being dangerous, like his father.

Crowe only said, "Keep your eyes closed."

"God. Damn. It."

Crowe called out again into the dark and waited. He could hear the blood whomping in his head.

The insects, hushed by the crash, were slowly resuming their chorus.

Then the man's eye went dead, a lifeless matte.

An optical illusion, Crowe convinced himself.

Nerves.

Still he waited a moment until he was convinced he'd seen a mirage, that his mind was playing tricks.

It was another half hour before they reached the harbor. By then Heidi was so scared and angry she was no longer speaking to Reed Crowe. She stayed pilled into herself like a kid in a middle-school tornado drill.

The harbor lot was empty save for Crowe's brand-new orange hatchback. Before he got a chance to rope the skiff into its berth, Heidi was already out of the boat stalking down the length of the pier. She went straight to the hatchback and slammed herself inside and stayed there.

Crowe off-loaded the bale. He was running on adrenaline alone. He was sore-boned and his legs felt like gelatin. He wondered what his next move would be.

He knew he would call the police about the crash at a gas station pay phone. He would disguise his voice to sound older than he was and he would try to keep the fear and guilt and uncertainty out of it.

And the excitement.

He would mention nothing about the weed. He would hang up before they had a chance to ask about anything.

Paranoid they were already on his trail, Crowe glanced over his shoulder as he shoved the bale into the trunk, but the road abutting the harbor was empty still of morning traffic, such traffic as there was in this outpost.

Morning was beginning its first blush over the tops of the trees. A baleful wind moved through the pines. Crowe could not shake the feeling the trees were watchful. Reproachful.

When Crowe got behind the wheel he reached for Heidi. At first he thought she was crying but she slanted away and said, "Take me home. Now."

Her voice was choked with anger.

Crowe knew her well enough to know any words he said now would be wasted.

But while trying to banish from his mind those burning bodies, those ravaged faces, the angry dead eye watching him in the dark, Reed Crowe said to Heidi Karavas, "This is going to change our life."

And he thought it was so, knew it was so, a certainty he felt in blood and bone as still sopping, reeking of the sulfur swamp, he drove them home.

CATEGORY ONE

GROTTO

(1980)

THE SINKHOLE

IT WAS A THREE-ASPIRIN MORNING, THE day after the anniversary of Reed Crowe's daughter's death, the eve of his ex-wife Heidi Karavas's return to the island after one of her long trips abroad, and something was amiss. So amiss that Crowe stopped stirring the sugar in his Café Bustelo and set down his spoon on the kitchen island and pondered what it was.

His head, like a Magic 8 Ball these days. The pot, the wine. YES. NO. MAYBE. TRY AGAIN LATER.

Mostly the latter.

Sometimes he wondered if he wasn't losing his mind, like his mother, living almost five years now in a Fort Lauderdale nursing home. Early onset dementia.

Now Crowe looked through the Gulf-facing windows of his beach house, scratching his beach bum beard, blinking groggy blinks behind his green-tinted aviators.

Yes, something was off. Something was peculiar. Crowe couldn't place what.

A nervous tinselly light dappled the ceiling and glittered on the terrazzo floor. Brighter than usual, the sun. Sharper.

He sipped from the blue enamel FLORIDA MAN MYSTERY HOUSE mug, the coffee still so hot it scorched his lips. He cursed, set the mug down.

Then he noticed the blank wall next to the television. Where a framed watercolor by Lily, his deceased daughter, usually hung, there was now a bare nail.

Crowe got up from the kitchen island stool and went to where the painting lay facedown on the floor. He picked it up. The glass and frame were unbroken. A watercolor of Crowe, fishing, on a little dinghy in the sea. Below the boat Lily had drawn a coral reef with anemones and parti-colored polyps. A school of bright tropical fish swam toward Crowe's line and hook. The fish had exaggerated smiles, human teeth.

Crowe put the painting back up, straightened it. "Otter," he said. The girl's nickname.

He was not usually a superstitious man.

But even with the painting back on the wall, Crowe sensed something off. He scratched the scruff of his beach bum beard, contemplated what it was.

He put on his rubber flip-flops and scuffed outside in his boxers and bathrobe.

A brilliant cloudless morning, mid-April, the south Florida sun in his hair and on his scalp. Almost tourist season. Almost spring break.

Almost fucked, between the Emerald Island Inn and the Florida Man Mystery House, his businesses, if you could even call them that, falling to ratshit. All of his debts piling on.

But a beautiful day yet. The mellow spring breeze riffling the sea oats on the sand dunes.

Crowe was halfway across his small garden, its menagerie of cacti and succulents in terra-cotta pots, when he halted.

The lime tree with the red hummingbird feeder, vanished.

For a wild second he thought the tree stolen. He wondered what kind of reprobate would go to such lengths.

Before long he realized this an addle-brained notion.

It was a sinkhole.

A sinkhole. In his fucking yard.

The state was riddled with them.

Honeycombed.

And now here was one just like they showed on the news, on his property.

FLORIDA MAN WAKES UP TO HOLE HALFWAY TO CHINA IN HIS BACK-YARD

Crowe toed up in his zories for a closer gander. Where it once stood there was now an unimpeded view of Florida beachfront. He could see the plank board path wending among the hundred-year-old dunes. And beyond the dunes the expanse of sugar-white beach, the bottle-green Gulf rolling soft and tranquil like it always did before spring heated up and summer storms made the water moody.

Crowe stepped to the edge of the chasm and peered down. He couldn't see bottom. Couldn't see the hummingbird tree.

Just an ink black crack, a zigzag seam of darkness.

"Holy motherfucking blue shit," Reed Crowe said.

Arms akimbo, face vexed, Crowe glanced around. He went to the patio table and fetched the conch shell ashtray full of joint ends and chucked it into the hole. Down it clattered and clacked, maybe twenty-five feet, maybe thirty, before hitting bottom.

He wanted to chuck other things down the hole, and he could have easily pissed away the whole morning in this fashion, but there was no time.

It was ten A.M. and he was due at the Florida Man Mystery House.

THE FLORIDA MAN MYSTERY HOUSE

THE FLORIDA MAN MYSTERY HOUSE, ONE of those dubious roadside attractions in this part of the state, a remnant from the era of tin can tourism, before HoJo and Holiday Inn and oh-Jesus-Christ-Mary-Mother-of-God Disney World. Now the highway billboards for the Mystery House were so faded, the paint so thin, the paper so flayed and shredded, the palimpsest of old ads showed underneath.

You had to wonder if the place was still open.

It was. Barely.

But in its heyday the Florida Man Mystery House boasted about a dozen big billboards all along the Florida highways.

I-75, I-95, I-4.

Two on Alligator Alley.

Even a few on the newfangled turnpike.

Now, these days, the Florida Man Mystery House was more of a place you happened upon by accident. A place you stopped to stretch your legs. A place where you stopped to take a piss, a dump. A place where you got out of your pea-green station wagon with the wooden siding because you couldn't stand another moment in the sweltering car with your batshit family.

A picayune operation, the Florida Man Mystery House. A skeleton crew. Just Reed Crowe, Wayne Wade, and Eddie Maldonado, aka the Coca-Cola Kid, a Mexican teenager from outside Emerald City.

Beginning of April, Eddie showed up asking if he could sell refreshments off Crowe's boat. The kid offered to pay for part of the gas, plus half the soda earnings, cash. Crowe saw no harm. Told the kid just the gas money was fine. If times weren't so lean, he might not have asked for that much.

And now, this morning, in his orange hatchback en route to the Florida Man Mystery House, Crowe passed one of the billboards. He gave the shabby-looking advertisement a look of rue.

The old-time tiki font faded and birdshit-spackled, the attractions almost illegible.

GO SPELUNKING IN THE DEEPEST [BIRD SHIT] OF
[BIRD SHIT]. OUTER SPACE [BIRD SHIT]. AMAZING
ODD [BIRD SHIT].
COCA-COLA. TAB. ICE-COLD [BIRD SHIT].

Riding shotgun was a head of lettuce, for Bogey the tortoise. "See that, man?" Crowe asked the lettuce. "Ice-cold bird shit. Now I'm jonesin' for ice-cold bird shit. How 'bout you?"

BATHROOMS CLEAN!
LONG DRIVE BEFORE ANOTHER [BIRD SHIT] ONE!
SEE BOGEY THE 200-YEAR-OLD TORTOISE!

"Fuckin' Wayne," Crowe muttered.

A refrain of late: fuckin' Wayne.

Wayne Wade, Crowe's childhood friend and factotum of Crowe's moribund enterprises.

Wayne Wade with three DUIs.

Wayne Wade, always in arrears with a bookie or a weed dealer. Wayne Wade, fired from every pool hall and sports bar and wing hut in the county. And eighty-sixed from over half of those. Places where even the pill heads and cokeheads kept their jobs.

Lately Reed Crowe thought he needed a big long break from Wayne Wade. Several months at least. He hated feeling this way about his lifelong friend, but there you had it. Everywhere he turned, Jesus Christ: Wayne. Wayne at the pool hall. Wayne at the Sea Cave Arcade. Wayne at the Rum Jungle. Mostly it was at the Rum Jungle these days, because Wayne was eighty-sixed for life from Chill Norton's Pervy Mermaid on the other side of the bridge.

There was also Reed Crowe's other business. The Emerald Island Inn. Two stories, a salt-crusted old Florida motel if there ever was one, stucco of turquoise and cream and pink, narrow cement balconies connecting the rooms. Towels and beach shorts and bikini bottoms hanging on the railing, Florida Gator and Florida Seminole kids crowding the public beach with their coolers full of beer and their cheap tourist shop beach chairs that broke four days after you bought them.

More than half a century ago when they built the causeway from the mainland to Emerald Island, the inn was erected near the public beach, between the water tower and the lighthouse. There was the Rum Jungle tiki bar, the Blue Parrot diner, the bait shop, the minimart. These were the few concessions to tourism on the island. The rest of Emerald Island was divvied up into big multi-acre lots belonging to the locals. And beyond these big chunks of land, on the southern half of the island, was primordial wilderness, the nature preserve. One of the last bastions of undeveloped beachfront this part of Florida.

Decades ago the island's big coral reefs were a popular destination for snorkelers and scuba divers, but in the late sixties a freighter carrying insect repellent and rat poison demolished the reef. One of the major tourist attractions, gone. Now the coral was dead bone, the hydra-headed gorgonians bleached white.

Fewer and fewer came the snowbirds. The sportsmen and yachtsmen and anglers. The convalescents who sought the tropical climate, the sun and the salt air and the long walks on the beach, to restore their health.

To some of the more misanthropic natives, this was just as well.

With a passel of other itinerant part-time employees and a few part-time maids, Wayne Wade managed, if that was the word, the old Emerald Island Inn. A mistake ever to mix business and friendship.

A few times a week, part of his routine, Crowe drove to the motel and saw to business, made repairs.

King Canute fighting the tide.

The dog shit in the small playground with the merry-go-round and the slide. The ice machines on the three different floors always on the fritz. The dirty, salt-grimed windows. The garbage full of reeking rancid bait.

The rooms with the fraying rattan and wicker furniture. Toilets and sinks forever clogged. Tubs scum-ringed.

The community barbecue, infested with palmetto bugs. The ice machine, a fuck zone for rats. The vending machine, cobwebs inside, those chalky Necco wafers nobody liked, dubious-looking pickles swimming in cellophane packs full of chartreuse brine.

And so on.

Reed Crowe would ask, "Wayne, could you please get the burnt horseshoe crab out of the grill?"

"Why'd somebody put a horseshoe crab on the grill?" Wayne Wade would ask from under his oversized Miami Dolphins baseball cap, the rattail of his brown hair hanging through the hole in back.

"I'm on the case, Wayne. I've been canvassing a search. Knocking door to door."

And now, for the rest of the drive, Crowe's thoughts turned from Wayne and the Florida Man Mystery House and the Emerald Island Inn and remained on the sinkhole. He pictured the whole house swallowed.

"What about the house?" he asked the head of lettuce.

"The cats?"

He convinced himself they could surely sense something like that coming, the bubble of their internal level off plumb.

Just as Reed Crowe had felt that morning.

Just as Reed Crowe had felt lately.

It was going to be a bastard of a summer for sure.

In the parking lot were station wagons with New York and New Jersey plates. An orange VW with a Canadian tag.

A respectable showing, these days, for the Florida Man Mystery House. Maybe twelve, fifteen people on this outing.

Crowe picked up the head of lettuce and got out of the car and went across the limestone and crushed shell lot lugging it under his arm like a Harlem Globetrotter with a basketball. Already sweltering. By the time he reached the gift shop, his forehead was sopping.

In the gift shop Wayne Wade stood behind the register. In plain view on the counter sat an open can of beer. His Walkman was clipped to the waistband of his jorts and the puffy orange headphones were clamped around his neck. Crowe could hear the tinny spillage of music.

Ramones. "Teenage Lobotomy."

Pointing his chin at Crowe, Wayne Wade told one of the tourists, "That's the guy you wanna talk to, mister. CEO of the operation."

The man turned his beery bulldog face to Crowe.

"Howdy," Crowe said. Thinking, Fuck me.

The man said, "You should get clearer signs. Wasted a lot of gas."

Crowe apologized. Told the man he had a point.

"But don't you got no dang number on the sign?"

Crowe kept the phone number off the billboards deliberately. Last thing he wanted, a bunch of assholes calling. And almost always the callers were assholes. Nutty assholes. Eighty-five percent of the time. Some half-drunk, half-crazed father from Peoria at wit's end on a Florida vacation that was not going according to plan.

From some godforsaken pay phone near Alligator Alley they'd call Crowe for directions they couldn't possibly follow. And Crowe wanted no part of them anyway, the hotheads near apoplexy, the station wagon dads with too many Charles Bronson and Clint Eastwood movies in their heads.

Now Crowe said to the harried father, "You didn't see the number?"

"I'm telling you, I got outta that car. I parked. Right, hon?"

Hon agreed.

And Crowe knew that the man had a point. Hell, he'd been riding Wayne Wade's ass for how long about the signs? Goddamn years.

"Get you a gift shop souvenir, mister? Get you a tchotchke? A gewgaw?"

"No need for gewgaws," the man said.

"How about a beer?"

The man's wife said to her husband, "It's ten-thirty."

"It's a vacation," said the man. He glanced quizzically at the head of lettuce cradled in Crowe's arm. "A beer would be good."

"My kind of man right there. Where you from?"

"Boise, Idaho."

"Never heard of it," joked Crowe, going to the cooler. "This your son?" He looked at the kid, a matryoshka version, one of those little Russian nesting dolls, smaller-sized, of his father. "Wanna beer, kid?"

"Hell, yeah," said the kid.

"Billy," the kid's mother said. "You want red steak tonight? Behave."

The family finally went and wandered amid the shabby bric-a-brac. The ball caps and the T-shirts and the mugs. The snow globes with the mermaid figures inside and with FLORIDA! written on the base. The backscratchers made of tiny alligator paws and the necklaces made of shark's teeth.

The mothers and fathers and kids looked sunburned, sweaty, gypped.

Crowe would be the first to admit, a certain squalor had settled of late. Creaky weather-swollen planks, windows opaque with cobwebs and dust.

A swatch of flypaper, speckled with dead horseflies and mosquitoes, helixed above the door.

Once the tourists were out of earshot and wandering the Mystery House trail, its pell-mell shacks and shanties full of chintzy exhibits, Crowe fetched to the register. His thoughts had been on the sinkhole, and now there was this shit to deal with.

"Need you to fix that billboard," Crowe told Wayne. "And those signs. People get turned around, off the highway."

"Good morning," said Wayne.

Crowe lowered his voice. "Don't give me that shit."

"Something about that Eddie I need to say," Wayne told Crowe.

"Hear me? The signs, Wayne. Who gives a shit about Eddie?"

"Today? Ninety-four degrees." He dug into his armpit with his thumb.

"Well, that's why I've been telling you," Crowe said. He lowered his voice. "And now here you go. Tomorrow it'll be a hundred degrees. Or you'll find some other excuse. Go paint it."

"Now? I gotta get the costume on."

"After the costume."

"After the costume. I'll have a stroke."

Crowe noticed again the beer flagrantly out in the open. "Hey, how about the goddamn can?"

"Tsch." Wayne set the can down on the floor. Then a look of petulant crafty triumph overtook his face, a notion having occurred to him. "It'll take two seconds. I'll blast the ever living fuck out of it with a fire hose."

"Whatever. Sure."

"Two seconds. I'll take Gary Jupiter's truck and you'll see."

"You're gonna drive a fire truck. You're gonna hot-wire a fire truck. Please. Do it. You'll end up in prison for life. Please. I beg of you."

"Some thing to say. I'll get him a six-pack and he'll drive it. Then I'll blast the fuck outta that sign."

Crowe told him he was doing no such thing.

"I wanna tell you about Eddie," Wayne persisted.

"Goddamn it, there's a sinkhole in my backyard."

"What? Hell's that gotta do with me?"

"Wayne." Crowe pinched the bridge of his nose.

"Listen, he's been stealing those Coca-Colas and Dr Peppers." Then, seeing Crowe's questioning face, Wayne said, "Yeah, they're stolen. From Red, White and Blue Liquor."

"Bullshit."

Wayne made another face, a small satisfied simper rising on his lips. He raised his hands and showed his palms as if to absolve himself.

Before Wayne Wade could press further, a voice said, "I'll do it, Mr. Crowe." They looked. It was Eddie, standing beside the rack of rubber snakes and spiders next to the gift shop door.

Crowe told the kid, "It's Reed, Eddie, please."

"I'll do it, Mr. Reed."

"What, Eddie? Just Reed."

"The signs," said Eddie. "I'll clean them."

Wayne snatched up the swatter, swiped viciously at a horsefly. "Kiss ass," he muttered.

"You'll do it, Eddie?" Crowe asked the kid.

"Yes. Five dollars?"

Crowe looked at Wayne. "Five dollars? See this, Wayne. Initiative. Incentive. What's the word?" Crowe snapped his fingers. Pointed at Wayne. "Gumption."

Wayne Wade's face was red. His goober teeth showed. "Oh, reverse psychology now," Wayne said.

Crowe, still lugging the head of lettuce, went to the back of the shop and exited out into the oddity trail. "Five bucks," Crowe said as if musing to himself, pitching his voice, "that's a bargain."

Crowe went down the footpath that drew a figure eight around the Mystery House attractions. In the middle of one of the loops was a concrete UFO, a Permastone igloo-shaped enclosure with hundreds of little portals made from the bottoms of green glass bottles. And in the middle of the other loop was the buried kiddy pool where Bogart, a humongous gopher turtle the size of a golf cart, made his nest several months out of the year.

The three or four other months, Crowe had no idea where Bogart went. A mystery.

Maybe he had some old lady turtle somewhere.

But going on fifteen years now, the stubborn old sonofabitch always came back, lumbering and settling into the pea soup water as if returned from a mere stroll.

Crowe figured him one hundred and fifty years old, maybe more. The two hundred on the billboard: probably slight hyperbole, but possible. Old Bogey's back was covered in a fur of moss and there were deep nicks scarred on his shell. From alligator's teeth, perhaps arrowheads from way back.

The turtle would eat anything. Pumpkins. Chef Boyardee out of the can.

And now Crowe gave the turtle the head of lettuce. Bogart turned to it, wrapped his serrated beak-like mouth around the lettuce. Bogart sheared off half in one bite.

A few of the tourists watched as Bogart chowed down. Crowe told them, "Get your gewgaws before the boat tour if you wanna, folks. Don't forget to say goodbye to Bogart the turtle. Poor guy's only got another hundred and fifty years to live. Might be your last chance."

Outside Eddie had the SS *Merman* already started at the dock. Crowe climbed aboard, got behind the wheel.

The round-faced Idaho-looking tourist family filed up the gangplank. Eddie took their money, five dollars a head. A honeymooning young black couple joined. Then another family, a snowy-haired Scandinavian couple, with two daughters.

The youngest was around the same age his daughter, Lily, would have been now. On the cusp of puberty.

Crazy to think.

Time was getting away.

Even in the small patch of shade under the Bimini top, it was hot enough to raise sweat on his brow. Crowe swiped his forehead with his wrist. Ten-thirty in the morning and already the heat was a blue-ribbon sonofabitch. He didn't want to think about what the summer had in store.

Eddie untied the mooring rope from the dock cleats. Bow, then stern. Soon Crowe was steering away from the Florida Man Mystery House, headed into the hothouse jungle of the Everglades.

The shacks and sheds drifted away behind them.

Crowe delivered his customary spiel on autopilot, a folksy automaton.

Still thinking of the sinkhole, still picturing his house swallowed whole, Crowe talked about de Soto and Ponce de Leon and the fountain of youth. He spoke of shell Indians, how they regarded the manchineel tree as grand inquisitor. How it was believed Ponce de Leon was felled by an arrow dipped in manchineel juice.

The chupacabra. UFOs. The fountain of youth. The devil's chair of Cassadaga. The demon of round cypress.

Mermaids, pirate treasure, haunted sinkholes, cases of spontaneous combustion.

Pirates. He talked about pirates. Gasparilla.

"Legend has it," Crowe said, "Gasparilla before he died buried his treasure somewhere off the Gulf Coast. Could be here. Could be in Tampa. He did write a secret code on a stone. This is confirmed fact. Wild, right? To this day? Still haven't figured the dang thing out."

Here Crowe turned away from the wheel, fished out of his madras shorts a laminated square of paper, business card–sized.

O-X-NXW-W-VER-VAR-LEGUA I/IO O-X-SWXW-VER-VAR-HASTA X, said the typewriting. Another Florida cracker legend, this of Gasparilla the pirate secreting his stash somewhere among the land of ten thousand islands.

Crowe handed the card to a fat kid with Red Hots gunked in his braces.

"Any one of you figure that out," Crowe said, "split the loot with you."

"Dr Pepper!" shouted Eddie. "Pesticide!"

"Pirates are gay," Billy from Idaho said.

"That's it, no red steak," said Hon from Idaho.

Crowe said, "What? Pirates? You know how many women pirates had, man? They had concubines. Harems."

"What's a harem?" asked Billy.

Crowe wanted to say, *More pussy than you can handle, you fat little shit,* but instead he said, "More girlfriends than you can handle. Whole mess of lady friends."

The mother asked the boy, "You want your red steak tonight, Billy? Cool it."

The Lily-aged girl, studying the card with the code on it, furrowed her brow, handed the laminated slip of paper to her father.

"Coppertone girl ointment!" shouted Eddie.

They serpentined their way through the labyrinths of tamarind and strangler fig toward the place where the interior opened into the Everglades.

The Lily-aged girl said, "Scary." Something else had caught her attention. She pointed at a tumorous bole sprouting from a pine tree. "What is that?"

"That's a catface."

See, Crowe thought. Not all of them are little shits like red-steak Billy. He asked the girl what her name was. Mellicent.

Crowe explained to Mellicent that turpentiners slashed pine trees to sap them. The deep cuts in the wood looked like V's, or cat mouths. When the holes scarred over with bumps and swells and the resin petrified, what looked like deformed faces peered from the tree trunks.

"See how it kind of looks like a face, Miss Mellicent?"

"Spooky," said the girl.

A few tourists snapped pictures of the tree.

"Coca-Cola," shouted Eddie, walking the length of the boat with the cooler on his back. "Ointment. Pesticide."

Finally they reached a place in the crooked canal where the water broadened out into a slough of water cabbage. Nailed onto the trunk of a gumbo-limbo tree was a pointed plank-board sign.

SKUNK APE CROSSING, it read.

Crowe cut the motor.

The chant of insects. The drone of cicadas. The hum of gnats.

Hidden in one of the hammocks was a deer stand where Wayne in his bogman costume—an ape outfit, but made of moss and peat, accoutered with pockets where he could secret his whiskey flask and marijuana pipe and pornographic magazines to while away the time—waited to come charging out of a swamp lily patch.

"Now's a good time to put on that 'pellent, you got some," said Crowe. "And if you have none, Mr. Eddie has some to offer."

"'Pellent, Dr Pepper, Coca-Cola, ointment, Coppertone."

Now Crowe, casting his voice, "You folks familiar with Bigfoot? Miss Mellicent, you hear of Mister Bigfoot? Well, we got our own version this part of Florida. Dude usually hangs around here."

And on cue Wayne screamed a bestial scream, crashed through waist-deep water toward the boat.

The tourists flinched and gasped.

The Lily-aged girl screeched.

"It's okay, folks," said Crowe. "Only Wayne."

Wayne took off the head of the costume. Miserable-looking in the heat. He started climbing the starboard ladder onto the boat, the head cradled under his arm. "Hi, folks," said Wayne.

And Crowe, on script, "Put that head back on, would you, Wayne? You're scaring the kids."

THE SKULL

THE NEXT PART OF THE MYSTERY tour was the grotto.

To reach it on the mainland you had to venture off-road and drive down a washboard limestone trail. And even then that was only half the way. Then you had to park the car because the land turned to swampy mush. Then you had to put on mud boots and slog through the brambles and bracken until you reached a ferny clearing bowered over with huge-limbed oak. A place where the shadows smelled like rain and peat and Spanish moss.

By water, the route was much simpler, accessible by high-floating, low-bottomed boats such as the SS *Merman*.

Crowe nudged the boat up to the dock. Wayne still in his bogman outfit sans head tied the mooring rope to the cleats.

Crowe said, "Watch your step, folks. And keep hydrated. Pace yourself. Don't forget your sunblock. If you got a bucket of ice to dump over your head, even better. Don't wanna end up like Wayne."

"Coca-Cola," said Eddie. "Dr Pepper. Ointment. Pesticide."

The tourists trooped out of the boat and down the gangplank. They went down the grade, Crowe leading the way over the boardwalk through clutches of paurotis palms and saw grass.

Grasshoppers and katydids flew.

The Lily-aged girl squealed. Round-faced Billy from Idaho swung at the flying insects with his fists.

His mother made a few more red steak threats. "Go ahead. You'll watch us from the hotel window walking to Steak and Ale tonight."

At the bottom of the path they reached a choke of rocks concealing the bunnyhole of the opening. "Watch your heads now, watch your heads," Crowe told the tourists. "Don't wanna end up like Wayne, kids. No life, I tell you, being a bogman. Miss Mellicent, you might wanna take note."

They filed into the first chamber. A room of dripstone and flowstone the size of an airplane hangar lit by string lights and miners' bulbs.

At the cavern entrance was a milk crate full of small flashlights and pickaxes. Crowe told the tourists to help themselves. The kids, lugging their tools, split from the group, flashlight beams cutting through the cloistered mineral-smelling dark.

Before long one of the tourist kids shrieked. A macabre sound in the cave. People whipped their heads, gaped pop-eyed.

The Lily-aged girl wandered off into one of the far corners.

Before these excursions Crowe secreted fossils and bones here and there for kids to find. Like an Easter egg hunt. Arrowheads and sharks' teeth and woolly mammoth molars.

Now he went over expecting one of these. A palmetto bug, a lizard, something ordinary.

But what he saw shocked him.

A skull.

A human skull, sheathed in mud and lichen. A lone clicker beetle darted out of a nostril hole and scuttled into the other. Tendrils of wispy gray hair, still tied in a ponytail, hung from the crown.

The head lay on the ground in a niche that must have freshly opened since Crowe's last tour. Likely the same seismic disturbance that had opened the sinkhole in his backyard. Almost certainly.

They happened from time to time, new nooks and crannies yawning wide in the limestone sinks of Florida, usually nothing life-threatening or dangerous.

But this.

The tourists crowded behind Crowe, gawking.

Crowe was agog too. Thankfully they couldn't see his face.

He ran his hand through his salt-stiffened beard. He composed himself, or tried to. He put on what he hoped was an approximation of a showman's smile. He turned. Chuckled a forced odd chuckle. "Looks real, right, missy ma'am? Just a trick."

The Idaho father remarked that it looked awful damn real.

"Doesn't it, though?" Crowe said. "Made in China."

The young black fiancé said, "That looks way real to me. Sick."

Outside, Eddie was yelling, "Ointment! Lotion! Pest control!"

"Fifty bucks. China. Sorry I gave you a scare there, girl. Might've gotten more than I bargained for, huh? You like hermit crabs?"

Crowe made toward the exit. Hoped to God he didn't sound as rattled as he felt.

Reluctantly the tourists followed, casting doubtful glances behind their shoulders at the skull.

Back on the SS *Merman*, Wayne Wade, now changed back to his T-shirt and jorts, asked, "What's all this about a skull?"

"Nothing. Prop."

Wayne Wade screwed up an incredulous eye.

"Wayne? Let me think. I gotta lot on my mind. Let me be alone with my thoughts, okay?"

The sinkhole. Heidi's imminent return to the island. His mother in the goddamn nursing home. All the goddamn bills.

He had enough to worry about without goddamn Wayne Wade.

THE PERVY MERMAID

WHEN HE GOT HOME THAT AFTERNOON from the swamp tour Crowe moved all the potted plants in the small garden. He moved them so they sat arranged around the small chasm in his backyard, circumscribing its perimeter. The cacti and succulents and hearty tropical flowers a warning barrier.

Crowe sat in his folding beach bum chair stroking his beach bum beard while studying the hole. He tossed in pieces of bone-white shell. Tossed in little pebbles and chunks of coral.

The skull and the sinkhole. It almost sounded like the beginning of one of those tall tales. One of those Florida Man stories Reed Crowe was reading about all the time, especially lately.

Florida Man beats chess opponent with brass knuckles after losing game. Florida Man urinates on uncle's coffin during funeral service. Florida Man caught fornicating in SeaWorld exhibit. Florida Man, coke-addled, calls 911 to ask for number for 911. Florida Man tries to conceal stolen ham in rectum, fails. Florida Man arrested for teaching parrot death threats made to IRS. Florida Man armed with iguana robs herpetophobic mini-mart clerk.

Now the feral beach cats slunk and sniffed around the chasm, their tails arrowed down.

Some growled. Others looked at Crowe as if he was responsible.

The cats were the descendants of felines brought in from the early days of sugarcane. Those days, the days of the first old Conchs, the rats chewed their sugarcane crops to shit, gnawing acres to stubble.

All the poisons they tried didn't work, so the sugar barons brought in cats from the south. They had their field hands sail to the Keys and corral as many strays as they could find. Poor souls in the middle of the night chasing after ferals in the mosquito-plagued islands, in the wild Florida dark. They loaded the cargo ship with hundreds. Tabbies, Russian grays, tortoiseshells. Never mind the surreal trek back home, the reek of cat piss and shit, the hissing and clawing that kept the crew awake, the fleas feasting on them, the mosquitoes, the insects on their skin so many they looked like they were in blackface.

Once loosed on Emerald Island the cats feasted and fucked and ran amok. Multiplied. Before long there were hundreds. To this day their descendants inhabited Emerald Island. And the same posse of thirty or forty stuck to the eastern tip of the island around Crowe's house.

He recognized a host of them by sight.

Many of the cats took a shining to Crowe and he to them. He gave the cats names. Lulubelle. Lady Marmalade. Leibowitz. Dr. Dynamo. Beelzebub. Frank. Elvis. Fats Domino. Carlos the Jackal. Edwin Patridge the Third.

Crowe said to the cats, "Don't look at me, man. Nothing to do with this shit. Maybe it was you? How about you? You, over there, you do this?"

They eyed the hole from a distance, noses working.

His thoughts drifted to Heidi, what she'd say about the sinkhole.

Then he thought about their last conversation before she left. So stupid.

What he said, for instance, to his ex-wife, in January, before her departure for Rennes. Her first art residency, at last, after years of watercoloring Emerald Island beachscapes, after moving on to still-life sketches of wading birds on the island, and then slowly after that finding her own style.

She kept a gallery of her paintings in her arts-and-crafts bungalow during tourist season.

And one day a few years ago a yachtsman bought one of her paintings, hung it up in his living room in Manhattan. The yachtsman threw a New Year's party; 1977, this was.

An art critic from *The New York Times* attended the celebration, where Heidi's painting, hanging above the man's couch, caught his eye.

But that was it. For years. Until, by fortuitous coincidence, the art critic vacationed in Emerald Island a few summers later. One of those rare men who remained true to his word, he made it a point of visiting Heidi's shop, where he was impressed anew with Heidi's budding style. The art critic knew people at Columbia University, who knew people at NYU, who knew people at the consulate, who knew people at the Franco-American Institute in Rennes.

One thing begot another.

And on the eve of Heidi's departure, Reed Crowe, about to turn thirty-three in October, felt an urgency he hadn't felt in years. Heidi, his ex-wife, the mother of their child, was thirty-one.

"Maybe you should stay here," Crowe said, meaning that maybe they should start over. This before her ten-hour flight across the Atlantic was about to depart from the Miami-Dade airport.

He clutched her shoulders at the boarding gate. He was always struck anew by her beauty before she left him—her Mediterranean tan, her sun-kissed dark curly hair, her big wonderful ass—but only when she was going away.

Heidi shook her head.

Thinking she misunderstood, Crowe went on, "Everything. Us. Let's try again. Life on the island."

He meant another shot at marriage.

Another child.

Another shot at life.

"How dare you," she told him in a rough shaking whisper. Ire burned in her eyes.

Crowe was dumbstruck. He asked his ex-wife what the matter was.

"You're something else, you know that?" Heidi told him, and with that she shouldered her carry-on and turned and joined the queue filing into the plane.

He knew it best not to follow. Her stiff shoulders, her indignant clipped stride.

Even her knock-out ass looked somehow angry.

Only later that evening did it occur to him why Heidi reacted the way she did. Only later did he realize it was selfish and misguided to say what he did before such a titanic sea change in her life.

These things were on Crowe's mind when his friend Chill Norton finally arrived later that afternoon in his dump truck full of oyster shells. Chill, the proprietor of the Pervy Mermaid just beyond the outskirts of the township. It was beyond Crowe who would eat all-you-can-eat raw oysters in an all-nude strip club on a Friday night, but far be it from him to question his own good fortune.

After the two-ton cacophony of the shells had ceased, and after the hole was filled, Chill asked, "This place insured?"

"What you think?"

"Oh man."

"No shit."

Crowe was off the books. A cipher. A nonentity. Like many under-the-radar types on the island, he paid his taxes, as little as he could get away with, and as for the rest, he was self-sufficient.

The sun was setting tangerine and bronze and they popped fresh beers, swatted away mosquitoes.

Chill asked Crowe how Heidi, Reed's ex-wife, was doing.

"In Rennes," Crowe told him.

"Fuck's that?"

"France."

They tipped back their beers, watched the cats watching them from within the jungle foliage hemming the backyard.

"Hey, assholes," Chill told them.

HENRY YAHCHILANE

HENRY YAHCHILANE HEARD IT TOLD BY the slow-witted man at the Rum Jungle.

If memory served, the dimwit man was in the employ of the man known as Florida Man. Something Crowe. The man who owned that ramshackle attraction on the mainland. The Florida Man Mystery House.

A shithole.

A bonafide tourist trap if he ever saw one.

Once in a while, during his long evening beach strolls on the island, Henry spotted Crowe in his Hawaiian bathing trunks or madras shorts kicking through the waves. Slouching along, head down, hands shoved in his pockets. The bright tourist shop T-shirts with the dumb slogans. Too baked to give a fuck.

The sun-scorched hair, the witness protection beard.

The zories, the loafers.

A silly man, Henry Yahchilane considered him. An egghead.

Sometimes he'd think, Oh, there goes the egghead. There goes the idjit.

Nonetheless they'd tender amiable half-waves from a distance. Like all the other islanders.

This guy, Crowe's de facto factotum, had a reputation for running at the mouth. And that night after chasing his third tequila shot with his third beer, the man in his typical shitmouth torrent said, "Yeah, he had this fuckin' head. I don't know, man. A skull, not a fresh head."

A coterie of regulars was giving him an ear. Beach bums. A ship captain or two. Salty dogs.

Yahchilane listened too.

Yahchilane pegged the guy as a nincompoop. His choppy rube's haircut, from the looks of it self-styled. Either that or clipped at the Salvation Army, where every second Sunday in Emerald City they gave out free haircuts to the needy.

Yahchilane often saw the nincompoop around the pool halls just outside of Emerald Island. He saw him in the Red, White and Blue Liquor store scratching his Florida Lottery scratch-offs at the counter as the owner with the pocked greasy face watched with unconcealed spite. And he'd seen him a few times in the wing hut way outside the county limits, wheeling and dealing with a bunch of pill heads and cokeheads.

And he'd see him driving that death-trap contraption, an ad hoc moped which was really just a BMX bike with a weed whacker engine attached. Yahchilane got stuck behind the idjit because passing was impossible on the two-lane road because the idjit was weaving in and out and Yahchilane's van was so big he knew he'd clip him.

The guy would fetch daredevil looks over his shoulder, motioning him to pass, leaning over the chopper-style handlebars.

"Egghead," Yahchilane would say, watching the man swerving and wobbling in the headlights.

And what did the islanders know about Yahchilane?

Much of it was common knowledge, simply by virtue of the fact that the island was so small, the population so scant, and Yahchilane's stay here so long.

A true local. When Henry Yahchilane was born, it was the tail end of an era when his forefathers, tanners and plumers and traders, lived off the land. This before the days of conservation. After Roosevelt and Audubon and all of them. After the oil magnates and Henry Flagler the investor and the railroad men laying tracks across the state. After the government started hacking away at the swamp, draining the Everglades, devouring the land with steam shovels, flooding their land and homes.

After forced immigration and extradition, those years when chickees were taken apart, whole villages packed in huge wooden crates, loaded on freight trains, and transported across the United States and reassembled in Nebraska, Oklahoma, Texas. Even Canada. These places for the Seminoles who'd known only the subtropics of Florida most of their lives might as well have been the moon.

Uncles and aunts and cousins named Eagle, Deer, Panther, all estranged and scattered to different points of the compass. Like dander, like dust.

Yahchilane's family, at least, was spared this misfortune and indignity. His family hailed from Seminoles from the tip of Florida to the north of Okeechobee, relatives scattered in Brighton Reservation and Big Cypress.

The new roads in Florida brought the tourists, and ushered in the so-called tin can tourism age. Droves of Americans trekked south in their Model T's and Studebakers, deep into the jungly terra incognita of the state.

In those days, Florida was still an exotic place. The primordial subtropical wild. The closest a red-blooded American could get to Timbuktu without leaving the country.

Tourists treated the natives as an attraction. Uncle Joe wrestling his alligators in the muddy slop pens. The wigwams and chickadees. The hides and pelts at hokey souvenir shops. Beads and trinkets. Wallets with beads. Patchwork purses.

Tourists took pictures of their children with a so-called Indian chief. For a few bucks, they could try on a so-called authentic headdress.

Yahchilane then was of an age that his memories of this era were clear. Post–World War II ecotourism. The thirty-foot billboard outside of Hialeah. The pylons made to look like totem poles flanking the entrance. The village enclosed by palmetto fronds. Bananas, sugarcane, sweet potatoes, chickens and pigs and dogs. The animal safaris. The monkey shows. The alligator wrestling.

As the tourists openly stared, the Seminole families sat painting rawhide calfskin drums.

The Seminoles stared wordlessly back.

One of Henry Yahchilane's uncles, a drunk and pothead, muttered nonsense. The tourists took it all as gospel. As if they were privy to something sacred, secret, solemn.

The toddlers got the most money from the tourists. They would walk up to the tourists in their patchwork outfits, hold out their hands without a word, palms waiting. Sometimes Henry would make more money in an afternoon than his father with all his wood carvings and hides and hunting in a week.

Henry sat with his mother and his older brothers in the shade of their chickee huts. The tourists snapped pictures with their Brownie cameras and Polaroids. Without permission.

If it was one of his days off from the department store, Henry's father would sit in the shade of the hut and not move an inch aside from his constant whittling. He would not shake hands, even when the tourists offered them. And they did. Often.

Little Henry Yahchilane rattled his tin cup for tourist money while his dad kept mum and hawked his bird whistles and tomahawks and knives.

His family was a dramatic bunch predisposed to loud quarrels and sometimes outright fistfights. Disputes over land, government, alcohol. Certain relatives seemed almost to relish being bitter and angry. They clung covetously to grudges as if they were their lifeblood.

Even before puberty hit he knew. Yahchilane wanted no part of federal restitution save for being left alone. He wanted no part of the tribal councils and politics. That fraught and fractious world of self-appointed goodwill ambassadors. Village managers and treasurers and spokespeople.

Not Henry Yahchilane.

Yahchilane had a few estranged nephews. Listless ne'er-do-wells one and all. The father and the mother's fault. Both dipshits. Their run-ins every few years were the only times they communicated. Emerald City was a small place. Inevitably their paths crossed. And when they did, words were exchanged. On more than one occasion, punches thrown.

The other Yahchilanes, including Henry Yahchilane's older

brother Cy, took the government reparations money. They had kids and a family and they took the money and within a year they had squandered it on drugs and stupid shit like a seven-thousand-dollar Fender Twin Reverb Amp and when they asked Henry for a loan, blood being blood, he denied them because he had no money.

The goofy man with the rattail said, "He found a real human head. Okay, go ahead. Laugh. Laugh. No, I wasn't giving head. Fuck you guys. I'm trying to tell you, a real whole human head."

They went on like this for a while and Yahchilane had already tuned them out and was about to order another beer when he heard the word "grotto."

The severed head was found in the grotto, the man who worked for Crowe was saying.

Yahchilane tensed. Forwent the last beer. Laid down his money and shoved off his stool and left the bar.

MIDNIGHT JAUNT

WORRIES SWARMED AT CROWE THAT NIGHT, hectoring him awake. Heidi. The skull.

He wondered whether he should call the cops. Quickly dismissed the notion, knowing the crooked ways and crooked justice that prevailed in this crooked place. Conch law. Laissez-faire. He thought of local Sheriff Schaffer, the crookedest crook of them all.

Crowe forewent sleep. He got dressed and crossed the Intracoastal bridge at midnight, spade and pick in the trunk of his orange hatchback.

He was on his way to the grotto, to see the skull, to see what else the collapse uncovered.

On the way, Crowe stopped at Red, White and Blue Liquor.

Krumpp was next to the standing ashtray smoking a long menthol cigarette outside the RWB, a repurposed Pizza Hut with the trademark roof, when Crowe came scuffing out of his beeswax orange hatchback.

"Sergeant Krumpp!" said Crowe.

Krumpp grunted and twisted out the cigarette and went inside, keys jingling. Crowe made a face behind Krumpp as he followed inside. Krumpp the immutable, always the same car salesman slacks, roomy and pleated, keys jangling from his hip's belt loop, like some kind of grim jailer.

No one ever robbed Krumpp because he never got through the police academy and thirty years later he was just waiting for the next guy to rob his store so he could blow his head off and talk about it on the television. Lord knew how many guns he had stowed behind the counter under the register.

Crowe, to avoid RWB Liquor in Emerald City, restocked his sundries—beer and wine—at the big Kmart in Fort Myers, but sometimes, circumstance—such as the need to get ripshit drunk—necessitated a visit to RWB Liquor.

Like tonight.

Inside Crowe went into the beer cave—the frozen-type arced above the door of the walk-in—and got a twelve-pack and went to the counter.

"You got a new guy working for you I hear," Krumpp said.

"How are you, Krumpp? How's life?"

"He work on your boat?"

"Wayne?"

"No. Sells sodas? The kid."

"Working for me? I ain't a conglomerate."

"Whatever, that kid stole those sodas from me."

Crowe looked at the door. The cooler. At Krumpp. "Then I feel kind of bad. That's kind of a long way."

"You think it's funny, I got a business to run."

"How would somebody steal sodas from you? How?"

"The delivery guy from Hialeah, he was in the beer cooler one minute, and one minute later, some Mexicans are speeding off in a white Ford truck."

"Some Mexicans."

"Dark people, what I saw."

"Where were you when the soda guy was delivering?"

"The beer cooler."

"That doesn't make sense."

"It doesn't make sense because maybe you're stoned, hippy."

"Whoa, Sarge, how'd this escalate so quickly?"

"I got a business to run and you're crackin' fuckin' jokes."

"I didn't steal your sodas. Why you so mad at me?"

"Talk to the kid."

Crowe said, "Seems like an okay kid. I'd venture to even say good. Wouldn't peg him as belonging to any soda syndicate."

Krumpp smacked Crowe's change onto the counter.

"People saw a white truck and it was full of Mexicans and your boy was on it."

"He's not my boy. Two, sounds like your fuckup. Three, what people?"

"There's your change."

Crowe stood there. "What's your deal, man?"

"Have a good night."

After Krumpp's, Reed Crowe drove out of Emerald City and went down the narrow two-lane that cut straight through the pine flats on the edge of the county. There was a turnaround that was easy to miss to someone unfamiliar with it, especially in the dark, but Crowe knew the old logging trail. He bumped the hatchback off the road and took a shell road into dark Florida scrubland. Where the land became impassable, where his car tires couldn't find purchase in the sand, Crowe parked his car.

Then in the half-moon night he walked down a faint horse trail that wound through the wire grass and long leaf pines and sable palms, shovel and pick and trowel in a canvas bag slung over his shoulder, Coleman lantern lighting the path.

He went carefully, mindful of turtle burrows and crab holes. If his foot caught and he tripped: Fucked. Certain doom.

He recalled what he once heard about Amelia Earhart on talk

radio. An aviation historian hypothesized Earhart's remains hadn't been found because there were none. The coconut crabs had gotten to her. Torn her apart, dragged the bits and pieces into a thousand different hidey-holes.

Next time he would tell someone before his excursion.

Maybe Heidi, when she was back from Rennes.

Whole weeks passed these days where they didn't speak. He wondered if she was seeing someone else. Wondered if she'd tell him if she was. If it was over between them. He hoped not. They used to say I love you to each other, but that was a long time ago, in their days of romance. Before their girl died.

Sometimes they were on good terms. Every so often they slipped when they were drunk and slept together, which they were trying to give up, because it only confused them and led to problems.

Other times, they would go out of the way to avoid each other, that six months out of the year Heidi was on the island.

The other six months, she traveled.

She scrimped and saved and before the last time she left, she had other news to share. She'd sold a canvas.

She invited Crowe over for dinner, to celebrate.

Heidi and Crowe were still learning to be friends.

Now, Crowe was hunching into an inner chamber of the cave when he heard a sound like distant thrashing rain. The dim lantern was set on the ground before him. He stopped. The sound grew louder. His disorientation was such he couldn't tell if the noise was coming from inside or outside.

Then he was beset by a cyclone of leathery wings. A blizzard of bats.

Hundreds, maybe thousands, flapping all around him.

Rodent squeals pierced his ears. He rolled into himself like a pill bug, hugging his knees to his body, ducking his head between his knees.

When the onslaught ceased there was a sudden shocked silence. His voice, *fuck fuck fuck,* echoing into the limestone bowels of the sinkhole.

For a minute he thought a heart attack would kill him. He would rot here and they would find his skeleton years from now, decades from now, if even then. A hunting dog nosing through the bracken would pick up the scent of his remains. What the crabs and turtles left of him.

But he caught his breath, his slowing heart herky jerky like a broken toy. He slapped the dirt off his body and raked his shaking fingers through his hair, his beach bum beard.

"Good goddamn," said Reed Crowe.

Reed Crowe, half-assed spelunker, picked up his tools and went toward the hole.

In the canvas bag with the tools were dishwashing gloves. Crowe slipped on the big yellow rubber gloves and lifted the skull with both hands. Blew a beetle off. The bug buzzed like a busted party favor and smacked the dirt. It stayed on its back, working its angry legs.

Crowe turned the skull this way and that, holding it far from his body. Hamlet examining the skull of Yorick.

On the back of the skull was a large crack, a missing shard of bone.

Beaned, this dude. Either that or he fell from a great height.

Unlikely.

Florida, flat as a billiard table.

Then Crowe saw it. The eyetooth, gold.

The tendrils of hair, the remnants of a ponytail.

Reed Crowe knew then that the skull was Jerry Vogel's, an old Conch who'd gone missing about a decade and a half ago, in the sixties, around the time of Hurricane Betsy.

Jerry Vogel, a notorious pain in the ass. The bartender at the Rum Jungle until he left for Puerto Rico on his yacht with two college girls and a ton of cocaine.

Until the big storm of 1968. His yacht, dashed to smithereens. Sunk. The insurance, invalid. Whatever damage, it happened out of the zone of coverage.

That yacht was everything to Jerry Vogel.

And once it was gone?

Vanquished Jerry Vogel returned to Emerald Island.

There were only two bars on the island and Jerry Vogel was already banned from one of them. And damned if he was going to drink alone on his shitty houseboat for the rest of his life.

So the Rum Jungle it was, where his ex worked. His ex, whom he'd left unceremoniously, cruelly. His ex, who had a new boyfriend named Henry Yahchilane.

Jerry Vogel told his ex, "I made a mistake."

The ex told him, "You must be kidding."

"Don't forget the vows."

"You forgot. You forgot our vows. Party over. Too bad."

"Sickness and health," Jerry insisted.

And he kept insisting for weeks, angrier and drunker by the day, until he disappeared for good.

Now Crowe put old Jerry Vogel's skull back down. It glared up at him. He took off the gloves. He put the gloves on top of the skull to cover it up. He shook his head. Put on the gloves again. He picked up the skull as if it were a bomb that might detonate, holding it far away from his body, averting his twisted face. He shoved it into the canvas sack.

And it was then that Crowe saw something else in the same collapsed alcove. A gleam of obsidian in the dirt. At first he thought it was the back of a big shiny black beetle, some cave insect, but when Crowe nudged it with the toe of his shoe, it didn't move.

He picked it up. At first he mistook it as a chess piece.

Examining the stone closer to the lantern, Crowe saw that it was a stone figure. An artifact of some kind of idol or god wearing a crown that looked like a nest of snakes.

Crowe held the carving close to the lantern and when the light caught it he saw the angry face, the overlarge mouth with enraged teeth bared, the angry brow bent in a V. "Well, what the fuck, brother," Crowe said softly in the quiet in the cave, and giving the face a final look he slipped the carving in the pocket of his madras shorts.

GROTTO

THE GROTTO.

For years Henry Yahchilane thought it a safe hiding place.

Say the place was discovered. You'd be a fool to try to descend its depths, the crater was so perilous, its walls so sheer and plumb. Even a novice spelunker would be a fool.

But Yahchilane knew another way, another route, and this evening he took it, sweeping his walking stick a pace before him through the bracken. His other hand a tight-fingered spade thrust into the pocket of his jeans.

Right at the witch hazel bush and left at the moat, another right through the cabbage palms and the mangrove tree. Then you crossed an old cedar plank spanning a brackish ribbon of creek and at last in the clearing in the middle of the slash pine you saw the hole in the ground, the grotto that led underground to another grotto, and that into another.

A cave system.

A karst.

After leaving the Rum Jungle, after hearing the nincompoop blathering on about the skull, Yahchilane drove across the bridge and through Emerald City to a place on the outskirts of town where he knew a path that led through the Florida bracken to the grotto. He parked his van on the shoulder of the road, took the faint trail with flashlight in hand.

Yahchilane squatted at the edge of the clearing. He stayed that way in the purpling shadow of a ficus tree. The metallic ratcheting of the bugs in full chorus.

He watched Crowe from a distance as the man shoveled possessed.

He lit a cigarette.

After a while Crowe smelled the smoke. His head stuck gopher-like out of the hole in the ground and pivoted. His eyes were white in his tan dirty face with the beach bum beard.

Yahchilane stayed where he was. Exhaled smoke through his nose.

He rose from his crouch.

"What're you up to?" Yahchilane asked.

"What you mean?"

Crowe looked at the shovel in his hand.

"Yeah. No shit. What for?"

Crowe leaned his shovel against the lip of the hole. "Is this your property?"

Henry Yahchilane told him it wasn't.

Crowe was breathing heavily still from his work. He leaned on the handle of his shovel. Raked his fingers through his sweaty hair. "Well, man. I don't see how it's your business."

Yahchilane took the last few drags of the cigarette without speaking. He flicked the cigarette to the ground and heeled it out. Turned.

"Hello?" Crowe said.

Yahchilane strode away into the buggy jungle night.

"Hello?"

GROTTO CLOSED

WHAT DID REED CROWE KNOW ABOUT Henry Yahchilane?

A war veteran. Decorated.

This the Emerald Island residents knew, which also gave Henry Yahchilane latitude.

And rumor was that Yahchilane hailed from one of Florida's vanished and vanquished tribes.

Ais. Jororo. Calusa. Tequesta. Jaega. Timucua.

A loner about fifteen, twenty years older than Crowe. Nothing wrong with that. Plenty of loners on Emerald Island.

He was seen always dressed in a denim shirt laundered thin and near colorless. The shirt was always tucked into the jeans, no belt. His hair looked dried wet and it hung in stiff black loose curls about his face. Like maybe he bathed in salt water. His fingernails were long. But clean underneath. Scrubbed. The hands of a banjo player, perhaps, a guitar picker.

People took him to be in his early fifties, about twenty years older than Crowe.

He took up all kinds of odd jobs throughout the county to make ends meet. He cleaned pools, hung wallpaper and Sheetrock, shingled roofs, paved asphalt, seal-coated decks, dragged dead animals out of attics, hauled trash.

Mostly he was known as a snake handler.

The resident ersatz herpetologist. Part-time. One of Henry Yahchilane's many odd jobs around the county.

It was in the third or fourth year of his tenure at the Emerald County Zoo that a team of scientists discovered a small island two miles off where they were studying the encroachment of nonnative species. This being a loci of the nonindigenous species horned vipers and black mambas, puff adders and forest cobras. Boomslangs and kraits.

At one point the state offered Yahchilane money to get the snake population under control.

Staving off the inevitable.

Fool's errand that it was, Yahchilane did as they asked. He spent a good many hours corralling them. The state was paying for it.

Hey, it was money.

In the tiny city hall that was housed in a moribund Emerald City strip mall Yahchilane stood before the city council every year arguing against the state-sanctioned Florida Python Challenge. He also advocated closing the town zoo.

The Florida Python Challenge, each year the Fish and Wildlife Commission offered a bounty to the hunter who caught the biggest snake. A second cash prize to the man who collected the most.

A disaster waiting to happen, Yahchilane had argued. This on record in the local weekly paper. And he made no short order telling the city council so.

Plus, he needed the money and no one else wanted the job.

The board, "Let's not be dramatic." This their gist. Of course they wanted the pythons gone. They were in their yards. And they wanted the tourism.

Never mind the black bears and the alligators and the crocodiles and the cougars. The countless other perils of the Florida wild.

———

Another thing about Henry Yahchilane was an anecdote of such legend and renown just about everyone on the island knew it. Just about everyone on the mainland too.

There used to be some disparaging talk about his lineage. The typical Florida cracker badmouthing. De rigeur bigotry. Early seventies, this was. Around that time, there was a commercial on television night and day. The commercial about pollution, the commercial with the gaunt middle-aged man, Native American ostensibly, crying on the side of the road, tears trailing down his craggy face.

One night at the Rum Jungle some loudmouth from Cooper City, Jerry Vogel, gave him lip, calling him Chief Crybaby and Chief Boo-hoo-hoo.

There were plenty of eyewitnesses. Reliable eyewitnesses.

Jerry Vogel called him Tonto. Called him Chief Boo-hoo-hoo. The man, belligerent on tequila, the last-place contender of a red-fish tournament, a blue-ribbon asshole, would not quit.

Yahchilane sat placid as stone on his stool. "You're gonna get hit," he warned plenty of times.

"Boo-hoo-hoo." Vogel was toweling a beer mug and he placed it in the overhead rack.

"Okay," Yahchilane said. "All right. Watch it."

"Chief Wah-wah-wah."

Finally Yahchilane put down his beer and turned on his stool and looked fully at the man.

Vogel, sussing the gravity of the situation, said, "Cooper City. Better get away, Cooper City. Shit."

The man looked wider-eyed at Yahchilane. Then he slammed his beer down on the bar and picked up a cocktail napkin and wadded it in his fist and flung it to the sand. "Boo-hoo," the man started.

Yahchilane socked the man so hard, a full right hook, that the man's eye popped out and hung by a vein.

A thirty-thousand-dollar hospital bill in Hialeah to have the eye put back in his skull.

Thereafter people gave Yahchilane a respectful berth. And there were no more Indian remarks.

At least within Yahchilane's earshot.

Unless the man had a death wish.

The man's name was Jerry Vogel.

A jack-of-all-trades, Henry Yahchilane.

A renaissance man. With a perpetual slit-eyed scowl. A face that preempted being fucked with, his. A face that suggested he consorted with bad company. That he was perhaps the bad company itself. If he kept any company at all.

Ask the locals, though, Yahchilane was congenial enough. Taciturn, but not impolite. He held doors open for people. He said "please" and "thank you" and "yes, ma'am" and "no sir," but in a toneless flat voice. A manner that kept conversation to the minimum.

He didn't start trouble. To most locals this was fulfillment enough of his civic obligation.

Reed Crowe's reasoning about the skull: Nobody was looking for Jerry Vogel and nobody cared that he was gone. Few people remembered him. And those were the people he'd done wrong.

Not much of a legacy.

If Crowe called the police—small-town bumble-fuck Florida police around here, what a joke—then Crowe would have to show them where he'd found the skull. Which meant they'd never stop poking around. No doubt questions about the legality of the Florida Man Mystery House would come up. Codes, laws, safety, insurance. A never-ending quagmire.

Emerald City, so sequestered in this jungly corner of Florida, operated more as a commonwealth. A jury-rigged skeleton crew upheld the laws in Emerald City and Emerald Island. Laws as mandated by public decree, within reason. If somebody wanted to erect a bat tower in his backyard, fuck it. If somebody wanted to use their John Deere tractor as a mode of transportation for seven years like Ward Kennedy—no relation to the Boston Kennedys—fuck it.

In the morning before leaving for the Florida Man Mystery House tour Crowe rummaged in the carport and found an old empty Johnnie Walker box. He tore off one of the sides and in black ballpoint pen wrote GROTTO CLOSED *until further notice.* This seemed somehow insufficient. So Crowe added, in his sloppy caveman's hand, *We're sorry for the inconvenience. Sincerely, Management.* Near the bottom he started running out of room so had to cram in the last part.

The smashed-up handwriting looked like a dispatch from someone desperate and deranged.

A madman's ransom note.

Whatever. Reed Crowe nailed the scrap of cardboard onto the date palm tree outside the gift shop.

He decided he would stay away from the grotto for the time being.

Wait until Yahchilane, whatever his deal was, forgot he saw him there.

Before going into the gift shop he walked through the picnic area, went to the dock where Eddie was prepping the boat. The Dr Peppers, maybe Eddie didn't steal them himself, but one of his relatives? A distant cousin maybe. Whatever, Eddie probably bought them cheap somewhere. Ill-gotten, from an obscure remove.

Crowe mentioned this in so many words. The kid was immediately defensive. His look turned dark and hooded. His pimpled brow lowered.

"I'm not accusing you of bullshit," Crowe said, "but you gotta look at it from my perspective."

"I'm no robber, mister."

"Hey, listen, I've shown you hospitality."

"I ain't no robber."

Did the kid think he was racist? Jesus, he hoped not. How did this shit get turned around? "Eddie? All I know is somebody stole a bunch of sodas from Red, White and Blue Liquor."

For a moment they kept silent, both of them breathing scraping angry nose breaths. A billion bugs sang in the fierce green wilderness around them.

"You know the place? Krumpp? The guy's a wannabe cop, so I'd tell whoever to be careful."

"I don't know where the colas are from."

"Not the good ship lollipop, Eddie."

"Don't talk to me like a boy."

"Well, I'll talk to you like a man then. You sell stolen stuff on my boat again?"

"I don't like this shit you make fun of my English."

"That's not what's happening here. Just watch it, is what I'm sayin'."

Eddie shook his head. Crowe barely understood what he was trying to say.

Crowe was already rattled by his exchange with Eddie so he was doubly startled when he went into the gift shop and saw Henry Yahchilane.

Yahchilane was at the register and without a word paid the fare. With a final hard sidelong glance at Crowe, he exited the gift shop and went outside and began wandering among the Mystery House exhibits.

The cobwebby screen door squawked closed on its rusty hinges. Crowe glimpsed through it a few downtrodden tourists scuffing along the trail, walking into one of the pell-mell shacks and then on to the next. Yahchilane, attired as Crowe always saw him in denim and boots, strode over to the tortoise pool and stood for a time looking at Bogey with his thumb hooked in the belt loop of his jeans.

"When he get here?" Crowe whispered to Wayne.

"Tonto? Been hanging here ten minutes."

"Christ."

Crowe went with his cantaloupe to the mystery trail and fed Bogey the tortoise. Yahchilane was now perusing the exhibitions with the passel of tourists. The cabinets of curiosities, the dinky exhibitions, the jumbles of junk.

Plaques with talking plastic fish. A stuffed peacock. The beer cans of the world collection. Specimens floating in formaldehyde in apothecary jars. Octopi, squid, a baby shark. Meteorites encased in glass cabinets and ensconced on shelves. Crystals, an Ordovician cephalopod, a mastodon tooth. Like many things in Reed Crowe's

life, the place started as a lark. A repository for his odd random find-
ings. Over the years he'd accumulated such a tonnage of junk he
figured he had enough for a kind of ad hoc roadside attraction.

So he made one.

One corrugated shed contained mannequins made to look like
robots. Another room featured a mural of old-fashioned Ben Cooper
Halloween masks. Another room full of glow lights and growing
magic rocks. Another room full of tiki stuff. Masks, spears, monkey-
head coconuts. Another yet, toy soldier dioramas depicting the ad-
ventures of Ponce de Leon and José Gaspar the Florida pirate. The
Great Seminole War.

And now, where Crowe had his grotto exhibit displaying what
he'd found in the cairn over the years, Yahchilane lingered.

During the ravages of the Great Depression, when Reed Crowe's
relatives were living in tent cities and shacks throughout the South.
Hoovervilles, the New Deal program. One long-dead uncle went
south to Florida. There he became a de facto archeologist, one of
the first men in America to unearth indigenous artifacts. Burial sites
and shelters and stone figurines.

Most of the time Crowe's grandfather had no idea what he was
looking at. Getting paid to dig. People starving in other parts in the
country, and here he was getting paid to dig holes in the ground,
why question his luck?

Some of the artifacts he gave to the government. Some he sold to
collectors and museums.

A few he kept for himself.

Yahchilane looked at the Tinkertoy contraptions and the cheap
dioramas. He spent some time examining the exhibits, lingering at
the glass display where Crowe kept the finds from his digging.

Finally Yahchilane went into the cryptozoo shack, studying the
strange menagerie. From the wood-paneled walls a host of fey creatures gazed. A lizard-headed bat. An antlered human skull attached
to the body of a lapdog. A frog with eagle wings. A two-headed goat.
A panther with human ears and grinning dentures. A snake-necked
monkey with a forked tongue.

They stared from their nooks and crannies with catawampus
eyes.

Some were rigged with buttons. These, of Crowe's design. Press a buzzer and they'd tell you a joke. A skunk with a leprechaun's green top hat said, "Let me outta here. This guy's bat, no, skunk, sheet." A snake-necked monkey with a forked tongue that said, "Come over here, baby, kiss me."

"Sick shit," Yahchilane remarked to Crowe. "You make it?"

"What're you trying to start, mister?"

Yahchilane shot a breath through his nose. He strode away, joining the tourists straggling across the picnic rest area toward the boat. He walked the length of the gangplank, his size making it quake. He gave Eddie the money and sat on the far end of the bench stern and portside, away from the tourists. An Asian couple honeymooning. A young Canadian family from Quebec.

The tourists eyed Yahchilane.

The Canadian kids were brazen with their stares.

Henry Yahchilane paid them no mind.

Crowe chugged away from the Mystery House pier into the calm dark-water canal canopied by mangroves and cypress. Bugsong and birdsong. Pondskaters embroidering little lacy wakes on the surface of the water.

Eddie walked up and down the length of the boat, carrying the cooler on his bare tan back. "Coca-Cola, dollar," he said. "One dollar. Ointment. Coppertone."

"Four colas," said the Canadian father. The sunburn on his face was peeling. He and his wife seemed to use the same hair dye. A port color, blackish gray at the roots. The kids were middle-school-aged and looked parboiled too in their Disney T-shirts.

Canadian accents.

The man gave Eddie a five. Told him to keep the change. Eddie reached into the ice and pulled out four cans, two in each hand, his long fingers wrapped.

Yahchilane, his gigantic hands resting on his splayed knees, stared with vatic intensity at trees, the jigsaws of broken green light falling through the leaves.

"And here you have the anhinga, an odd bird, the anhinga. Some say serpentlike."

Crowe heard his voice, his faltering delivery. This man's presence, Yahchilane, made him self-conscious. Nervous.

Crowe singled out a girl. "Name, young miss?" He thumbed
sweat off his forehead.

"Crayola," she said.

Crowe was certain he'd misheard—his hearing, worse and worse
every year—but it didn't matter. Now people were getting up and
crowding starboard.

A big manatee rolled in a clear water spring.

The Canadian boy asked what the deep scars raked along its back
were from. It looked like someone had taken a three-pronged hoe to
the manatee's elephantine hide.

Crowe told the kids the truth. Propellers.

"Oh no," said the young Canadian girl with pigtails. "Poor Mr.
Manatee."

"He seems to be getting along okay," said Crowe. This didn't
seem enough. He added, "We all got scars, right?" He wondered if
he sounded whacked. The Yahchilane man had him nervous.

The Canadian father pointed at the mangroves with his chin and
asked what the plants with the far leaves were.

"Mangroves."

"No, the plants on the plant."

"Water plants. Mother of a thousand plants."

Yahchilane cleared his throat.

The tourists looked. Crowe looked.

"Alligator plant," said Yahchilane. "The devil's backbone."

The Canadian girl asked, "It is evil?"

"No, ma'am," said Yahchilane. "Just doing what it does."

The plants had been a gift from Crowe's mother some years ago.
One single leaf. A jade-colored succulent leaf as fat as a chandelier
crystal. He recalled the plastic bag, foggy with the leaf's sweat. They
were at her kitchen table, and she'd made him his favorite. Gnocchi.
His twenty-fifth birthday. Long ago now.

"Mother to a thousand trees," she'd told him. "Even someone
with black thumbs, presto."

She was right. Within months the plant thrived and blossomed.

Begot other fat-leaved plants. And before the season was over the backyard beach garden was teeming with pots filled with the alien-looking clusters.

And after his mother was committed to the home Crowe would spot the plants popping up here and there on Emerald Island. The wind spread them over the dunes and the pine flats. Sprinkled them around mailboxes and at the edge of parking lots. They proliferated. Within the span of several years, he saw them all over. He even saw a patch growing in the gravel of the standing ashtray in front of Krumpp's liquor store.

And now here they were in the swamp, the plants, Yahchilane pontificating about them.

"What's your name, sir?" the girl named Crayola asked.

"Yahchilane."

"Are you a chief?"

"No. Nothing like that now."

The earnest pigtailed girl with the freckled face and PAC MAN FEVER T-shirt wrote in her notebook. The pencil, one of those big huskies, the superthick ones. BIG CHIEF, it said on the side.

BACK FROM RENNES

HEIDI KARAVAS, BACK THE FIRST NIGHT from Rennes, was in her bungalow kitchen sautéing Amatriciana sauce—Bordeaux in the wineglass, Michael Jackson on the honeytone radio—when she heard something, someone, treading outside.

She turned down the radio. Set the wooden spoon down in the ceramic flamingo holder.

It was the gait of a man, large, long-strided, scuffing in the oyster shell drive.

The man went up the porch steps. A heavy stride. A big man.

The screen door squealed ajar.

Then there was a knock. Firm, three times.

It was after nine, late enough and dark enough that the automatic porch light was switched on.

Heidi's heart skipped. She wondered who it could be. "Reed?"

"No," came the voice, gruff and deep. A middle-aged man's rasp. "You open?"

"Open? Please go away. I don't know you."

"The bookstore, lady. The sign says open. It's glowing."

It took Heidi a moment to realize what he meant. Many were her various beach jobs to make ends meet over the years, as was the case with many of the natives, and the small used-book store had been one of the few to fall by the wayside.

She stepped to the door and looked through the peephole. In the wan porch light his face was in chiaroscuro, the deep creases, his wedge of nose throwing a shadow like a sundial.

She recognized the man from the island. Yahchilane something. Always polite.

Heidi opened the door a half-foot. The burglar chain still fastened. "Hello."

The man stepped back. Moths and june bugs fluttered through the corona of the porch light. "I apologize," he said. A low deep voice, the accent studied, almost bland.

"Just, you caught me off guard."

"I apologize, ma'am," said the man. "I'll come back business hours."

He turned, began to walk.

Heidi unlatched the chain, opened the door wider. She peered outside. The sign, glowing blue. "It's my fault," Heidi said. "Forgot to turn off the sign."

His stride slowed but he kept going. "I'll come back another time."

"What're you looking for?"

He paused, half turned. "Archeology book. Picture guide." His thumbs were hooked in his jean pockets. "Another time," he said, half-lifting a hand in valediction. "Evening."

Then went down the drive, turning south at the access road in the quarter moon dark.

RILING THE BEEHIVE

CROWE WENT TRUDGING THROUGH THE SPIKY Florida scrub toward the grotto, the canvas bag slung over his shoulder. One hundred feet of nylon boating rope was coiled inside, pick and spade propped over his shoulder like a work bound miner of yore.

Surprising, but despite all these years in Florida, despite his sundry cracker enterprises, he could fashion only a few reliable knots.

Basic boating knots, fishing rig knots.

Other knots, he compensated. Improvised.

And now around the trunk of a gumbo-limbo tree he fashioned a knot so byzantine, so cats-cradled, he was certain it was sound.

He assumed a tug-of-war stance, leaned full-bodied against the rope, testing it with all his might.

Satisfied at last Crowe went to the lip of the hole and peered down and then did an about-face. Backward, like a spelunker, he descended.

He'd dropped a few feet when the rope went suddenly loose and limp. Something gave.

The rope unspooled, the coarse braid burning through his fingers.

For what seemed a long and surreal spell Crowe plummeted. When he hit bottom he was jarred like a ragdoll. Pain jolted through his bones.

Amid myriad agonies, needles of pain along his neck and arms. Splinters of fire.

Hornets. A tempest of hornets buzzed around him. And now three or four dozen yellow jackets bulleted against his face, his arms. He glimpsed the mango-sized hive among the rocks on the cavern floor. Still more wasps seethed from a crack down its middle.

The more he swatted the angrier they grew. The blitzkrieg gyred. Stingers stabbed through his sweated T-shirt.

A poison prick to his earlobe.

His brow.

His elbow.

Crying caveman cries into the Florida night, Crowe fumbled and picked up a rock and blindly swung. He smashed insects against the cavern walls. When the stone crumbled apart he picked up another and lambasted anew.

And when he had most of the hornets pounded into jelly, he started jumping, fingers raking dirt as he clung for purchase. Pebbles hailed into his eyes and mouth. He grabbed the thick white root of a strangler fig and grabbed at another and then another.

Above him the plum and mango of dusk. He swatted at the hornets still clinging to him and stabbing their stingers through his skin.

In the twilight he staggered up and went through the brush toward his hatchback.

In the bathroom mirror he regarded his face with revulsion. The wheals and bumps like bunches of grapes growing under his skin. His right eye shot through with vermillion.

His head was a furnace with fever. His heart knocked catawampus.

All the poison.

He called Heidi. He tried explaining. His throat was swollen. His speech garbled.

It had been a while since they'd spoken. Their last phone conversation ended in an argument.

Now Heidi asked him, "Who is this?"

Crowe garbled out the words. "Do. You. Have. Antibiotics."

"Reed?"

"Hornets." He said it a few times before realizing she might have mistaken him for an obscene phone caller making a lewd proposition. "Horny," it sounded like.

"Are you drunk?"

"Hornets."

"Drunk."

"Anti. Biotics."

"Stop fuckin' with the phone."

"Anti! Biotics!"

It was a few minutes before Heidi understood the gist, and another long ten more until she arrived at Crowe's beach house.

When she first saw him she was aghast. She led him to the bathroom and sat him down on the fuzzy-covered toilet seat. She still knew the places of all the things, all the first aid stuff. She daubed his face with peroxide-soaked cotton balls. With Q-tips she swabbed the wheals with Mercurochrome. "Why do I do this?" she asked.

"Sorry."

"Why do I get pulled in?"

"Sorry."

She stooped on her knees and stuck Band-Aids on his cheeks and forehead. He smelled the faint musk of her skin, the eucalyptus and jasmine of her shampooed hair. That Heidi smell. He could feel her body heat, she was so close.

"We can be friends."

They'd had the discussion many times.

Crowe looking up like the elephant man. The pathetic, woebegone sight of him. Wretched.

Heidi laughed. Tried to stifle the laughter, couldn't stop.

"Not funny! Hurt!"

"Dummy."

"Hurt. Don't laugh."

She was laughing.

Crowe garbled out, "See, we can be friends."

"Then stop being nasty."

They were quiet for a time. Their faces close together. Their breath mingling.

I FOUND A HEAD

NEXT MORNING HEIDI CAME TO CHECK on Crowe. She found Reed Crowe in the backyard lounging in the hammock between the coconut palms. He was wearing a light poplin beach shirt, the buttons at his stomach open where one-handed he balanced a sweating bottle of Hamm's. He had on green aviator polarized sunglasses. A ukulele lay beside him. He had the sliding glass doors thrown all the way open and the hi-fi was playing Neil Young.

"Are you stoned?" Heidi asked. Clamdigger jeans, her white halter showing her tan shoulders.

"Yes."

"Nine in the morning."

"To you."

"To the planet. You got work in an hour."

"Like this? I got Wayne to handle it."

"Surely you're kidding."

Inside the house he turned down the music, changed the record to Fleetwood Mac. Then he went to the kitchen and poured an Arnold Palmer for Heidi. One of Crowe's prized possessions, one of his most cherished creature comforts, was a small freestanding icemaker at his wet bar. He gave her a full scoop of the small artisanal cubes she loved.

"Well, welcome back, Heidi," Heidi said.

"Welcome back, yeah, welcome back."

As she sipped at the diner booth in the sunny alcove, she looked over the archeology book on the table. The crude sketches of the grotto system, of Crowe's own design, on grid paper, the kind from trigonometry class senior year.

"What is this now?" Heidi asked. Wary already.

Crowe, wearing his sunglasses still, sat across from Heidi. Licking his joint, twiddling the paper between his fingers. "Nothing."

"Up to no good."

"I wish. There's no no good 'round here."

"It's called bad, I think."

"Let me write that down."

Heidi's eyes were still questioning.

Crowe, "Okay, if you really want to know."

"Oh god."

"You want to know? Just don't freak out."

"Reed."

"I found a head."

"Human?"

"Yeah."

"No, you didn't."

"A skull. Old."

Heidi was silent. Her face was stricken. She put down her glass, sat back. "Are you stupid. Call the cops."

The cops. Crowe almost laughed. Schaffer, his corruption and ineptitude. A laissez-faire spirit prevailed on the island. The islanders would have no other way. There was no need for meddlesome authorities. They caused little trouble among themselves. There were few people and places and things to trouble.

"It's old old, like artifact caveman shit."

Heidi slapped her hands on the table. "Reed, tell me you'll call."

"Yeah."

"Yeah. Yeah. You're a foggy-headed buffoon is what you are. Yeah." Then, something occurring to her, "You into some funny business with that Yahchilane guy?"

"Who?"

"You know who damn well."

"Native fella?"

"He came looking for a book the other night."

"Sounds like a weirdo."

"He came looking for an archeology book and here you are."

"Hey, listen," Crowe said. He looked troubled, wanted to change the topic.

"Oh god."

"That stuff at the airport. It wasn't fair."

Heidi looked at Crowe, took this in, forgot about Yahchilane and the archeology book.

SPRING BREAK

TAIL END OF APRIL, THE ANNUAL spring break horde filled the rooms of the Emerald Island Inn and scrummed the beach. College students from the state universities who for one reason or another couldn't make it down to Fort Lauderdale.

Every day Wayne could be found hustling among the young sunbathers, the beach revelers. From as far up as the motel Crowe could hear his yodeling cracker voice. His "woo-hoo" cackling. He was in high heaven.

Crowe would catch him loafing around the sea-facing catwalk connecting the rooms. Forearms folded on the railing, scrawny, tube-sock-clad ankles crossed, a spliff smoldering between his pinched grubby fingers as his eyes slavered.

One particular girl on the beach, Crowe noticed, Wayne had his eye on. A willowy blond girl, pixieish, bird-boned. Small nipples on bugbite breasts poking through the apple-green top of her two piece.

"I were Sheriff Schaffer," Crowe said to Wayne, "I'd cuff your ass right now."

"Hotter than a Hawaiian volcano," Wayne said to Crowe, pinched gray eyes on the girl through wraparound shades.

"Child."

"Eighteen at least."

"A child."

"Tell that to her body." He stroked his rattail, took a toke from his spliff.

"Jesus fuck Wayne."

"Since when's this Disney?"

Crowe was blasting the lime stains off the stucco side of the Emerald Island Inn with a spray hose when he saw and heard commotion on the beach.

Near the water a passel of college kids were playing volleyball. There was a net set up near the water. The sounds of their game, the *thunk* and *thwack* of the ball, their taunts and cat whistles, drifted from a distance in the afternoon. The mellow surf.

Crowe wasn't paying them much mind until there was a scream from the beach.

"Something's wrong, dude," Crowe could hear some kid saying, "something's fucked, oh holy shit." The young man was talking to his friend, who was telling him to shut up and relax.

Crowe dropped the nozzle and sprinted.

On the beach a bocce ball match stopped. Then a game of Frisbee. Now a full-fledged audience was gawking as two young men hauled the young blond skinny girl. The bird-boned pixie of a girl Wayne had his eye on. Her nose was bleeding. Her head was slack on her rubbery neck. She was stumbling and mumbling and her eyes were half-mast.

But she was alive. And ambulatory, as two young men dragged her away from the water up to the dunes.

"It's all right, folks," Crowe called. He waved. "Everything's okay. Everything's cool. She's gonna be okay." He waved some more, smiled like a warped game show host. "Enjoy your day. We got this."

Crowe followed the trio. "I don't want any of this shit at my motel," he said in a hissing whisper.

"Okay."

"I need you out."

"Come on, man."

"Out."

The kid looked at Crowe. "All right, mister."

"I'll call the cops myself. If that girl dies in my motel, so help me God."

The college boys were so shaken they had no fight in them. "Okay, mister, we're outta here, just, come on? Ten minutes, dude?"

"What room you in?"

"Two eighty-one."

"Well, get the fuck going. Quick."

The girl would be fine, Crowe saw. A savage gleam was already rising in her eyes. Defiance. And aimed toward him, of all people, as if he was spoiling her fun.

"Oh, eat my ass," said the girl.

"All right," Crowe said.

Crowe was at the checkout desk examining the Emerald Island Inn ledger, seeing what room the girl was checked in to when the phone rang.

A man said, "I hate to be the party crasher." It was Sheriff Schaffer.

Crowe told him he had the situation under control.

"Certain things I'm willin' to overlook. Whatever the shit you're peddling, no."

"You come over here, Schaffer. Search. Search my house." Crowe wondered how Schaffer caught word so quick, figured it must have been one of the older tourists. If not, then one of the locals.

"I'm getting calls," Schaffer said.

"I'm inviting you."

On the checkout desk was an avalanche of mail. Catalogues and circulars and weeklies. And bills. The fucking bills.

A horsefly started buzzing around Crowe's head and Crowe swatted at it but the fly came back at Crowe with vengeance and doubled fury. Crowe grabbed an issue of *Time* magazine from the stack— PARADISE LOST, it read, in kind of retro postcard font, over a picture of Florida State—and whacked the thing away until it loop-de-looped out the cracked-open door.

Schaffer was still talking. "I can't be having any of that shit going on now. Whatever cocaine bullshit you got. Whatever crack bullshit. You hear what's going on down south?"

"I'm inviting you. I'll mail you an invitation. Come on over."

By the time he'd finished talking the line was dead.

Crowe went right away to Wayne Wade's room.

"That girl out there. You give her any shit?"

"What happened to knocking?"

"Wayne, you sell any shit to that girl?"

"Home office call you or somethin'?"

"Cut the shit."

"I sell shit. That's what I do, Reed."

"Cocaine. Pills. Heroin."

Wayne Wade stroked his rat-colored rattail, turned away from Crowe's rancid look.

"Man, you're wiggin'. I don't know what else to tell you. Wiggin'. Some thing to say."

"Tell me the truth."

"I can't control what the kids're bringin' to the island."

"Now they're kids. Not so long ago, grown ladies. Now kids."

A poster tacked up on the wall caught Crowe's attention. *Scarface*. Crowe stalked over to it as if intending to rip it down. Instead he stood with his arms akimbo, grimacing. On the picture was Al Pacino in a pinstripe coke lord suit, brandishing a tommy gun, his face twisted, dusted with cocaine.

Crowe asked Wayne Wade, "Are you some mental defect, this shit?"

"My room." Wayne was sitting at the end of the bed on the grungy conch-patterned bedspread, knees spread, his unlit cigarette lipped. "Decorate it how I like."

"I'm gonna tell you something."

"Get the fuck outta here, Reed."

"Any woman comes here, she's gonna think you're a serial killer."

COOL PAPA LEMON

THAT SPRING A RARE SERIES OF thunderstorms slammed the coast. One right on the heels of another, three in swift succession. And an odd red tide washed up from the sea depths, seaweed and wrack spangling the high tide line, thousands of burgundy wigs infested with white crabs tiny as lice ranged up and down the beach. After that poison purple jellyfish filled the shallows, so fewer people filled the rooms of the Emerald Island Inn.

Meanwhile the receipts and debts and bills mounted. There was the upkeep of the Emerald Island Inn to consider, the colossal power bills during the summer, the air-conditioning units always straining and rattling against the heat. And there were the bills for his mother's care Crowe had to pay. The monthly fees for the nursing home.

Crowe was always loath to dispatch Wayne Wade on any serious errand. Let alone one felonious. But circumstances demanded once more this spring. What with the recession and the middling business of late at the Florida Man Mystery House. What with the upkeep of the motel, the property taxes. The interest rates, the late fees, the penalties.

Everybody over the bridge, the old Conchs, got a post office box, since Myrtle was the sole employee of the U.S. Postal Service for both Emerald Island and Emerald City. Unless it was a special circumstance, an emergency, Myrtle let the old Conchs get the mail their own asses, as she was wont to put it.

It was so ill-used, the post office, when you stepped inside, motes of dust swirled in the fuggy wood-paneled room. When the sunlight struck through the front glass of the converted Payless Shoe store, the dust rising through the old blue carpet looked like luminescent spore.

The mailbox was one of those old brass jobs of yore. And one could walk in the post office whenever they pleased. The place was kept open 24/7, all days of the year. There was nothing to steal.

"King Canute fightin' back the waves," Crowe would say to himself.

These days nightmares about his mounting debts kept him awake. Sometimes his dreams seemed to consist only of a floating blackness, some kind of embryonic space in which he floated astronaut-like with his only company Myrtle the mailperson's voice in his head, sweet, but with a mocking motherly edge, "You got mail, Reed."

It was after one of these sleepless nights in spring, brought upon by just such a visit to the Emerald City post, that Crowe woke and raided his ganja stash in the kitchen freezer and parceled out chunks of marijuana into ziplock bags. Halves and ounces. They no longer fucked with quarters. And so adroit was Crowe with this task he no longer required a scale. He did it by sight, touch.

With the small bags in a king-sized Swap Shop plastic bag, Crowe drove to the Emerald Island Inn and went to Wayne Wade's so-called office, a room he'd appropriated years ago as a makeshift break room and headquarters.

He rapped on the door. Nothing. Loud AC/DC on the boom box. "Dirty Deeds Done Dirt Cheap."

Crowe kicked at the door.

The music was quickly turned down, an angry twist of the knob.

"What now," Wade said, birdy pique already in his voice.

"It's me."

"No shit. Open."

Crowe found Wayne Wade atop the bedcovers with his legs crossed and his back against the headboard and his grimy Miami Dolphins cap crooked and low on his head. His arms were crossed behind his head with belligerent insouciance.

He was expecting an upbraiding for one thing or another.

Instead, Crowe said, "Gonna need you to go to Fort Lauderdale." As if it pained him. And he was wincing, though Wayne Wade couldn't discern it behind the shaggy beach bum beard.

"Fuck yeah," said Wayne Wade, already rising from the bed.

Wayne Wade was several years ago eighty-sixed from the Elbow Room. So those few spring nights on the Fort Lauderdale beach strip he frequented the Mermaid Lounge. Lurking in the wings, hopped up, juggling his body from foot to foot with a kind of contained bristling energy, waiting for an open spot at the bar. And then quickly he would jackrabbit into the space and vouchsafe a stool. The elbows of the much bigger men at the bar would crowd him in.

He'd nurse his Budweiser beer until the dregs were room temperature, awaiting the next mermaid show. Every forty-five minutes the women in the silver-scaled bikini tops and big costume tails would dive into a pool, twisting and turning in the water like balletic seals. A fifteen-minute routine. You could see them through the glass behind the bar. Four Florida girls with spring break tans and sorority girl teeth.

Wayne Wade had his eye on the skinniest of the quartet. A gyring, ringlet-haired nymphet.

Next to Wayne Wade was a hunched man in an oatmeal-colored Members Only jacket. He was staring without expression at the swimming costumed women. They blinked into the dim bar, eyes open in the chlorine water, the corners of their smiles birthing strings of bubbles like necklaces.

Wayne leaned and mumbled to the man. "I got pixies."

"Fuck off."

"Love beans. Scooby Snax."

"Who do you think I am, mister?" His face reddened. His eyes were intense, goiterishly abulge, behind big boxy bifocals.

Wayne Wade figured the man had misunderstood. "Snow? Maybe that's your thing."

"I'm from Kentucky. I don't need your Florida shit."

"Only askin' if you like partyin'. Chill, dude."

"Fuck off."

"Kentucky tight ass."

The man's hand shot as quick as a snake for Wayne's scrawny throat.

The barkeep lifted the bar flap and moved in swiftly, wedging himself between the two.

And in this manner the matter was decided. Wayne Wade was yet again banned from another Broward County bar.

Wayne Wade, sunburned after three days of spring break reconnaissance, moved like a jackrabbit amid the beach mob, among the towels and the Igloo coolers and the boom boxes.

"I got barrels," Wayne Wade would sidemouth to the Grateful Dead–looking people.

"I got snow," he would sidemouth to the kids in the pop collars and designer shades.

Mostly, it was snow kids were crazy about these days.

With the pockets of his jorts bulging Wayne Wade tippy-toed and jack-be-nimbled among the oiled buttocks and legs and stomachs, leering from behind his wraparound sunglasses. Among bright orchards of beach towels and umbrellas were young women in their neon pink bikinis. He smelled their aloe, their coconut oil. Their watermelon gum.

The spring breakers shot him looks. This man in checkered Vans and red-striped tube socks. A tie-dyed tank top that said I WRESTLED A BEAR ONCE in a kind of clawed, ripped-out font.

Wayne pssted and whispered, "Barrels. Scooby Snax. Snow."

A man's thunderous voice said, "Hey!"

Wayne Wade looked and saw two hulking men who he reckoned plainclothes detectives moving toward him.

Wayne ducked and scrambled away. The men quickened. Wayne's checkered Vans spat out clods of sand as he veered to and fro among the sunbathers and spring breakers.

One of the policemen caught up with Wayne and poleaxed into him. For a moment scrawny Wayne Wade was airborne, flying sideways. Then he was pinned down by an officer into the sand as dozens of people gawked. His face was mashed as he flailed and kicked, his goober teeth showing in anguish.

"Touch your nose to the ground . . . no, your left . . . on your knees, stop right there . . . hands on your head . . . don't move . . . don't move, squirt . . . spit out the cigarette, small fry . . . What's in the orange bag, sir? Is this a knife? Another knife here? What's in the orange bag?"

The other cop, cuffing Wayne Wade, "Oh boy, this ain't your day, sir. Now stay still. Because it still can get a whole lot worse."

POINCIANA

TWICE A MONTH, EVERY OTHER SUNDAY, Crowe visited his mother. The Poinciana Nursing Home was in Fort Lauderdale, on the opposite coast of Florida, a three-hour drive across the dicktip of the state. South down I-75, east across Alligator Alley, north up I-95.

Before going to the nursing home Reed Crowe went to a place called Fran's Chicken Haven on Federal Highway and Glades in Boca Raton, the best fried chicken ever in his considered opinion.

His mother's too.

They sat at one of the white concrete benches near the hibiscus garden in the nursing home commons. Picking at the chicken and macaroni salad. Wiping the grease off their fingers and lips with paper napkins. Watching the anhingas in the pond with the fountain in it. Sipping through straws their fountain ginger ales from the giant Styrofoam cups before the ice got too melted.

They talked about random things. The weather. The crime in Fort Lauderdale and Miami. Oprah Winfrey. Crowe's mother, Shelly, loved this new talk show host Oprah Winfrey.

There was no longer much family left living to speak about. Her kin scattered like dandelion thistle. Good-hearted, wholesome Scottish Conchs, a tight-knit clan, but now all over the map and with Fort Lauderdale so deep south it was just about the tropics.

Her room was large and sunny. And always when Crowe visited there were other people in her room. At least a few of her retirement village friends. A nurse or two. And if it wasn't in her room he found her, it was in the aquatic center or dining room or garden. The bingo hall.

Sometimes Crowe would have to explain things to her like a child. This was in the beginning, when Crowe was telling her the truth. But it was too difficult, because he'd have to tell her the truth over and over again. Every visit.

"There's been an accident, Mama," he used to say, willing patience into his voice.

She'd lift her head off the pillow of the nursing home bed. She blinked at him, her foggy emerald eyes uncomprehending. She thought he was talking about a broken bone, a knocked-out tooth.

Not life or death stuff.

It was almost as though he needed to tell her his life story every time he saw her.

A Magic 8 Ball, his mother's head. Much like his, except the wine and pot was probably to blame. Except was it? There was no way of knowing, since Crowe eschewed the doctor. He saw Dr. Vu as little as he could.

He had a troglodyte's fear of doctors.

Other times his mother mistook him for her high school sweetheart.

Other times, she'd recognize him as her son and he'd have to explain where Otter was all over again.

"Otter?" she asked. "Otter's in the hospital? Is she in the hospital? Is she on this floor? Let's go see her. We'll get ice cream sundaes."

This time, his mother asked, "How's Otter?"

Her roommate was watching *Sanford and Son* on the television. The theme playing.

"She's good."

"I keep on forgetting the grade."

"High school," Crowe would say.

"My. Already? Already? And what schools, what schools is she going to? She will be going to school, right? A home wife, no life for Otter."

"Elizabeth, this is the big one," said the character Fred Sanford to his son. "Elizabeth, this is the big one."

Twenty minutes later, Crowe's mother asked, "And Otter? How is Otter? She's in school today?"

Crowe said she was, just as if he hadn't answered the question minutes ago.

"I miss her." She sipped her ginger ale through her straw.

"She misses you too," Crowe said.

IN THE CLINK

IN THE BROWARD COUNTY JAIL, IT was bologna sandwiches for meals. Baked beans. Apple slices, the flesh long turned brown.

The smell. The smell, by god. In the way of a lavatory they had a single aluminum toilet, flat out right in the open, for some twenty-five or thirty criminals. Some mere miscreants, others shrieking bedlamites, still others outright murderers.

All with one pot to shit and piss in.

One guy, a grown man with an abnormally small head, coconut-sized. Wayne Wade would have placed from Alabama by his accent was bashing his head into the bars over and over again. "Mama. I need you. Mama. Mama."

"Stomp that motherfucker's head like an acorn," one black man said. He was tired of the caterwauling.

"Do it," said the guard down the hall.

"Stomp that motherfucker's head flat as a pancake," the black man said.

"Do it," said the guard.

When the black man rose and the small-headed man turned and noticed, he at once realized the gravity of his situation. Coconut head or not, he wasn't so dim-witted after all. He shut up and went to the corner where he sat despondently.

Mostly the men were taciturn. Their hard-bitten faces said, *Don't you fuck with me.*

Florida men of the hardest sort.

Still, there was occasional palaver.

"What they got you for?" said one man to another.

"Ridin' a horse on I-95."

"Bullshit."

"No shit. I didn't know you can get a DUI ridin' a motherfuckin' horse."

"How can you get a DUI on a horse? No, you cain't."

"Oh, yes, you fuckin' can."

"You ride a horse. You don't drive it."

"No shit."

"That don't make no sense."

"No, it don't."

"You should'a called your lawyer. You got fucked."

"I did. I did call my lawyer. And as soon as I get outta here, I'm gonna kill him."

Wayne watched and listened all the while from his corner, one bony butt cheek hanging off the edge of the hard metal bench.

"You mind scooting over a bit?" he asked the man next to him.

Nothing.

"Hey, buddy?"

Nothing.

Wayne gave up.

He tried not to look at the faces. He didn't want to invite trouble. The merest glance might set off god knows what. He did not want his head stomped like an acorn. Or a pancake.

It was among this motley crew of felonious riffraff that a man by the name of Hector Morales, alias Catface, was ushered into the overcrowded holding pen by a bullfrog-faced bailiff. The man, Hector Morales, wore a bespoke Panamanian suit of fine butterscotch silk. His face was ravaged with scars. The face looked like a mass of scored putty.

There were a few cat whistles once he entered. A few double takes. A few looks of unguarded repulsion. The kind of naked wonderment a child might wear after beholding roadkill. An animal slaughter on *Mutual of Omaha's Wild Kingdom.*

"Ugliest motherfucker I ever seen," said one man. This the same big bald black man as earlier.

At first Catface seemed not to have heard. He stood with a kind of prim soldierly vigor, but looser in bearing, his loafers spaced evenly apart, his arms clasped behind his back. He stood this way for thirty seconds, until the clocking of the bailiff's footsteps retreated down the hall and then turned.

Finally Catface turned and went up to the man who'd made the remark.

"Yes. That's me. How es you?" He held out his hand for a handshake. The "how es" cartoonish, lampooning himself.

The man cast a dubious look around at his cellmates. "You dig this ugly motherfucker?" Then, turning to Catface, he said, "Get lost."

Catface kept his hand out. "No shake?"

"You better get lost before you get stomped."

"Stomp?"

"Smash your buttfuck ugly bacon-looking head like a grape."

Catface kept his hand out, no change in his posture. He appeared almost a statue, frozen in this amiable stance. A petrified city park mime.

The cellmates watched, their craggy felonious faces waiting to see how this episode would unfold. Another story of the many in their books, this.

When the black man rose from the bench ready to belt him, Catface lashed out.

Wayne Wade did not see the blade. No one saw the blade. It must have been a razor, playing-card flat, secreted in some fold of his bespoke clothing. A hidden pocket. The blade was out like a catclaw and then it vanished just as quickly, but in the interim the man's arm was slashed deep at the wrist.

The man screamed and blood was everywhere. Spraying. The man was so enraptured and repulsed by the sight of his own blood that he'd all but forgotten the catfaced man.

Then the man with the face like a vivisection started clapping rhythmically. He stomped an alligator skin shoe against the concrete floor. In a mellifluous throaty tenor he hummed a few bars of a familiar song. Then he sang, "Miami Dolphins, Miami Dolphins, Miami Dolphins number one."

Wayne Wade marveled, how quickly the Cuban roused the whole motley lot of them.

Catface gestured between claps.

As soon as one man stood and tentatively started to sing then another man joined and then five voices became seven and before long most of the reprobates in the cell were stomping like a group of revelators, smacking their hands, stirring up a gospel tent racket.

"Yes," they sang, "we're the Miami Dolphins, Miami Dolphins, Miami Dolphins number one."

The bald man banged his head on the jail cell bars. He kept wailing for his mother.

The criminals crooned on, their voices drowning his. "We're in the air, we're on the ground, we're always in control."

The guard shouted from down the hallway. "All right, assholes."

His footsteps approached, a peevish clip. But then they turned away, and his own singing trailed off. "And when you say Miami, you're talking Super Bowl."

Their voices grew. Their stomping. Now the chorus was so loud Wayne Wade's tinnitus flared up. A shrill treble trembled in his inner ear.

"All right, assholes," the guard said again, but now there was a smile in his voice. He joined in. "Miami Dolphins, Miami Dolphins."

When the chant reached a crescendo, the scar-faced man stepped onto the supine man's skull. He pressed down with his loafer.

The voices started to peter. But then the Cuban motioned preacher-like, gesturing expansively with his arms in exhortation.

Uncertainly the men resumed their chant.

"Miami Dolphins, Miami Dolphins, Miami Dolphins."

They watched, some enthralled and others aghast. Mostly, though, and most frightening to Wayne Wade, they looked indifferent.

As though they'd seen worse. Far worse.

The Cuban stepped harder, harder.

The man's head began to cave like a rotting gourd, his berserk yelling drowned out by the hollering.

Then the eyeballs popped out of the man's skull. His swollen tongue lolled out with a gush of blood. With a final wracking spasm the man went still.

Dead.

The Miami Dolphins chant abruptly stopped.

"Mama!" wailed the bald man.

The noise drew the guard back and they could hear his big bulge of keys jangling against his thigh.

The men, eyes dropped noncommittally to the gray institutional concrete, would say nothing when the guard came.

He gaped at the bloody pulpy mess on the floor. "What happened here?" he said. "What the fuck is this?"

The motley crew kept mum.

"All right," the guard said. "All right, you fucks. Have it your way."

"Chuck!" the guard yelled.

"Yeah," Chuck, the youngest and newest guard, the lackey, said back.

"Get a mop. Somebody's head got smashed."

The young man's aggrieved voice came down the hall, "Oh jeez, you gotta be kidding me."

NGANGA PALO MOYOMBE

HIS NAME WAS HECTOR MORALES, ALIAS Catface, the man with the scarred face. A Cuban refugee from the Mariel Boatlift. Late April 1980, aboard one of the first waves Castro sent after the Soviet Union collapsed and cut off Cuba's goods. Around that time Jimmy Carter granted a certain number of Cubans asylum. Castro, feeling betrayed, crammed the boats bow to stern with reprobates. Here you go, Jimmy.

Child molesters and serial rapists and drug warlords.

The immigrants who were trying to come legally, they had to wait for the lottery.

The criminals, they got a first-class ticket.

Catface, the man with the face so maimed even the most self-possessed people did double takes, was on one of the first boats.

His face, like it had been shredded with a pitchfork, sewn back together by a maniac surgeon.

The day's ride across the water was a hellish odyssey. The biblical heat, the heavy chop of the waves roiling his guts. All of them massed and stinking on the boat, standing room only. Seasick men scrambled for a place to puke but there was nowhere except over the gunwale and sometimes they didn't make it in time.

One reedy straw-hatted man got sick on someone's sandaled feet.

The man in sandals stabbed the straw-hatted man in the gut with a box cutter. The man staggered off to a corner and sat whimpering with his back against the gunwale and his hand clutched to his stomach, his blood seeping blackly through his fingers.

The other men kept their distance.

Nothing to be done.

After he slumped and bled out and died a few men consorted and finally threw the dead man overboard into the water. The man floated facedown, his white shirt so dirty and old it was the yellow of aged ivory. The khaki pleated pants, the sewn-up back pocket. A lone seagull lit on his back and watched the boat frothing away into the distance as the men with tight sun-cured faces watched the bird.

A picture of the landing of Catface's boat was on the front page of the *Miami Herald*, commemorating his first legal step on American soil. Men young and old and middle-aged shirtless and filthy from the journey stepping off the boat onto American soil. Men with hard-bitten faces. In the background among the mass of people, among these faces, was a visage so warped it appeared an optical illusion. A smudge on the lens. A trick of light.

No.
Catface.

Oh, what a strange and twisted journey it was that delivered him to America. How far his travels from the domino tables of his youth, the hardpacked yard with the scraggly chickens and the slat-ribbed dogs, the droughted citrus trees reared against the dun hills.

Catface's father, a farm worker, believed him cursed.

One morning Catface's father found a small black cauldron left on the doorstep of their shack overnight. An occulted-looking thing likely crafted by witches in some old twisted wood. The cauldron was spiked with railroad rivets and barbed wire and sharp rusted metal, wrapped around with chains and old-fashioned padlocks. Amid the rust and dried blood were feathers, a small rodent bone, a hoof.

A nganga, the cauldron.

Black magic. The black arts.

And this, a scary grimoire. The nephew knew it too.

"Nganga Palo Moyombe," he said.

"Enough, boy," Catface's father told his nephew. "Get that fucking thing away."

"How?"

"Up your ass, boy."

"Where?" the nephew asked.

"I don't care. In your mother's ass. Get it out."

"Should I get gloves?" The kid would later describe the nganga to his friends as a rusted metal octopus. Tentacles of barbed wire and chain and razor blades.

Hector Senior said, "That thing will blast this whole neighborhood into eternal hell."

Catface, Hector Junior, was born with a cleft palate and Hector Senior, his father, a degenerate gambler and drunk, was convinced black magic was to blame.

And believing his firstborn son cursed, Hector Senior tried to drown him when he was eight months old. One day when the mother was at the market he plucked the mewling ugly baby out of his crib and carried him out of the house and threw him into an irrigation canal. As if he were a sack of cornmeal.

And while the infant choked and cried he strode calmly back to the house, poured himself a jam jar full of rum, sat in the recliner listening to futbol on the transistor radio.

The mother, when she returned, was apoplectic. "Where's Junior? Where's Hector?"

Hector Senior, indifferent, blasé, "No idea, woman." He picked up his flyswatter. He took a vicious swipe at a buzzing horsefly. Missed.

Catface's mother, Esmerelda, "You were supposed to watch him."

"I did. I was."

"Well, he's gone."

"You told me, woman."

Hector Senior swiped at the fly again and this time the insect went flying into the blades of the fan. There was an angry chattering like a misrouted BB and then the insect corpse pinged against the cracked stucco wall and fell to the floor.

Junior's mother, "What did you do, you bastard?"

The father, sheepish, got off his recliner, searching around the room behind the furniture.

The mother, "He's gone."

"I'm looking, woman. All right?"

"You did something. What did you do?"

"Fuck, woman. Watch it."

The mother's voice was soft, barely audible. But it was tight and trembling with anger. "You did something, you did something, I know it. Where is he? Where is my child?"

Hector Senior gave his wife a dark hooded look. "Watch it. Look at me. Watch it. Don't doubt it. Now find your child."

They searched the little adobe house. Nothing. And with each passing minute the mother grew increasingly frantic.

Hector Senior, for the first time in his life, was frightened of the woman. What she might do. But then, when he saw what he saw through the kitchen window, his legs gave. They buckled and he held on to the edge of the chair to steady himself.

His child. Hector Junior.

The child had swum out of the canal and had come back home all this way. Now he was under the blighted mango tree, crawling through an ant pile, his face and arms and legs teeming with insects.

The mother flung open the door and went running to the child across the scrubby hardpacked yard.

Among Catface's associates in the syndicate, the rumor was that he was touched. So they always treated him warily, gave him wide berth.

Look at what happened to the man in the Everglades, for instance. The airplane crash, the fire. Even that he survived.

So by 1980, once Catface was conducting business in America, he had already vouchsafed a reputation.

Within his first few months in Miami, he killed three men, all by hand, all by knife. He made enough from those killings to buy a brand-new midnight-blue Mustang convertible, cash.

He drove the Mustang right off the lot with the price sticker still in the windshield.

From the auto dealership he drove to the Holiday Inn where he had a young black couple duct taped naked to one of the beds. They'd stolen a kilo of cocaine from one of Catface's cohorts.

The man was a pimp and aspiring drug dealer, the black girl his whore. They were naked, injected with psychedelics. For days they insisted they had no idea where the drugs went.

"Shatter every bone in your body," Catface told them. "One by one. Es ever heard of the stapes? Baby bones in ears? One by one. Work my way to the femur."

On the third day, the pimp finally told Catface all he needed to know.

Catface sliced their throats open with a filleting knife anyway.

———

In the summer of 1980, Catface took residence in the Mutiny Hotel. The room like a captain's quarters, a mahogany ship wheel mounted on the wall. The balcony, shaped like the prow of a ship, overlooking the horseshoe-shaped bay with hundreds of pristine gleaming white boats. Yachts as big as three football fields combined.

The room was called the Emerald Island suite. This remarkable coincidence would not strike him for many years to come. And what a mazy twisted path would it be, the culmination of that fortuity, that coincidence, so improbable as to seem nigh occulted, like providence.

The early eighties were a time of anarchy in Miami. Race riots. Massacres. Rapes. Shoot-outs. Holdups. Drug deals gone wrong. So many murders, so many citizens shot and stabbed and slaughtered in the streets, the Miami morgues were crammed full. The city started stacking corpses in a Burger King freezer.

The Hotel Mutiny was the epicenter of the Miami madness, where criminals of every stripe conspired and consorted. Murderers. Arms dealers. Mercenaries. Assassins of overthrown narco-republics. Gunrunners. Dictators deposed from third world countries and ad hoc Panama republics.

Men with names like Tarantula, so nicknamed for the spider-shaped birthmark on the side of his neck. Yoyo, on uppers and downers. Barbo Rojo, a man with a green parrot on his shoulder, a golden grenade clipped to his belt.

Some of the men were twice as big as Catface, assassins and henchmen and outright coked-out murderers. Yet they treated him with a certain deference, nigh servile.

Si, senor. No, senor. Perdón, senor. Si, si, de nada.

Looking Catface in the eyes, but not for too long.

Downstairs was a private club where you had to be a special member. Members got a special gold card with the club's winking pirate logo.

Catface had the card, the cigarette lighter, the medallion on his necklace, the signet ring. The key with the fob that was also embossed with the pirate face.

It wasn't only his appearance that gave people pause. If it wasn't for his face, he would be a handsome and formidable man.

His black grayless hair, his widow's peak.

His even white smile, a game show host's.

His finely tailored bespoke clothes.

But his face.

And it wasn't only his face.

A feral black energy crackled around him. An occulted charge.

It was a miracle he was here, really.

He was so high and out of his mind near the end of his stay in Cuba that his last memories were loose-leaf, scattershot. A constellation of impressions. The grubby embassy. The rib-skinny dogs in the street, gnawing on chicken bones. Riots between Castro loyalists and the rebellion.

Busted jaws, broken hips, children wailing in the pandemonium.

Propaganda on leaflets, everywhere.

A busted cafe window. The owner beating someone's head in with a bocce ball mallet. Then the man's brother later coming to gun the man down to succotash with an AK-47.

One night one of his cohorts hired a blind prostitute. Thinking it was just the face. She went with Catface to the Elbow Room in Fort Lauderdale, a private booth, to see a rock-and-roll singer Catface understood to be Timmy Boffett.

Jimmy Buffett.

A man opened up for Buffett, a comedian who smashed watermelons with a sledgehammer. Catface understood him to be the "melon hombre."

After his show Catface requested that the man he called "Timmy Boffett" come to the table.

He did. A man in a Hawaiian shirt and a lobster-red sunburn,

escorted by a small entourage of bodyguards and security and restaurant personnel.

"She likes the concert and I like the concert," Catface said.

Buffett, still recovering from the shock of Catface's face, still in
the grip of his handshake, "Well, thank you, sir."

"The real Mr. Timmy Boffett. Why not you play the lime in the
coconut song?"

Buffett laughed a fake laugh.

Catface still hadn't relinquished his hold, clutching the hand
though he'd stopped the pumping of his arm. "Why not though?
Your best song."

The smile fell off Buffett's face. "It's not mine, dude."

"Of course it is."

Catface sang it. People turned in admiration. His singing voice
was a mellifluous tenor. But then they saw his face and their eyes
went holy fuck and then they turned quickly away. The singing
stopped with the abruptness of a switched spigot and then Catface
resumed in his rough whisper. "Everybody wants lime in the coconut."

Buffett puffed up and started to pivot away. "Hey, fuck you."

Catface kept his hold.

Buffett tugged.

Catface kept his hold.

Buffett cocked his fist.

Catface sprung and took Buffett's right arm. Yanked him back
and pinned his head to the table, cheek mashed against the surface.

"Pardon?"

Buffett was hissing spitty breaths between gritted teeth.

The personnel, "Sir, sir, senor, please."

Catface would not let go. He took out a switchblade, flicked it,
pressed the blade against Buffett's neck, the tip poking the flesh with
just enough pressure to birth a quivering ruby of blood. "Request
from the crowd. Lime in the coconut. From Mr. Timmy Boffett."

And Buffett then moaned a few bars of the song.

But ten minutes later the cops came into the Elbow Room and
arrested Catface for aggravated assault.

LIKE A GRAPE

NOW, HECTOR MORALES, THE CATFACED MAN, was looking around the jail cell for a space and finally sat next to Wayne Wade.

Wayne looked up, willing his glance anywhere besides toward the catfaced man. On the ceiling he saw a gecko in the corner licking drops off the water pipe. Its eyes looked like golden BBs in the shale-gray light of the cell.

When Wayne looked down again he saw that the catfaced man had his hand on the thigh of his butterscotch silk trousers. On his pointer finger was a gold ring with an insignia. Wayne recognized it from the news. It was the pirate logo, from a place called the Mutiny Hotel.

He'd seen the stories on the television. The machine gun massacres, the machete slaughters.

Catface must have noticed Wayne's attention. "You like that?"

"Sorry, mister?"

"The ring."

"That's a real nice ring."

"You know what that es?"

Wayne's voice came out in a dry nervous click. "Oh yeah, I do."

"Es okay, you can look, amigo."

"Okay, sir."

"Hector." The man extended his hand.

Warily Wayne took it. Then he relaxed when he realized it wasn't a ruse. The man's hand was soft, manicured. But the handshake was firm.

"And your name?" Hector asked.

"Wayne Wade."

"Oh, these es a bunch of motherfuckers in here, Mr. Wade?"

Wayne Wade agreed this was the case.

A short while later the bailiff's voice boomed down the hall and called out Wayne Wade's name. He'd made bail.

Once they were in Crowe's baking hatchback, Crowe asked Wayne, "How many times have I told you? No hard stuff." He was apoplectic.

And Wayne, drained, exhausted, famished, still shaken up from his encounter with the scar-faced man, said, "Reedy." He stank of jail.

"Don't Reedy me nothing."

"Can we just get going?"

"Cool Papa Lemon," Crowe said.

"You're wiggin'. Come on."

"Cool Papa Lemon, that shit I seen on the news. Was it you?"

"Holy shit, Reedy. Listen to yourself. Can we get goin'?"

"We're gonna have a long, long talk, Wayne."

Crowe was backing out of the space when the door of the municipal jail swung open. The glass caught the late afternoon light and sent an amorphous specter of reflection gliding across the hatchback's windshield. Crowe was temporarily blinded. The scar-faced man, just released on bail, was the first to see Crowe. When Crowe's eyes adjusted and he glimpsed the man, he near recoiled with shock.

The man with the scarred face locked eyes with Crowe. As if he were struck by some ineffable déjà vu.

The man recognized Crowe somehow.

Crowe pressed harder on the gas, shot out onto the access road, peeled away. He kept one eye fixed on the rearview mirror.

"That guy know you?" asked Wayne.

"What? No."

"Looking at you real weird."

"Weird lookin' guy."

"Yeah, he was. Seen him kill a guy, maybe kill him, right in the cell. One of them Miami guys on the news."

"Kill a guy? Jesus. In the cell?"

The afternoon light was in Wayne Wade's eyes and he squinted, put down the sun visor. "In the fucking cell. Yeah. So maybe we talk shit tomorrow? Right? Thank you."

Crowe told Wayne not to get wise. Then he asked how the man killed the other man.

"He smashed the guy's head. The eyes went flying and everything."

"Punched him?" Crowe asked.

"No, he stomped him. Not stomped him. It was, I don't know, he just stood one-legged, you know? Stood on the guy. Like some weird yoga pose. Put all his weight on the guy's head, and pop like a fuckin' grape, man."

Crowe stroked his beard anxiously.

"So," Wayne said, "how was your night, man?"

They were silent for a while, hot asphalt whining beneath the tires.

Crowe asked Wayne what the guards did.

"Shit their pants. Nothing. Craziest thing of it all. You could see the blood on his pants. Right there. Cuff to ankle. The guard could see it. No doubt in my mind. They didn't do shit. Nobody did shit. And the guy's head, like a fuckin' grape."

SPRUNG

AS THE HATCHBACK SHUDDERED AND COUGHED and bucked out of the lot Catface ran to his car. There was a kid around twenty-five at the wheel, caterpillar mustache. His face registered a double shock. It was the kid who'd sprung him out of jail. Catface jerked open the door so hard that the kid clutching the handle almost flew out of the car. Still clinging on to the handle the kid tried to compose himself and started rising, but it was too slowly. Catface grabbed a fistful of the Haitian kid's silk gigolo shirt and when that tore he grabbed the thick gold chains around his neck and hauled him one-armed out of the car. "Bailed your ass," the kid protested. He cursed and fell on his side and elbow onto the hot asphalt.

Before he could rise Catface was behind the wheel. He stomped the gas and took off shrieking. He shot out of the lot and onto the two-lane access road and gave chase.

He was closing in on the hatchback. At first the driver waved him onward, thinking he was someone else. Or not knowing who he was. What he was. That dirty hippy look of dishevelment about him, he was likely oblivious. Just look at the scuffed-up dirty pumpkin of a car, the crooked bumper, the duct tape on the passenger-side mirror.

As Catface closed closer still, closer yet, he saw the man's green Polaroid sunglasses in the mirror.

Then the orange hatchback shot forward, doubled the distance. Catface in the Mustang could have breached it in an instant but something black shot into the road as quick as an apparition. A black snake the size of a fire hose.

He ran right over it.

The carcass of the thing thumped and thudded and rattled against the undercarriage. It caught in the chassis and the car started skidding. Sidewinding wildly. Catface went swerving, tried to straighten the car. The road was arrow-straight and flat, new asphalt, and around it was a veldt of saw grass.

No exits within sight.

Nowhere to go.

He could have easily had the man who left him burning in the swamp, but for the fucking snake.

The car's right front axle got mired in the muck. It got stuck. The wheel span and shrieked and threw ropes of mud and slime.

Catface kicked the brake and the car slewed to a stop.

Catface got out of the car. He watched the hatchback disappearing west. Going, going, gone. Vanished, not so much as a speck left on the heat mirage quivering of the horizon. Catface spat curses in the profane heat.

Then he heard the distant siren coming from the east. He looked. The small rack lights of a police car glinted jewel-like in the tropical glare.

Catface screamed in rage. On the asphalt lay the bifurcated body of the snake. Cut in half, the snake still whipped and hissed. He stomped the skull. It popped under the heel of his alligator shoe.

Then Catface composed himself. He got back into the car and put his hands on the wheel and watched the cop car coming closer in the side mirror. He waited with the driver side window open.

The heat. The bugs. The gnats. The sulfur stench of baking mud.

The cop car nosed behind the car with the stolen tags. The officer, Nate Sternberg, got out of the car. He caught a glimpse of the man's face in his side mirror. Minced meat. A half-cooked hamburger steak with eyes and a mouth and a feline stub for a nose.

Nate Sternberg asked for the man's license and registration.

"Of course," Catface said. He reached for the glove compartment.

"Both arms where I can see them, sir."

With one hand held up and the other opening the glove compartment Catface kept his eyes on the young officer.

Smiling crooked eyes. None of the features on the face plumb level.

He handed the documents over to the officer. All fake, all fraudulent.

Catface saw the man's hand trembling.

The young officer said, "Sunglasses off, sir."

In the Florida glare Catface's ugliness was shocking. But amid the scarred-over face was a congenial smile. Kempt teeth straight and white.

"May I ask why the stop, officer."

"A moment," the young man said. His eyes drifted from the license to Catface's face. From the registration to Catface. Even his eyeballs were slightly atremble, aquake with fear.

Now Catface was regarding the small black bugs flying around the officer. There were dozens everywhere, every one of them paired with another, every one of them mating while flying in the air. Catface, friendly, curious, "What are these things?"

The officer said nothing.

Now the man was writing on his clipboard.

"What do you call these bugs, officer?"

"Lovebugs."

"Lovebugs?" Catface chuckled.

"How about I ask the questions?"

"Why are you getting upset?"

"Sir."

"Why are you shaking?"

"Hands on the wheel, sir."

"I comply. I do everything you ask."

"No sudden movements."

"Lovebugs," Catface said.

"Hands on the wheel, sir. I'm warning you."

"Looks like they are a'fucking," Catface said. "Why not fuck-bugs?"

The officer reached for his holster.

Within an eyeblink Catface like a magician produced one of the wafer-thin daggers secreted in his shirtsleeve. Quick as a cobra the knife slashed. The man's neck gushed. His voice gurgled. He fell to his knees even as his hand was still reaching for the belt.

Catface stepped out of the Mustang. He took off his shirt, draped it on the driver's seat. He dragged the officer's body by the legs to the edge of the marsh. He pushed the body with his shoe and it rolled a few times until toppling into the bog where green scum and algae swallowed him.

Catface then got behind the wheel of the cop car. He put the car in neutral, cocked the wheel so the tires swiveled swampward. Catface then stepped to the back of the car and pushed it until it lumbered and sank into the muck.

MICROFICHE

CROWE TRIED TO FORGET THE MAN'S face. He tried to banish it from his mind. He could not. The face burned like a fire in his head. It was graven in his brain, cattle-branded.

Somehow he knew the face. And he knew from the way the man's eyes lit on him from across the parking lot, the way his eyes looked away from him, cut back to him, switchblade quick, that the man somehow knew his face too.

For days nightmares about the catfaced man hounded him in the wee hours. He would wake in bedsheets tangled and sweaty. He would wake on the couch shouting pleas, flailing his limbs as if fending away an attack.

Sometimes he found the feral beach cats gathered anxiously outside near the sliding glass door. Peering inside with their reflective yellow eyes, drawn by his thrashing and shouting.

Blood knocking loud in his head he sat on the edge of the sofa. He set down his half-moon television-watching glasses on the coffee table.

He'd fallen asleep watching Johnny Carson.

As he caught his breath, he glimpsed his spooked reflection, bathed in the blue wash of the test pattern, in the glass. The dark sand dunes beyond, the darker darkness of the Gulf.

His heart slowed.

He watched the cats relax. Oh, that guy.

They scattered.

He went to the kitchen and poured himself a glass of ice water. He downed it in three big gulps. He poured another. Then he went back to the den and sat on the couch, put his elbows on his knees and his head in his hands and he said, "Get your shit together, man."

After his next visit to see his mother at the Poinciana, Crowe on impulse visited the Broward public library. Inside he sat in the periodicals section at one of the carrel desks and looked up old editions of *Miami Herald* on the microfiche machine.

Images flickered past. Lurid headlines.

Grainy green, pixilated photographs of shoot-outs in front of the Fort Lauderdale Burdines. Refugees landing in jury-rigged boats ashore Key Largo, Islamorada.

The *thunk-thunk-thunk* of the microfiche machine caught people's attention in the stale air-conditioned hush of the building.

Thunk, thunk. Crowe zooming in and zooming out onto the negatives, a quick carousel of images.

Other patrons glanced peevishly from their carrels.

There was no way he could quiet the machine. He apologized nonetheless.

Thunk.

Dadeland Mall Massacre.

Thunk.

Castro, "I'll flush the toilets of Cuba. Send all the criminals to America."

Thunk.

Morgues overflowing in Dade County. The Dade medical examiner's office storing corpses in a refrigerated Burger King truck.

Thunk.

The narcotics war between Cuban and Colombian dealers. Some guy, a local Venezuelan resident who'd immigrated to avoid such mayhem, "They'll kill your wife. Your kids. Your neighbors. Your dog. Your plants. They'll kill your pet rock."

Thunk.

Disembowelment by sword at a Cooper City car wash.

Thunk.

The green microfilm blurred past. About thirty minutes into his search he stopped.

It was an article and picture about a shooting near the Hotel Mutiny, Miami Beach. Police tape sectioned off a street. In the middle of the street was a body draped in a white sheet. Across the street on the far sidewalk a crowd stood to rubberneck. Among the heads and faces Crowe saw him five or six heads deep.

The catfaced man in the custom-tailored summer suit.

Unmistakably him.

Right there, in plain sight, peering from between the breach of bodies and heads.

How could anyone miss him?

Could they just not bear to give him a second glance? Was he that unsettling to behold, that maimed and deformed?

Crowe went to the reference desk and returned the box of microfiche to the librarian.

"Sir? Sir? Are you okay?"

Reed Crowe already had his back turned. He held up a hand, a two-fingered wave. He thanked the woman for her help.

He walked outside in the muggy Florida afternoon. Said, "Fucked."

One morning when arriving to the Florida Man Mystery House Reed Crowe found the new kid Eddie dragging the garden hose from the side of the lavatory building, across the caterpillar grass, across the bucked-up tamarind fig tree roots, to the pontoon boat.

He was blasting the swamp crap off the boat. He'd already washed the mildew off the hard top. Scrubbed the tourist benches. Washed the slime and mold off the Bimini top of the console.

Crowe went down the dock and saw Eddie in the water of the canal, wakeboard shorts and scuba goggles on. He was brushing the barnacles and beards of algae off the hull.

Crowe couldn't believe his eyes. "Eddie, Eddie, what're you up to, buddy?" He was looking down at the skinny kid in the tannin-tinctured water.

"Five dollars?"

"Five dollars to clean the boat? That's the best bargain I ever heard in my life."

"Wayne should be doing this."

"Why not?"

"Why doesn't he? He'd contaminate the Everglades."

"Sorry?"

"He'd pollute the water."

"Que?"

"Good work, Eddie," Crowe said.

Crowe went into the gift shop for the express purpose of breaking Wayne Wade's balls. He found him behind the counter with an issue of *Fangoria* magazine.

The spring door squawked back on the hinges and Wayne looked up. "Uh," he said in the way of greeting.

Crowe pointed his chin at the door where through the cobwebby screen, past the giant tamarind fig, past the picnic pavilion, sat the SS *Merman* at its dock. He said, "See that?"

"Huh," was all that Wayne said. His mouth tightened around his toothpick, ticked to the side of his face like it did when he was peeved.

What tourists there were idled by the knickknacks and gewgaws. One kid in a Space Invaders T-shirt and straw cowboy hat was whacking his chubby brother upside the head with an alligator back-scratcher. "Keep it up," their father was telling them. "We'll see what happens at Uncle Barry's tonight when I fire up the grill."

Sometimes the things Crowe overheard from these tourists, he had no idea.

He was still waiting for a response from Wayne. "I said see that, Wayne?"

Insolently Wayne flipped a page of the magazine. "Spic in the water. Amazing. Ten stars."

"Doing shit you should have done five years ago."

"Tell me then. I'm not a mind reader."

Crowe stood there staring at Wayne Wade.

"You're not, eh? Try."

"Oh, fuck you." Wayne flicked an annoyed glance upward. He hissed dismissively through his toothpick. His eyes went back to the magazine.

"See, there. Don't underestimate yourself."

Now he could hear Eddie starting up the boat, the cough and splutter of the balky engine from a distance.

A few startled terns winged over the mangroves.

Crowe went over to the Mystery House entrance and called out, "Five minutes, folks."

The small passel of tourists began to herd toward the gift shop.

Crowe went back to the register. Wiped his sweating forehead with his thumb. "When's the last time you tuned her up?"

"Okay, Reed. I get it."

"Boat sounds like fuckin' Chitty Chitty Bang Bang."

In the following days Eddie became a steward of sorts, attending to the maintenance of the boat, attending to chores long gone ignored and neglected. Always coming back at you with some excuse, Wayne Wade. And if Reed Crowe dunned him about it, he'd sulk the rest of the day.

Not so with Eddie. So the *Merman* chores became his. Crowe started paying Eddie twenty dollars a week.

Their excursions were twice a day during the spring, once at ten in the morning and the other at two.

But during the summer that dwindled to one excursion. The bugs, the heat.

So the tours went on. As he cruised the waterways and canals Crowe delivered his spiel about Florida, all the native flora and fauna. He pointed out turtles and manatees and alligators. Wetlands, pinelands, hammocks, prairies.

There's a roseate spoonbill. Pete. He owes me twenty dollars.

There's a great blue heron. Cornelius. He's going through a rough time with his old lady.

There's an asshole. Wayne Wade, ladies and gentlemen. Beyond hope or salvation, but please feel free to tip the help. Even feel free to tip Wayne Wade.

EDDIE

CROWE CAME TO LEARN PIECEMEAL THAT Eddie was here on a visa, a night student at one of the Broward Community College satellite campuses. He was saving for his family back in Juárez, and in the meantime staying with his abuelita and cousins.

Crowe asked the kid, "You drive all the way out there? Broward Community?"

"Yes, sir."

"I would have never thought," Crowe told him.

"Why not?"

Indeed, it was a good question. One to which Crowe had no answer. "Good for you, Eddie," said Crowe.

A big part of him wanted to apologize for Wayne's behavior, though it was out of his control. Or was it, really?

As the summer wore on and heated to a boil, problems proliferated. Mother of all plants.

Wayne Wade often came into work hungover or stoned or both.

One day during the Florida Man Mystery House boat ride, he missed his bogman cue.

"Legend has it," Crowe called midway during the boat tour, Wayne's cue to come charging out of the swamp hammock in his bogman costume, but there was silence within the mangroves. No bestial roar, no animal bellow.

Crowe cleared his throat.

Insects buzzed electric in bracken.

Whut-whut-whut, went a whacked-out bird from the jungle deep.

The sweaty tourists blinked and waited. They looked wretched. Their faces were an unhealthy glazed ham pink. They batted away mosquitoes and midges. They fanned themselves with brochures.

"Ointment," Eddie said. "Root beer."

Their faces said it all. If only they'd chosen Disney instead.

"Yes, legend has it," Crowe said again, pitching his voice louder.

Then there was a huge splash in the water, as if a man had belly-flopped from a diving board into a shallow pool. A sickly human moan came from within the bracken.

A phalanx of tourists stood and grouped starboard, wondering if the commotion was part of the tour. They glanced questioningly at Crowe, who wore a poker face.

Finally Wayne Wade emerged from the muck and mire toting the gorilla head in the crook of his arm. With his other arm he groped around for purchase but it was all lily pads and swamp cabbage as he foundered through the bog.

His rattail was loose, so his lank sparse hair was in a weedy tangle. His eyes were bloodshot, conjunctivitis red. Dried vomit like a bib was fanned on the front of his costume.

"Looks like the bogman got a touch of the heatstroke," Crowe said. He winked expansively from behind his green sunglasses, so the tourists could see. What few were looking. Almost all the people were gawking at Wayne.

"That man's drunk," said a man with a large Rottweiler-like face. For some reason the man made Crowe think of a Louisiana constable. Mr. Rottweiler Constable was not amused. "I got children here," he said.

The two husky boys, brothers, seemed elated. They grinned grins that were stained blue from Polar Pops.

"Hydration," Eddie yelled tonelessly. "Ointment. Ice-cold water. Hydration."

Wayne stopped sloshing midway to the boat and went still. His face moiled. He retched and a bountiful spate flew.

Crowe preempted the tourists, their complaints, "Of course all you folks'll be getting your refunds."

MELEE

WHEN CROWE ARRIVED TO THE FLORIDA Man Mystery House a few days later it was to a melee. From a distance he could see two men fighting, duking it out beneath the enormous strangler fig tree. Ringed around them was a score of tourists.

There were evil-looking charcoal clouds shoving inshore from the Gulf. Already the day looked fucked. They'd have to leave in five minutes, max, to make the tour safely before the storm.

And now this.

Crowe parked and jogged across the lot. Above the heads of the tourists, in the midst of the fracas, an aqua-blue Miami Dolphins cap flipped in the air.

Crowe knew the cap well.

Wayne Wade's.

Crowe parted through the tourists. "Pardon, folks. Pardon, ma'am."

Eddie and Wayne were in a tangle, flailing. Eddie had Wayne in a headlock. They were spinning about, throwing sloppy punches, almost tripping on the heaved-up roots of the tree.

Crowe wedged himself between the two like a wrestling ref, shoved them apart. They were in each other's faces, bloody-mouthed, cursing.

"Fuck's wrong with you two?" Crowe said in a vicious whisper.

Reluctantly the men staggered apart. Wretched-looking, pummeled. Wayne had gotten the brunt of the blows. The right side of his face was already swelling. His cap was smashed where the ground was slick with mud and deliquescing fig jam.

"The cap, signed by Bob Griese, ruined!" Wayne wailed. The thin cloth of Wayne's T-shirt—FLORIDA BEER CAN CONVENTION—was ripped at the sleeve.

The tourists were agog.

Crowe led the pair to the squalid public restroom.

"Look at this place," Crowe complained, glancing rancidly about. "Gloryholes. Spider webs. Green fuckin' slime. And you're duking it out there."

The men said nothing. They stood tensely, like they still had fight in them. Wayne with his soda straw legs, his knees scuffed and dirty. The flesh around one eye was swelling purple.

Crowe asked the men what happened.

Still nothing from either one of them.

"One of you idiots is gonna tell me."

Eddie's head snapped up. "Hey, fuck you."

Crowe stepped back, flung up his hands, showed his palms. "Whoa," he said. "Hey, let's calm down."

"Don't tell me what to do. I'm not your wetback."

"Eddie? I don't know what you think, but? Hey? You think I'm your enemy? Is that what you think?"

They were both looking at the ground, the grubby mint-green hexagonal tiles. Their breaths were loud and scraping in the small space. A sink was leaking, slow steady silvery plinks.

Crowe's face turned rancid. "Smells like bona fide pig shit in here and you guys are doing whatever the fuck out there." He turned to Wayne. "Wayne, tell me what this shit's about."

"Kinda way is that to ask?"

"You wanna scroll from the queen?"

"That. That." He shook his finger, prosecutorial. "That way of askin' right there. What's that? Like I'm your employee."

"Wayne. I got people out there. Families. A couple of kids scared half shitless."

Wayne opened his mouth, goober teeth showing, chin lifting, scrawny neck corded and red with indignation.

Before Wayne could speak, Crowe pointed at him. "Fuck whatever you're gonna say. I got shit to do."

"I'm the villain?" Wayne asked.

Wayne's high wheedling voice was still going on when Crowe started walking out.

"Am I fired?" Eddie asked.

"What? No. No, Eddie. Why'd you be fired? Forget it."

Then Crowe was out of the restroom and addressing the crowd in his corny game show host voice. "All right, folks, let's get you some godforsaken tchotchkes."

CHOCOLATE BUDDHA

A GRUFF IMPASSE REMAINED BETWEEN THE two men. A grudging truce. They exchanged nary a word aside from bare necessity. "Boat," Wayne would say, reminding Eddie to get the Florida Man Mystery Boat ready. Sometimes it was a shrill roistering whistle that he sounded through the gift shop door. It rolled across the picnic area beyond the huge strangler fig tree and it reached the boat and then it whanged back with reverb, bouncing off the curtain of rank jungle green on the far side of the canal.

"Watch," one would say to the other if they were about to collide during their errands. Not even bothering with the "*it.*"

So few were his responsibilities that Eddie spoke only when in dire need. Some random emergency. "A little girl shit in the bathroom, on wall," he said.

Wayne, his face a vaudeville parody of vexation, said, "You gotta be fuckin' kidding me."

Then one night in Red, White and Blue Liquor, Wayne Wade was fetching a six-pack when two Mexican kids Wayne recognized as friends of Eddie's came into the store.

One of the guys was big as a behemoth. The other skinny and tall with tattoos on his forearms.

Wayne started down the aisle. But with the two Mexicans walking abreast there was so little berth that Wayne Wade knocked into the big Mexican. Or the other way around.

Whatever, the collision nearly knocked Wayne Wade out of his checkered Vans and on his ass. He slewed sideways, knocked over packages of Goody's headache powder. Condoms.

But he regained his footing and kept hold of his six-pack.

Wayne's expression went quickly from bewilderment to embarrassment. "Watch it, goddamn it," he said.

The Mexicans went into the beer cooler.

By the time he fetched up to the register back again on sea legs, his face was maroon with rage.

Behind the register, the owner Krumpp was smiling faintly.

"You see that?"

"Yeah. That's why I'm laughing."

"You gonna let that happen in your store?"

"No. Pick it up."

"What?"

"Pick that shit up. I ain't your granny."

"It's the spics done it."

"You walked right into that guy. I saw it."

"I had the right of way."

Krumpp studied him from behind his tinted glasses, his acne-scarred face scowling. "Look at your pupils. I was a cop, I'd arrest you on the spot."

"I'd commit you to the asylum, Krumpp."

"I'd shoot you dead."

"Fuck you, Krumpp."

"You know what, maybe it's you I gotta worry about."

"You're stroking, Krumpp. You're fadin' fast. You're wiggin'. Go to the doctor."

"Hey, fuck you. Two, shut the fuck up. Three, let me listen to Shula." There was a small transistor radio playing. They were talking about replicating the perfect lossless season of 1973 this year.

Wayne stomped down the aisle. He made a show of picking up the merchandise and putting it back on the racks. When he returned to the register, digging wadded one dollar bills out of his jean shorts, he said, "Happy?"

"Four," Krumpp said, "get the fuck out."

The Mexicans, each toting six-packs, were chuckling low and secret when they came out of the cooler.

Wayne took his change and went out of the store. He stood waiting, brooding in the jungly Florida twilight. A fingernail moon hanging above the tops of the sand pines and palmetto scrub.

When the Mexicans came out, Wayne Wade said to the big one, "I might be small, but fuck you."

The big Mexican pawed him aside, kept walking.

Wayne Wade followed on his heels, smacking his chest. He'd put his six-pack down by the standing ashtray.

"I might be a small piece of shit but I will destroy you. You can't take me down. Think so? Let's go. You can't take me down."

"Go home," said the man.

"Fuck you. My mama died right on over down there, down the street."

The big man's friend said, "Go home, jefe, you're stoned."

"What'chu call me?" Wayne Wade grabbed at his side for his jackknife. "What'chu say?"

"Nothing. Friend. Dude. Man. That's all it mean."

"You can't win because I can't lose," Wayne went on even as the men walked away toward their pickup truck.

"Because you know why? My mama died right down the street in a car crash. I never once needed her help. She'd help me if I needed it. She'd kill you, her spirit. She's standin' right behind you."

"Loco," said the smaller one.

Wayne Wade, full of Dutch courage, dizzy-drunk, charged with his knife.

The big Mexican turned. "You're on crack, jefe. A knife? Shit."

"So let's go. I live for this shit right here. Swing."

Wayne lunged.

The sumo-sized Mexican man, usually a paragon of patience, so much so his friends had nicknamed him the Chocolate Buddha, swung. He swung a big right hook to the underside of Wayne's jaw that sent him flying. He was socked off his feet, flung backward. It was like a cartoon. Any other man of Wayne's featherweight size would have been knocked cold. But dazed though he was Wayne, no doubt coked up, or cracked up, scrabbled up from the ground with an uncanny insectoid energy.

He tottered toward the pair of Mexicans with his fists up. Spat out little pieces of teeth like shrapnel. After a few wobbly steps he slewed sideways and sat with his back against the garbage dumpster, chin dripping bloody drool onto the front of his Panama Jack shirt.

The two Mexican men had their doors open. The skinny man got behind the wheel. The man nicknamed Chocolate Buddha said, "I tried to warn you."

"Fuck you, fat tubba shit." Wade's lips bubbled blood.

"You need an ambulance?"

"Go eat your mama."

He climbed into the rusted blue truck and slammed the door. The truck lurched away, turned onto the two-lane blacktop and geared down the flat straight road.

Wayne kept muttering in a bloody drunken slur with an audience of five or six stars shining above the incandescent-lit lot. The bugs filled the jungle night with their lusty song.

All this time Krumpp stood waiting behind the glass door, his calfskin holster with its firearm dangling at his hip. Only when the blue truck was a ways down the road did he step outside. He walked halfway across the lot in his tasseled loafers, the sweltering night air fogging the lenses of his gray-tinted glasses, so much was the difference between the air-conditioned cool of the store and the muggy jungle night.

"You need an ambulance?" His pitted face squinted.

"No."

His glasses defogged. "Then move your ass. You ain't exactly a glowing advertisement for business."

DIGGING A HOLE

AS SUMMER SHOWED SIGNS OF WANING around him the hillocks grew in the grotto clearing. Reed Crowe pried and hacked through roots. He heaved great clods of earth.

He grew to look forward to these mornings and evenings. An odor of warm turned earth and hummus, somehow evocative of childhood. His insect repellent.

As he dug he was sweating so much he peeled off his sodden shirt and wrapped it bonnet-style around his head, the knot under his chin. No one was around to tell him he looked ridiculous. Crowe in the skim of lamplight laboring with the shovel under the big spring-glutted leaves of the banyans and cyads.

The clearing around the cavern's entrance looked ravaged by gophers, groundhogs. Trenches and holes of varying depths.

In the grottoes he came across troglophiles. Millipedes and cave frogs and newts and salamanders. Larvae so ghostly pale they seemed to glow. Tiny translucent frogs no bigger than a fingernail. Eyeless worms. Anthropoids with palpating feelers and antennae. Pale spiders with huge red eyes and white hairs sticking from their legs.

Some nights he'd find two or three fossils.

All kinds of bones. No more of them human.

So far.

He found cane and bamboo and charcoal in the pits. Hawk skins. Old feathers turned to jerky. Fish bones and shark teeth. Cups made of shells.

Every so often, sweating and out of breath with his heart racing, he'd lean on the handle of his shovel to rest and light his joint and peer into the restless Florida dark.

Stridulating insects. Croaking frogs. Piping alligators. Cawing nightbirds.

Sometimes he rose and got dizzy-headed and worried about his blood pressure. His arms tingled from shoulder to fingertips. He wondered about his heart. He thought of his father, felled by a heart attack at fifty-five.

BIG GORILLA FIREWORKS

THE FIREWORKS EMPORIUM OUT ON THE edge of the county had been open as long as he could recall. A hangar-like building of sheet metal painted blazing red and yellow, jutting up from the ferociously green Florida landscape like a hematoma. A fifteen-foot inflatable gorilla hulked beside the door, glowering with its fangs bared.

BIG GORILLA FIREWORKS, yelled the sign.

Three exclamation marks.

Crowe in Polaroid sunglasses and flip-flops wandered the tall wide aisles among the spinners and poppers and rockets and mortars. The tang of gunpowder. Remembering coming here as a boy with his father.

Every so often Crowe stopped to inspect one of the packages of rice paper with screaming cartoon animals and Chinese lettering. And every so often he'd pick up one of the explosives and consider it. Toss it in his wire basket.

A kid wearing a Pink Floyd shirt, the one with the prism, came up to Crowe, asked if he needed any help.

"Ya'll got any of those M-80s?" Crowe asked the kid.

"Oh, they outlawed them, mister." Braces, his face stippled with acne like a pelting of buckshot. "Swap shop. Gun show. Only places you'll get that stuff now."

Crowe reached for one of the brightly colored boxes on the shelf. Black Cat. "Combine some of these, added them up?"

The kid's grin snagged on his braces. "Oh, I can't recommend anything like that."

"I want to blow the shit out of my ex-wife's birthday party."

"Far out."

Crowe asked him, "How you people stay open, man? No offense." Crowe looked around. No one else. "I just don't see it."

"One guy'll come in here and really make your day."

"What's the most you ever saw one guy spend?"

"Seventy-five grand."

"Grand?"

"Yessir."

"Grand."

"Yessir."

"Man. Was he crazy?"

"Coked up."

They were still chuckling when the kid rung him up at the register. The kid told him he had to sign his name, spelled out, and then his signature, and the date, on a list that was on a clipboard. The law.

"I gotta put my full name down middle and all?"

"Just sign a name."

"Any name."

"They don't check."

Crowe wrote down a bullshit name out of nowhere. Gerald Macandu Macnamarra.

"Hey, what happened to the older red-haired fella worked here?"

"My dad."

"Gary?"

"Yessir. He passed."

"I'm sorry to hear it. What's your name, son?"

"Barry."

"Barry, I'm sorry."

"Thank you, sir."

"I'm real sorry to hear it."

KABOOM

THAT EVENING AT THE WORKSTATION IN the garage Crowe sat under the bug zapper knifing the small firecrackers apart and making a pile of the gunpowder. The transistor radio was tuned to Miami, a station playing afrocuban.

A can of Hamm's sweated at his elbow. Before him on the table, a book, *The Poor Man's James Bond Vol. 1* by Kurt Saxon, lay open. An acquisition from an underground bookstore and porno magazine stand and metal detector repair shop in Fort Lauderdale. He'd picked it up out of idle curiosity and read the back. *ABOUT THIS BOOK: It is bad to poison your fellow man, blow him up or even shoot him or otherwise disturb his tranquility. It is also uncouth to counterfeit your nation's currency and it is tacky to destroy property as instructed in Arson by Electronics.*

Instant purchase.

Now the book was open to a page with a heading that said "Cannon Cracker Composition." Illustrations of dynamite pipes, their construction. *The cases for crackers are rolled similar to rocket cases except that paste is used only . . .*

Pain shot through his thumb, a small loud spike. He leapt from the stool. The knife clattered to the floor. Sucking his bleeding thumb he hobbled cussing to the bathroom and bandaged his hand.

He was still working later that night, insects popping against the zapper, when the rain came crashing down all at once like a broken water main.

A luna moth as big as a hand fluttered languidly and clung to the garage wall.

In the crushed shell driveway, small green tree frogs hopped, shiny as gewgaws in the floodlights. Beyond was a vale of night so black and profound it might as well have been a dropped stage curtain of black velvet.

Crowe every so often glanced up and couldn't shake the feeling the darkness was looking straight at him.

Glowering.

Next night he took the homemade explosive to the grotto and set it alight in the rocks, scrambled away. Watched from a distance under the trees in the lavender and plum sunset.

He heard the crackling hiss.

Bats winged above him, snatching insects out of the air in soundless swoops.

Nothing.

Bugs flying from stalk to stalk in the clearing, grasshoppers and katydids flitting off, diaphanous sparks in the late slant of sun.

Nothing.

Some bird about ten yards away going, *yuk-yuk-yuka-tuk-tuk.*

Then the detonation, the noise rolling terrifically into the night.

"Holy fuck, man." Crowe cackled.

Surely people for five miles square heard.

A hail of stones. A mushroom of gunmetal smoke.

Birds winged into the night, screaming in rebuke.

Still chuckling, ears still ringing, he ducked through the rubble and went into the chamber.

The limestone boulder, gouged and charred.

But the passageway, still blocked.

Crowe put his hand on the rock, still warm from the blast. There was a lingering bite of gunpowder in the air. Crowe would swear his skin caught the kiss of a draft. There were a few cracks in the rock, horsehair-fine. He would hold up his palm a centimeter from the stone, keep it there until he thought he felt the sigh again.

A SURPRISE PACKAGE

ONE NIGHT A DIMINUTIVE METALLIC CLACKING pulled Crowe out of sleep. One of the cats fooling around with the mail slot, he thought, groping blindly for a throw pillow. He flung it across the room.

He was drifting back to sleep when small tinny clicking started again.

Crowe reared upright on the couch and blinked into the dark. No cat in the room.

But Crowe saw the mail slot pried open. And an eye peering at him through the hole. A human eye.

His heart flipped.

Before he was on his feet he saw something fall through the mail slot. It looked like a two-foot length of black rope. But when the mail hole snapped shut and the rope hit the floor it started moving. A quick liquid squiggle across the room. A scaly whisper against the terrazzo floor.

A snake.

It whipsawed across the room and jettisoned toward the couch. Crowe reached for another throw pillow and flung it. The snake stopped, knotted into a tangle, tasted the air with its tongue. Then it unraveled and slithered to the corner of the room where it curled up behind the potted ficus tree.

Crowe stood. "Who is it," he said, aiming for menace. Gelded, even to his ears.

"Shit's there? Fixin' to get shot."

He went to the foyer closet and got his aluminum baseball bat and flashlight. Then at the door he shouted he was coming out. He brandished the baseball bat with one hand and flung the door open with the other. No one. He stepped into the night. Scanned the yard with the flashlight, the feeble beam catching the elephant eared plants fringing the yard. The few ghost-pale geckos sipping dew off leaves.

Wind gusted off the ocean and rustled the sea oats.

Crowe waited, squinting into the dark.

Back inside he got the broom from the kitchen. In the corner the snake was still knotted into a tight coil. Crowe nudged the snake with the broom bristles. The snake hissed, tightened its knot. Crowe pushed it again and it unraveled. It slithered across the terrazzo and over the door's threshold and into the sand.

He waited. The humid night. Tropical flowers breathing their hot breath. Lizards and frogs rustling in the leaves.

THE MENTAL CENSUS

THE NEXT MORNING WHEN HE WOKE Crowe wondered if it hadn't all been a bizarre dream. The snake wriggling across the floor. The scaly whisper across the terrazzo.

But no, there it was in the morning. The broom propped against the writing desk.

Crowe, "What the fuck, man," scratching his beach bum beard, scratching the bird's nest of his crispy sun-bleached hair.

While the coffee was still brewing he rummaged in the garage for superglue. Then he went out to the side of the house where he started gluing the mail slot shut.

Out of commission anyway, a remnant from days of yore before navigable roads on the island, when the barefoot mailman delivered letters the old-fashioned way, lugging his satchel down the length of the beach. Besides notes from neighbors and Heidi, the mail slot was out of commission. His mail was routed to a post office box across the bridge on the mainland. Sometimes Myrtle the mail-woman would make special deliveries across the bridge, but those were packages, not letters.

When he was done gluing Crowe tested the metal flap with the crook of his finger. Sealed shut.

A few of the cats had slunk up to him, curious about his activity, and as they walked in circles with their tails up and their eyes on the mail slot, as they tipped their noses up, sniffing, Crowe said to them, "Guys're like Wayne, you know. Useless. Earn your keep."

In the coming days Crowe tallied his enemies. A mental census.

Were there any?

Did he have any?

A panoply of faces drifted through his mind.

The man with the scarred face.

The denizens of Emerald City and Emerald Island.

Various beach codgers. A metal detector enthusiast researching the legend of Gasparilla the pirate. A square-headed trivia junkie, the island auto mechanic and boat mechanic. Another man with a face pockmarked like stucco who won the lottery in the 1970s and had a very young beautiful Vietnamese wife who everybody left alone because the pockmarked man was said to be in the Witness Protection Program. A mean Mississippi woman, a wino, a marine biologist prone to maudlin bitter crying when drunk, and Crowe would listen for a time. Some of the best sex he ever had in his life.

There were tour boat captains. There was a burnout or two. There was a hippy couple, camping granola types, barefoot, dread-locks. There were the drifters-through that stayed for weeks at a time at the Emerald Island Inn. There were the anglers and the hunters, less and less often these days. And the investors.

Who would put a snake in his mailbox?

There was Josie Regent the Irish-Italian guy who ran the angler's shop and bait store. Short-tempered as hell was the worst you could say about him. Usually he was very drunk and jolly.

There was a retired bird-watching couple who were studying the

migratory and mating habits of blue herons for a book for some aca-
demic avian society. Oddly, they reminded Reed Crowe of birds. The
man a stork or egret, leggy and long-necked with a convex beakish
face, a bony ridge of nose. The wife like a puffin, a small tight ball
of a woman, very affectionate and jolly and always calling everyone
pumpkin or honeybun.

The island had its fair share of hermits and cranks and there
were more than a few people who you couldn't imagine surviving
elsewhere.

There were strange guys, sure, like anywhere. There was that
taxidermist he bought his weird shit from, no doubt that guy was
scrambled in the brain. He used to live in the Emerald Island Inn.
But he had kicked no one out of there. He had slighted no one.

Then there was a hulking man, a half-assed body building type,
with a shockingly small head. The head looked like a baby pumpkin
on an overstuffed scarecrow. What in blue royal fuck, Crowe thought
the first time he saw him. He later felt bad about it. The man's name
was Lloyd Barret and he was fully functional and normal. Articulate,
well-read, a suave radio voice. A retired art therapy professor from
FSU. And an avid spearfishing enthusiast.

And of course there were women. Barmaids and waitresses and
single mothers and divorcees. One retired scuba instructor. Another
equestrian.

Every few months they'd bump into each other at the bar, get
drunk, joke and laugh. Four or five times out of ten fuck.

Most desired a long-term commitment no more than he. Kindred
spirits, that way.

Crowe was still wondering who it could be, wondered if it could
be the man named Henry Yahchilane.

THE SEA CAVE ARCADE

THE SEA CAVE ARCADE. HENRY YAHCHILANE was known to frequent the
place, always with a roll of quarters in his jeans pocket. Overkill,

since a few coins would last him the whole evening on the pinball machines.

Yahchilane could keep a ball careening for hours at a time. Every now and then ducking and grabbing his beer and taking a quick pull and then setting the beer back down before shooting upright once more. All with the liquid alacrity of a yogi.

Then he would slap at the flippers again, the ball shooting up chutes and banging bells. The scoring reel flipping in a wild blur.

Next door to the Sea Cave was a putt-putt course, too hot to play on during the long Florida summers. The chlorine-reeking tourist kids would bang and flip-flop into the arcade. They'd look Yahchilane over, elbow each other, consort in whispered voices, but would give Yahchilane wide berth.

His inscrutable black squint. Two knife slits cut in clay.

And at night, when they turned on the black lights in the Sea Cave, when the Day-Glo jellyfish lit on the walls, he looked even spookier. His teeth and his slivered eyes stained lavender in the black light.

The kids stuck around the flight simulator. The air hockey table. Centipede and Asteroids.

Those rare occasions the kids did bother him, Yahchilane spooked them.

Asked them strange questions without prologue, "I see you're looking at me, but can you imagine me in ten years looking at you?" His thumbs hooked in the saggy jeans.

Another time, to a teenage hippy girl who'd bumped into him and caused him to miss his ball, "Patchouli. Invented to mask the smell of the dead."

Yahchilane was playing Kiss pinball one Friday evening when Crowe barged into the Sea Cave Arcade.

Crowe went up to Yahchilane. His eyes and teeth glowed lavender.

"Hey, Yahchilane."

Yahchilane said nothing. He played ball. He slapped the buttons and the ball caromed.

"Hey, Yahchilane."

"What."

"What's your deal, man?"

Yahchilane slapped the buttons, said nothing.

"You work in the serpentarium," Crowe said.

Yahchilane shook his head and told Crowe, "Go home, egghead."

"You work at the serpentarium. I know it. You put snakes in my mailbox, Yahchilane?"

Now, a minor miscalculation, a misfire, the ball clunked down the shoot. "Hey, fuck," he said.

Yahchilane turned his fierce black squint on Crowe.

"Whatever you think, you're wrong," Crowe said.

DOWN IN THE HOLE

WHATEVER YOU THINK YOU'RE WRONG.

Yahchilane turned the words around his head for days. He replayed how Crowe said it on loop, the inflection, the tone, the volume.

Whatever you think you're wrong.

He thought about the words during the weekend when he played pinball in the Sea Cave Arcade.

He thought about the words when he shingled roofs under the Florida sun.

He thought about the words when he cleaned the reptile cages at the serpentarium.

Late one Wednesday after a thunderstorm had cooled the air and the jungly bracken, Yahchilane came down the path with his mage stick. He paused a distance away from the cave.

Crowe. The fucking egghead.

It was still light yet but two tiki torches were lit around the cave's mouth to fend off the mosquitoes.

Yahchilane propped the stick against a gumbo-limbo tree. He

came charging through the fiddlehead ferns. When he got to Crowe he lifted him whole off the ground. He scrabbled and kicked like an upturned pig in a slaughterhouse.

He kicked at Yahchilane's shins.

Kneed Yahchilane's balls.

Yahchilane let him go.

Crowe crawled away on his hands and knees. When he looked over his shoulder Yahchilane was getting up.

Crowe picked up a rock. Grapefruit sized.

He pleaded, "Yahchilane! Yahchilane!"

Yahchilane was deaf to his entreaties. He charged like a stevedore.

Crowe's first swing with the rock Yahchilane ducked and dodged. But as Yahchilane rose from his crouch Crowe swung again and this time the rock cracked him upside the head. There was a sickening hollow knock. A crunch of bone. Yahchilane groaned. A spurt of blood erupted from his temple. His eyes rolled and his knees buckled. He looked like he was about to fall. He shook his head and his eyes found their focus again.

They seared on Crowe with murder.

He lunged at Crowe. His callused thick fingers gripped his throat. Crowe felt blood ballooning to his head. Heard the dull hollow roar of his pulse. His vision swam and started to go white.

Yahchilane's seamed visage eclipsed all. The deep lines bracketing his mouth. The sharp cheekbones. Hair matted and sticky with blood. Teeth gnashed and crazed in his blood-gored face.

Yahchilane seized a fistful of Crowe's hair. Crowe pulled, but Yahchilane's grip was tight. Crowe pulled harder, his shoes shoving against the cavern wall for leverage. When he wrenched away, a hank of his hair was ripped out at the root and left in Yahchilane's hand. Yahchilane threw the clump aside.

They came at each other again. The men locked arms like wrestlers. They went twirling and spinning and tripping.

They floundered. They flailed.

"Cocksucker."

"Motherfucker."

"Fuck your heart."

"Fuck your mother."

Then there was a rumble and their curses were cut silent and suddenly there was nothing beneath them, the rocks holding them up toppling.

Down they went in free fall, helter-skelter.

They slammed to the ground, another cave below the one they were in. Now they were in a chamber beneath the chamber. Some kind of burial site. A crypt. An orchard of old bones. Some ten or twelve skeletons scattered around.

Crowe scrabbled back, slapped at his clothing. Hopped about, but everywhere there were bones. Brittle, clacking. Scowling skulls. Here and there a tea-colored rictus.

Beetles and roaches scattered, scurried under clavicles and hip bones.

Crowe reached blindly on the ground for another rock but came up instead with a large brown toad.

Crowe mashed the toad into Yahchilane's face. The toad croaked and let loose a blatting fart. Its intestines squirted out of its mouth and asshole. The black and green guts ran into Yahchilane's mouth. His face twisted in disgust. He gagged. He retched. Bile exploded out of Yahchilane and spackled Crowe.

Crowe backed away retching and wiping his face with his fingers. His gorge rose. He knelt and puked.

Finally they staggered from each other and sat with their backs against the wall of the cave. Fifteen-odd feet separated them.

They stayed put, catching their breath, the rasp of their gasping loud in the sepulchral space of the cave. They regarded each other with battered and busted faces. Teeth missing. Hair sticking up, sweaty and bloody.

The cave was the size of a small hangar. Crude petroglyphs marked the walls. Memento mori drawn by hand in blood upon the stone. Crowe recognized familiar figures. Alligators and bobcats and warrior hunters. Pictures of corn.

As with the sinkhole in his backyard that opened that past spring, Crowe surmised, there must have been a similar shift in the earth many hundreds of years ago. Perhaps thousands. And the sinkholes and the limestone collapses sealed off the inner chamber, turning it into a big time capsule.

An ossuary.

A burial ground.

The walls were sheer plumb. Impossible to gain purchase. Still for a while Crowe tried desperately, clinging, thwarted, clinging again, thwarted.

Meanwhile Yahchilane watched the floundering futility of it all.

Out of breath Crowe looked at Yahchilane. Gasping, hands on hips. "Nothing? Zero? Just gonna sit like a lump'a turd?"

Yahchilane didn't answer.

Rocks were scattered about the cavern floor. Some no bigger than baseballs. Others loaves of bread. Others horse saddles.

Yahchilane saw Crowe assessing them. He said, "If you think about coming at me with another of those rocks, I'll fuck you up dead."

Crowe gathered and stacked the bigger rocks. Once he had a stack about three feet tall he stood upon it and jumped high. He grasped at an outcropping of rock, but the limestone broke apart.

Crowe fell and he reached for something to grab but there was nothing and he hit the ground on his side.

A fresh score of agonies erupted throughout his body.

Crowe wailed.

He picked himself off the bone-littered cavern floor. He sat on one side of the cave and Yahchilane another, their backs against the limestone. Their faces were swollen and gashed with cuts in the tenebrous light.

Crowe's broken nose was swelled like a kiwi.

Yahchilane's lip was split, a fat purple worm bisected.

For about an hour Crowe shouted for help before finally tiring and giving up, slouched in defeat.

"Why, Yahchilane?"

Yahchilane was silent.

"You think I gave a shit about Jerry Vogel?"

Yahchilane's eyes lifted. His expression stiffened.

"Hello?" Crowe said. "Earth to Yahchilane?"

"Why do you keep on saying my fuckin' name like that, egghead? There's two people in the cave."

"You really thought I didn't know about Vogel?"

Yahchilane was silent.

"Half the island suspects, Yahchilane."

"I didn't do anything to Jerry Vogel."

"Everybody wanted Jerry Vogel dead. You did the world a favor."

There was a spell of silence.

Nightbirds.

"Some people the world is better without."

It was true. Jerry Vogel, some people might have balked, raised their eyebrows at the dubious, old Conch way of meting out justice. But such people knew nothing about life in Emerald Island. And such people weren't acquainted with Jerry Vogel.

Emerald Islanders were. All too intimately. Vogel's mother was dead. He had no wife or kids or much of a family. No one noticed him missing. No one gave a shit except for a few of his fair-weather friends.

Jerry Vogel had no shitstorm friends.

And you could say Jerry Vogel had it coming. It was only a matter of time.

Hubris.

The Colombians wanted nothing to do with him after his boat was destroyed. He asked for a loan, to buy another. They laughed in his face. When he threatened to snitch, they told him if he didn't shut the fuck up and disappear, they'd chainsaw him into a hundred pieces.

It was over for Vogel.

Vogel returned to Emerald Island vanquished. How close to the sun he'd flown, and now he was a burnout. A vagrant without a dime. For four years, caviar and cocaine and Dom and sex with eighteen-year-old Puerto Rican girls, now he didn't have a tin can to redeem for five cents.

And the home he left no longer existed.

Jerry Vogel wanted to return home.

Impossible.

But Vogel would not go away.

Vogel no longer belonged.

There was one man in town, Ziggy Schaffer, who cared. His friend. The sheriff.

One of the few people who never knew what really happened to Jerry Vogel. And didn't need to know.

Just as the laws sometimes worked oddly in latitudes and longitudes, so did lies and secrets. Who you told, who you didn't.

The Florida stars. The gibbering of small Florida animals and lizardy sounds in the leaf litter.

Crowe eyed Yahchilane. Just sitting there.

"I always figured you as a church bomber. I don't know why. I know you don't bomb churches."

Another silent half minute passed.

"Or who knows. Maybe you do. Bomb churches. But you know how you sometimes assume the worst. How you imagine things. Look, I don't give a shit. But you see a person over the years, you wonder. Course you do."

Zero from Yahchilane.

"Oh, there goes Yahchilane. With his walking stick. Where's he going? He gonna bomb a church? Fuck some lady in Panacea?"

Yahchilane leaned against the wall of the cave, his head tipped back, his legs drawn up. An arm draped across the knees. Craggy face limned in light. Long feet bare in the dirt. His boots off and resting to the side with white socks rolled and stuffed in their mouths.

Outside, an owl screeched, a small lonely sound in the night coming from a great wooded distance.

Knowing he was going too far, half hoping Yahchilane would sock him just to distract him from their doom, "You throw tomahawks at raccoons? That your hobby, Yahchilane?"

Finally Yahchilane spoke. "Hey. Watch it, that shit."

This time it was Crowe went silent.

Yahchilane, "Watch it before I rip your head off and shit down your neck."

LASSO THE POPE

SOME HOURS LATER YAHCHILANE WAS DREAMING of the war.

The flies and rats swarming over the bodies. Dogs and cats carrying away the chunks and gobbets of their masters.

No one was in charge. Orders were passed along, garbled in translation. A game of telephone.

Human beings.

Cooked like meat.

Sometime in the night Yahchilane awoke from nightmares to a thin trickling rain of dirt. Figuring it a roach or mouse or lizard, Yahchilane kept his eyes closed. He tried to fall back under, waited for the black dreamless smother. Wished away nightmares.

But then there was a ripping sound, like fabric rent asunder. Then there was an industrious rustling.

Yahchilane cracked his eyes open.

At first he thought the man was in the middle of a perverse act. In the darkness Crowe was manhandling something resembling a tuber, his hands twisting and working.

But when Yahchilane blinked away the rheum of sleep he saw that Crowe was holding on to a carrotlike white root he'd ripped from the gullet of the hole.

Crowe was knotting together a crude rope. Already he had four or five roots tied together.

"Fuck're you doin'?" Yahchilane asked.

Their eyes met briefly, a rancid glance. Crowe was the first to break it.

The birds were just beginning to sound their dawn chorus. The first pink-gray blanching the sky. Against this backdrop, the pine tops, just the silhouette of their crowns, so deep they were in the hole.

"Rope," said Crowe.

"You're making a rope."

"Go back to sleep."

"You think you're gonna escape with four roots tied together."

"Ever hear of a lasso?"

Crowe's face, riddled with mosquito bites, was filled with so much rue and conviction that Yahchilane leaning back in his corner laughed. "Spider-Man," he said.

Crowe's fingers didn't slow.

"Lasso what?" Yahchilane asked.

"The Pope."

The rose and plum of morning was just beginning to turn the sky aglow. Rousing doves cooed their liquid babble from a distance.

GIVE ME YOUR BELT BUCKLE

AT NOON, THERE WERE SEVERAL MINUTES when the sun came straight down through the leafage of the trees and beamed directly down into the grotto.

A plane stitched a thin contrail against the glaring sky. It passed overhead, its roar silencing the bird and bug sound. Crowe in his brain-dead fatigue found himself staring at Yahchilane's sterling silver belt buckle. Oval, inlaid with filigree. So old it wore a patina of tarnish.

"What," Yahchilane said.

Crowe rubbed his beard speculatively. Flakes of dried mud fell. "Let me see your belt buckle."

"No."

"Lemme."

"Why, egghead?"

"I'm gonna run away with it? Fly outta here and pawn it?"

Yahchilane waited.

"Flash a signal," Crowe said.

Yahchilane waited more.

"To a plane?" Crowe said.

A taciturn, one-syllable chuckle.

"I'm trying. I'm trying here."

"You think someone in the plane is going to notice a belt buckle from two miles away. A belt buckle in the jungle."

Crowe swept his parched tongue over lips dry as trace paper.

"Addle-brained."

Crowe didn't argue otherwise. He leaned his head back against the cool cavern wall in gloomy rue.

Another night in the cave.

Amazing, Crowe thought, how Yahchilane could sleep at a time like this.

Every now and then Crowe heard the scuttle of roaches and beetles. Darting, pausing, darting again.

He heard the burrowing of creatures that would eat them as soon as they got the chance. Moles and rats. Turtles. The huge coconut crabs that dug underground warrens down to fifty feet. Those crabs would make quick work of them with their pincers. Shear their faces into mincemeat.

Sleepless late that night, Crowe saw on the cavern wall his handprint, of blood, from when he tried to climb out.

Years later should some archeologist or spelunker come picking among the ruins they'd find his bloody handprint dried on the rock, a spread hand somehow desperate, beseeching through the ages.

"Yahchilane."

Zero from Yahchilane.

"Hello?"

Nothing.

"Why a snake in my mail slot, Yahchilane?"

"Fuck're you talking?"

"Not gonna call the cops at this point."

Yahchilane shook his head.

"Why, Yahchilane?"

"Why what, egghead?"

"Why'd you put a snake in my mail slot?"

"Brain's goop from drugs."

Now it was Crowe's turn to brood. In a broken voice he said, "What a way to die."

Crowe thought of his mistakes.

He thought of Heidi.

He thought of his dead daughter, Otter.

He thought of the babysitter, her life going on. As it should have, he knew on a deep gut level, but still.

And it was his fault, leaving the pot there. The babysitter got stoned. The babysitter invited her boyfriend over. The boyfriend and the babysitter fucked around on the couch while the child was in her bed. The child wandered off through the back door and she went into the neighbor's backyard. Into their pool.

How often in the past had Reed Crowe pinioned himself on the torture rack of guilt going over the minutest details.

It stymied Crowe to this day.

It just didn't make sense.

How Otter could have gotten out and how Otter could have drowned.

Why would Otter sneak out in the middle of the night to swim?

And say she did, how would she drown?

She took after her grandmother Shelly. Crowe's mother, a mermaid at the Weeki Wachee Mermaid Show, nineteen, when Reed Senior met her.

Lily was the child's name. But they called her by her nickname, Otter. Not only because of her acrobatic swimming in the water, but because the first time she laughed, as a baby, it was at a trio of dancing otters at SeaWorld.

Would his child have drowned if he didn't have that pot in the freezer, if the babysitter hadn't found it?

You had to wonder, mother of a thousand plants, one tendril of circumstance begetting another.

Mother of a thousand mistakes.

Their faces were shadowy and scary in the dark. Nightmare faces. It was three or four hours past midnight.

The night was sweaty and buggy. The insects were trilling.

Crowe couldn't sleep. Mosquitoes hummed in his ears.

Crowe watched a palm-sized luna moth drift down through the cracked roof of the cave. It floated languidly toward him. Mistaking the paleness of Crowe's eyes and the farmer's tan of his bare chest as some kind of glow or luminescence.

The moth was about a foot away from Crowe when it sensed he was nothing worth further investigation. It flapped softly away, up and out of the cave.

Crowe caught Yahchilane watching the moth too. Maybe a similar thought was passing through his head. A dumb shithawk moth able to escape, and here they were.

Yahchilane looked away, tilted his head back against the wall, shut his eyes.

Crowe, "Question, Yahchilane."

Yahchilane's eyes stayed shut but Crowe could see the little ticking movements beneath the lids.

"Yahchilane," said Crowe.

With his eyes still closed, "Shut up."

"Why sever Vogel's head?"

Yahchilane slowly opened his eyes. The slits stayed on Crowe without blinking. The expression on his face telluric.

The cicadas and crickets droned on.

Crowe asked again, "Why sever the head, Yahchilane?"

"You think I severed the head?"

"Yeah."

Yahchilane shot breath through his nose.

Crowe set his jaw. "I'm not a sick fuck who severs heads."

"Talk to me again that way. Your head'll get knocked clean off."

Yahchilane settled back. He looked at Crowe stonily for a time, as if assessing. "Coconut crabs carried those bones away. Whatever had meat on it, they carried it away."

The image of the crabs carrying away the gobbets of flesh, hauling away minuscule bones in their pinchers, would not leave Crowe's head.

He belched and coughed up phlegmy strings that tasted like acid.

There was nothing in his stomach to throw up.

When the fit subsided Crowe lay on his side and pointed his face at the cavern wall. He shut his eyes and tried to sleep. Tried to banish from his imagination the clickety-clack sounds of crab claws.

They were quiet for a while. Crowe dozed. His empty stomach was keeping him awake. His stomach was gurgling its own acid. Crowe was in a semi-sleep, head tipped on the limestone wall, when he heard eating sounds. Munching, swallowing.

Crowe cracked his eyes and looked through bleary slits. When he saw Yahchilane grab a fat white grub from the dirt wall and palm it into his mouth like a peanut Crowe dry-heaved.

There was nothing else to eat now. Root and grubs and if they were suddenly to develop pica dirt. Yahchilane already scoured the cavern for edibles. Old muscadine grapes. Purslane. Acorns.

Yahchilane swallowed the grub. Looked at Crowe.

"Jesus Christ," Crowe said.

Yahchilane found another wriggling grub. Pinching it with pantomimed delectation, like a bonbon, he dropped it in his mouth. Munched while keeping a steady stoic eye on Crowe.

Crowe marveled. "Maniac."

Yahchilane said nothing.

"Maybe there're some roly-polies around here," Crowe said. "Lemme look."

"Wanna know something?"

"Bugs taste like chicken."

"You're a pussy."

"'Cause I don't eat beetles and shit. Fuck yourself."

"You're a pussy and an egghead."

A big wind moved through the trees.

They were silent again.

Next morning Yahchilane woke to Crowe talking in his sleep. "Otter. Otter."

Crowe lay curled on his side like a child, his hands groping.

When Crowe awoke Yahchilane was still watching him.

A groggy moment passed and then Crowe seemed struck by fresh horror. The reality of their predicament.

He stood. He shouted.

He shouted his voice ragged into the vast Florida pine flats.

When he tired and his voice frayed, Crowe slumped on the floor of the cave.

With a small quick movement of his Swiss army knife blade Yahchilane cut off a piece of root. He tossed it with a disdainful flick of the wrist, without looking, at Crowe. The same way you'd toss a scrap at a dog. The snip landed in the dirt at Crowe's bare feet.

Crowe looked up, incredulous.

A trick, perhaps.

But he was delirious from hunger.

Their jaws worked bovine, grinding the white-green roots.

"Thanks," said Crowe after a while. Swallowing was hard, his throat so raw and dry.

Yahchilane said nothing but there was a simper on his face.

Let him laugh, Crowe thought. Like I'm the freak.

Crowe assumed the grinning was over, but then it started again.

Crowe couldn't help himself. "Real funny. Fixin' to die in a hole with a bunch of bones."

The frogs. The crickets. The other small swamp vermin trilling and fluting.

"I know who you are," Yahchilane said at last.

"The guy who you attacked in the woods for bullshit?" Crowe slapped at a mosquito on the back of his neck.

"Seen you on television one time."

Crowe wiped the smear on his shorts. "That's right. Johnny Carson."

Yahchilane was still grinning.

"Go back to sleep, man," Crowe said.

"Cops were arresting you," Yahchilane said.

Crowe was silent.

"Television show, public service announcement," Yahchilane said. "They were mashing your face. They were mashing your face against the pavement."

Crowe, yes, once he was on television, his arrest televised locally as a cautionary tale. A "remember to stay off dope, kids" kind of deal.

"Look, it's you," his mother said.

This was one of his most recent visits at the nursing home.

Crowe glanced at the television. At once he was incredulous. The man's resemblance was remarkable. Uncanny, really.

Crowe watched with mounting shock. Struggling to maintain his poker face. Wondering if he was wigging out, hallucinating.

Not only did he and the man resemble each other. They could pass for brothers.

Crowe stepped closer to the television.

Twins, Crowe thought. We could pass for twins.

It was then that Crowe realized with shock that the man on television was him.

"You two could be cousins," his mother said.

There he was on the television, in an Ocean Pacific shirt he owned, in Bermuda shorts he owned, in the very same flip-flops he was wearing now. There he was, getting his face smashed into the hood of a car.

Then he wondered if it was legal, airing this footage. Knowing himself, he'd probably signed the forms. If he didn't recall the incident being filmed—hell, if he did not then why would he remember forms?

"Your hair is much nicer than his," his mother remarked.

Crowe decided that instant he would burn that Ocean Pacific shirt and those Bermuda shorts.

He stepped to the television and switched the channel to *The Price Is Right.*

That television footage, Crowe wanted to explain the intricacies of the story, how he came to find himself in that situation. He wanted Yahchilane to know, for the record, that he wasn't some asshole who liked to get his head pounded into pudding on national television. But Crowe knew his story would fall on deaf ears. He wouldn't be halfway through the first sentence before Yahchilane said shut up egghead or some such Henry Yahchilane thing.

What set him off the night he was arrested was when Heidi said, "Maybe you cursed her." Meaning the child.

Meaning Otter.

They were in the middle of an argument. Drunk. A red wine argument, one of the worst kinds. He couldn't remember how the blow got started or how it whipped up so quickly into a full-blown tempest.

They were still raw. Seven months after the child Lily's death.

"What?" Crowe stood from the kitchen table, hurled the wineglass into the corner where it shattered. "What? What?" His voice was ferrous, strange-sounding, so heart-torn was the grief.

At the kitchen table Heidi flinched. Slanted her body away from him.

"What? I cursed my own child?" His voice bereaved. Berserk.

She stared quiver-eyed at her glass. Her mouth drawn shut.

Days later she would apologize. Tell him she meant something different. Something like karma.

Karma. Curses.

All the same.

He'd lost her.

She was just as lost to him now as Otter.

Three days in.

The men had relieved themselves in the farthest corner of one of the cave's alcoves. Like cats they buried their waste, kicking dirt over the hole. Wiping their asses with ferns torn from the cavern walls.

Their stench filled the cave.

"We're gonna die, Yahchilane," Crowe said. "Don't you care? You don't got any ideas?"

Yahchilane coughed.

"Bet you want one of your cigarettes right now," said Crowe.

Crickets and frogs and toads. The whine of mosquitoes and gnats.

Yahchilane coughed again and he rose and he cupped his hand and scooped water from the puddle in the stone and he drank it. He sat back down.

The skeletons around them looked accustomed to their presence. And they to theirs. No longer menacing. Now they were benign.

Just old bones.

"Whose skeletons you think?" Yahchilane asked Crowe.

Crowe said nothing.

"Seminoles. Calusa. Shell Indians. Worked out on a railroad. They buried them here. Out in a pit."

"That's not historical fact."

"It's exactly true."

"Rumor."

His grandfather started a nutria farm. A farm of overgrown rats in Louisiana. Grim times. Grandpa Heath jounced out of Idaho in a shanty wagon with all their meager worldly belongings in tow. The wife and kids and dogs and Rudolph the pet canary in his brass wire cage crammed between the tottering boxes and trunks. His father and aunts amid the bedlam. No uncles.

For three years or so Reed Crowe's grandfather sold pelts. A lucrative enterprise, for a while. There was a need for fur coats, imitation, fashion being what it was at the time. But the coats started falling apart. They wouldn't even last a whole winter before tattering away into fuzzy clumps.

Word got around. Manhattan ladies no longer bought the nutria coats. That was that for the nutria.

When the nutria enterprise proved ill-fated in 1923 the family again pulled up its stakes and embarked for the swampy thickets of Florida.

Millinery and moonshining.

For about a decade, the women in the big cities, so far away from this sweltering longitude, wore exotic feathers, sometimes whole birds, in their hats and bonnets. If you were in Gotham at a certain time in the late 1800s and looked down the length of Madison Avenue or one of those haute boulevards, you'd see all the feathers and birds in hats.

His kin were opportunists. No denying. In the right place at the right time. The time of land grants and manifest destiny.

Florida was the back of beyond in those days, trackless wild full of a million hazards. These were the days of the industrial revolution, of road and railroad building. Many a contractor promised to tame the land. More than a few gave up defeated and humbled. More than a few took the money and ran.

Outlaws. Refugees. Desperados. Pioneers. These were Crowe's kin.

His grandfather was a construction foreman after pluming was outlawed. The Tamiami Trail. Then he decided to embark on his own enterprise. For every mile of road he built into the jungleland of Florida, the government granted him ten acres.

Their reasoning: Who the hell would want it?

And for decades, no one did. This before the boom of tin can tourism after the war. Before Florida became an exotic tourist destination.

So Crowe's relatives built miles of road into terra incognita. And they took the land. They took plenty of it.

Including Emerald Island.

And it was Reed's father, Reed Senior, who oversaw the bridge from the mainland to the island. But before then, there were the roads to lay across the wilderness. How were the roads built?

That was a story.

A story involving the first Calusa Indians and then Seminoles and Miccosukee. And the story also included the great floods and hurricanes. The great sicknesses.

Reed Crowe had no doubt the roads were paved in the blood and sweat and tears of Indians. And blacks.

Slaves under a different name.

So, if there was such a thing as curses.

If there were such a thing as karmic retribution.

As far as he was concerned, his birthright was an accident, a mere coincidence.

Which absolved him.

"It could have been the flu," Crowe said to Yahchilane.

"They worked on a railroad and they didn't want to pay up the money and they killed him."

"And you think I have something to do with this."

"No."

"I'm implicated."

"We're all implicated."

Crowe put his finger to his lips and gazed skyward as if absorbing a great profundity. Then, "Riddles. We're dying here. Fuck's it with you?"

"Hey, watch it, egghead."

They looked at each other.

"Watch the tone. I'll knock your fuckin' head off."

They were silent. A yammering bird went *yuk-yuk-yuk* over the surround-sound bugsong.

Crowe, "You think I care about Vogel? I don't give one jack shit about Vogel."

It was their fourth day in the grotto when at dawn the sound of an engine roused them from sleep. Diminutive and bug-like in the Florida immensity. Crowe knew too little about engines and their workings to identify the kind of motor, the horsepower.

But Yahchilane could. He could tell the engine belonged to a Jeep. About two or three hundred yards away Yahchilane could discern this much.

Yahchilane asked Crowe if he knew anybody who drove a Jeep.

Crowe said he did. Heidi.

Whoever it was had driven as far as they could because the engine abruptly ceased. Whoever it was, they'd parked because they'd made it as far as they could in the marshy ferny bracken of the Florida pine flats.

For ten minutes both men shouted their voices ragged and raw.

Then, so faint and distant, so high and reedy Reed Crowe feared it might be a hallucination, a voice.

A woman.

There was a quickening of her steps.

"Reed?" said the woman.

"Heidi," screamed Crowe.

Then Heidi was peering down at them as they peered up at her.

Filthy woebegone revenants, faces bruised and bumpy and bloody. Eyes crazed. Mouths swollen, caked with dried mucus.

"Lord Jesus Christ," said Heidi.

Heidi returned to the island to find Crowe's house locked and empty. The backyard stray cats, their food and water dishes empty too.

Not like Reed, dunderhead though he often was.

And that note, no letter, no answer when she called his number.

Maybe Crowe was out of town on business, she figured. Visiting his mother. Shacking up with one of his girlfriends.

Reed Crowe, who knew.

But then she remembered the visit from Henry Yahchilane, the man asking for the archeology book.

She remembered the skull.

Reed's digging, the artifacts.

Maybe he's in trouble, she thought.

And when Heidi discovered the men trapped in the grotto, she came back with a ladder and rope. Once the men, battered and half-dead, were in her Jeep, she told them she was taking them to the hospital.

"No way," Crowe said, one eye swollen shut, his top lip split. Black blood dried all over his face. "Can't afford it."

Heidi driving them through Emerald City, looked at him sharply. "Can you afford being dead?"

Crowe, crammed between Heidi and Yahchilane in the middle of the front seat, said, "Inflation these days, probably not."

"You two stink," Heidi said.

Neither of the men denied it.

As they were passing Red, White and Blue Liquor, Yahchilane asked Heidi to stop.

"For beer?" she asked incredulously.

"Cigs."

Heidi shook her head, bumped the Jeep into the lot and parked in a space.

"Grab me a beer?" Crowe said.

Heidi and Crowe watched Yahchilane hobble wretched and mud-spackled and bloody into the store. They watched the man behind the counter, Andy Krumpp, the owner, gawk at Yahchilane. Yahchilane looked every bit like a man who'd escaped a mine collapse.

He went to the cooler, fetched three tall boys. Then at the counter he paid for them and a pack of cigarettes.

Back in the car, Yahchilane gave a beer to Heidi and Crowe and kept one for himself.

"Mind?" he asked, before he lit a cigarette.

Heidi shook her head. She took one for herself, lit it. She cracked open her window and Yahchilane cracked his. The sound of tires singing on asphalt filled the cab.

Heidi and Yahchilane were smoking and they were almost to the Emerald Island bridge when Yahchilane laughed his short gruff laughter.

Crowe eyed Yahchilane, swallowed from his beer.

Heidi asked what was so funny.

"Krumpp," Yahchilane said. "When I walked into his store."

AGE OF THE REFUGEE

(1981–1984)

RUM JUNGLE

THE MEN MET ONLY ONCE AT the Rum Jungle and they agreed to leave the remains of the Seminole Indians be. This bothered Crowe at first, leaving the bones out there like they were nothing, nobody knowing about them, eternal anonymity, but Yahchilane pointed out that the bodies were where they wanted to be. "We got no other way of telling, do we?" Yahchilane asked him.

"I suppose not."

Jerry Vogel, another matter.

Yahchilane knew Crowe would never approach Schaffer about the matter because he had his own proverbial skeletons, and vice versa.

Everybody had secrets this part of Florida. Somewhere so small, word got around quickly, so you had to keep certain things to yourself. Emerald Island, if one person knew, everybody knew.

So mysteries would remain about Reed Crowe and Yahchilane and Vogel. About Schaffer.

"Just tell me, what happened?" Crowe asked Henry Yahchilane.

"He came at me. It was self-defense. But Schaffer wouldn't'a thought of it that way."

Crowe stroked his beach bum beard. "No, he wouldn't have either."

NIGHT OF A THOUSAND CASKS

THE REST OF THAT SUMMER HEIDI would come over in her clamdiggers and culottes more nights out of the week than not. Her white poplin shirts tied calypso style. They drank and they talked and they shared joints in the beach twilight. Over the weeks their tans grew darker, her tan lines he so loved. They listened to the discography of Fleetwood Mac. *Rumours* and *Tusk*. Crowe moved his big Bose speakers so they faced out the open sliding glass doors.

The tiki torches kept the insects at bay.

In the dusk the beach cats chased scuttling tailless geckos.

Sometimes Herman the heron would flap in like an apparition from the dark and stand back at a distance, waiting for pompano scraps, redfish leftovers.

Crowe would make ceviche, grill African pompano on the backyard grill. Heidi made Cuba libres.

Every so often Crowe would go over to the spot where the hummingbird tree once stood. Making a show of it for Heidi, he'd toe the spot. Then he would set down a tentative foot, slowly. Then he would stomp his zorie. Then he'd stomp both.

Crowe drunkenly romped for a while like this.

Heidi kept telling him, "I wouldn't if I were you."

"Why not?"

"You're tempting fate."

"I thought you were the big explorer."

"I'm not going to go jump into a volcano like an asshole."

"This is solid ground."

"Says who?"

"I got it checked professionally."

"Oh yeah. Who?"

"Chill Norton."

"Oh god. Now I really got to get my ass off this chair. You're gonna believe Chill Norton? Chill Norton's the scientist now. You might as well just pack up and move. We're going under."

"Seismic tests. The newest technology."

On one of his moonlit jaunts Crowe saw in the distance a few square containers washed ashore. He quickened his step.

Four old wooden crates. Maybe crab traps. Maybe not. Maybe he'd lucked upon one of those fabled marijuana or cocaine bales of yore.

Oh man, he hoped. Wildly hoped.

Crowe ran, crashing splay-footed and awkwardly through the surf. His plastic tumbler with the seashell applique slopping white wine and ice cubes.

He pawed one of the boxes apart one-handed. The thin wooden slatting and the sodden timber snapped easily. Crowe in his excitement flung the plastic tumbler onto the beach. Then he tore the wood with both hands and glimpsed the corner of a paper label.

"Oh goddamn," Crowe said. "Oh man."

Crowe reached. The cool curve of a wine bottle. Intact. The dark emerald gleam of wine filled colored glass. There was a label flaked and frayed, the color of tea-stained ivory, so old. Crowe could hardly read it in the dark. French, calligraphy. 1838, said the label.

Crowe glanced about. No one around for a mile and a half in either direction. The moon on the lace of the surf. The pretty luminous curd feathering in boomerang shapes.

Still Crowe ran. He sprinted. He ran himself gasping and he got a wheelbarrow out of the garage. Like a maniac crazed with a plow he shoved through the sand. An ordeal. The whole thing an ordeal, back and forth four times with all that wine, bottles clanking, all the weight, the sand, the wheel getting stuck in the sand, Crowe thinking he would die of a heart attack by the end of it all.

He put three of the crates in the garage. He shoved the crates under the workstation table. He hid the crates under a deflated rubber pool. The fourth crate he opened, the old cork still intact after all this time, and he tried it straight from the bottle, a small sip, very small, keeping it in his mouth, tasting, thinking he might have to spit it out.

But the wine was good. A taste of old berries and nutmeg and smoke. It was like time and age. You tasted the centuries. The spice of time.

He called Heidi. "You're not gonna believe this."

Heidi came.

Then some neighbors came and then some others and after a while half the island was getting shitfaced and they spent many hours on the beach drinking one entire case of the wine. They burned a driftwood pyre on the beach. Someone dragged out Crowe's hi-fi equipment onto the back porch and blasted the music so loud you could hear the bass and beat even halfway down the beach. Motown. They danced. Their shadows elongated and capered on the sand. They made up idiotic songs about wine. *Wine, wine, won't you be mine, well, you are mine, all mine, wine, wine, wine . . .*

After everyone straggled off, Crowe and Heidi stripped off their clothes. He lay with his back in sand as she rode on top of him.

The flames danced, fitful wraiths. A pocket of sap popped, a spray of blue and green sparks spluttering up. The sparks helixed and scattered like fireflies.

A sweet salt breeze played on their skin, balming their sunburns, keeping the mosquitoes at bay, drying the spit of his wine-sticky kisses off Heidi's nipples.

THE GOLDEN BRIDGE

END OF SUMMER HEIDI TOLD HIM she was leaving again for Europe, Amsterdam, for how long she wasn't sure. This time, she was not only helping transport art from gallery to gallery throughout Europe, but holding her own art show, a collection of her pieces, at the Franco-American Institute in Rennes, France.

In Heidi's bungalow on the eve of her departure he went among the paintings hung on the walls of her small gallery. Flame-colored celestial blots. Overheated colors. Startle colors. Mother-of-pearl phosphorescence. To someone else they might have looked very similar, the smudgy spectra, but to Crowe they were all very different.

Crowe stopped at one of the canvases. "What's this painting?"

"The Golden Bridge."

"Heidi."

"What?"

"This is something else." He meant it.

"You really like it?"

"I love it. Why *The Golden Bridge*?"

"You're high."

"No. Yeah. A little. I like what I like. Tell me about *The Golden Bridge*."

"Is there a moment of the day you're not doped up, Reed?"

They were getting along, and then she told Crowe how long she was going abroad.

Crowe felt his heart drop at the news, but he acted happy for her. Part of him was. She'd been through so much. Their child. Him.

They toasted their wineglasses, sat down to a meal of conch fritters, one of Heidi's specialties.

After dinner, while they were washing the dishes, Crowe took her by the shoulders, tried kissing her.

She leaned away. "Don't."

"Come on. Who cares?"

"Who cares? We have to stop this."

"But if it feels good?"

"No."

"Just no?"

"Yes."

Crowe tried again. And again Heidi leaned away.

"All right," Crowe said. "Shit, Jesus."

She pecked him on the cheek. "Here," she said, taking him by the hand, leading him to the painting. *The Golden Bridge*. "It's for you."

Crowe teared up.

"Oh, Reed."

"Please don't go, Heidi." He hated how desperate he sounded, but so it was.

"Oh, Reed."

On her bed was a modest hardshell suitcase. Into it she'd crammed her clothes in fastidious little rolls. Amazing, how much she could cram in such a small suitcase. Crowe could never accomplish such a feat.

"You gonna water the plants?" she asked.

"Come on."

"Well, are you? I need to know. Because if not I have to make the call tonight. I'm serious, Reed. I won't be making calls from Europe. Let's not shit around."

"Well, I walk by every day."

"So yes."

"Yes. Yes."

But a month or so after she left, it was Crowe's habit walking toward Henry Yahchilane's barrel-shaped house. The other way, toward the bridge, was Heidi's folk art bungalow. Bright as a children's storybook, cobbled together with mirror shards and broken glass and mosaics made of ceramic bits of pottery. A bottle tree in the backyard. A garden of tropical flowers.

Unmistakably Heidi's abode. And the sight of it made Crowe miss her.

Which he resented.

So he got either Eddie or Wayne to water Heidi's plants for him. Eddie did it for free. Wayne, though, "Gonna pay me?"

Sometimes while on his evening jaunts his thoughts wandered and he imagined Heidi with other men and other bedrooms. Her mouth on someone else's. Her eyes looking at strangers with the kind of unguarded longing they used to share.

Other men inside of her.

He had his fuck buddies on the mainland. Women who sold jams and jellies and marmalades and Florida honey. Women who waitressed at the Rum Jungle. He felt great affection for them. Friendly love. No romance, but they flung and flailed at one another out of a kind of animal abandonment. Which was precisely the point.

And if anything, the women were usually less sentimental than he. Yes, this was a different time, all right.

But with Heidi whenever he walked there was some reminder. If he came across a piece of driftwood he'd carry it home. If he came across a piece of sea glass he would pocket it for Heidi.

Fuck her, he'd say. Bitterly, when drunk and alone at night when one of their old songs played on the record player.

But he meant it in neither head nor heart.

In the morning he'd take the piece of sea glass out of the trash and wash it in the sink and place it with the others in the big mason jar that sat on the driftwood table next to the reading chair in the sunroom of his coral beach house.

Heidi sent him postcards. She sent him pictures. But less often each year. Fewer each time she went away.

She waxed rhapsodic about her travels.

The museums and opera houses and brasseries of Paris. Amsterdam, the hash bars and canals and van Gogh museum. The pyramids of Egypt. Sea caves of Scotland. Ice castles of Salzburg. The blue deserts of Sinai. The wild wonders and huge oddities of Australia. The crabs in Christmas Island. Jerusalem, Bangladesh.

He thought she would tire of her journeying with age.

If anything, the opposite.

There was once a time when Heidi invited Crowe along for her trips.

"I can't," he'd say.

"You're a grown man who's never been to Europe."

"That flight, no way."

"I don't know why you're stuck there."

"I'm not stuck here."

And he didn't think of it that way.

Crowe loved the old beach house. Its simplicity. Cypress and Ocala lime block and floor-to-ceiling windows. He loved the coffee table and shelves made from driftwood. The jars of sea glass, the hunks of coral. He loved opening all the doors in the spring and fall, letting the trade winds breeze through.

He loved the terrazzo floor, how it kept cool during even the hottest summers, its foot-deep gleam. How he always saw new patterns and shapes in the tiny chips of quartz and mother-of-pearl and abalone shell.

And Emerald Island. Emerald Island was the Rum Jungle and the Blue Parrot diner. Emerald Island was where all his ghosts lived.

Emerald Island was where the light fell on Heidi in a poetic way. The tang of citrus and dried ocean salt on her lips in summer. The sheen of coconut oil on her body, her shiny sun-brown hips, her eyes mossy hazel and aglow in her tan. The big brown macaroon of her nipple in his mouth as he entered her and she moaned in his ear.

STAY IN ONE PLACE

WHAT IS IT SHE ALWAYS SAID? Stay in one place long enough, the old adage went, the world came to you.

Horseshit, Reed Crowe knew. But in his three and a half decades on earth, he'd witnessed wonders.

The Perseid meteor showers. A solar eclipse. A few lunar eclipses too.

And once he saw what he would swear was a Soviet submarine. At first he mistook it as a whale. But then he saw the gleam of metal and heard a large engine straining and he saw the periscope emerge from the water, a cyclopean stalk eyeing him from a distance. Alien.

Crowe threw up his hands. "Hey, I don't give a shit."

The periscope inched down. The gray hump of the submarine sank back into the depths. Then the vessel was gone, vanished back into the Gulf.

Another time he saw lightning strike a pelican as it flew midair. He was fishing and lightning cracked like an incandescent whip out of the clear blue sky. Unpredictable Florida weather. His heart jolted as if horsewhipped. Even from his beach chair Crowe felt the heat on his face. By the time it hit the water the bird was cooked. It hissed like a hot cast-iron skillet and a puff of steam rose from the surface.

James Caan. One day in the late seventies Crowe saw Caan, Sonny Corleone himself, flying a Japanese box kite with his toddler son. Nice guy, asked for a cigarette. Crowe didn't have one, but Caan told him a Polack joke nonetheless.

Sophia Loren. If it wasn't Sophia Loren, then her doppelganger in beauty. A woman wearing a green and white banyan-patterned two-piece. Cinnamon skin, Persian eyes, amphora figure. She walked barefoot by him, French manicured toes, and he said hello and she said hello. Then he was left with her effluvia, her musk. He waited for hours sitting in his beach chair to see her again. To maybe say something, anything, because he knew he'd regret not. And it would be a story. But she must have taken another route because she didn't pass him again.

A huge school of incandescent jellyfish in the shallows of the Gulf. They glowed with sapphire bioluminescence. Like a constellation fallen to earth. Like a planetarium under the sea.

And one night he saw a UFO. Not a weather balloon, not some mysterious celestial phenomenon, not foxfire or aurora borealis.

A UFO. Bona fide.

A lozenge-shaped vessel, like a flattened blimp. It hovered low on the horizon among the stars and the lights of distant ocean liners and oil tankers. After ten minutes of perfect stillness, it zipped away, meteor quick, leaving only a lingering scribble of light on his retina.

O-X-NXW-W-VER-VAR-LEGUA $^1/_{10}$
O-X-SWXW-VER-VAR-HASTA X

WAYNE WADE WAS DEAF TO REASON. Ten at night, worked up in a fervor, words coming out of him in a torrent, telling Reed Crowe on the phone that he had to come over pronto. Wayne had something big, something incredible, something fucking mind-blowing, he wanted to show Crowe.

A revelation, Wayne said.

Strange language. Even for Wayne Wade.

It was a few months after Heidi's leaving.

"Tell me who's speaking, please," Crowe said. Stoned. Wine-headed.

"Stop shittin'," Wayne said.

"Private line here. No soliciting."

"Fuck you. Come over."

"Reveal your revelation tomorrow."

Wayne was obstinate.

Crowe got into his beeswax orange hatchback and drove two miles north in the primal dark of the island. The headlights did little to dispel the darkness. Ordovician insects flitted in and out of the beams. Flying beetles the size of walnuts. Gargantuan cockroaches and palmetto bugs. A chartreuse green katydid.

Beyond the light's reach was pure pitch black. This night, a new moon. Steep sand dunes, tall as escarpments and generations old and sculpted by time and tempest, flanked the narrow road. This dark and late, Crowe could have been driving on the dark side of the moon.

When Crowe got to the trailer Wayne was apoplectic with excitement. Pacing. Wild-eyed.

"You on something?" Crowe asked him. Grabbed a beer from the mini-fridge. Sat at the Formica table.

"No."

"Coked up, man?"

"No, man, no." Then, Wayne sat across from Crowe with his own fresh beer. Popped it. "You remember that code you're always talking about?"

Crowe stroked his beach bum beard. Leaned back, scratched his stomach. "Code?"

O-X-NXW-W-VER-VAR-LEGUA 1/10 O-X-SWXW-VER-VAR-HASTA X, was what Wayne Wade wanted to show Reed Crowe. He'd come across the letters and numbers, seeming gobbledygook, carved upon a rock near the grotto. He'd written the code, whatever it was, on the back of a mini-mart receipt which now sifting through all the scrap and trash on the counters he couldn't find.

No surprise. Wayne was known to clean his house with a leaf blower. He'd open the two side doors and let the machine rip, blasting the trash out the doors into the yard. Gum wrappers, rolling papers, cigarette packs, fast-food bags. A bizarre sight, if you were witnessing from afar. As though a storm were raging from inside the house, blowing debris outward.

Now Crowe was about to tell Wayne he was going home when he

saw, or would have sworn he saw in the corner of his vision, the rooster clock on the kitchen wall move.

The trailer ticked and groaned.

Crowe, "That sound? You hear that?"

"Just the heat. Hold up."

"Your clock, it moved."

"You're high, motherfucker."

"I'll remind you, I'm your employer."

"Fuck off."

"Listen. Shut up. Listen."

Then the cataclysm was upon them as swift and violent as a mortar blast. And Crowe and Wayne were in free fall, everything in the trailer topsy-turvy in the air. Like one of those fairground rides where the floor plummets from under you. Some surreal alternate universe where furniture could leap on its own volition like Jesus-drunk revelators.

The toaster oven and ashtray and green glass bong shaped like a dragon's head. The beer cans and the table between them. The chairs in which they sat. Crowe and Wayne themselves.

The bong struck the back of Crowe's head and shattered. The walls buckled and warped. The sofa went tumbling and flying. Windows imploded inward. Glass shards flew. Bulbs busted. The electricity flickered and went black. A pipe popped. A spring of well water sprung. There was another rupture. Foul, septic.

In the midst of this tempest, Crowe caught vertiginous glimpses of Wayne's anguished face. His mouth stretched in a soundless scream.

Wayne close.

Far.

Close again.

Like a Halloween horror fairground ride.

Then it was over in a huge jarring *whomp*. They lay like rag dolls on the floor.

Twenty-odd feet above them was the opening of the chasm. The roof was sheared off, rolled up like the top of a sardine tin. Florida sky gazed down upon them. Prehistorically dark. Crowded with so many stars you could barely make out the constellations. Oddly tranquil, after the half minute of bedlam.

Wayne's dumb doggish eyes fixed on Crowe through the darkness. Wayne lay with the upended trash bin atop his back.

"Wayne," Reed Crowe called.

Wayne, thunderstruck, said nothing.

Debris settled. Glass pieces fell and shattered and slid. There was moaning and groaning of metal settling. The mini-fridge was canted with its door yawed open. Jars and bottles slid and hit the floor and rolled and busted.

"Wayne," Crowe said.

"Somebody bombed us," Wayne said.

Crowe coughed. Pain knifed through his ribs.

Another jar shattered.

"We're gonna die here," Wayne said. He coughed. Spat. "Fuckin' lip. Shit."

"Did you break anything?"

"Somebody bombed us."

"A sinkhole. My rib. Shit."

They rose groaning and cussing. They were covered in dust and bloody nicks.

Panic overcame Wayne. "Holy shit. We're gonna die here. In this hole."

Dirt and pebbles fell. Then the sound diminished to a trickle of scree.

Crowe rubbed the back of his head. Felt warm blood. He looked at his fingers. Black and slick with it.

"We're gonna die down here."

"Wayne? Whole damn island probably heard. Somebody's on their way."

True. The dinky siren was coming from the Emerald City side of the bridge. And dogs were barking in the distance. His far-flung neighbors' dogs.

Wayne's half-concussed gaze roved the ground. Searching.

Crowe, "You okay, man?"

His eyes flicked dully. "Huh?"

"You okay? What you lookin' for?"

Wayne shook his head. "Nothin'. I don't know."

SHIT ON A SHOEHEEL

AFTER WAYNE WADE TOOK UP PERMANENT residence at the Emerald Island Inn, the summer dragged on like shit on a shoeheel. Days upon days passed of what-the-fuck-are-we-doing heat.

A few times Wayne and Eddie almost came to blows. All over nothing. Bullshit. A wrong word, a wrong glance, a wrong facial expression. An RC Cola thrown by Eddie into the garbage bin just a little too loud and close for Wayne Wade's refined taste.

Crowe had to wedge between them, pry them apart.

It was always Wayne's fault. Always.

Crowe would warn him to drop it.

Wayne wouldn't.

Crowe would snap. "Listen, you apple-headed son of a bitch, you think this is funny?"

"Fuck you."

"Fuck me. Hey, I've got news for you. There's a HELP WANTED sign up in Arby's. Saw it yesterday. Free to go explore your options."

Wayne asked him what side he was on.

"Mine."

Some days so few tourists showed that it would have been a waste to make the trip. Crowe offered nonetheless, acting contrite and hangdog, as if the greatest disappointment were his, "Oh, we don't mind going out, folks," all crestfallen, "that's why we're here."

Arms akimbo, head hanging. Like he couldn't bear it.

"On the other hand, you know, lightning," gesturing at the black swag-bellied thunderclouds, "what're you gonna do."

Almost always the tourists had sense enough, mercy enough, to forgo the boat tour.

Other days they had no choice but to cancel the tour. The rains of summer crashed down. Downpours that turned the ground to mud within half a minute.

They'd eat their brown bag lunches under the awning of the picnic table, waiting for the storm to break. Jawing their white-bread sandwiches in grim silence as white rain roared down around them. Even the strangler fig tree looked defeated with its drooping festoons of moss.

Crowe would often have to let Wayne and Eddie go early. He'd tell Wayne Wade to go clock some hours at the Emerald Island Inn.

"Got something to do today," Wayne, who was on the payroll for four hundred a week cash, told Crowe about eight times out of ten.

"That right? Like what? Move out of your motel room? Where you've been staying gratis? When's the U-Haul coming? Sign me up."

Wayne caught Eddie grinning over his ham and cheese sandwich. "Something funny, pussy lips?"

"Wayne? You better get on your bike and go. I'm telling you."

And with bristly chin jutted upward, Wayne Wade would rise and stalk away and go about his half-assed way through the day's errands. With indignant dispatch, making a show with the broom, chucking errant beer and soda cans into the trash like they'd insulted his mother.

If it wasn't Wayne Wade and his bullshit, it was the kids Crowe had to contend with.

And holy shit.

The sugar, the heat, the hormones, the pent-up energy from being cooped up all those hours in the van.

Who knew what the fuck their deal was, but the kids were pure blue-ribbon menaces, no denying.

They snapped one another's ears with rubber bands. They gave one another Indian burns. Wedgies. There was some new thing called titty-twisting. There was a lot of titty-twisting. They called one another shit-for-brains and dick-nose and butt fuckers. The boys let off stink bombs in the back of the gift shop. Brothers got into outright fistfights. They balled up Little Debbie snack cakes so they looked like big pieces of human feces and they left the grotesque boluses near the restrooms as though someone hadn't quite made it in time.

BOSTON BLUTO

THE DAYS OF THE FLORIDA MAN Mystery House wore on. The days at the Emerald Island Inn.

One day they launched into the savage green Everglades, Crowe steering the boat away from the Florida Man Mystery House, and over his shoulder Crowe glanced at the passengers through his sunglasses. One young woman elbowed her husband in his side. *What a gyp.* Or, *Why are we here again?* was the impression Crowe got.

There was another man, older, with buzz-cut red hair and a red angry bulldog face. He kept patting his forehead with sodden wads of Dairy Queen napkins. His wife, also redheaded, looked on the verge of heatstroke.

Cicadas shrilled.

"What's your name, missy ma'am?" Crowe asked a young girl wearing a sun visor.

"Olga," she said.

He said, "What's those you wearing, missy ma'am?" Crowe pointed at her shoe. "Those're neat."

The girl looked dubious. The girl told Crowe they were called jellies. They weren't for boys. Or adults. Just girls.

Crowe looked down at his battered brown docksiders, the barrel lace of one of the boat shoes untied. He left it alone.

"How 'bout captains?" Crowe asked. "I can't wear 'em? No jellies for Captain Crowe?"

"No," she said. Peeved, as if he was a party crasher about to bum rush her shindig.

"Maybe I can wear jams?"

"It's your life, mister," Olga told him. She seemed fatigued of the topic.

Olga's father, Otto, nodded. "It's a free country."

Crowe turned away and commandeered the wheel. Feeling old, out of it before his time. Or maybe it was after his time and he didn't even realize.

These kids, he thought.

Jellies. Pac-Man. Rubik's Cube.

Crowe just didn't know what the fuck anymore.

The pontoon boat cleaved through a patch of swamp lilies. The dragonflies stirred and flitted, translucent wings sparking in the late morning slant of sun. Through the mangroves shafts of light streamed. The dragonflies fluttered back onto the big white flowers.

Crowe eased the boat around a bend and started down the next mangrove tunnel.

Small mammalian life moved in the woods. Snapping twigs, crackling leaves.

"Jellies," Crowe heard himself saying into the PA system, "that reminds me." He cleared his throat explosively. A few tourists jerked. "You folks wanna hear something I heard on Jacques Cousteau the other night? Jellyfish can technically live forever."

The tourists blinked, waiting. A few looked like, *This man is without a shadow of a doubt on drugs.*

Crowe went on. "Technically, they can. They could. A million years, maybe more. If they didn't have any predators. Without predators, they'd be immortal. Same with coral. Coral can live forever."

"But didn't Emerald Reef die?" Otto asked.

"That's right, yes, it did. A tanker scraped over it and that was it for the reef."

"What kind of tanker?"

"Insect repellent, if you can believe it. Roach spray."

"That's depressing," said Olga.

"Yes, it is, missy ma'am. Yes, it is."

Then, as if she wanted to rescue him from the awkwardness of the situation, as if taking mercy on his soul, the girl with the birthmark shaped like Cuba on her knee pointed to a place in the mangroves. On one of the trees was a place in the bark where a tumorous bolus grew. It resembled a face. A goblin face, bumpy and warped and melted.

The girl with the birthmark asked, "What's that? Spooky."

"That's a catface, missy ma'am."

Near the end of the Everglades tour Crowe was helming the wheel, boating back to the Mystery House, when he was startled from his stupor. A man with a Boston accent shouting angrily, "Is that true? He did? He did what? His dick?"

Crowe looked. Already a big bearded man who looked like Bluto from *Popeye* was standing off his bench seat, a fistful of Wayne Wade's Dolphins jersey in his grip.

Crowe dropped his can of Tab and threw the boat into idle and ran over and put himself between the men. He shoved Wayne away. The man let go but kept glaring like he wanted to rip Wayne Wade's head off and kick it soaring over the mangroves.

Wayne Wade sat.

The man told Crowe in no uncertain terms that Wayne had exposed himself. His genitals. To his daughters.

"Say what now? Like full-on?" At first Crowe thought he misunderstood. He shook his head.

"That man showed his goddamn dick to my daughters. He knows exactly what he did."

Crowe looked at the daughters. Two redheaded preteens who looked mortified. Then Crowe looked at Wayne, sitting red-faced and sheepish and abashed with his head lowered and with his pecker in his pants.

His shorts were high-hemmed red rayon jogging shorts with white piping.

"Wayne, go steer the boat. Get us back. Let's get these people back."

Wayne didn't move.

"So help me god, Wayne."

Wayne went quickly to the wheel.

"Honey, please," the man's wife pleaded. Also redheaded. None of the kids had inherited Boston Bluto's black-haired genes. Maybe Bluto was their stepfather.

The wife continued, "This was supposed to be a vacation. Honey. Take a pill. It's just too hot for this."

"Please, sir," Crowe said.

The man was beginning to deflate.

"Daddy, please," said one of the girls.

The miserable methane-smelling heat. The gnats. Crowe swatted a nimbus of them away but they came right back.

"Yes, Daddy, sit and take a pill. We're okay."

Finally the man sat.

"You need to fire that man. Something's not right."

"I do. I fire him every day. Sometimes twice."

When they got back Reed Crowe drew Wayne Wade aside in the gift shop. They stood behind the postcard rack.

Wayne said, "I guess it fell out. Shit."

The sweaty tourists slouched back into the shop.

Crowe said in an angry whisper, "I don't wanna hear it. I don't wanna even start to imagine." He grabbed Wayne's shoulder. How long had it been since he'd seized him this way, shook him like this? Years. Probably around after when his girl died. When he was lost in the black monsoon of drunken depression. Now Wayne jerked righteously away, knocked into a View-Master. It fell off the shelf and clattered onto the wood-plank flooring.

Crowe pointed close to his sneering red face. "I want you to go and I want you to hide because that's the kind of guy we're dealing with here. He'll come back in here with an axe. Get lost and get lost quick."

Wayne Wade snuck through the back of the gift shop to the mystery trail.

The Boston family filed back into the gift shop for their refunds. Crowe tendered them the money and apologized at least a dozen times. He apologized to the other tourists just as many times. To the other vacationers Crowe gave complimentary alligator claw backscratchers.

As the Boston family plod out of the shop, Crowe called after them, hand aloft, waving from behind the register, "Again, folks, my apologies. Grab you a Mystery House shirt on the way out?"

Boston Bluto scoffed but didn't turn. "Shirts? To wipe my ass?"

COMPLAINT BOX

BESIDE THE GIFT SHOP EXIT HUNG the customer remarks box. An old-fashioned, wall-mounted community suggestion box of the cast-iron variety, an antique painted to look like a frog. A child's drawing. It gleamed bright cartoon colors of green and yellow, cherry red for the tongue.

Lily's frog. Lily's painting.

Tarnished now, so many years had passed, but there it would remain as long as the Florida Man Mystery House was standing.

Crowe blamed SeaWorld and Disney World and all the other big Florida attractions.

The waterparks with putt-putt and go-carts and arcades. Chuck E. Cheese, ShowBiz Pizza.

Crowe blamed those too.

Oh, yeah, and the fucking Sea Cave.

Kids were tuning him out these days more than ever before.

They seemed hopped up too. Ritalin they were calling this new shit, but it was basically speed. Truck driver amphetamine pills painted a different color and called a different name.

These kids, to Crowe, were just unbelievable. They sounded ready for the mental ward. "Mom. Mom. Mom. Dad. Dad. Dad."

Just because they wanted a Popsicle or needed batteries for their Pac-Man.

Goddamn speed freaks at eight years old.

"You got AIDS!" said the kids to their younger brothers and sisters. "You were found in the orphanage. The AIDS orphanage! I found semen all over your bunk bed!"

AIDS jokes, evidently, were all the rage these days with the kids.

Maybe it's time, Crowe would think. Maybe it's time to forgo this whole kit and caboodle.

All that summer the tourists wrote on the remark cards with the little green golf pencils, on occasion throwing surreptitious looks over their shoulders.

As if Crowe wasn't standing right there crunching on his Granny Smith apple.

As if Wayne wasn't standing behind the register thumbing his nuts.

Finally they'd shove the cards into the frog's mouth. Usually they were chucked straight into the trash without so much as a glance. But morbid curiosity one day compelled Crowe to gander.

There were just so many.

There were the usual crude drawings of pussies and dicks, courtesy of the kids.

And there were many references on the cards to the "little fella." Or to the "small man." One remark referred to Wayne Wade as "small fry," which gave Crowe a chuckle.

Small fry seems a bubble off plumb.

Obviously a tax scam, said one remark card. *Get help,* said another. Another said, *You ramble but you seem like a nice man. Maybe a little more pizzazz?* Another said, *It said grotto on the sign and there was no grotto and my kids were looking forward to it and i can promise you i will not be returning and you both reek to high heaven of something probably marijuana.* Another said, *You guys are obviously on drugs and it's amazing no one's sicked the FEDS on you yet.*

Crowe wondered what the people expected. Kansas's World's Biggest Ball of Twine. It wasn't like he was running the Massachusetts Plumbing Museum. Some kazoo shrine. What did these motherfuckers expect for five dollars? He wasn't asking for their mortgage and their firstborn like Disney.

Some days he wondered why he still bothered. Aside from the obvious need to get out of the house. Out of his head. Off his ass.

What else was he going to do at this point, take a correspondence course in stenography? Spearfish? Conquer Poland?

He supposed it was the only time in his life he still felt boyish, these trips into the Everglades. The thrill of not knowing what you'd encounter. The critters and creatures and oddities. The feeling of a jungle safari into the heart of the unknown. And once in a while on these trips there would be a kid who reminded him of himself as a boy. And once in a while there was a little earnest inquisitive girl who'd remind him of Lily.

It would ease his worry about the state of the world, the fate of man, the purity of her heart.

"Oh really, mister, you're a real captain?" one pigtailed Japanese girl said. "Oh wow, can I take your picture?" Later, "Captain Crowe, what's the weirdest thing you ever seen out here? Captain Crowe, you ever seen a real live monster?"

Crowe had to turn away, he was so choked up.

Soon the nights grew too hot to dig. Even the nights: heatstroke hot.

But in Crowe's dreams he still spelunked. That boyish part of him never went away, even after the cave collapse with Henry Yahchilane. In his dreams he explored the nether regions of the grotto, discovered new alcoves and caves. In his dreams he tunneled and dug and he crawled within chambers that gave way to other chambers. On hands and knees he went through rocky labyrinths.

One night in one of these spelunking dreams Crowe came upon a grotto where there was a large silver puddle in the middle of the floor. The water was as shiny as a mirror. He crawled to it, parched, like a desert revenant to an oasis.

He was halfway to the puddle when a child's forearm shot out, tiny hand grappling the air, seeking rescue.

He'd wake with his voice shredded and red and raw from screaming, his arms reaching, his hands clasping.

After three straight nights of such dreams he went to Dr. Vu for sleeping pills.

Absolutely not, was the doctor's steadfast stance.

"Maybe I should get a second opinion."

Dr. Vu told him it was a free country.

This was neither the answer Reed Crowe was hoping for or expecting. "Where am I going to get a second opinion within driving distance?"

Dr. Vu rattled off a list of names from outside Emerald City. There was Herve Cordele in Naples. There was France Beauregard on Sanibel Island.

Crowe said nothing.

Dr. Vu told him, "Exercise."

Crowe said he was active.

"More. Exercise more. And don't mix all this stuff. Booze, pills, pot."

In his mint-green gown Crowe shifted on the paper-lined examination table. "I'm not a sot," he said. "Assumptions. Do you know that Krumpp at Red, White and Blue Liquor the other day called me a hippy?"

"I am familiar neither with this Krumpp nor this liquor store."

She wrote.

He eyed her askance. Her tiny ears. The shiny straight black hair that threw off the white light of the room. The catty unimpressed eyes behind round-framed glasses.

"Doctor," he began.

"No," she said.

1983

THAT SEASON MUCH OF THE NEWS was about Operation Everglades. A dragnet of Feds swarmed a town outside Naples, busted a bunch of boat captains and their loaders. They'd gotten greedy, reckless. Fifty thousand cash a night if you were a captain, ten grand if you were a loader.

Crowe could understand.

Hard to blame them.

The captains would launch their boats from the mainland late at night, rendezvous with giant freighters stationed several miles off the coast. They'd load and ferry the cargo back to the mainland, where they divvied it up in the wharfs and fish houses. From there the drugs were transported all over the state in trucks and vans.

Mother of all plants.

Little towns like Everglades City, population five hundred, give or take, local yokels were suddenly driving Ferraris and Porsches. Speedboats. Jet Skis. All bought with cash.

Only a matter of time before someone with a big nose sniffed something rotten in Denmark.

And, now, the reckoning.

Crowe was on one of his evening strolls when he saw the raft far out beyond the ten-fathom sandbar. At first he thought it was a large piece of driftwood. Maybe an abandoned pirogue or canoe.

He sat up near the big sand dunes where the breeze kept the mosquitoes at bay and he lit up a joint and watched. He had it half-smoked when he saw a head.

And then another.

Crowe looked around. No one on the beach. Desolate. The orange-red fire of the wild Florida sunset. The ocean calm and shining pewter in the evening.

The gnats and no-see-ums buzzing at Crowe's face and ankles.

He swatted and swiped.

He went ankle-deep into the surf and cupped handfuls of seawater and dribbled them over his head. Then he waded out into the water up to his knees. "Hey," he said through cupped hands, "hey, man, hello."

The heads lifted a bit and turned. Hard to tell how many from this distance. And Crowe, stoned and nearsighted. "Hey, you folks okay?" he called across the water.

Four heads now he counted.

Crowe slogged out into surf. A wave smacked the roach out of his fingers. He waded farther. Another wave smacked and soaked his nuts.

He saw black hair. Dark faces and necks. Victims of shipwreck, perhaps.

Crowe splashed out to the people.

An old man. A young couple in their twenties.

All of them wore ragged tattered clothes, filthy. Their lips were parched, flayed. The girl regarded him with eyes glassy and fevered and frightened. The old man looked nearly dead.

Crowe smelled their stink of sweat and piss and shit.

"Okay," he said. "Hey, man, I promise. Okay, it's okay, man."

For the life of him he couldn't at the moment think of a Spanish word. Not that he knew many.

He clung one-armed to the lip of the boat, pulling it, fighting against the undertow. A jerry-built thing, a sardine boat with a Port-O-Let door for a roof. A jib, a sail. The hull buoyed by all manner of junk—plastic milk jugs, child floaties, Styrofoam containers.

It seemed to Crowe a very long time before his toes grazed the sandy bottom. And then he hopped for a distance before his feet fully touched.

Staggering high-kneed he dragged the dinghy the rest of the way through the surf, pulled the small boat a few yards up into the sand. All he could manage before collapsing. He gasped and coughed, the coppery bitter sting of seawater filling his mouth and nose and eyes.

The young black-haired man who was missing the top of one ear toppled out of the boat and tried standing. He took a few slewed steps sideways before his legs fell from underneath him. He stayed on his side groaning. Bare-chested, slat-ribbed. His stomach protruding in that malnourished way.

"Es bien," Crowe said. "No policia." You learned a bit of Spanish, this far down into Florida. It was all around you. The radio. What you heard in the stores south of Emerald Island.

Even Crowe, as challenged as he was with learning the language, knew enough to talk to the refugees.

"Un amigo," Crowe told them. "Comrade."

The young woman had black hair and green-hazel eyes. The girl, her sister Crowe assumed, resembled her.

They wore makeshift hats of cardboard and straw.

Cubans, Crowe knew.

They must have launched with the intention of shoring south. But the storm rerouted them and their boat jettisoned here.

The girl, in a Mickey Mouse T-shirt, was yammering in fevered sleep. The old man muttered a prayer in Spanish, his voice thin and frail.

Crowe told them in broken Spanish to stay put. Mimed with his hands.

Needless. Stupid. They were going nowhere. They were half-dead.

AN UNEXPECTED REUNION

HE COULDN'T CALL THE AUTHORITIES. HE couldn't call a doctor. Couldn't call Heidi because she was away on one of her vision quests.

Irrational, the anger, he knew. But so many of his feelings toward Heidi were.

He loped up to his house. Still catching his breath, a cramp searing his sides.

He thought about calling Wayne Wade, holed up over in the Emerald Island Inn ever since his house went in a sinkhole.

No. Definitely not Wayne.

And he thought about calling Eddie, but he didn't like the idea of involving the young man in trouble.

He called Henry Yahchilane.

"What," Yahchilane answered the phone.

"Yahchilane," said Crowe.

"Yeah."

"It's Crowe."

"Yeah, egghead. What."

The men had not spoken for several months, if not a year.

Crowe told Yahchilane about the Cubans.

"Okay," said Yahchilane, hanging up without another word.

Crowe put them up in the Emerald Island Inn. He tried giving them two separate rooms for space, but the Cubans wouldn't have it. Separation anxiety. And after all that time on the cramped dinghy, the room with the two queen beds and the color television and the mini-fridge probably seemed palatial.

From the depths of one of Heidi's closets Reed Crowe scrounged out a miscellany of clothes. Blouses and skirts and beach hats. Sarongs and wraps. T-shirts. Panties. What he scavenged would have to do until a proper trip south. Emerald City was so small, he'd probably draw attention, suddenly buying a lot of girl clothes. "He was out there buying clothes, oh yeah. Reed Crowe. Strawberry Shortcake stuff. Guy's finally gone off the deep end." He was sure he had some of his girl's old clothing stored away somewhere, but the girl was probably too big, and honestly Reed Crowe was worried that just the sight of the clothes, just the smell, would crack his heart in half.

The Cubans got washed and fed. And the next morning Yahchilane drove his van to an outlet mall in Hialeah where he bought clothes for the family. Clothes that didn't look picked out at random from a mini-mart or gas station.

Crowe told Yahchilane he'd reimburse him.

"Unnecessary," said Yahchilane.

It turned out Yahchilane knew Spanish. Fluent. He spoke to the family. The young woman in her twenties did most of the talking. The old man so fevered and addled in his bed they could make no sense of his ramblings.

From Yahchilane Crowe learned that the old man was the grandfather of the two young adults, who were siblings. The young girl was not their sibling. The girl was the young woman's. The young man, Marlon, was the girl's uncle. The girl's father was dead now five years, a casualty of the Castro resistance.

From Yahchilane, vis-à-vis Nina, Crowe also learned after a few days that Marlon started as a cigar roller and had gotten into some trouble with contraband rum which led to other troubles with bad people in the city.

The young man couldn't keep still. Kept getting up and parting the seashell print curtain and peering out the window as if expecting an ambush.

They filled the tiny room with Spanish language magazines and newspapers. A hot burner for café con leche. The transistor radio playing telenovellas and the Spanish broadcast of baseball games.

Those first few days Crowe was certain the old man would die. His eyes were glassy and ablaze with fever. His past was coming back to him. He spoke to people who weren't in the room. People long dead. People in his memory.

Standing close Crowe could feel the sick animal heat wafting off him.

Crowe got Yahchilane to explain to them that they could have adjoining rooms, leave the connecting door open between, but even this they refused. They were overwhelmed and afraid. Sticking together had gotten them here.

A miracle they made it this far.

They wouldn't chance a hair.

They played board games at the small Formica table. They watched television and listened to the radio. Still the young man kept restlessly pacing, peering out the peephole as if awaiting the authorities. Someone else.

Crowe tried to convince the mother, Nina, that the girl, Mariposa, should not be so close to all of this. And all this time in this small room, like a jail cell. But they would not separate.

Mariposa would sit on the edge of the bed watching PBS, one of the only channels the old wooden television sets got out this far into the Mangrove Coast. She watched *Mr. Rogers*. "Won't you come to my neighborhood?" On one of the episodes, Mr. Rogers had a civilized disagreement with a neighbor. The neighbor, a mean-spirited old man with beetled brows and a rancid-looking mouth, would often bellow the refrain, "America, love it or leave it!"

This was the first American phrase Mariposa learned fully. "Love it or leave it!" she would say.

"More pizza, Mariposa?" Crowe would ask.

"Love it or leave it," she'd say.

"How do you like the weather today, Mariposa?"

"Love it or leave it."

"Have your orange juice," Nina would tell her daughter. Their English getting exponentially better by the day.

"Love it or leave it," Mariposa would say.

FORT LAUDERDALE

TWICE A WEEK YAHCHILANE WOULD DRIVE them in his root-beer-colored van to the radio station in Fort Lauderdale, WIOD, where every week they posted a list in the lobby of those Cuban refugees who'd safely reached American shores. Nina and Marlon would look at the list with wild hope, looking for their aunts and uncles and cousins. And when they didn't first see a familiar name among them, they'd look over the list a second time, something deflating inside of them as if a nozzle was leaking air, as if somehow in their haste their eyes had failed them.

It was Nina who had saved them all. Piecemeal Reed Crowe gleaned this from the young woman, from Marlon, from Yahchilane.

Nina who read a page of the Bible, King James Version in English, every morning. Nina who woke before dawn so she would have the extra hour to herself. Days she had worked in a nail salon for rich Cuban women.

Nina's hands were rougher than Crowe's. Sometimes, while struggling to make a point, while trying to remember a word, she'd place her hand on his knee, tapping. Or flutter her hand on his forearm, fingers palpating.

Those first few days Crowe learned Nina worked in a nail salon so long that she would never forget the chemical stink. No, she vowed for the rest of her life to cut her fingernails and toenails the same way her mother and grandmother did, with old-fashioned clippers.

She scrimped four years of laundry money, sewing fishermen's shirts, mending their filthy underwear, stitching their reeking socks, to buy the sardine boat. From Havana her family set sail, bound for Miami. But the trade winds and the El Niño knocked them off course.

They veered adrift.

And while at sea they saw a host of makeshift boats. All abandoned or capsized.

A few with dead people. Some with dead children.

Nina clamped her hand over her daughter Mariposa's eyes.

And it was only later still that Crowe discovered their reason for leaving. Marlon, the brother, had gotten on the wrong side of the pro-Castro, anti-rebel forces. Drugs and guns and street crimes.

The news didn't surprise Crowe. The brother's young feral energy. The coiled anger inside him ready to spring.

Nina told him she never had an inkling she would end up here in America.

Some days being here still felt like a fantasy, she said, a dream. Here there was air-conditioning and hot water and most shocking of all a phone, right there, a phone in her own room. They could call anyone in the world they liked.

In Havana there was only one phone in the lobby of their apartment complex. A pay phone for hundreds of people. The line of people waiting to use it was often ten or more deep and it could cost a whole day's pay just for a two-minute conversation. Most of the time you couldn't hear, the noise, the yelling, the shoving, the street noise.

Another night Nina and Crowe were down by the water alone when he offered her a drag off the joint he lit. He did so with a lot of goofy semaphore, hand signals.

"No, never."

It was the first time Crowe heard sternness in her voice. But it was not the first time he felt self-conscious in her presence.

He snubbed out the joint and put it in his pocket.

They sat quietly beyond water's reach, on the edge of the high tide line. The sinking sun made a golden bridge on the ocean. A squadron of pelicans flew past, hovering low over the bronze water.

Feeling suddenly awkward Crowe focused with unusual intensity on the bright cherry-red balloon of a spinnaker on the far ocean horizon.

Nina kept glancing behind her shoulder at the motel. Always worried about her child, her brother.

Crowe said, "Your brother keeps a tight eye on you."

"More other way around."

The woman seemed so much older than her years. Not in appearance, but in maturity. It was a quality that Crowe found himself immensely attracted to.

There was a southwest breeze keeping the insects at bay. A strand of her pure black hair whipped in the wind and stuck to her cheek, and her eyes caught the light and glowed a mossy green.

She glanced over her shoulder again. Now her brother was on the back porch, leaning with his arms draped and crossed over the railing. He was watching them. When he saw Crowe turning and watching too the brother shoved away and went back into the room.

Crowe, thinking, She is beautiful, said, "Does he dislike me?"

"Dislike?"

"Me, muy mal?"

"No, scared."

"Scared, a new land. Yes."

"Old land too. The people from. Our brother work with evil man."

Nina looked around the beach, pointed at one of the cats, a marmalade-colored cat, that was slinking among the dunes after a green anole lizard. "Gato," she said.

"Cat?"

"Catface they call the man."

Crowe wasn't sure he understood. "He looks like a cat?"

She gestured at her face. "Marks," she said. "Hurt."

"Scarred," Crowe said.

"Yes, scarred. Mark. The scar, they look like? What you say?" She mimed with her fingers.

"Whiskers?"

"Yes. Yes. Yes."

"Catface. He was born looking like a cat?"

"Scarred. Plane crash? In water? Trapped?"

Crowe's mouth was suddenly dry. His heart cold as clay. He no longer cared, at least for the moment, so much what Nina thought of him. "A big plane?"

Little gesture with two of her fingers. "Piqueño."

Crowe felt his blood pressure. "Where?"

"Somewhere in Everglades. Many years ago."

SOMEWHERE IN THE EVERGLADES

SOMEWHERE IN THE EVERGLADES, NINA TOLD Crowe. A plane crash.

How long ago was that? Decades. Not hard to keep track, considering that was almost certainly the night his daughter was conceived. One might say the night the entire course of his life was conceived. The first seed of the mother of all plants sowed. One event unfurling after another. One tendril begetting the next.

And just when you thought you had the weed ripped out at the root, out sprang another shoot.

That night twenty years ago, after taking his soon-to-be-wife and later-to-be-ex-wife home, Reed Crowe motored his skiff back to the scene of the crash. Part of him knew it was a risk. Part of him knew it was dumb. Already he had more of the pot than he ever needed and then some.

But shitting away all that money?

Those men dead in the swamp, the weed belonged to no one now.

It would belong to the first man with the gumption to take it.

Bits of flaming wreckage still steamed and hissed in the black water. The crabs and the alligators and the frogs hemmed in on the floating bodies. But at the sound of his motor the creatures dispersed and retreated to their hiding places, watching him from a cautious distance.

Crowe cut off the motor and waited. He listened. Just the black terra incognita of the Florida swamp. The last diminishing gurglings of the bog as it sucked the plane down.

Crowe went from one bobbing plastic-wrapped parcel to the next, oaring his way around the brimstone, hoisting the packages over the gunwale. Every so often he had to draw close enough to one of the bodies that he could smell their brisket stink. The odor of singed hair and the chemical stink of burned clothing. And a few times he glimpsed the fire-ravaged faces.

Once, he could have sworn he saw the eye move. He thought he saw the eye roll in the moonlight and he called hello into the dark and then there was no answer. The eye went still and the body was still.

He went on into the night.

All that pot he sold over the years. All that pot he smoked within plain sight of the locals and the tourists here on Emerald Island. All those regulars who came back year after year.

Flagrant.

Taunting.

Unwittingly, but still.

No wonder, then, if someone could easily trace it all back to him. Even some thick-witted sonofabitch.

FISH HEADS

SOON AFTER THE CUBANS SHORED ON Emerald Island, the old man's condition worsened, his coughs sounding like wet BBs shaking in a coffee can. Standing three feet away Crowe could feel the scorch of his fever. He could smell the grim gray sickness of him among the other smells of people living in too cloistered and hot a space.

If they didn't get him to a hospital, Crowe knew, the old man would die.

The county hospital nearest Emerald Island was impossible, as they'd ask too many questions, ask for documentation and forms. He might as well rent a plane, advertise on a flying banner.

They would have to go down to Miami, where the doctors were less suspicious and asked fewer questions.

No matter how much the air-conditioning labored, the room stayed fuggy, warm enough that there was always sweat on your forehead.

Not good for the old man, nor for the kid.

The girl sitting there on the bed with her dolly, the old man dying on the other bed.

The dolly, a gift from Wayne. Wayne kept bringing the girl candy and coloring books. Kept making jokes with his face.

Maybe it was his imagination, but Crowe didn't care for Wayne's long glances, or where they settled. Mariposa's chest in the VISIT FLORIDA T-shirt just beginning to bud.

"You want me to take the girl out for a walk?" Crowe would ask Nina.

"You ask that already," she said, sterner every day. More herself. Her early temerity he'd mistaken as shyness. "And I say no."

Now he understood she'd only been scared, overwhelmed.

Strangers in a strange land. Of course. And like any rational people they were doubtful of his intentions, this bearded man in the middle of nowhere Florida. No wife or child of his own. Associated with another man, rattailed, of dubious repute. And associate to another man, Native American, who was more inscrutable than the aforementioned combined.

Anyone in their position would be wary.

But after a week, as they convalesced, their personalities showed piecemeal. Crowe observed the change as they became less tentative.

The television and radio played constantly, often at the same time. Telenovellas, *The Price Is Right*, *Mutual of Omaha's Wild Kingdom*, *Sesame Street*, *Mr. Rogers*. The girl, Mariposa, was transfixed. She absorbed catchphrases. "Good morning, America," she'd say. "Love it or leave it." "Have it your way." "Three, two, one, contact." "Won't you be my neighbor?"

The girl was an ace copycat.

Her favorite was something called "Fish Heads," off the radio. "Fish heads, fish heads," she'd sing in her accent, "roly poly fish heads."

"My god, stop with the fish heads," Nina would say. But with a little smile.

The girl would giggle and go on, "Eat them up yum, fish heads."

In the mornings the girl would go down to the beach with the mother and in the shade of a beach umbrella Mariposa would write in her homework books with her crayons and pencils. She would feed Herman the heron grapes, cherries. Then the seagulls would come in wanting their share and before long a mob would dive-bomb after the girl and she'd go off squealing and running as the birds cawed and wheeled.

Marlon, chain-smoking, would pace and watch from the balcony. He smoked so much, you couldn't help but notice his pinkie finger missing, the scarred nub that barely jutted out of the palm.

One time Crowe asked Nina what happened to Marlon's finger. Trying to be casual, discreet, "Was it work?"

She scoffed. "Work? Marlon? If only. If only he'd just stayed at the cigar shop."

Seeing Crowe's questioning expression, she said, "The accident happened when he wasn't working. When he was doing other kind of work. The wrong kind." Nina left it at that, cursing under her breath, shooting her brother a private look of disdain. Even her moles, somehow, looked incensed.

So there you had it, Crowe thought. That would have explained Marlon's temperament, his perpetual state of unease.

Most days you could find him playing a short, agitated game of solitaire at the Formica dinette table, the door kept ajar to air out the stifling room. So hot that summer that the wall unit air conditioners rattled as if suffering emphysema.

Portable fans rotated feebly in all the rooms. If the sea breeze was coming in cool off the ocean then people opened their windows and the conch-pattern curtains billowed.

After a game of solitaire, Marlon would smoke a quick cigarette. Then inside again for another quick game of solitaire. Marlon would spend whole afternoons in this fashion. A cuckoo bird executing ingress and egress in a deranged, off-kilter clock. Out the back door for a cigarette, inside for a game of solitaire, out the front door for a cigarette, inside for a game of solitaire, and then back to the ocean-facing side again.

After lunch and *Mr. Rogers* it was naptime for the girl. Afternoons they spent in the room with the grandfather. The mother and brother and girl said prayers and Hail Mary's. They tidied up the room, which was crowded but orderly, all the victuals and provisions, all the canned goods and pill bottles and lotions, neat and orderly on top of the vanity and television and bed stands and Formica table.

The only main alteration made to the room was the crucifix hanging above the old man's makeshift convalescent bed, and this addition made only after Marlon asked permission and borrowed the hammer and nail.

SANTERIA

OFTEN DURING HIS ERRANDS CROWE WOULD catch Wayne Wade snooping and sneaking around their room. Crowe would tell him to mind his own business. Then Wayne Wade would scuttle off chastised and mopey for a while with his broom and dustpan. But after a spell he'd invariably return, the room the center of his daily orbit.

"You see all that voodoo shit?" Wayne said to him one day, leering at the Cubans' motel door. "Candles and shit. Little dolls."

Crowe knew of what Wayne spoke. On one of the nightstands Nina had erected a makeshift shrine. Ceremonial herbs and beads. Pictures of the saints. Scraps of yellow and red cloth.

Crowe said, "What's it to you?"

"What's it to me?" Wayne gave him a gummy grimace of incredulity. Yanked the bill of his soiled Miami Dolphins cap. "Voodoo, I'm talking."

"They're religious."

"That ain't religious. That's batshit."

"Saints. They're called saints."

They stood a few doors down on the mezzanine. They lowered their voices when Crowe pointed his chin at two fat kids standing at the vending machine.

Wayne asked in a harsh whisper, "And you don't think it's batshit crazy? At least admit it's a fire hazard, all that crap burning near the wall."

Crowe still said nothing. He made a mental note. The candles. The candles might pose a fire risk. Not that he was about to admit so to Wayne. He would talk to Nina next time he saw her.

Crowe looked at Wayne. "I don't want you skulking around the room anymore."

"Skulking! What the fuck is skulking?"

"Read a book, whipdick."

The fat boys overheard and laughed. They watched in their swimming trunks, chewing their candy bars.

Wayne Wade shot them a look. Then shot Crowe a look. "Something to say."

"Stay away from the room, Wayne."

"I don't like bein' talked to like some kind of errand boy."

"Wayne? I got news. I could give a flying shit."

PICK YOUR BATTLES

FOR A WHILE THERE WERE OTHER near altercations between the men. None of them devolved into violence, but Crowe knew deep in his nuts it was only a matter of time.

Invariably he tried to reason with Marlon as much as he could. Everybody had their limits. Crowe couldn't blame the kid.

He would draw the young hotheaded man aside, separate him from Wayne Wade. "This is not a threat. This is just simply a fact I'm about to tell you, okay? They'll put you in a detention camp—but it's really just another kind of prison. They'll separate you."

Marlon said nothing. He was looking down at the ground, away from Crowe, composing himself. His breathing through his nose was a heavy rasp. His arms were folded tight around his chest, his hands clamped under his armpits as if he didn't trust what they'd do if he let them free.

"It's not Disney World. They'll throw your ass in jail. And your sister. And Mariposa."

Marlon scratched the side of his nose, a quick agitated gesture. Tucked his hand under his armpit again.

"It's no camp. I know you know it isn't. I know you know better than me. But what you think happens? In those camps? Kids get lost. Kids get, shit, I don't even want to imagine much less say it. You get me, Marlon?"

"I just don't want to see this man. I don't like him."

"All right. I got it. But, just, you know? Pick your battles. Ignore him. You want Schaffer around?"

Grudgingly Marlon shook his head, the desire to knock the piss out of Wayne Wade still making him grind his jaw.

DOGGY DOCTOR

IN THE LITTLE ROOM THE STINK of the old man's sickness was overwhelming. The stench of incontinence, night sweats. The air-conditioning strained and rattled futilely against the cloistered stuffiness. Leon Caesar Arango's breath was weak and trembling, rotten with fever. While half in dream he muttered to ghost-friends and ghost-relatives, people from his past long gone. He slipped in and out of consciousness. He slipped in and out of truth and dream. He slipped in and out of time. One moment he was back in Cuba guarding his mule from thugs. The next he was sitting in his open-air kitchen with his wife as she cooked tostadas on the cast-iron skillet, drinking black coffee as the morning pearled the sky and yard birds pecked at his feet. The next yet, here he was, in this strange cramped room among his grandchildren suddenly grown, one with a child of her own he could barely recognize, and about him strange boxes and cans, brightly lit, slogans he couldn't read.

Crowe raided his medicine cabinets for antibiotics and pain reliev-ers. He raided Heidi's. Yahchilane raided his own bathrooms, though he couldn't recall the last time he went to the doctor. This, despite his persistent sludgy cough.

The expiration dates on all the labels, long past. Decades.

They debated whether to enlist Dr. Vu. At very least confide in her, asking if she was amenable. *I got this friend, see, Dr. Vu.* One could never be too sure, this part of Florida. You never knew where a person's allegiances lay.

These reprobates and renegades, these beach bums and misan-thropes and runaways: Often their only allegiance was to them-selves.

Finally they confided in Myrtle the mailwoman, who knew an old girlfriend on Marco Island. A vet. Otherwise, there might be a spe-cialist in Miami, a real doctor, but that would entail traveling to see the doctor, a trek down south. A reasonable journey if you were able-bodied and healthy. A risk if you were old and sick and had to ride in the back of a near-stranger's van.

Marlon was outraged. Crowe could understand little of his Span-ish, so quick and angry, but Crowe surmised the gist. His grandfa-ther, treated like a dog. A literal dog. Dying in the care of a doctor for dogs. A vet.

BIG CYPRESS

IN THE MORNING THE SIBLINGS FOUND him stiff in the bed and Nina came to the front desk of the Emerald Island Inn and told Crowe. There were no tears in her eyes. Her voice was composed, calm. Her black hair was braided back.

"Where's the child?" Crowe asked Nina.

"In room."

"With the body?"

Nina seemed surprised that Crowe was surprised.

It was the brother, Marlon, who lost his bearings, his bawling from the room alarming the neighbors.

Marlon was so worked up and loud that the motel guests called reception to complain and Henry Yahchilane reasoned with him. A day would not have made a difference. Not even a week. And say by some miracle they could have procured the best doctor on the Gulf Coast of Florida. No matter the man's expertise, the advancement and acuity of his instruments, nothing could have cured congestive heart failure overnight.

"Somebody passed," Crowe said to people who asked what the matter was. "They're upset."

"My god, somebody died in here?" This from an Alabama man who sounded as though a murder were committed. As if Crowe committed the murder himself.

"Yes, people die in motels, man," Crowe told him. "I don't know what to say."

The siblings argued outside on the landing. The young girl Mariposa was in the motel courtyard pool, splashing on the steps in the shallow end.

"They want a Catholic burial," Henry Yahchilane explained to Reed Crowe at the stairs. He was smoking a cigarette.

Crowe, "It's not happening."

Yahchilane jetted smoke out his nose. "No shit."

Marlon pointed at Crowe, cursed at his sister.

"Why's this dude screaming at me?" Crowe asked Yahchilane.

"His father just died."

Nina said something in angry whispered Spanish to her brother. He set his jaw, hands on hips, pacing in tight circles. She took him by the forearm and led him around the corner of the landing, where the vending machine and icemaker were.

While Yahchilane and Crowe were waiting in the room with the old dead man and the girl, there was a knock on the door. Crowe answered, kept the chain hasped.

Wayne.

"What's goin' on in there?"

"None of your business, Wayne."

Wayne glanced over Crowe's shoulder at the old man in the bed. Eyed the shrine, the religious paraphernalia.

"That guy looks dead."

"He is dead."

Wayne stared.

"We're figuring out what to do," said Crowe.

"Man, I told you you were getting into some fucked-up shit."

"Just go back to the desk. Do whatever you do. Do nothing."

"I'm managing the place."

Crowe unfastened the chain and stepped outside. He got close to Wayne and said in a lowered voice, "It's my place." He shut the door behind him.

"The cops. People on the island have been talkin'."

"Who?"

"People."

"Bullshit."

"Krumpp. Red, White and Blue Liquor."

"Fuck him. Who's he, ambassador?"

In Henry Yahchilane's van they transported the old man's body to the Seminole reservation outside Big Cypress. Yahchilane met with a second cousin who would make sure the body was properly interred.

"I thank you, Horace," Yahchilane said.

"Oh, it will cost them."

Both men stood close together but their arms crossed in the discount cigarette shop.

"I was hoping for a favor, Horace."

"This is a favor."

Yahchilane asked about the logistics.

Horace gestured: better not to ask.

He saw the look on Yahchilane's face. The looks on the Cubans' faces. "There will be proof," Horace reassured them. "From a confirmed Catholic priest."

They settled on a price.

When Crowe learned how much it was he was shocked. More

than Crowe could afford. He was glad Yahchilane offered so quickly, since Crowe was self-insured and these days almost always nearly broke.

INDEPENDENCE DAY

A FEW WEEKS PASSED BEFORE THE siblings' gloom lifted. On Fourth of July night Mariposa laughed for the first time since her great-grandfather passed, pirouetting on the beach, twirling, pinwheeling her arms with sparklers in her hands. One green, one red.

Dusk. A painting of a night. Volcanic Florida pastels. A ghostly sliver of moon.

There were three big beach dogs, Labrador and retriever mixes, Myrtle the mailwoman's, and they frolicked around the girl, snapping playfully at the sparks, snouts chomping air.

Crowe was watching the girl and then he was watching the mother, Nina, watching the girl, when something broke in his heart. The toss of her shiny black hair over her brown shoulder. The whorl of baby hairs on the nape of her neck. The fine complicated muscles of her arms.

The woman was beautiful.

Once in a while the dogs ambled away for a sprint or two, sniffing in the sand, chasing a ghost crab into its hole.

Myrtle and her girlfriend, Moe, watched from their Coppertone girl beach towel, drinking wine spritzers from the bottle. Bartles & Jaymes.

And some of the motel guests and quasi-permanent itinerants drank and barbecued around the pool. A fat kid in a Pac-Man T-shirt cannonballed into the pool. "Thad, you got the buns wet. You better hope that dangdog store's open on the Fourth 'cause you just soaked the buns."

The sharp tang of gunpowder, from fireworks, hung in the air. The smell of chlorine and burning charcoal briquettes.

A rare July night breeze kept the mosquitoes and sand flies and no-see-ums at bay.

Herman the heron, about as high as Mariposa, stood back at a wary distance, knee-deep in the slackening tide. Mariposa at first would chase the bird but Crowe explained to the girl that he'd come to her if she didn't scare him away. Just give him time, Crowe told the girl. And after a time, Herman did strut up to her, a yellow eye on the sand castle she was making while sitting pooch-bellied by the ways.

"Hermano," said the girl that first time.

Every so often from one of the small balconies of the Emerald Island Inn, a bottle rocket or a Roman candle would streak color against the darkening night. The chemi-luminescent fire reflected in the small chop of the water. The trails of smoke tattering apart, but the haze staying in the becalmed night, dulling the emerging stars.

It was dark and a few people had started a bonfire with a stack of driftwood on the beach. The small girl, Mariposa, built no differently than a toddler boy except for the missing privates, wore a two-piece bathing suit and she found pieces of driftwood up and down the beach, running to toss them into the fire.

She was throwing the fourth or fifth stick into the mounting fire when Crowe spotted Wayne Wade sitting a distance up the beach. He was looking straight at the girl. Crowe looked away. Waited a beat. Then he looked again at Wayne Wade, whose eyes were still on the girl. Whose eyes stayed on the girl.

Crowe counted ten Mississippi's inside his head. Still Wayne's eyes went up and down the girl's length. It wasn't a dreamy abstracted stare. It was a roving riveted stare.

Wayne at last noticed Crowe. His glasses propped up on his head, his green eyes fixed sharp on Wayne.

Wayne looked away. Crowe didn't.

Wayne got up after a minute, his posture stiff, that of a man watched.

Next night at the Rum Jungle Crowe told Wayne, "Watch how you look at that girl."

A trio of seagulls were lunging, trying to get through the wire cats-cradled over the picnic tables, but the birds winged away

thwarted. Myrtle and Moe were drinking with their trivia and kara-
oke friends at the other end of the bar. Their three big shaggy beach
dogs frolicking in the sand.

Wayne had a half-finished grouper sandwich in the newspaper-
lined basket before him. He took a belligerent swig from his beer
bottle. Then he set his bottle down a little too hard. "Fuck you."

Myrtle the mailwoman and Moe and their several friends glanced.

"Watch it, would you," Crowe said.

Crowe half-waved at the women. Grinned a friendly kernel-
toothed grin. He looked at the dogs, play wrestling in the white sand
tinted under the big-bulbed Christmas lights. "Nothin' better than
three old dogs in the sand," Crowe told the women.

"Better than two old dogs at the bar," said Myrtle.

Crowe pointed a finger gun across the bar at Myrtle. "Pow."

Wayne, low-voiced, swatting viciously at a gnat, said, "Accusing
me of bullshit."

"I'm telling you cool it. Eleven years old."

"I'll look where I like. I'm not gonna fuck her."

"They'll kill you. Believe it, Wayne. That brother. That mother.
That mother especially."

"Like'ta see 'em try."

Crowe said nothing. He drank his beer.

"Sure doesn't look eleven," Wayne said. When Crowe said nothing, "You think she looks eleven."

"Doesn't matter, Wayne. She is. If she looks forty, she's still
eleven."

"Wonder if they lyin' about her age," Wayne mused.

"Why the fuck would they do that, Wayne?"

"Legal reasons."

"Legal reasons? Think about what you're saying."

"Sucker us. Make us more sympathetic."

"Wayne, let me just be in my head awhile. I want to be in my
head with my thoughts if that's okay."

Marlon started shuttling back and forth, spending six days out of
seven in Miami working on the docks for shippers and wholesalers

who couldn't care less about his citizenry or papers. All for two dollars, three dollars an hour if he was lucky. From one end of the city to the other he'd take the public bus after twelve days of working in the malign Florida heat to visit the radio station once a day. This in the midst of one of the most violent summers in Florida history.

The things he saw on public transportation. The things he saw on the streets. It reminded him of Cuba. Those last days, people beating one another with rocks and baseball bats in the streets. People stabbing other people because of a stolen chicken.

Yet amid this pandemonium he visited the radio station once a day, shouldering into the throng, scanning with the rest of the Cubans the names of those who'd made it safe to shore.

Most of the men and women turned away dejected, faces stricken.

Months went on this way, once a week Marlon bussing back to Emerald City to check on his sister and niece. Yahchilane would pick him up at the bus depot on the edge of the county line.

Crowe tried to keep the young woman and the girl occupied. He took them to the tiny zoo, which the girl and mother were right to find depressing. Yahchilane had warned him against it. "I hate that place," Yahchilane said.

He was right, the arthritic and spavined creatures cramped in their piss-smelling cages.

MR. CLOWNFISH

OVER THE COMING WEEKS, THEY SPENT so much time together, Crowe was convinced he might love her. Both she and the child.

He would think about Mariposa, saying, "America, love it or leave it." Saying, "Peanut butter and jelly, love it or leave it."

One breezy afternoon they were on the bayside of the island, Mariposa out of earshot, standing in her zories at the edge of the seawall, balling boluses of stale bread from a Wonder Bread bag. The sheep head and the parrotfish that usually gnawed on the barnacles with their hard chitinous beaklike mouths finned up to her.

"I want you to know I care for you," Crowe told the girl's mother. They were sitting thigh to thigh, knee to sticky knee.

"I thank you," she said.

Reed Crowe waited a moment. "Do you know what I'm talking about, though?"

"Yes. I understand." She cut him a look. "I said I did."

Mariposa, in the background, said, "Hello, Mr. Clownfish. Only bread. Love it or leave it."

Crowe said nothing. His insides knotted.

"I will always be very glad for you. You have helped us. We thank you. We are grateful."

Reed Crowe kept quiet, digging his fingers through his beach bum beard, scratching the scruff.

LOVE IT OR LEAVE IT, HERMAN

HE HINTED ABOUT MARRIAGE IN A roundabout way. Of course he did, all those long summer days on the beach or on their road trips to the Swap Shop or to the radio station WIOD to check the list of names of the Cuban refugees who'd safely arrived ashore.

Mostly, it was when they were sitting beside each other on the beach in the long evening hours, those nights when there was enough of a breeze to keep the voracious no-see-ums and mosquitoes at bay.

One night, emboldened by two glasses of wine, expansive after a long day with Nina and Mariposa at the ShowBiz Pizza place, he forwent subtlety altogether. Or so he thought.

"Maybe it would help to get married for citizenship," he said. "Say if you were to find the right person."

"I'm Catholic," she said to him. There was a certain stoniness in her voice, as if she was talking to a child. He wondered if she was maybe misinterpreting him.

Their bottoms were in the sand. Herman the heron was legging in the shallows nearby, Mariposa saying, "Love it or leave it, Herman!"

"What I mean is, a compromise."

As soon as the word "compromise" left his mouth, her eyes snapped at him. They were very white in the gloaming, almost aglow, against her beach tan.

"Com . . ." she said, her lips reared back and showed her long white teeth.

"Compromise, a convenience."

"I know what you mean." Her eyes were upon him now with a kind of fierceness. Scorn. They were black and steady and they kept on his eyes without blinking.

"After this? Compromise? Never. Do you think I'm weak?"

"No."

"Why would I compromise then?"

Reed Crowe glanced away, scratched his beard. The last light of day was bleeding into the world's edge. Seafowl flew northward in three-score chevrons. He waited until the birds were out of sight before he said, "I never said you were weak. Never thought of it."

Her eyes were still latched onto him fiercely. "Why compromise?"

He shrugged, gestured with an upturned hand.

"Why?" she insisted.

"They might send you back."

"What, you report me?"

"No, no, of course not."

Thirty yards or so away, Herman the heron winged off into the dusk. Mariposa called after him, "Phone home!"

"I will never compromise." She gestured, a broad sweep of the horizon. As if to say, *I conquered all of that.*

"I have made it this far. I've gone this far." Her chin was jutted upward at the fiery-edged clouds.

Crowe swatted dejectedly at the gnats.

"Midges comin' out," he said.

"Never," she said.

BLACK HAIR FALLING

AND AS THE DAYS WENT BY and their personalities showed, so did Nina's beauty.

Her intense eyes. The luster of her hair. Her long legs and fulsome hips. Her ripe chest.

On a few occasions, Crowe told Wayne to cool it, his lascivious stares so flagrant.

Whenever Nina caught him looking at her long and sideways and funny, she would say, "What? What is it? What do you want?"

Her look was reprimanding, scolding. Her temper was showing now too. Despite the circumstances, when you thought she would have practiced discretion.

Sometimes she got so pent up that guests would come out to the sound of her angry Spanish, watch her tempestuous exchanges.

Wayne would rear his head back incredulously. He'd let loose a high and loud "Wow!" His eyes would rivet once more upon her ass, her breasts, her legs. Her curvaceous length.

"Spicy!" he'd say.

One day Crowe heard Wayne and Nina yelling outside. Nina was cursing Wayne out. And Wayne was chuckling his high yodeling chuckle. He was holding a spray hose and was watering the hibiscus bushes around the Emerald Island Inn sign.

Wayne acted like the nozzle was a phallus and swiveled his hips, letting loose a wild meandering spray. "Whoa, nelly," he hollered.

Through the lobby windows Crowe watched Wayne squeezing off wild sprays of water like ejaculate.

"Goddamn idjit," Crowe said. He walked out from behind the check-in counter and went outside into the foul heat and confronted Wayne.

The sun was so bright off the limestone it smarted his eyeballs.

Nina had her middle finger shoved in Wayne's face. She gave Crowe a curt sharp glance. Then she strode across the glary parking lot to her room and slammed the door, leaving Crowe to wonder what the hell he did.

Crowe said, "Don't make that lady uncomfortable."

Insolently Wayne would not look at Crowe. Now he was blasting water from the spray hose upon the stucco front of the building.

"You hear me?"

Wayne sucked an eyetooth, as if trying to loose some gristle. He blasted a wasp nest hanging like a grape cluster on the rain gutter.

Crowe smacked the nozzle out of Wayne's hand. The metal spray gun went flying and clattered in the dirt.

"Hey!" Wayne said. "What the fuck?" He slanted away, goober teeth showing in incredulity. His eyes were pinched and irked beneath the overlarge Miami Dolphins cap.

"Then listen, goddamn it."

"What's it with you and that lady?"

Before Crowe could answer, they heard a woman shouting. "Hey, you! You, cabeza de mierda!"

They looked. Nina stood on the catwalk outside her room and she leaned over the second-story railing. She was holding scissors. Without a mirror, looking straight at Wayne with those eyes so intense they seemed kohl-rimmed, she snipped off a hunk of hair.

"Wow," Wayne said.

Another shiny black clump fell.

"Nina," Crowe called.

Another clump.

"You don't wanna do that."

"Nina," said her brother from within the room.

"Shut up," she told him without looking.

She looked at Crowe as she scissored off more. "Oh, why not?"

"You don't wanna do that."

"I'm doing it. So I do. It's what I want to do. Obvious."

Polaroid glasses riding low on his nose, Crowe turned to Wayne and glared. His head was hot and pounding in the hotcake heat. He felt his blood pressure in his temples.

This man, this idjit, would give him a heart attack yet.

Wayne said, "I'm cuttin' her hair? I'm the one who invented scissors?"

Crowe hollered to Nina again. "I don't know what that's going to solve."

"You wipe your ass, don't you?"

Crowe had zero clue what to say to this. He stood there wincing in the sirocco heat, arms akimbo.

Snip, snip, snip went the busy scissors.

BORIS KARLOFF

LOW TIDE HE SOMETIMES WENT HUNTING for shells with the girl. Tulip shells, whelks, angel wings.

The water was so clear and tranquil certain nights you could see beneath the water the rills and scallops of the sand. The ghostly sand crabs scuttling sideways with their claws raised. Their movements stirred up little cloudlets of sand. The baitfish moved through the shallows, flocks of flashing silver-blue needles moving in sync.

One evening, with just as much clarity, his very first childhood memory struck him. It was of strolling along just such a sandbar, kicking through the foot-deep water, flicking big conch shells into a tin pail. His mother would pay him ten cents a shell because of the conch inside. He remembered the heft of the pail, the sun in his hair warming his scalp, the taste of shaved lemon ice in his mouth.

Crowe decided it was time, past time, to visit his mother.

There were wild budgies on the loose in Fort Lauderdale. That afternoon you would hear them cawing in the seed and berry-bearing trees flanked along the Intracoastal Waterway. A bright green flock of about a hundred.

Crowe's mother, Shelly, asked, "Remember Boris Karloff, the budgie?"

Crowe did. Surprising, the things she would remember.

There were things he hoped she forgot for good. The beatings.

Near the public grounds gazebo under the big fat sea grape tree was a group of old octogenarian men playing bocce ball. The clack of the balls carried over to where Crowe and his mother sat. The sound of their New York City accents. Mostly Jews and Italians, a few Greeks. A small group of old Cubans played dominoes at a picnic table.

Behind them stood Pier Sixty-Six, the white crown of the rotating bar twenty-five or thirty stories high.

Crowe remembered the Fort Lauderdale of his youth. Fort Lauderdale and Miami, there was still wilderness between them back then. Pockets of swampland and saw grass when you got off I-95.

He remembered a time when if you took US 1 to Boca Raton there was nothing but Bermuda cottages and the odd Spanish-style mansion. Now all that territory was built up. High-rises of glass and stucco for the snowbirds and retirees.

Now, the Atlantic, you only caught glimpses and flashes between the palm trees and condos.

Crowe asked his mother, "Hey, Ma, great-grandpa who laid the railroad tracks?"

"The Thompsons?" She sipped from her big Styrofoam cup of ice and ginger ale.

"The Crowes."

She shook her head. "Grandpa Crowe?"

"His company. Who laid all those tracks with him down there?"

"What railroad? What on earth? Oh, don't get me started about the Crowes."

ANOTHER HAVANA

ONE AFTERNOON REED CROWE WAS ON his way home from the Hoggly Woggly when just before crossing the bridge he saw the sign. At the last turnaround, a gravel shoulder, it stood gaudily new among other handmade signs.

DON'T TURN EMERALD ILAND INTO A HAVANA, it said, hand-painted, on cardboard.

ILAND.

Stupid pig ignorant sonofabitch, Crowe thought.

He slammed the brakes and bumped onto the shoulder of crushed shell and limestone where there was a small picnic area by the shallow edge of the bay. Standing on the shore in rubber boots was an elderly black man with a cane pole. He watched as the door of the orange hatchback flew open. He watched Crowe get out and stalk over to the sign. He yanked it out of the ground.

Crowe noticed the man watching and tendered a nod from behind his big green sunglasses.

"How you doin'," said Crowe, pitching the sign into the trunk.

"How you doin'," said the man.

On the way back to the Emerald Island Inn, the sign in the hatchback trunk, Crowe tried to give Wayne the benefit of the doubt.

Increasingly difficult these days.

Wayne was doing Duncan yo-yo tricks behind the register when he found him. "You calling me stupid?"

Crowe stabbed his sunglasses up his nose with his finger. "You know what, Wayne, you know what? Yeah."

For a time Wayne said nothing. His small pinched eyes working angry and upset behind the glasses with the smudged lenses.

Crowe, feeling bad, "This time you forced me. Sometimes you just got to call things as they are."

"Now I know the truth," Wayne said. "What a thing to say. You goin' round calling me a fool. Well, I guess I am."

"How'd this shit get turned around? You do something fucked, now I'm the villain."

"You don't even know it was me, that sign."

"Wayne. Eye-land. Remember? Eye-land?"

Wayne asked what he was talking about.

Crowe shot out a scoffing breath. "The way you spelled it. And your handwriting. I know your handwriting, Wayne. Don't shit in my face and tell me it's Thanksgiving."

"I ain't gonna be made a fool of," said Wayne.

"You want the cops here? The government? Think. Think, goddamn it."

Then Wayne grinned.

"I don't get it," Crowe said. "I don't get you."

"Mark my words, I'm right about this one. You're wrong."

"You're fired, Wayne."

"Yeah, right, whatever."

He slipped an envelope across the Formica top like a blackjack dealer. "Love letter," he said. "Ma Bell."

A bill, already opened.

"Came in the mail this morning. Myrtle had to special deliver it."

Crowe looked at the envelope. Pink, a warning color. Then he looked at Wayne. Still grinning.

Crowe, shaking his head, filching out the bill, "Fuck's wrong with you?"

Crowe saw the figure, moved the bill closer to his face to double-check: $545.77.

Phone calls to Cuba, Havana.

Five hundred forty-five dollars and seventy-seven cents from the Cubans' room.

Crowe looked up from the bill at Wayne. Still grinning. "Fuck's so funny?"

"I tried to tell you, man," Wayne said in a kind of singsong, "I tried and tried." He raised his hands in the air as if letting a hot potato drop.

One ass cheek on the wicker-topped stool, the other lifted as he tooled with a glow-in-the-dark Duncan yo-yo. *The Gong Show* played on the little portable black-and-white television. The unknown comedian with the paper bag over his head. The shepherd's cane hooking around his neck.

"No wonder this place falling to shit."

Wayne still yo-yoing, "Where do I start?"

"Sweep. Look at this." Crowe gestured at the floor. A dead palmetto bug. "You just gonna leave a dead roach?"

Wayne said he didn't see it.

"It was there yesterday."

"Tell me. I'm not a mind reader."

Crowe, "Sweep. And put some Visine in your dumb goddamn eyes."

Wayne, "Some way to talk."

Crowe went to the Cubans' room with the bill in his hand like a summons.

The brother, Marlon, at last understood. Nodded. Opened the bedside drawer and took out a ziplock bag full of quarters. He gave the bag to Crowe.

"Money for phone," Nina explained.

At first Crowe was incredulous. Maybe they were mocking him. The brother, at least. But then he saw their earnest faces.

"Hundreds and hundreds of dollars," Crowe attempted.

From his vehemence the seriousness of the situation must have finally struck the brother and sister.

The brother kept talking to her in Spanish, with increasing anger. Crowe asked Nina who they'd been calling.

Nina shook her head. Shouted at her brother. Pointed her finger.

"I did not," the brother screamed. "One call is all."

Marlon started searching the room, overturning cushions. He rifled through drawers.

He was talking about the number, that much Crowe could gather from his limited Spanish and from where he stood.

He'd lost a number.

It was a scrap of paper he was searching for, a list of contacts he'd brought all the way from Cuba.

"You lost it," Nina accused him.

"I did not lose it. I traveled across the ocean with that paper." The brother was indignant.

"You lost it, you fool. Stupid. Paper and ink. In the ocean." She told him he should have gotten the numbers tattooed. If he had half a brain.

Marlon's frustration mounted into indignation. Why the few calls he made would add up to so much.

Marlon, so quiet, what Crowe knew about him he'd gleaned from the sister, who herself was taciturn. Crowe knew he was swept up in an anti-Castro force. As a new recruit he crop-dusted the town with anti-Castro pamphlets. By stealth, in the heat of night two or three hours before dawn. Nina talked about the persecution. The anarchy. Imprisonment. Neighbors backstabbing one another to spare their families, their sons and daughters.

Now, Marlon thought the quarters, the brown paper bag of quarters he'd squirreled away, would be enough. And when his sister insisted it wasn't enough, his indignation erupted into anger. Their voices grew hot and quick and loud, Spanish obscenities volleyed back and forth.

Estupido. Estupido. Cabaza de mierda.

It was fifteen or twenty minutes before Marlon and Nina seemed to puzzle something out. They went to the window and looked outside down at the pool where Mariposa in her watermelon one-piece sat on the second step of the shallow end and splashed her hands.

Wayne Wade was at one of the patio tables in the shade of a striped beach umbrella, watching the girl.

The girl seemed suddenly wary and shy of Wayne, but maybe it was Crowe's imagination.

SLAUGHTER ON GOOSEFUCK AVENUE

CATFACE SAT ON THE EDGE OF the hard motel bed, tugging on his black silk socks. He got a toothpick out of his alligator skin wallet, put it in his mouth. He picked up the remote, turned on the television.

On the television, Jack Horkheimer, aka the Star Hustler, strolled down the catwalk of cosmic stardust. Members Only Jacket, mustache, toupee.

Every week on WPBT2 out of Miami, PBS, Horkheimer the astronomer would give you the astral run-down. Comets, meteor showers, planets, constellations. "Greetings! Greetings, fellow star gazers, and this week, yes indeedy, we have quite a doozie."

The doozie was the Jupiter Effect, a once-in-an-eon astronomical occurrence. All of the planets in a row, aligned on one side of the sun.

He delivered this news with great excitement. His voice like a summer stock actor's. Hands clasped before him. Fingers wriggling. Brow beetling.

"In ancient times," Horkheimer said, "some believed the Jupiter Effect betokened the end of the world! Seven planets in a row!" He mentioned something called syzygy. Then, "And remember to keep looking up at the skies!"

He turned back from where he came, strolling away on that fanning cosmic ray like the yellow brick road.

That night, after Horkheimer's broadcast, riots broke out throughout Miami.

Looting. Drug trafficking. Human trafficking.

Criminals went about business with nigh impunity. Meanwhile, coke orgies in the clubs. Uzis, semi-automatics, bazookas, grenades sold from the trunks of DeLoreans.

Catface was watching the commercial, tugging on a sock. A guy was dancing down the street. Right down the sidewalk. Some kind of cha-cha, because his diarrhea had gone away. He was cha-cha-ing down the street high-fiving the mailman and the butcher and the baker and the candlestick maker because a pill had solved his diarrhea problem.

Catface stuck a toothpick in his mouth, chewed. He imagined killing the man. The man cha-cha-ing up to him on the street. He flicking out his knife and ripping him open like a shoat. Blood everywhere in the street. An abattoir. Everybody horrorstruck, their mouths agape.

Slaughter on Goosefuck Avenue.

The thought, so clear in his mind, made Catface chuckle.

The gold-plated phone beside the bed rang and he picked it up. He listened, toothpick rolling in his mouth.

"Goo," he said. "A girl, you say? A girl called? Southwest Florida. No name? Small motel? Hello? That is all you have. I see. She was phoning home?"

CATEGORY THREE

CATFACE

(1985–1986)

HOLIDAY ROAD

INTO THE SAVAGE GREEN JUNGLY HEART of Florida Catface drove, looking for the island where he'd crashed so many years ago.

Looking for an island that had a pink and purple sign.

Land of ten thousand islands, they called this place.

In his travels Catface had fights major and minor. Catface usually needed only to reach into his inside coat pocket and produce a blade with a grease-jointed movement as quick as the flick of a scorpion tail. A few men he had to cut. In the parking lot of a pancake house in Cape Coral he stabbed a man for calling him a quote unquote shit-ugly spic.

"Cheeseburger in paradise," Catface crooned, toothpick in his mouth, as he knifed him in the gut. "Wasting away in Margaritaville. Oh, yeah, baby."

A move Catface might have forwent had he not been high as a weather balloon after freebasing in the IHOP bathroom.

Onward he drove.

Some places were no bigger than glorified fishing hamlets.

Now here was one. Captiva Island.

An ice cream parlor, an antiques emporium, a taffy shop in the thoroughfare. A shop of gewgaws, the door propped open with a hunk of coral. Inside was a ladder-back chair, upon it sitting a human-sized sponge man. Some marine equivalent of a scarecrow made of sea sponges, an effigy, sea shells for its eyes and mouth and nose.

At the four-way intersection in the center of town, Catface braked his stolen canary-yellow Buick and surveyed the scene. The late afternoon sun fell mellow on the storefronts and awnings. The windows glared bronze.

The somnolent hour close to supper.

Spread out on the cream leather passenger seat next to Catface was a Rand McNally map. Catface was studying it, toothpick switching from one side of his scarred mouth to the other, when he glanced up and saw a tourist family beginning to cross the road. A young middle-aged couple with two young daughters old enough that a kind of petulant boredom had cemented on their faces. One daughter was around nine. The other about fourteen in a halter top and hoochie shorts.

When the father saw Catface his expression curdled.

Catface took off his sunglasses.

Then the man's mouth gawped.

Catface's very white wide eyes cut to the daughter and lingered on her tawny legs. He flicked the toothpick in his mouth. He meant the look as instigation. Nothing else. Little girls were not his kink.

"Your daughters," Catface said to the man. "Thumbs up. Meet you at the movies."

Some odd combination of anger and fear seized the man's face. "What about them, mister?"

"Hey, why so angry?"

"Don't ever talk about my daughters, mister. Don't even look at them."

The man's wife was tugging on his hand. And you could tell he wanted her to. He didn't want to be the hero, not this time. "Come on, Richard," she told him.

Now Catface's toothpick angled speculatively, the toothpick staying pointed upright in the corner of his mouth, his eyes squinted and assaying. "Are you a hero?"

The man didn't budge.

"Adios mios," Catface said. "I think you are."

The man got pissed again. "Fuck you, buddy."

"Richard!" said the wife.

The older girl was grinning. Braces.

Catface said, "Your daughters, very bored. Take them to Disney World."

"What!"

"I take them to Disney World."

"You're not taking them anywhere!"

"Hm. How much do you weigh?"

"Weigh! Fuck you."

"Why rude? That es not goo. I just ask."

"I weigh two hundred and thirty pounds, mister, and if you're saying something about my weight, I'm working on it."

"Huh."

Silence. Catface stared with his toothpick moving.

The man could stand the impasse no longer. "Look," he said, beyond exhaustion, a pissed quaver in his voice, "it's not a contest."

"Oh, it is," Catface told him.

The man was dejected, baffled.

Which irritated Catface. Plus, the drugs, the bugs, the heat. "Everything is a game, conyo. Everything. Crossing this street is a game. I can run you over. Everybody out to win these days. I'm playing a game. You're playing a game. What else is there, conyo? Games! I win everything, conyo! Girls, Uncle Hector wins everything! Go with Cuban man with big fat cock who take care of you, bonita, si?"

Catface often wondered what kept these guys ticking. After thirty, as good as neutered and euthanized.

Married? Over.

They all needed a good long weekend of rawboning in a Nevada whorehouse.

Finally Catface grinned his jagged grin at the man. A beaming game show host smile, but mutilated. And in broad daylight. Reeking of some kind of weird drug that smelled like a burned-up shower curtain. "Thumbs up! Meet you at the movies!" He poked up a thumb.

"Richard!" said the wife again to her husband, who was standing there like a lawn jockey, but stupider. And no cojones.

And as if in confirmation of this, the woman finally got her husband to move away, the girls following quickly, the encounter burned in their brains forever.

Another memory for the Kodak slide carousel.
. FLORIDA TRIP 1985.

Catface watched them go to the box office of the tiny beach town movie theater. The father, still casting angry red-faced looks over his shoulder, paid for his family's admission and they went inside. Catface parked the car and paid the meter and barely noticed the ticket-taker's shaking hands as he paid the two-dollar admission. By the time he got into the theater the lights were down and the curtains drawn. Catface sat in the back.

No one took notice of his ingress.

During the advertisements Catface freebased in the back of the packed theater.

On the screen, a cartoon played. Anthropomorphic characters—popcorn, candy, soft drink—danced a kind of jitterbug in a conga line.

"Let's all go to the lobby," they sang. "Let's all go to the lobby."

The air was already thick with cigarette smoke. A hovering gray haze like chalk dust.

No one noticed Catface smoking at first. But then someone whiffed a gamy steam in the air and looked. Their eyes widened with the double shock of seeing the man. His mutilated face, his bespoke caramel suit of Panamanian silk.

Catface stared back.

Five minutes into the film Catface was lighting up his pipe again when an usher wearing a maroon coat with gold piping on the sleeves came down the aisle. He pointed a flashlight at Catface's face.

Catface turned. A prison escapee in a spotlight.

People looked Catface's way again. The pimple-faced usher gawked. The father from the crosswalk turned and when he saw Catface he jerked and then his posture went completely rigid with shock. It was as though he expected a bullet fired through the back of his skull any moment.

Toddlers started to cry. One boy shrieked.

The usher jerked the beam away and hurried out of the theater.

Heads turned back to the movie.

Catface stayed put.

The heads kept resolutely forward, the necks stiff.

A couple of families waited a few minutes before leaving. Others stayed the whole duration. And when Catface, lighting his glass pipe again, yelled, "Fly, conyo, fly" as the boy Elliott soared off into the sky on his bike, the alien in his handlebar basket, no one dared turn.

"Phone home, conyo!" Catface yelled at the screen. "Phone home, baby!"

Catface came to know America in a way he hadn't before.

Cape Coral. Naples. Sanibel.

He meandered through the southwest quadrant of the state, looking for any sign that would stir his memory. Point him toward the man he sought. He veered oceanward where the back roads took him through small Gulf Coast hamlets.

Land of ten thousand islands, they called this place.

Catface knew he had to be careful. Sometimes caution required changing cars. He hotwired a Bonneville and went onward into the heart of Florida.

Dogs, particularly the large slobbering breeds, loathed Catface on sight. Labradors and Dobermans and even docile retrievers would rear their lips back and show broad expanses of black gum and angry spittled fangs. They'd break into frenzied baying. They hurled themselves at him. Owners would have to yank their pets back on their leashes.

And there were many glum children with brazen stares in Florida.

In restaurants, people stared. Catface stared back. He could go without blinking for almost a minute.

The people would wither under his gaze. Grown men, truckers, Hell's Angels. Priests.

Catface after a while would return to perusing the local paper. He'd started in the beginning of his trip with the *Miami Herald*. Then it was the *Sun Sentinel*. Now, the *Fort Myers Beach Observer*.

He read about AIDS. The bloodbath murders in Miami. He read

headlines about Florida men. FLORIDA MAN ARRESTED FOR CANNON-BALLING ONTO SEAWORLD ORCA. FLORIDA MAN NAMED RONALD MCDONALD WANTED IN CONNECTION WITH FAST-FOOD HEIST.

For weeks he worked his way up the coast, staying in motor courts and lodges. Stiff pillows, cheap mouse-brown curtains, scotch-guarded plaid sofas. At night, smoking crack, he'd look out the window of his room at the gravel parking lot, a sign saying VACANCY spelled out in aqua and pink neon.

Every so often a couple headed to their room would pass and, seeing Catface's face through the glass, they'd start. They'd glance quickly away, and you could tell by their postures, the slightly faster clip of their walk, that they were waiting until they were safely behind the locked and bolted doors of their rooms to talk about what they'd just witnessed.

A few people were perspicacious enough to notice his ring, his necklace. Especially in the strip clubs they recognized the necklace. The logo from the Mutiny Hotel. Particularly barkeeps and strip club managers and especially exotic dancers.

The cops. Rather than arouse their suspicions the necklace seemed to elicit from them a kind of craven deference.

Onward.

He saw myriad tourist traps and roadside attractions.

Cabins on stilts. Mango's. Chachi's Cantina. Big Bahama Mama Raw Bar.

Onward.

Chapels by the sea. Coral castles. Lighthouses. Sea oats whispering in white-sand dunes.

Sunday cracker enterprises. Honey. Oranges. Mangos.

Onward.

MANURE FOR SALE, said one sign, handwritten, a scrap of cardboard on a picket.

A man selling manure, Catface thought.

America, Catface marveled.

This part of Florida, so far down south, brown guys with accents, not so unusual. Brown men wearing Miami suits of linen and poplin specially tailored for the heavy heat of the south, very unusual.

The farther north he drove, the more suspicious the looks he received. They might have fucked with him, these Florida men the farther north he went, the farther away from Miami.

But then they saw his face.

His face spared him.

Kids gawked. Toddlers cried.

What had been a curse was now good luck.

Waterparks and miniature golf courses and mermaid shows and jai alai frontons. Boat tours and fishing charters. Jungleland, Indian casinos, strip clubs, seafood joints, monkey sanctuaries, myriad roadside oddities.

He crossed the vast saw grass prairies north of Miami and took I-75 north. The exits few and far between. The small communities with cookie-cutter stucco homes behind stucco walls, retention canals and ponds like moats.

Then the vast wilderness again. The jagged saw grass marshes, their silhouettes reared against the twilight like black construction paper cut with toy scissors.

The billboards. Strip clubs. Asian spas. Bungee jumping. Scuba diving. Deep sea fishing. Spelunking. Walt Disney World. SeaWorld. The Mermaids of Weeki Wachee.

A hand-painted billboard for a parrot circus where cockatoos and macaws performed stunts and tricks. SEE MISTER PECKER LIVE, said the sign. Three exclamation marks.

Jai alai.

Seminole Indian casinos.

The monkey safari.

The Baboon Lagoon.

The serpentarium.

The Pirate Tour of Gasparella.

Swamp tours. Snake hunts.

The Florida Man Mystery House.

EXCURSIONS

YAHCHILANE'S VAN WAS A FAMILIAR VEHICLE over in Emerald Island as well throughout tiny Emerald City. His face, familiar. A few new Cuban faces, though, would draw notice from the locals, even if they were in Henry's van. Especially if they were in Henry's van, known loner that he was. So while they were driving through the island and the coast, Nina and Mariposa lay in the back. The root-beer-colored van had little submarine-like bubble windows, but they were tinted. The other windows had the shades drawn.

"Think of it as an adventure," Crowe would say to the girl of their excursions.

"Que?" asked the girl. Mariposa was confused. She said, "Silly."

Like he used to for Otter, Crowe would pack brown paper bag lunches for the girl. Peanut butter and jelly sandwiches in ziplock bags, a banana, one of those glass apples with the juice, a cookie wrapped in tinfoil. Always something else wrapped in tinfoil, though Crowe insisted the girl leave it for last.

Once it was a pine cone. Once it was a yellow rubber dishwashing glove. Another time it was a small canister of WD-40.

"You're silly, Mr. Reed."

"Love it or leave it," Crowe would tell her.

"Leave it," said the girl.

They went to Miami Beach and South Beach to scan the faces. They sat on the benches among the art deco motels and restaurants and bars and the sports cars and the hordes of scantily clad women.

Nina by comparison looked almost nunnish and prim.

Nina in her apricot sundress, her white sandals, watching the passing faces. The constellation of moles and freckles showing on her neck and her shoulders and her arms. They looked as intense and stubborn as her somehow. No, not stubborn. Unapologetic.

The moles polka-dotted the dark burnished gleam of her shoulders.

To Crowe everything about the woman was a vision.

They continued watching the parade of South Florida through the windows. So many faces, so many scantily clad bodies.

Crowe remembered when he was a boy, the time when Miami Beach and Fort Lauderdale were veritable shtetlach. Kibbutzim. They'd picnic there when he was a kid, before his father started beating his mother. Before his father got into all the trouble with those Dade County criminals.

Back then, Yiddish was more common in the streets than English. Holocaust survivors living there called the place Little Jerusalem. And for a while, it was a mecca. A sun-kissed halcyon Xanadu. What the old men and women so much deserved. A place so different from the camps it was like an afterlife.

Collins Avenue was another Broadway, another Vegas Strip. Jackie Gleason, Frank Sinatra, those kinds of guys played on Tuesday nights to packed houses. Shit, it wasn't like the old coots had a job to report to in the morning.

But things had changed.

The times had changed.

The McDuffie riots. The "Paradise Lost" issue of *Time*. The boatlift.

All that round-the-clock coverage on television, that new cable channel CNN showing all that gruesome and gory footage, you'd think Miami was San Salvador. You'd be just about half-right.

But the water. The fucking water. That looked the same, for the time being.

Here was the Florida sun and glittering water of the beach. The convertible cars coasting along the strip, red Mustangs and yellow Camaros gleaming like candies. The art deco buildings and stucco homes like pastel macaroons, pink and yellow and turquoise. And here were the new downtown skyscrapers standing on the edge of the water.

He remembered when the place was an outpost. Now? A different country.

Shit, almost a different century.

Crowe tried not to look too long at the women, for the sake of the girl, for the sake of Nina, but he stole glances. As did Yahchilane.

And Mariposa. "Bonita," she said about a willowy golden-haired girl in a Hawaiian print bikini as she crossed the walk before them at a stop sign.

"Hussies," Nina told her daughter.

Then Nina caught her brother ogling and hissed a curse.

And then Marlon grunted something back.

Everywhere you looked, another group of women who looked like sauntering pinups. Oiled-up and tanned bodies, curves spilling out of bikinis. Some of the garments looked painted on. Others were three dinky triangles of bright cloth near diaphanous.

"Hussies," Nina said again.

"Bonita," Mariposa said again.

At the Swap Shop Nina Arango and Mariposa forgot for a spell that they were strangers in a strange land. Forgot they were refugees. Probably because nobody looked at them like they were. Here were Haitian and Mexican faces. Vietnamese and Native faces. And faces they might have glimpsed in the streets of Havana or Santiago de Cuba.

The Arangos stopped at stalls and kiosks to survey the wares. Clothes, sunglasses, cassette tapes.

Crowe had lent the mother and daughter money. He had no expectation of ever seeing it again, but Nina insisted that it was a loan and kept careful tally of what she owed, down to the penny, scribbling the figure down on the little Emerald Island Inn notepad with the little Emerald Island Inn pencil.

They came upon a cluster of Cuban booths and vendors. The glistening bright heaps of papaya and mango and passion fruit. Another vendor selling tres leches and churros and café Cubano. Someone's tinny radio played soukous guitar.

Crowe followed behind the Arangos, Nina holding Mariposa by the hand.

Mariposa tugged her mother toward a toy vendor. Mariposa seemed to have no interest in the Cabbage Patch dolls or the Monchhichi. She went to the windup monsters and bugs. The plastic dinosaurs.

Nina told her it was too expensive, to pick another toy. How about this doll, or this stuffed unicorn?

But Mariposa wanted Lite-Brite. Crowe insisted on buying the toy for the girl. Nina said no. Crowe told her it was a gift. But as Crowe paid the cashier, he saw Nina reach into her purse and withdraw the pad and pencil. She added a new number to the list.

Crowe was still trying to buy the toy when he saw the scar-faced man in the Havana summer suit of cappuccino silk coming his way.

When Crowe saw him, his heart gave a little frog hop.

The man first saw Yahchilane. He cut his assassin's eyes Yahchilane's way as if daring him to take another look. Yahchilane didn't.

Then his eyes lit on Crowe and they widened briefly and cut away but there was something in his posture and his bearing that told Crowe that he was waiting to look again.

And then he did, keeping his stride, but his keen studying gaze fixed on Crowe.

Crowe seized Yahchilane's arm. "This way," he said. "Come on."

Yahchilane jerked his arm away. "Hey, egghead. What's your deal?"

Crowe cut away and changed direction, moving in a half-trot, and Yahchilane reluctantly followed. Back in the van, Yahchilane asked Crowe if he knew the man with the scarred face.

Crowe said nothing, ducking in his seat.

"Get going," he said.

"You wiggin'?" Yahchilane said. "We gotta wait for them all."

The Arango family filed into the van. Yahchilane started the engine. Steered them out of the massive crowded lot and turned them toward the interstate.

"You knew that guy."

"No," Crowe said, half-believing himself.

INFERNO

CATFACE SMELLED THE FIRE. HE SMELLED the fire before he saw it.

The stench of burning sulfur in the air.

The Everglades was on fire but he was trying to catch the man riding along in the van and somewhere along the way he must have turned off, because now this.

"Fuck, fuck, fuck," Catface screamed, racing the stolen car.

The smoke got so thick, a gray apocalyptic cloud, he had to slow the car.

Finally he had to pull over to the side of the road and close his rooftop. He got back in the car. He rolled up the windows and closed the vents.

Through the bug-smeared windshield he saw smoke boiling against the glaring Florida afternoon. The voracious fire roiled demonic. An inferno.

But Catface drove on.

A few miles outside the conflagration Catface came across a makeshift convoy. Some Lilliputian beach hamlet's chamber of commerce turned into an ad hoc deputation of park rangers. A gold Buick was parked so it blocked most of the road. Standing alongside the car was a pear-shaped man with a mustache and red-haired secretary ten years his junior. The woman had on a beige woman's suit and her top was mussed.

From what Catface could discern, the pear-shaped man had a raging hard-on.

The two had been at it. At first they feigned nonchalance. Then when Catface drew closer in the car and when they glimpsed his face, their expressions dropped.

Catface came to a stop and rolled down his window.

"Hello, sir," said the pear-shaped man.

"Hello, sir," said Catface.

"You can see for yourself, up ahead."

"Yes. Fire."

"Crazy."

"Looks crazy," said Catface.

"You prolly wanna turn around."

"No."

The woman said, "There's a fire. You can't just drive through."

"I will try."

The man, "Well, it would be suicide."

"It woo scar me?"

"What?" the man asked.

"It woo scar? The fire? Not goo?"

"Gonna have'ta insist, mister. Ain't about to let some man kill himself."

"Insist what?"

"Insist you turn around."

Catface asked the man what started the fire.

The man had not anticipated this line of questioning. He palmed the sweat off his face. "Just my job here. Why this grief?"

"What started the fire?"

"Lightning. Probably. This time of year."

And as "year" was leaving the man's mouth Catface said "Goo luck!" and stomped on the gas and the car was off like something sling-shot.

Mud flew, spackling the couple's legs. In the side mirror Catface saw their stunned faces.

Catface laughing darkly shot down the road into the heart of the inferno.

BIG CAT GAS

CATFACE SAW THE BILLBOARDS FOR MILES on the highway. Time flayed and weather worn, but legible through the fungi and lichen and vine, the occasional gang graffiti tag. Cuban, Colombian.

BIG CAT GAS! COME SEE DORIS "THE BIG CAT" AT MR FONG'S WORLD FAMOUS GAS/CIGS/ICE COLD BEER!

At Mr. Fong's Big Cat Gas Catface went inside to prepay. A diminutive Asian man, presumably Mr. Fong, was smoking on a stool behind the register. Flipping through a magazine and about to draw from his cigarette. When he saw Catface his arm halted midway to his mouth. The small bitter lines around his mouth massed and ticked.

Catface asked the man if there was a problem.

A wizened bitter gnome, childlike in stature, the man shook his head. He put down his magazine. *Gallery*, read the front. A large breasted cherub-mouthed gringa was splayed atop a cheetah-covered bed, fully nude. Her fulsome ass and titties, her fuck-me-daddy lips and eyes.

TRACI LORDS FULL FRONTAL INSIDE!

Young for Catface's taste.

"Shit her," said Catface.

The man's baggy neck quaked roosterishly. "What!"

Catface looked around the mini-mart for a door. "Lavatory."

"Closed."

"Why?"

The man drew from his cigarette, exhaled a quick irked puff. "Night."

"Give me the key."

"Look, why problem?"

"Give me the key."

The man gestured, the cherry of his cigarette toppling. "Too many problem. People, funny business." Another fierce head shake, the chin wattle wagging in sympathy.

"Give me the key."

"No."

"Give me the key."

The man fell into a fit of coughing. Angrily he held up a finger. The coughing did not subside. It got worse. Angrier still, the man groped under the register and slapped the key onto the counter. Still hacking the man gestured with a nicotine-yellowed forefinger. He looked like he was about to fall apart like a dollar-store egg-timer.

Outside Catface stuck the gas nozzle into the stolen Bonneville's tank and flicked the automatic lever and kept the gas pumping.

Adjacent to the gas station lot was a clearing where concrete dinosaurs stood in the tall weeds and grass, behind them the black-green jungly wilderness of Florida. A Mesozoic tableau. The hulking gray shapes of the dinosaurs in the dark.

Catface looked at them.

A T. rex. An Edmontonia. A brachiosaur. A stegosaurus.

A few others Catface could not identify.

He remembered their shapes and names from the burn ward. The picture books he used to flip through that whole year he was bedridden, bound in traction.

After gassing the car Catface went to the lavatory to freebase. He lit the small portable butane torch and the flame lit the white rock. Catface sucked in the smoke from the pipe. Exhaled. Within moments, the rush rocketed to his head.

He felt like he could break a fist through the concrete wall. Shit lightning.

Every particle of him was vibrating. Every atom of his body felt on the verge of cumming.

Catface went to return the key and pay for the gas. "Where is the big pussy?"

"What!" The man's scrotal chin accordioned when he recoiled.

"Big cat."

A fresh-lit cigarette smoldered in the man's mean crimped mouth. His sweaty forehead looked jaundiced. "Look, you use bathroom. You got gas. Why problem. Good night."

"Where is the big cat?"

The man's nostrils worked and he seemed to smell the burned chemical odor wafting off Catface. "Sleeping!"

"Where?"

"Why problem?"

"Where."

"Other side of building!"

Catface stood looking at the man.

"Something on fire. Funny business. Why problem."

"I don't like you," Catface said.

"Who care?"

"You should," Catface said.

Outside, on the other side of the building, Catface found the pen. An enclosure of chicken wire, not much larger than a dog kennel. Sleeping inside was a big black cat, slat-ribbed and shit-slathered. A Florida panther. Its haunches and sides were piebald from living so cramped.

Catface stepped forward, touched his fingers to the metal mesh. The animal's piss and shit stench hit him like a slap to the face. Gnats clouded around Catface's head. Absentmindedly he slapped them away.

"Right away!" cried a voice in the night.

Were Catface a jumpier man he would have startled. Instead he only looked, fingers still hooked around the mesh.

It was Mr. Fong, loping toward Catface with hand upheld to stop him. "Get away right now from the cage!"

The big cat sniffed Catface. Cracked an eye. Moaned. Stirred. Cracked its other eye.

Mr. Fong now held a small pearl-handled pistol and was pointing it level at Catface. Catface jerked his arm. A dagger materialized in his hand. One of many such blades secreted on his person, within the folds of his tailored suits.

An assassin's legerdemain.

Then the blade was whistling through the air like an evil insect.

Mr. Fong howled. The gun dropped and clattered to the pavement with two of his fingers still clutching it.

Catface's mad, cracked-out laughter rang into the night. He shucked the latch of the pen and flung open the door and stepped aside like a toreador. The door squawked on its rusty hinges.

Mr. Fong's eyes popped, custard-yellow and wide in the dark. He crabbed backward toward the mini-mart door. His two fingers and pearl-handled gun still on the asphalt.

The cat hesitated, regarded Catface. Growled.

Then it moved and slunk from the cage. It scuttled ten or fifteen feet, low-bellied, from the pen, moving toward the gas station door. Mr. Fong watched through the glass, his face shrieking.

The cat looked at Mr. Fong. At Catface. At the dinosaurs standing in the dark field.

Then the huge black cat pounced away, a sleek phantom through the grass zigzagging around the dinosaurs, keeping its distance from the concrete monsters as it rushed into the Florida wild.

———

Not even a full song had played on the Bonneville's radio since Cat-face drove away from Big Cat Gas when his headlights swept over the panther.

It lay twisted in the middle of the road, its spine snapped and its legs twisted.

He could see the figure of a man crouched above the car-struck animal. His posture indecisive. His car, with its emergency lights strobing, idled on the shoulder of the road in the saw grass.

Catface stopped the car in the middle of the road. Staggered out of the Bonneville as if gutshot.

He knelt with the man in the middle of the desolate road. Shell and pebblerock bit his knees like teeth.

Around them was saw grass and cattail and swamp as far as the eye could see. The two-lane road marooned and black-hole black in either direction, the only light from the skinny fingernail moon and the multitude of tropical stars. The headlights and taillights, minuscule, puny, against the massive Everglades night.

The panther's bones were broken in dozens of places. Its skeleton twisted, agonized. Gore spilled out its mouth and slicked its teeth crimson. Part of its stomach was split and its intestines slopped onto the pavement.

The young man, red hair crew cut, face freckled and raw from crying, cradled the big cat's head.

Their faces were stained in the red taillights.

"I don't know what to do," said the young man. His T-shirt, a polo, said, BIG GORILLA FIREWORKS.

The young man seemed to have trouble looking directly at Cat-face. Too much, this nightmarish man, this nightmare of a situation, this big cat smashed in the road. He shook his head. "He was running," he said in a stricken voice.

"He run across road."

"I mean he was right there. I didn't see him. Holy shit. A panther."

"Was he happy?"

The kid swallowed. Dry-voiced, he said, "What?" He shook his head in abject consternation.

"Happy?"

"Me?"

"The cat."

The young man looked down at the cat's face. Its blinks sluggard, its torso barely stirring with breath.

Catface asked again.

"He just jumped. He jumped in front of me and then? Shit, mister. I don't know what to tell you."

Catface saw the tears slicking the young man's face. He nodded. Withdrew a bolo knife from the inside of his jacket and told the young man to step away.

Catface slit the animal's throat. Its blood ran fast and thick onto the road. The puddle grew and spread. The cat's eyes grew sleepy and vacant and then a dull matte overtook them.

The scent of blood thickened salty and hot in the air.

The insects formed a kind of humming smoke. Mosquitoes and gnats and midges and no-see-ums.

No doubt there were other things waiting, lurking, in the bush.

Catface and the red-haired man stood facing each other in the road.

"Hey," Catface said, "you want feel better?"

"Pardon?"

"Feel goo?" Standing at the open door of his Bonneville Catface was lighting his glass pipe with the portable butane torch. He exhaled smoke. "Feel better?"

"It's okay. Thanks. I gotta get going, mister."

"It es help sometimes."

"I gotta get going, mister." The young man was hurrying away into his car.

"Don't be scare. He die thinking he going to heaven. He die running."

Catface was telling the kid to wait when the phone rang in the trunk. One of those cumbersome newfangled contraptions, what they called a car phone. This a DynaTAC prototype not even yet on the market.

Only one person had his number. Tarantula.

Catface was obligated, was required, to answer.

"Wait!" Catface screamed.

The young man halted. Half-turned, shoulders sagged with dread.

The bugs sounded orgiastic, insane. A bedlam of screeching. Beetles big as bats helixed in the headlamps.

Still the mobile phone trilled.

Catface popped the trunk and withdrew the leather black valise and he popped the latch and he brought the brick-sized receiver to his sweaty cheek. "Yes," he said.

He listened. "Fort Lauderdale? Tonight?" He listened again, batting away moths attracted to his tan silk suit one-handed.

He hung up. He cursed anew. A liquidation. Tonight, at Pier Sixty-Six Hotel.

Had the young man not been so distraught, had he not been crying, Catface would have filleted him right in the Florida jungle.

"Okay, the kids need to be pick up from soccer practice," Catface told the young man.

The red-haired man dashed to his car and did not turn back.

Catface put the phone back in the valise and the valise back in the trunk and then he got behind the wheel and executed an elaborate seven-point turn.

Then Catface in the stolen black Bonneville headed from whence he came, eastward toward Fort Lauderdale, away from the bearded man who left him burning in the swamp.

WIGGING

CROWE DID NOT FORGET THE CATFACED man. But after a week he convinced himself that maybe he'd imagined the whole episode. Maybe the man was scarred and in a suit, yes, but with all the violence in Miami? Maybe he was simply a man who looked like the other man he glimpsed that day at the Broward County jail.

Within a few weeks the episode was relegated to the back of Crowe's mind.

There were troubles enough at the Emerald Island Inn.

One day Marlon during one of his visits down from Miami came with Yahchilane to the reception desk on a night when Crowe was working. Yahchilane said that Marlon was going to kill Wayne Wade.

The girl. Wayne Wade had touched the girl. The brother, Marlon, had seen Wayne stroking the child's leg and had come running and chased Wayne into his room, where he was now barricaded.

Crowe pounded on Wayne's door.

"What now," Wayne Wade said, muffle-voiced. "My god. Fuckin' Chinese laundromat."

Crowe rattled the knob, cracked the door, but the burglar chain was latched.

"Let me in, imbecile." He kicked at the door.

A few doors down SnoBall Larry stuck his head out. Mellow as fuck, as usual. Zonked. "Hey, buddy."

"Hey, Larry," Crowe said.

Larry's stoner grin. "Thought it was my door."

"Nah. Just Wayne's."

"Oh, jeez man, good luck."

SnoBall Larry disappeared back into his room.

Crowe kicked at the door again, remembering some time ago when he asked Nina what the matter with Mariposa was. She had not been acting like herself. Quiet and withdrawn, sulky. Her eyes avoided Wayne Wade whenever he entered a room or came near.

"She thinks she sees faces in the wall," Nina explained to him.

Crowe told her he didn't understand.

"Eyes," she said.

Crowe shook his head.

"In the wood. The walls. She thinks she sees eyes."

"Bad dreams? Nightmares?"

Nina was adamant. "No, no. She's awake when she sees them."

Now Wayne called from behind his door, his voice high with pique. "Hold your shit, damn it. Whatever happened to privacy?"

Inside the room Crowe inspected the wall Wayne shared with the

Cuban family. With his hands on his hips, he studied the plaster and stucco for holes. He looked behind the potted rubber tree. He looked behind the television.

Wayne said, "Look at this," as if to another person in the room. As if there was a studio audience.

Crowe kept searching.

"What'chu doin'?" He was finally hovering behind Crowe, nervously stroking his rattail. "Lookin' for your mind? Lost that long ago, man."

Crowe moved aside the wastebasket and then he saw it, the gouged-out place in the wall. A hole the size of a gumball.

"What's this?" Crowe said.

"Should I know?"

"You make this hole?"

"Hole? There's a hole?"

Crowe gave him a look: *Don't bullshit a bullshitter.*

"Maybe call Orkin, man. Pest control."

"You did this."

"Why'd I put a hole in the wall I'd have to shove my face down that far? Yeah, I'm gonna stick my dick through that hole."

"Wouldn't put it past you."

"Some thing to say."

Crowe stood with his arms tightly crossed. "Tell me the truth."

"Believe what you want to believe."

"Did you touch that girl?"

"What? Who?" Wayne got up and went to the fridge and looked for a beer, his back turned to Crowe. The motel room was an ad hoc living space. The black light. The *Scarface* poster. The hot plate. The minifridge stocked with beer and knockoff Publix Dr Peppers.

Wayne was popping a beer when he turned and was surprised to find Crowe a few steps closer.

"Breathin' down my neck," Wayne said. He sat down, eyes angled away from Crowe.

"You touch her? Say your hand went the wrong place? An accident."

"Come on with this shit."

"Wayne, goddamn it."

"She got it all twisted around."

Now Crowe was pacing. Wayne stiffened in his chair, as if preparing to fend off an attack.

"My god, Wayne. My god." Crowe was breathing hard through his hand, which was clamped over his mouth as still he paced. "They're gonna kill you."

"Come on."

"Out, out."

"Out what?"

"Out by tomorrow."

"Here? Out from behind the desk."

"From the room. From the job."

"Bullshit. Reed, come on, now."

"First thing tomorrow."

"Reed, man. You're wiggin'. Where'm I gonna go?"

"Little girl. I'd kill you myself, you fuck."

"Some way to talk." Then, using his old childhood nickname, "Come on, Reedy."

"Get outta here."

Wayne brooded. For a moment he was slumped in frustration. His face the epitome of vexation and defeat. Then there were a few quick clicks in his eyes. Scheming already.

"Calamine lotion, Reedy. All those no-see-ums. Chiggers."

Crowe shook his head.

"I was putting lotion on the bites."

Crowe pinched the bridge of his nose.

"That's the confusion."

"Get outta here, Wayne."

"Reedy."

"You gotta go."

"Some thing to say."

"You gotta go."

"Reedy."

"No more Reedy shit."

"Some thing to say."

"Hear me? Pack your shit up and get the fuck out before I kick your teeth in."

———

Wayne Wade left Emerald Island and Emerald City. Like a latter-day hobo jumping a boxcar with his bundlestaff, except Wayne on his modified bike with his yellow neon knapsack bulging Quasimodo–style from his back.

Two weeks passed, three. No calls from Wayne, no begging, no remonstrations.

Crowe was surprised. Relieved.

Then one morning he was unlocking the sheds of the Mystery House trail exhibitions. There used to be no need, but these days, the economy, the crackheads, all the Florida men running amok, you never knew. Crowe was walking on the trail jingling the ring of keys and found one of the sheds broken into. The archeological exhibit. The metal door was hacked, mangled, crowbarred open. Crowe walked in, broken glass crunching under his zories. All the artifacts and trinkets gone.

Stolen.

Crowe had little doubt as to the culprit.

THE BIG BAD PYTHON RODEO

YOU WOULD HAVE THOUGHT A MAN in circumstances such as Wayne's, a man who'd been all but driven out of town by a torch-wielding mob, would have stayed away for good.

No.

Wayne?

Shit.

This was Wayne Wilson Wade. Triple fucking W. Yet, Crowe hoped against reason and precedent the man would stay away. Perhaps the idjit had accrued some modicum of common sense after all these years.

The football season was nearly halfway done, and the Dolphins were hopelessly in the hole, and Crowe was just beginning to think they'd rid themselves of Wayne Wade for good—whole days passed when he gave the idjit nary a thought—when he received a call.

He was outside pinning up his T-shirts and Bermuda shorts on the backyard clothesline when he heard the phone ringing in the house. He went inside and answered.

It was Henry Yahchilane. "He's back," he said, "the Python Rodeo."

"Sweet Jesus," Crowe said. Then he told Yahchilane to turn him away.

Yahchilane told Crowe that Wayne Wade showed up drunk, with a semi-automatic. It took Yahchilane ten minutes to talk Wayne into putting the gun back and locking it away into the storage of his moped.

"What the hell do we do?" Crowe asked Yahchilane.

Yahchilane said he'd worry about his end. "Just make sure to god Marlon doesn't get word. He'll come over and kill the guy. Shit, there'll be a shoot-out."

For the twentieth straight year Henry Yahchilane oversaw the ill-advised and misbegotten annual Python Rodeo in Emerald City.

The zoo people, eggheads that they were, had assumed him endowed with some kind of communion with nature because of his heritage. Now, twenty years later, he could boast this prowess. He'd become the person, by sheer accident, they thought they'd hired.

The chicken and the egg.

And this year, as always, a rowdy fraternity presided over the event. Beers cracked and swilled under the hot morning sun, a Florida Saturday. Knockoff cigarette brand cigarettes smoked. Skoal spat.

Some seven or eight dozen men.

You could smell their insect repellent and truck stop jerky. Their beer. Seagulls hectored around the oil drum trash cans, fighting for nachos and hot dog buns. Boom boxes played Buffett and Dire Straits.

There was a man at one of the small picnic tables, bare-chested, a scar running the length of his torso on the side. He looked like someone who'd lived through an autopsy. The small gaunt man went around shirtless nonetheless. Smoked cigarettes one after another. Pall Malls, filterless. The guy, "See, that's how we roll. That's how we roll in Florida. I don't know where you from, but where we is right here." He had a raspy phlegm-clotted laugh. "Don't matter who it is. This woman might have accused me of rape. I'd still rescue her. Kentucky? This guy right here, I don't know him, but he's my friend, see."

Around ten, just as the locusts were beginning to screech full-throated, a few men went off singly into the scrubby pine flats. They brandished sticks and held sacks and pillowcases. They clutched beers in cozies advertising oyster shacks and adult entertainment establishments.

Then groups of two and three and sometimes four scattered away from the picnic pavilions and went off on the hiking trails.

No supervision. No demonstration. No training.

What could go wrong, deep in the heart of wild, wild Florida on the outskirts of the Everglades?

Yahchilane went with Wayne Wade, who at ten-thirty in the morning was already drunk. Not beer drunk, but Jameson drunk. He'd already been starting problems at the pavilion, singing nonsense songs, shaking his ass lewdly in front of someone's twenty-five-year-old blond Mississippi wife.

"Cool it," Yahchilane told him.

"Ancient Indian wisdom," Wayne sung.

Yahchilane followed Wayne warily into the bracken, Wayne wailing a mocking rendition of the Florida State Seminoles Native chant song. If it wasn't for Reed Crowe, he might have throttled the moron then and there.

"Oh, oh, oh," he bellowed into the pine slash and cypress. The morning sun had turned late and the air murky and pollinate, a dingy yellow pall.

Wayne went stumbling along with his stick, whacking the ferns. "Oh, oh, oh."

Yahchilane eyed the back of the man's brick red neck.

"Hell you leadin' us?" Wayne asked him, glancing over his shoulder.

Yahchilane followed from several paces behind. His eyes were clenched against the sun chinking through the leaves.

"Watch your step."

"Let's stop here."

"Go right."

Wade veered right down a faint hiking trail.

"Why we goin' so far?"

"You want to win this thing, don't you?"

"Shitfire fuck I do."

"Not doin' this for my health."

"You lead me to where the snakes are, watch me."

They forged ahead, Wayne every so often slowing and cocking an ear when he heard movements within the branches and leaves.

"Nothing," Yahchilane said. "Keep going. I told you, watch your step."

"Oh, put a sock in your pussy. I know what I'm doing."

Anoles flared their necks like red warning flags. They moved up and down on their legs like they were doing push-ups. Then they scaled up the tree trunks and changed color from green to brown.

Farther they went into the thickets through cycads and banyans and fiddlehead ferns, Wayne scuffling along with a kind of belligerent invincibility, mindless of his steps. He wore not even the proper footgear, but checkered Vans with tube socks that went halfway up to the ragged fringes of his jorts.

They went onward around clutches of serrated saw grass. The smell of camphor trees was rank in the air. Cicadas droned.

Yahchilane saw it before Wayne. Along the path lay a snake long and slick, diamond-patterned. Like a loop of rope it lay in the sun on a bed of rotting leaves, the color of ferns and moss. It tightened its coil, reared back its head. Then with switch knife quickness the snake sprang out.

Before the snake loosed its venom-dripping fangs from his ankle Wayne Wade let out a shrieking howl.

A demented sound in this deep wilderness. But no one would hear him now, not where they were, not this far.

Of that Henry Yahchilane was certain.

He was about to warn Wayne but before he could the man was shrieking and hopping around the path. Then he was on the ground, red-faced and grasping at his ankle.

"Fuck. I've been bit. Fuck. Holy fuck."

Yahchilane watched from a distance.

Wayne's sweated face was contorted. "Did you see that thing?"

"Yes."

"What?"

"Snake."

"Yeah. Fuck. You fuck." Goober teeth showing. "What kind? Poison? Was it poison?"

"Yes," Yahchilane told him.

Wayne's face was woebegone, twisted. "I need help."

Yahchilane put his hands in his jeans pockets, thumbs hooked out.

Wayne screamed into the gigantic Florida wild. He writhed on the ground. Curdled spit foamed in the corners of his mouth.

Yahchilane watched with slitted black eyes.

Wayne threatened Yahchilane. He apologized. Cursed him. Apologized again.

Then he started begging.

"I'll give you whatever you want." His face was wild and sweaty, his snakebit eyes crazed.

Yahchilane said, "I don't know what to do."

"You're goin' to hell, cocksucker."

"Yeah," said Yahchilane.

Wayne shot a glance, half angry and half fearful. He rose and took a few mincing, hobbling steps forward. He fell onto his ass. He got up and limped a few more steps before stopping and falling over once more.

Henry Yahchilane had led Wayne Wade into a nest. A breeding ground.

This time Wayne stayed on his ass in leaves. Crying. Whimpering. His beige face looked snotty and spitty like a toddler's. "Please, please, Mr. Yahchilane."

As Yahchilane strode, his gait easy and long, Wayne's voice followed him, but it gradually diminished with each step, grew fainter in the green smother of the jungle, and mixed in with the wild drone of the insects, until falling silent within the vast acreage of summer-glutted leaves.

Word spread through the township. Crowe heard the news from Myrtle who heard the news from Eddie who heard about the so-called python harvest tragedy on the FM radio.

A man was bitten. A man was in critical condition.

No, a man was dead.

No, a man was on life support in Hialeah, Florida.

No name or identifying information until the next of kin was contacted, standard procedures followed, due course observed.

The Python Rodeo, cancelled out of respect to the victim. And out of concern for the safety of the hundreds of men who'd flocked to Emerald City for a weekend of life-endangering revelry.

Then the rumors came piecemeal on the phone, a puzzle none too hard to put together. Crowe heard from Eddie that Yahchilane strode out of the woods with no emotion, with the vague wariness of a man who'd done all he could do, reporting a man down.

A man snakebit.

Wayne Wade.

Late afternoon Crowe drove his beeswax orange hatchback to Yahchilane's shaggy-shingled barrel house.

The front door, no answer. The side door, no answer.

Crowe went down the garden-flaked path to the beach and found Yahchilane sitting in the sand a stone's throw from the water. He was smoking a cigarette, staring out at the water, low tide. From the tight set of his shoulders Crowe knew that Yahchilane sensed his approach.

Crowe, "What happened, Yahchilane?"

Crowe stood above Yahchilane. Yahchilane was still not looking at him.

"What happened, goddamn it, Yahchilane?"

"A snake bit the guy, what else is there to say?"

"How."

"Call Sheriff Schaffer," said Yahchilane. He drew deeply from his cigarette. Still not one glance at Crowe.

Crowe shot out a hand as if to grab Yahchilane's hair and rip it out by the root. But Yahchilane still without looking and with the cigarette dangling in his mouth caught Crowe's wrist and kept it seized in the vise of his hand.

He twisted Crowe's arm.

Crowe wailed on the empty beach. He fell to his knees. Contorted, pinioned.

Yahchilane let go and Crowe backed off a few paces.

Yahchilane flicked his cigarette in the sand and faced Crowe. His face rancid. His lank curls hanging sweaty.

Crowe charged at Yahchilane with his arms thrown wide. The green beach bum shades flew off his head.

Yahchilane wrapped him up in his bear arms and the two men lumbered and groaned and tottered like two rabid warring beasts.

They toppled. Yahchilane pinned Crowe and mashed his face in the sand. He grabbed Crowe's hair. Held him down.

Crowe felt the bite of small shells digging into his cheek. Like little fangs. Crowe kicked like a trapped anole in a beach cat's mouth.

Yahchilane said, "You gonna calm the fuck down? Gonna come at me again?"

Crowe breathed angry scraping breaths through his nose, his face mashed.

"Gonna let you go," Yahchilane said. "You come at me, then I'm gonna put you down. Quick."

Yahchilane stood up and tugged his denim shirt straight. One of the sleeves was ripped at the shoulder. Yahchilane let it dangle. He sat down where he was before. He fumbled with an already-swelling hand in his pocket for his cigarettes and took out the smashed pack.

He withdrew a cigarette. Broken. He flung it aside. He withdrew another. Broken. He broke off the end, lit the good half.

The men sat catching their breath. Crowe slapped the grit off his cheek. Little nicks of blood were welling, scoring his face.

Then Crowe put his elbows on his knees and his head in his hands and kept his face hidden as he made a choking crying sound. He did this for almost a full minute.

Then he took his hands from his face and looked wet-eyed at Yahchilane. "There were other options."

"No," Yahchilane said.

"I've known that man my whole life."

"I understand."

"You killed him."

"Nothing to be done," Yahchilane said.

"You're a sick fuck."

"Your judgment is clouded."

Yahchilane, staring at the water, sat with his shoulders hard and straight.

"I grew up with him," Crowe said.

When Yahchilane said nothing, when he only kept smoking, Crowe stood and lunged as if gearing for another attack. He swatted the cigarette out of Yahchilane's mouth.

Yahchilane glared. Crowe glared back.

Then Crowe with his beaten face hobbled back from where he came.

MELON HEAD

YET WAYNE WADE DID NOT DIE. Miraculously he did not die. And when Reed Crowe learned the news, a thousand new worries beset him.

What now? Would Wayne Wade go after Yahchilane? Would Wayne Wade think he was complicit, co-engineer of some diabolical plan? Would Wayne go after him?

Where in everliving blue fuck did they go from here?

Reed Crowe didn't have a notion.

Doubting himself, doubting Yahchilane, doubting every fucking thing that had happened in his life thus far, Crowe went through the rooms of the Emerald Island Inn.

The peepholes, at least one per room. Sometimes two or three. Behind the television, behind the thrift store wall-hangings of lighthouses and seashells. Behind headboards and nightstands and hutches.

Maybe mouse holes, he thought.

Termites, silverfish, some other kind of pest.

Hey, maybe it was normal wear and tear from the weather and storms.

He wanted desperately to believe this.

But going through the motel the more he discovered. The more he discovered, the more they began to resemble one another, dime-sized holes bored into the wall with a drill or file.

Identical.

Imagining Wayne Wade crouching, imagining him peering through the holes, imagining what he saw and what he did, Crowe went to the bathroom and knelt in front of the toilet and puked.

Crowe spent that night thinking about Wayne Wade.

Drinking alone. Brooding in silence. Looking out at the ocean from his BarcaLounger in the beach house sunroom, looking out at the night surf under the planetarium sky.

From his somber expression and his thousand-mile stare, Crowe might as well have been looking at a cinderblock wall.

Crowe marveled at how long he'd let this state of affairs with Wayne Wade go on.

Decades.

How was it possible?

Yet he was blind to so much of it, willfully blind.

Next morning Reed Crowe went to the intensive care ward to see Wayne Wade. If not for the rattail, if not for the telltale goober teeth, Crowe wouldn't recognize him. His face warped, his head swollen as big as a melon, his skin hived and blistered, his legs swaddled in gore-soaked bandages.

Crowe succumbed to a brief spell of pity.

He thought of Wayne's childhood. There weren't many kids who attended their little beachside school in Emerald City. It started as a damn one-room schoolhouse, for god's sake. But of course Wayne immediately became the brunt of the jokes, the punching bag.

There always had to be one, no matter where you went.

Now, looking at Wayne in the bed, he remembered all this, but then he remembered Mariposa sitting Indian-style on the edge of the motel bed, watching *Mr. Rogers*. Won't you be my neighbor? He thought of Mariposa watching *3-2-1 Contact*. He thought of "Fish Heads" by Barnes & Barnes. He thought of the girl who used to give him rocks and dirty socks for presents, wrapped in gift paper.

Within a half minute, the spell of pity dissipated.

"Well, Wayne," Crowe began. His voice was strained. "I'm sorry it had to come to this. I really am. But I think you brought this upon yourself. You can't speak. I know. The nurses told me."

Crowe shook his head. Looked down at the green and white linoleum. "I don't know what your plans are. I didn't want you dead. I didn't want you dead." Crowe looked up. "Know that. I just wanted you gone. Goddamn it, you should'a stayed gone."

There were tubes shoved in Wayne's mouth and nostrils and into his arms. About him machines blipped and wheezed. A heart monitor. A ventilator.

Now Wayne huffed like a bellows. He writhed in torment. The restraints around his wrists and ankles kept him in place. He was pinioned.

Crowe went on, "You get Schaffer or anybody involved in this, you know what's gonna happen. That's a promise. You'll die in jail. They'll fuck you raw in prison."

Wayne's eyes wept pus.

The blipping on the monitor quickened.

"I'm sorry. Bullshit, I'm not sorry." Part of Crowe wanted to grip Wayne Wade around the throat and end it right now.

Instead he backed away from the bed a few steps. He said in a hissing whisper, "When you get out of here you get out of here. They'll kill you. And I won't lift a finger. You hear? It's over. For good. Disappear. Get."

OPERATION TARANTULA (IMPROBABLE PALACES)

ONE MIGHT WONDER HOW A YEAR passed for a man such as Catface. They might imagine chapters of such a man's life passing in cinematic montage. Catface, with stiletto blade, hiding behind shower curtains patterned with tropical fish. Catface, with a bauernwehr dagger hiding behind hotel drapes and venetian blinds. Catface lurking in the wings of a dictator's palace or plantation or hacienda with his assassin's knife.

All vignettes pretty much true.

And an assassin's trade took him to improbable places. Midnight Cessnas to Medellin, to Los Cabos.

The world of dictatorships and coups and cartels.

But most people might not imagine such a man watching the *Pink Panther* films of Peter Sellers. Imagine such a man mailing a brown butcher paper envelope containing a brick of American money to the children's sick ward at Hermanos Ameijeiras Hospital, mailing bricks of one-hundred-dollar bills to the churches and the orphanages clustered along the banks of the Rio Grande.

Catface saw them on the news all the time these days. The refugees. He remembered being one himself.

He was one.

He would always be an alien. Here, everywhere. Not only in America, but in Cuba, his birthplace. Even there, especially there, he was alienated. There were some moments he felt an alien of Earth. And, like an alien, he felt immune to laws, impervious to human restrictions and mores.

Not when it came to those poor kids.

If they were lucky the kids ended up at a shelter on the Mexican side. Because the other side, without their parents? If the children didn't end up black market babies, they ended up camp detainees.

A dark world out there. A dark country. A dark time. He'd made the acquaintance over the years of many men who slavered over girls not even made it yet to their quinceañeras.

He gave such men wide berth.

Not for fear of them but for fear of what he'd do to them.

When Catface was in the company of such men, he got so high before he killed them that he believed he was an alien.

An extraterrestrial.

What was it those cabrona comedians were saying on television these days?

Cocaine: hell of a drug.

MR. VIDEO

IT WAS BY A SHEER STROKE of luck, finally, that Catface happened upon the information that led him to Reed Crowe. He was in a strip club near Punta Gorda, Florida, the Pink Pony, one of many such seedy establishments scattered up and down the coast, when a scrawny, cracker-voiced man on the neighboring barstool caught his attention.

It was a shadowy place so you wouldn't see the stripper's crow's-feet or C-section scars.

Nor, evidently, did the scrawny man next to him see Catface's scars because the first thing he noticed was the necklace. "Hotel Mutiny?"

Catface regarded the man. The man's lips clamped over his goober teeth. He had on cutoff jeans, a Timex watch, white-and-black-checkered shoes. A shark's tooth hung from his plated necklace. The plating was so cheap that Catface could see the faint green ring rimming his collar.

"That's right," Catface told him.

"All those stories true?" The man's eyes were half-lidded, inebriated.

Catface shrugged.

"I bet they're true. I'd like to check that place out. Man, oh man, I bet it's wild."

And now, finally, the man named Wayne Wade noticed Catface's face. A moment of clarity seized him. For an instant he was aghast. Then his face underwent a series of contortions. As if he suspected himself dosed, in the grip of some mind-altering drug.

Here was a man he'd met before, a man whose head was shaped oddly catlike, the scars on his face like bacon for whiskers.

Wayne Wade picked up the red glass votive holder to look at. The candle flame guttered. From the far end of the bar the 'roided-up bar backs shouted to Wayne that he was getting thrown out if he didn't put the candle down.

"Hey," Catface said, his voice cutting through the disco.

The man looked at Catface. Catface held up an imperious hand.

The bar back turned away.

"Man, you got the ring too, look at that," the scrawny man said, recovering from his shock. "You must be loaded."

The men had to speak over the loud disco pumping out the speakers. A black-haired woman with a leg brace moved topless around the stage pole.

Catface told him, "Not so much."

"You like history, mister?"

Catface told him, "It seems the older I get, the more interested I get in the past, and less in the future."

Wayne blinked groggy cracker blinks at him.

"Yes," Catface told him, "I like history."

Now the man flashed a grin. He rummaged in the depths of his jorts pockets. He set something on the bar before Catface.

The bar back inserted himself into the conversation again. "Hey, I told you, no sellin' shit in this place."

He was striding toward them. Catface stalled him with his hand. Then he pointed and said nothing. Just pointed.

The bar back started to puff up but then the raven-haired barmaid clutched his forearm and said, "Chet."

"Your name is Chet?" Catface asked the man. Catface's eyes widened in surprise for an instant before they slitted again. Through his toothpick he grinned.

Now even the man's eyes looked steroidal.

"Clit, get us another round."

The bar back took a scuffing step toward Catface with his fist beginning to bunch but the barmaid stalled him again with her hand. She whispered in his ear. The bar back's face changed. His eyes went to Catface's necklace, then his ring. The hulk composed himself.

Catface said, "Flex, baby, flex."

Wayne was not used to this kind of respect. Immediately his attitude changed. His posture inflated with pride. Now that he could laugh with impunity, he put some gut in it.

The disco blared.

The old-timers went back to lollygagging over their harvey wallbangers and gin rickeys. They leered at the girls dancing beside the neon-faced cigarette machine.

The object before Catface looked like a trinket or bauble of some sort.

"Native American?"

Wayne Wade hunkered, swung around a secretive look. Wayne told Catface it was. The genuine deal.

In the dim bar light it looked like a figure or idol. Catface thought of Kalki. Of Vishnu. He thumbed the rough-hewn stone amulet. A talisman of sorts made of hard black rock, grain like soapstone.

He rolled it in his well-manicured hand, held it up to his face for closer inspection in the wan bar light.

The figure, a humanlike effigy, had an overlarge, angry-looking mouth like the face on a tiki stump.

The statuette looked like it was wearing a wig made of black spaghetti. Maybe worms or snakes. Maybe tendrils of smoke. Catface pictured a chief or priest many years ago, from some prehistoric time, squatting aside a ceremonial fire, stroking the figure with his thumb as he was now, as if coaxing out a hex or curse, summoning a genie.

Catface asked, "Why you selling this?"

"Oh, employment opportunities run dry," Wayne said. Then, "You hirin'?"

"I'm an independent contractor, you might say."

"They used to call me Cool Papa Lemon." The man admitted this with visible pride.

"That right?"

"Yessir."

Catface called for the bar back. Motioned for two more drinks.

"Where you from?"

"You familiar with the coast?"

"Growing."

"Emerald Island, about fifty miles up from here. Little island."

Catface looked at Wayne.

The hulk set the drinks before them. Catface waited until he walked away and said, "You worked there."

"I did. Until I was fired."

Catface asked, "Where did you work?"

"Little motel. Mostly, though?" Again Wayne swiveled a secretive look around. "Grass."

Catface asked him if he grew it.

"No, just sold it."

"Your boss?"

"Grow it? Shit, no. That's the bitch of it, see." Another sneaky look around. "He found it. He just found it. Lucky, was all."

"You know, I might have been there. Emerald Island. Is the hotel pink and purple?"

Wayne had to consider this for a moment. "The sign is."

Catface remembered flying over a barrier island. He remembered a motel sign. This little he remembered in the moments before the plane fell apart and the fuel line exploded and they went down burning in the swamp.

On closer inspection, Catface believed he might have seen this Wayne before. He thought of all manner of people he came in touch with over the years. He could picture Wayne stepping in his zories and his too-short rayon shorts and Panama Jack T-shirt through the coconut-oiled scrum of people on a Fort Lauderdale strip beach. *I got hippie flips and love pills and bumblebees and Quaaludes and purple microdots.* If a cop stopped him, all he had to do was scamper away and duck into the jam-packed Elbow Room.

Wayne asked him now, "Hey, you like artifacts?"

"You already asked me that, amigo."

"How much you think this is worth? A hundred?"

The man reared his head back in surprise.

"Too little?"

"Too little. Florida lottery."

"Happy to oblige."

"You okay, buddy. You okay."

Catface pocketed the figure. They finished their drinks and Catface motioned two-fingered for more.

Now the dancers changed and there came onstage a young almost breastless woman who couldn't have been a few weeks older than eighteen, if that. And it was this young nymphet that the scrawny cracker's eyes settled on wolfishly. The tip of his tongue roved in the pocket of his cheek like a ball bearing.

Catface, cold rising to his eyes, studied the man now in a different way.

Catface looked at the stage. "Your type?"

"Oh yeah."

"We have very young girls at the Mutiny."

"How young?"

"How young do you think?"

Wayne leaned toward Catface, whispered, "I'm not only known by Cool Papa Lemon."

"Tell me more."

"You ever hear'a Mr. Video?"

"You're the one? With the cassettes? With the recordings, in the motel rooms?"

Wayne went silent. His lips clamped. He turned away with some secret proud knowledge, basking in his mystery.

DER KOMMISSAR

LATER IN THE EVENING, FROM THE depths of his cappuccino silk suit, the scar-faced man took out a small glass vial and sprinkled a neat line on the brass bar.

Wayne didn't move.

Catface motioned Wayne in the fashion of a game show host. "Por favor," he said.

Hesitatingly, Wayne partook.

"Por favor," Catface said again. "Please."

In the rubicund bar light they shared a few lines on the brass railing. Right in plain sight of the management, who stood at a re-move with the vexed and helpless faces of hostages.

A harried yellow-haired woman in a neon bikini lit a cigarette and looked away at a Miller High Life sign.

A pair of bikinied women were at the jukebox. A skinny girl wearing a thong was pressing the buttons.

A song called "Der Kommissar" played.

On the sixteenth bar, Catface leapt from his chair Michael Jackson style and executed a series of dance moves. The patrons had no idea whether to laugh or applaud or join along or watch in admiration. Everyone was so wary of Catface by then, so unnerved, they feigned blindness to the spectacle.

Everyone aside from Wayne Wade, who egged him on with the fervor of a revelator. After all the excitement Wayne Wade said he needed to piss and went to the bathroom.

Wayne was pissing at one of the urinals when Catface came at him from behind, grabbing his rattail. The man began to turn his scrawny neck and was in the middle of a curse and still pissing. He howled like a butchered goat. Catface was already whirled around and had the bloodied blade snicked back into the handle as Wayne Wade collapsed shrieking to his knees, groping the floor for his severed manhood.

And with the same stealth, like a cat burglar, Catface stepped out of the bathroom and went out the strip club exit, deafening disco beat following him outside into the sultry night, drowning out the man's screams.

DREAD ENVELOPES

NOW AND THEN, SMALL BEACH ISLAND and small beach city where they lived, Crowe saw Yahchilane. And Yahchilane saw Crowe.

One grocery over in Emerald City, a few bars on the island, a few on the mainland. Five restaurants, one on the island, four in the town.

Inevitable that their paths should cross.

One two-lane road extending the length of the skinny island like a spine.

One bridge connecting the island with the mainland.

Inevitable.

In those days of yore, before Crowe found the skull in the cave so many years ago, they might have exchanged a perfunctory greeting from afar. A small nod, a half-wave, a peace sign flicked off their steering wheels. The same courtesy they would have extended any familiar car or truck so few were the denizens in these parts. Perfunctory.

Now, nothing. Not so much a tick of the eyes, a middle finger.

And when Crowe did drive across the bridge he would pass the Lilliputian post office where on temperate days Myrtle sat in her aluminum beach chair in the lee shade of the building.

In December every time Crowe passed, there was Myrtle. She would stand and wave, try to flag him down. He would wave back.

The envelopes, how Crowe dreaded the envelopes. Resented the envelopes. He wanted to murder the envelopes.

The envelopes changed color. They went from plain white to a weird baby blue and then to an odd hot pink and finally there were red envelopes, which had to contain dire news, so these he ripped in half and then quarters and then in pieces so tiny they couldn't be torn any more and he shoved them unseen and unread in the garbage.

The envelope this time, a warning from the IRS. Back taxes. Legalese about property forfeiture. Legalese about outstanding debts from Reed Crowe, Sr.

Crowe's third or fourth trip that month across the bridge Myrtle stood and waved yet again and Crowe waved back but this time Myrtle trotted toward the road and gestured frantically, moving her arms in wide swaths like an air flight controller minus the glowing batons.

The charade was over, Crowe realized.

He slowed the hatchback and bumped into the lot.

When he got out of the car they hugged like old chums.

"Hell's your problem, Crowe?" Myrtle asked him. Thirteen years ago before Myrtle went full lesbian she gave him a hand job at a Christmas party. A vague recollection to them both, they were so drunk on the spiked cider and the eggnog. They never mentioned the hand job to each other again. Better that way.

Now, Crowe told her, "Myrtle, just throw it out, whatever it is."

"You know I can't do that, Crowe. Government duty."

"Well, leave it there in the box then."

"Like Schrodinger's cat."

Crowe blinked at Myrtle. Swatted the gnats away from his head. He had his shades on but had to scrunch his face against the fierce August sun.

"The cat in the box," Myrtle said. "That philosopher. I know I'm mispronouncing it, philosophy course, Broward Community College. There's a cat in a box, right? But maybe there isn't. It depends if you open the box."

"If a tree falls in a forest," Crowe said.

"Kind of like that. Cat waiting inside for you."

The mail was from a tax collection agency and threatened liens on Crowe's house and properties.

Word of Reed Crowe's predicament spread across the island like the mother of all plants.

Word must have reached Yahchilane because Reed Crowe had caught a small whiting fish in his hand and was trying to get it off his hook when he saw Yahchilane approaching from the dunes. Yahchilane topped the boardwalk spanning the sea oats and came long-strided, hands spaded in his jean pockets.

It was the first time they'd been face-to-face since the fistfight. Not since the Python Rodeo had they spoken.

"Yahchilane," said Crowe.

"Crowe," said Yahchilane.

Crowe tossed the fish back into the ocean and washed his hands off in the waves and shook the water off them and rubbed his hands dry on his madras shorts.

Yahchilane shared the news he'd come to share. Told Crowe that a surveyor had been staying in his motel, taking measurements of the island.

"You sure he's a surveyor? Not some wildlife photographer?"

Not hard to figure out, Yahchilane told him. The man had a hunter orange vest and a yellow hard hat and he had a grade pole and a surveying tripod.

"They can't do that. They can't just take over land you own for a pipeline."

"They sure as fuck can. They took my cousin's land away from him. And he's registered Native."

Herman the big blue heron legged into the water. He poked the water a few times with his beak and picked up the whiting. With the fish snapped up in his beak he winged off.

Crowe's beard by this time was fully white. His hands and arms and forehead were freckled with benign melanoma. He had not been to a doctor in some time and he was afraid to start now. The pot was gone. The stuff they had these days, too strong, mixed with chemicals. So he drank more. His face was ruddier, webbed with broken vessels.

Crowe asked, "How much they gave him for the land?"

"Four hundred dollars."

"Four hundred thousand?"

"Hundred."

"Well, there's no amount of money."

"It doesn't matter. Bet your ass they can. Take it right away from you."

"We'll see."

"Yeah, you will. Quick."

Crowe was silent.

"I think you're serious."

"There'll be a standoff, I guess."

"They'll poison you the fuck out of here, believe it," Yahchilane said. "They'll shotgun you out. Tear gas. Grenades. Won't even hide the fact. Shit, they'll televise the shit. Make you out one of those compound nuts."

THE PLANE, THE PLANE (WHAT WOULD AN ASSASSIN DO?)

CATFACE HIT THE ROAD, TREKKING UP the Florida coast via stolen cars. He was not afraid of taking his time. Other business to attend to on the way. And he knew the man Reed Crowe, the man whose name he learned from the rattailed degenerate known as Mr. Video, the cocksucker who'd left him burning alive in the Florida Everglades like a *pinchos de pollo,* was good as anchored to the island where he lived.

Crowe was going nowhere.

Also, there was the matter of what Catface would do after. Of course the thought had occurred to him. He had an assassin's heart. It burned in the core of him, a fiery gem. What did an assassin do after slaying his ultimate quarry?

He would have to find another. Monumental.

Who? The President of the United States, he supposed.

For now, though, Crowe. Reed Crowe. The roach.

In seedy beach-smelling motel rooms he watched the local news stations when he couldn't find *Three's Company* or *The Jeffersons* or *Fantasy Island.* Once in a while he'd take out the matchbook with the number for the Emerald Island Inn front desk. He would call it.

Sometimes a young man would answer and introduce himself as Eddie. Other times the receptionist was a woman named Bertha.

He wondered if these people would end up dead too.

Reed Crowe would certainly. And it would be heinous, slow. Delicious.

Catface would sit on the edge of the bed, phone cradled between shoulder and ear, one loafer dangling from his toes as he filed his heel with the emery board. Then he sanded the other, *shish-shish*, working the callus as hard as pumice.

Whenever Reed Crowe answered, Catface stayed quiet for a while.

Shish-shish.

"Hello?" he'd say. "Seventh damn time tonight. I got you on a trace." His breath nervous.

Then Crowe would hang up the phone. Catface would call right back.

Catface cupped his hand over the mouthpiece, turned his head away. Even his laugh was a menacing whisper.

On the television a rerun of *Fantasy Island* played. Catface rose from the bed with the phone stand in one hand and the receiver in the other. He twisted the volume knob on the television and put the mouthpiece up to the speaker as the midget Hervé Villechaize in his white tuxedo and black bow tie pointed up to the tropical sky and told his boss, "The plane, the plane."

Then Catface, full of savage glee, cackling goblin laughter, slammed down the phone.

PHONE CALL FROM HADES

THE RINGING PHONE JARRED REED CROWE out of shallow sleep. It was half past midnight, graveyard shift, and he was slumped on the chair behind the reception desk, the *Sun Sentinel* sports page spread open before him. Stuff about Coach Don Shula, quarterback Dan Marino.

No one said anything when Crowe answered. But on the other end of the line was a slow, measured breathing.

A presence.

Maybe it was a crank call. A wrong number.

"Emerald Island Inn," Crowe repeated. "Reception."

He was about to hang up when the whispered sandpapery voice said, "Reed Crowe?"

A man.

Crowe straightened in the chair. "Who is this?"

Silence. Still the raspy breathing.

Shish-shish.

"Wayne?" Crowe said.

He waited. He felt his blood quicken.

He said, "Wayne, this you?"

Then the man said, "Goo luck."

Crowe asked who in the blue motherfuck it was, but by then the dial tone was humming in his ear.

Crowe got up from his chair. He went to the lobby window and looked out. His ghostly spooked face was reflected on the glass, superimposed upon the island night. The Emerald Island Inn sign glowing pink and purple, the swaying palms and sea grape trees awash in neon.

Night. Just the night staring back at him.

He knew it was irrational, but Crowe expected the caller awaiting him beneath the porte cochere. Magically materialized, as if via teleportation or conjuration.

He stepped outside and for a while stood listening to the muggy dark. Moths and june bugs fluttered around the globe lights flanking the entrance. Their birdlike shadows gliding big upon the seashell lot.

The occasional nightbird, their shadows like model planes.

Bamboo stalks moved in the beach breeze. Chuckling, as if with dark rumor, a sinister secret.

SPEED TRAP

THE SMELL OF ORANGE BLOSSOMS. A grapefruit orchard flat and stretching far as the eye could see, an infinity of evenly spaced trunks as tidy as a watercolor painting. Horse fields. Boat launches jutting out into the waterways. A hand-painted billboard for a parrot circus where cockatoos and macaws performed stunts and tricks. SEE MISTER PECKER LIVE, said the sign. Three exclamation marks.

Occasionally he passed a lightning scorched cypress, always topped with a shaggy nest that looked like a wig made of hay and twigs and wicker. Buzzard nests. Osprey nests.

On the side of the road were the hides of run-over alligators. Hundreds of grasshoppers the size of ladyfinger bananas. One on top of the other, mating season.

This was the terra incognita beyond even the Indian casinos on the outskirts of the Everglades. The jai alai fontons. The massage parlors and tug-off joints.

So desolate this far out that often ten minutes would pass before he spotted another car on the two-lane road.

They'd shoot past each other, the wind of their passing making the Mustang shimmy.

Then alone again in the purgatorial darkness. Alligator and frog eyes glowing jewel-like in the saw grass. A raccoon flitting out of the headlights, a furry hind leg darting out of view.

The flattened remains of a boa constrictor, like a fire hose run over several times.

The flying insects so big in the headlights they looked like fairies. Pixies.

It was past midnight when Catface hit I-75, headed north. Fifteen miles outside of Emerald City he passed a weather-flayed billboard advertising THE FLORIDA MAN MYSTERY HOUSE AND SWAMP TOUR.

"Who Can It Be Now" on the radio, WSHE FM out of Miami.

Behind the billboard waited a police cruiser and after the midnight blue Mustang shot past, its klaxon bleated and its blue lights spun. The police car bumped onto the road and followed the car.

A speed trap.

Catface eased to a stop on the highway shoulder. Waited. His hands rested at ten and one on the wheel.

The cop car nosed up behind the Mustang. In the rearview mirror Catface saw the silhouette of the cop's head. The man scribbling notes on his clipboard.

Then the door swung open and the officer stepped to the car. He rapped his knuckles on the glass. Beamed a penlight into Catface's face and bent down to better regard him.

Catface rolled the window down halfway. The sweltering night air hit his face like a rag. Mosquitoes and gnats hummed. The frogs and crickets roared.

"Everything okay tonight, sir?"

"Yes, officer," said Catface. He looked straight at the officer. Hands very relaxed on the wheel.

The young man's expression jerked. Then his face ticked back to its composure. Or some semblance of it.

The officer, "Know why I stopped you tonight?"

Catface studied his badge. The name tag. Ziggy Schaffer, Jr. "Was I speeding, officer?"

The officer was about to answer but then looked at the thin gold chain of Catface's necklace. The first two buttons of his shirt were loose and in the V of his scarred chest rested a gold medallion. A logo of a round cartoon pirate face. Like the Mister Donut logo you saw around the South. The same jaunty wink, the same rakish slant of the hat.

"Is it you?" Schaffer Junior asked.

"It all depends."

The man's expression changed. "My mistake, sir," he said.

"No mistake. No problem. It es goo."

"My advice, watch the speedometer." A small tremble in his voice.

"Well, you have a goo night now."

"You too."

The officer waved him onward.

"Goo luck."

Then Catface went on his way. In the rearview mirror the officer already was turning to his car in the red stain of the Mustang's taillights.

WICKED PISSAH CATEGORY
SIX THREE-PRONGED SHOCKER!

SO VAST WAS THE TERRA INCOGNITA in this part of Florida that Catface drove for miles without seeing sign of civilization. About twenty miles away from Emerald Island, Catface's guts were twisted. Knots of hot agony. He had to take a volcanic shit. He sped up the Eldorado, his latest stolen car. He was about to pull over on the side of the road and burst out of the car and tear down his pants and relieve himself in the saw grass when he saw it evanesce on the heat-hazed horizon. A three-story windowless warehouse of sheet metal, fire-engine red, like an inflamed sore against the jungle-green backdrop of the trees.

BIG GORILLA FIREWORKS, the big black letters of the yellow sign exclaimed.

In the fireworks emporium Catface went to the clerk. The clerk noticed him at once and his face dropped.

Catface already knew the young man would die. He just didn't know how.

"I must use your bathroom," he said.

"No bathroom, mister. Sorry."

"Where do you relieve?"

"Where do I live?"

"Where do you relieve!"

"Pardon?"

These gringos and their bathrooms. Places more holy, more sacred, than El Cobre. Than San Lazaro. "Do you shits in your hand?"

The young man, shaking his head in mute consternation, was still out of sorts, reeling with shock from the sight of Catface.

"I'll buy big firework, okay?" Catface said to the young carrot-haired man, already striding toward the back of the building where there was a hallway. On one side was an office door, on the other a lavatory.

"Sir," the man called after him.

Catface said, "Big, big firework, hey, okay?" His voice was small and echoey in the vast space of the warehouse, tall aisles deserted of customers.

"I gotta ask the manager," the young man, weak-voiced, called after him. "Sir. Hello?"

In the bathroom Catface relieved himself. Then he washed up at the sink and cupped his hands under the spigot and splashed water in his face. He raked a comb through his hair. He blotted his face with a wad of paper towels and tossed them into the garbage. Then from his coat pocket he took out the butane torch and crack pipe. He lit a rock, inhaled the smoke deeply.

On the porcelain lip of the sink he left the torch with its gas still hissing like a snake.

When Catface emerged from the bathroom the young man had the phone picked up, finger poised above the rotary dial.

"Down!" Catface bellowed. A Pentecostal injunction.

The man's shoulders jerked and then he stood frozen, indecisive, still clutching the receiver.

In a voice still raised and hard, Catface said, "Put that phone down, conyo."

Now the man was shook. Catface could see even from this distance. The clerk set down the phone.

Catface went down one of the aisles, arms akimbo, surveying the wares.

"It's okay, sir," the man said in an odd, strangled voice.

"What's okay?"

"You don't need to buy nothin'."

"No, I want a big, big one."

"You already used the bathroom, no need."

"Grande."

"No need."

"In a hurry to get rid of me?"

"No, sir. No."

Catface went down one aisle and then the next. His alligator loafers clicked sharply. He clasped his hands behind his back. He whistled two bars of "La Chambelona." Then he hummed the Miami Dolphins rally.

The kid stood there.

He clapped and stomped. "Miami Dolphins, Miami Dolphins."

The kid, pale-faced, nodded.

"Miami Dolphins. Miami Dolphins."

With his chin, Catface motioned him to join. "Miami Dolphins," the kid said in bleak agreement. "Miami Dolphins."

"Greatest football team!"

Then Catface changed his tune. "Wasting Away in Margaritaville," he crooned. His voice echoed in the tiled space. "Some people say a woman there's to blame. No, officer, mi dick, motherfucker."

Catface moseyed with arms behind his back, surveying the wares. He passed a display of Black Cat fireworks, the howling black cat in the middle of the yellow logo. Catface eyed it, muttered something in Spanish.

Finally he stopped and selected from the gaudy shelves a large cinderblock-sized explosive: WICKED PISSAH CATEGORY SIX THREE-PRONGED SHOCKER! On the brightly colored box was a round yellow logo with a yowling black cat in the middle. Catface took the explosive to the register, toting it both-armed, it was so big and heavy. As big as a hatbox, as heavy as a bowling ball. Catface had to carry it at a fastidious remove, so as not to sully his clothes.

Catface studied the kid's T-shirt. Tie-dyed, with a big round yellow happy face on the front.

"I like that. I like that shirt."

"Thank you, sir."

"Good shirt."

The young man thanked him again.

"Happy face."

"Yes."

"You are happy?"

The kid's posture was befuddled, helpless.

"Are you happy?"

The clerk said nothing.

Catface showed the clerk the pirate logo on his necklace. "Hey, look, they hombres, see? Only mine's got one eye and isn't so happy."

"Sir," the young man said glumly. A look of dread twisted his face.

"I like your shirt. It's okay."

With that Catface exited the store lugging the firework. He was halfway across the lot with it when he whirled and went dashing back into the store.

Catface put the firework down on the floor. He unpocketed his lighter and crouched to light the fuse.

The clerk was saying no, no, no, but Catface already had the three-pronged shocker lit. As it sparked, Catface went scrambling away. A tittering jack-be-nimble.

When Catface was backing his car out of the lot, he could see the young man running from behind the counter with a broom. The pandemonium of fire like a miniature volcano. Jumping jacks of copper-green flame.

Catface, hurtling 120 miles per hour, had already put a mile between the car and the warehouse when a station wagon about three hundred yards away came toward him. Then the explosion came. He felt the force of the detonation buffet the car. He felt the heat radiating through the glass of his back windshield.

The kid must have just then thought all the mayhem over, the final flames extinguished to embers, when a drifting cinder kissed the butane gas and blammo, the inferno, the white hot instant of his death.

Now the column of fever-hued flame boiled and rose, a cyclone of psychedelic pumpkin orange and wild electric green.

The man driving the station wagon stomped the brakes, burning skid marks.

Catface glimpsed the family in passing. Their faces were shocked. Their mouths were screaming holes. There was a blond-bearded, sandy-haired father with his bottle-blond wife and three sunburned kids, all blond too. And there was a Labrador barking hysterical barks.

All of this Catface registered in a hot wild moment and then laughing he sped onward toward Emerald Island.

A FLOCK OF FLAMINGOS

CROWE FLIPPED THROUGH THE CHANNELS. A *Three's Company* rerun, the actor Richard Kline. A local access talk show, beamed from down in the Keys, called *Reef Talk*. A nature documentary, a flock of flamingos flying over a sunset-dappled bay.

Then Crowe flipped upon the rerun of the eleven o'clock news and sat up. They were showing the Big Gorilla Fireworks emporium engulfed in flame. It was a towering inferno, a boiling wicked column of fire. The camera shot was from at least a mile's distance.

Crowe thought of the kid Barry. "Oh Christ," he said. He ran his hand through his beard.

They were interviewing a deputy now. He couldn't look more haggard and harried. He looked as stymied as a second grader in algebra class.

Then neither could the next interviewee. Barry the fireworks kid, a little older now, a little more crinkled around the eyes, but alive.

Crowe felt a rush of relief for the kid. Kid, shit. A man now.

Watching the raging conflagration, Crowe said, "Look at that, holy moly."

THE BUCKET BRIGADE

WHEN SHERIFF SCHAFFER GOT THE CALL about the explosion he was coked out of his mind. "Yes, sir, oh sweet Jesus," he said, voice clogged with postnasal drip, "I got it." He hung up the phone. Cussed. Sniffed. Pinched the last scintilla of cocaine from his septum and shoved on his county sheriff hat.

When he stepped outside into the heat and saw the mushroom cloud of smoke billowing strong and unabated some fifteen miles away, he said in his salt-cured cracker voice, "Oh that dumb motherfuckin' kid finally blown himself up. Of all days."

The kid had always been a bit on the dim side. The bent spoon in the drawer, as his mother used to say.

And now.

Five miles away, he could see the fire tinting the sky. He passed people in Emerald City pulled over on the side of the road, standing on the shoulder, gawking at the spectacle. They tendered anemic waves. Grim-faced, he waved in return, the rack light strobing, his siren shrieking.

The sky was murky with falling ash. He flicked on his high beams.

About a mile from the fire, he parked on the shoulder and got out. A young officer, butter-haired, big-eared, was already on the scene. Officer Petrowski.

"Is this the craziest thing you ever saw?" he asked. Schaffer heard Polk County in Petrowski's voice. They wouldn't have him there, evidently, so they got rid of him in this outpost. This unincorporated part of Florida, a place of nebulous jurisdiction and jury-rigged justice.

Schaffer pinched the brim of his felt hat and doffed it but didn't answer the young officer. He put on his sunglasses to keep the sting of smoke out of his eyes. The road tar was gummy under his tooled-leather roper boots.

The flames by now were reduced to tufts but every now and then there was a new eruption in the conflagration. A supernova of fire. New black smoke boiled up demonically into the sky.

"Are you okay, Sheriff?"

Schaffer was damp-haired and harried and his porcine face was a choked livid red. He appeared a man on the verge of both lethal heart attack and heatstroke. "What? Why? Why're you askin'?"

"It looks like?"

"Should I get a lawn chair?"

"Looks like you're fixin' to laugh."

Fixin', definitely Polk County or thereabouts.

Schaffer shook his head. He felt a rush of blood to his face. By god, had he been smiling? He was conscious suddenly of his face and yes, he felt his muscles grinning. The sight of the fire, it was massive and gorgeous, it was true. You're high, Schaffer thought. Get the fuck out of here.

Schaffer blurted, "Well, son, look at what we got here."

"It's a situation, all right."

"God, look at those dummies in the helicopter."

"Sir?" The earnest bumpkin Petrowski disbelieved his ears.

Schaffer had said it aloud without intending. He palmed the cold sweat off his forehead. This shit they had in Miami, mind-blowing. And none of it he'd ever bought. He stopped cars with young adults driving, under any flimsy pretext, and if they had drugs in the car, which was almost always the case, he confiscated them. And if it was a woman by herself, he'd give her a choice. "Either you suck my dick, or you're going to jail for a long time."

Their looks would be horrified, disbelieving.

If you acted authoritative enough, Schaffer had discovered over the years, there was no limit to what some people would do or believe.

Schaffer would tell them, "Not only are you gonna suck my dick, I'm going to take a Polaroid. For my collection, see. And if you ever tell anybody about it"—here he would inspect the name and the address on the license—"I'll mail the picture to your grandma on Valentine's Day. How about that?"

So far Schaffer had collected forty-seven Polaroids, forty-seven different women, not an outstanding figure, given all the years he'd been on the job.

The helicopter hovered closer to the burning building. More would soon be on the way. They would want interviews with the firemen and they'd want interviews with Schaffer. About a mile away, where the air was so hot it quaked and shimmied, a squadron of county firemen were spraying borate. Their figures were wobbly in the mirage heat. Little more than a bucket brigade. Several men in turnout coats were a mile closer to the fire than Schaffer and Petrowski. They wore pack pumps and were spraying.

With the same authority Schaffer showed those young women over the years, Schaffer told the officer, "Listen, I want you to talk to those news people."

The officer seemed part surprised, part excited. "What you want me to say?"

"Shit, just say big fire." His heart pounded harder with each moment. He was not prepared for this. Not today. And he did not trust himself to appear before a camera. He was likely to come across as a whackjob.

Schaffer said, "I have seen many a damn strange thing in my time, son, and though this is one of the fuckin' strangest, it is also something I was expecting."

The young officer waited.

"That kid? Courting disaster for years. He left a Pop-Tart in the toaster too long. Lit a doobie. Who knows. But there's nothing to say that you can't tell them." Schaffer said this with great authority.

The young officer mentioned the string of crimes in recent months up the southwestern coast.

"And the guy decided to burn down the building just for the hell of it?"

Petrowski said nothing.

Schaffer clapped him on the shoulder as if he'd won a prize. "You take care of the interviews, how about that, kid? Have the girl at the station call your mother and get out the VCR. You gonna make her real, real proud."

"Really, sir?"

"Hey, fixin' to be her pride and joy."

"Thank you, sir, thank you, really, I won't let you down."

"Hey, diamond in the rough. You're gonna be a real good sheriff one day, son. Real good sheriff."

ROOM SERVICE

HE BROKE INTO THE ROOM AT the small motel and in the room Catface waited until night, the shift change. Then he called the reception desk and the man Reed Crowe answered. Catface, in his cordial and measured voice, said, "Problem with the water closet."

Reed Crowe was standing behind the check-in desk of the Emerald Island Inn when the call came from room 292. There was no one checked in to the ledger, unless one of the night clerks, one of Eddie's cousins, made a mistake, which was unlikely. They were good workers.

"You said you're in room 292?" asked Crowe.

There was a brief silence. A sound almost like a swallowed hiccup. Or a stifled laugh. "Yes," he said, whisper-voiced. "I need toilet paper."

Again, that strange choking sound, the noise of the man's palm over the receiver.

Then he hung up the phone.

Crowe not knowing what to expect locked up the reception office and went walking to room 292 with a few rolls of toilet paper under his arm.

Crowe knocked on the door and the man said come in.

The door opened and when Crowe saw Catface sitting in his suit upon the end of the bed his face drained bloodless. Algor mortis. Then, holding the toilet paper still, he angled to turn, ready to dash.

All flight, no fight.

But Catface stood, slapped his thighs as someone would if he was awaiting a belated friend who finally arrived. "Come in. Sit. Let's talk."

Crowe began to blurt.

Catface cut his finger across his throat and rattled his tongue on the roof of his mouth and made a hissing rattle.

"Close the door," he said.

He shut the door on the dark buggy swelter, the Florida night.

"Sit, conyo."

Crowe began to cross the room with the toilet paper.

"Put the shit down at the door," said Catface. "Stupido."

Crowe placed down the toilet paper and went to the twin bed farthest from the door. Dejectedly, he sat. His stroked his beard with a shaking hand.

"You think I left you there," Crowe said.

"You did. I know. Not think. Know."

"I didn't know."

"Oh, you did."

The men regarded each other for a moment, Crowe's eyes unable to settle for more than a moment on Catface's face.

He was at an abject loss.

"You're sure of something that ain't true."

"I said to myself, He'll forget me. But he won't forget my face. You saw me. You saw me. I was burning alive."

"I did not."

"I was alive in that swamp for days. I came out. I survived."

"I'm glad."

Catface showed his teeth in a clean even smile. He put a tooth-pick in his mouth. "No, you're not. You are the very opposite of glad."

Crowe said nothing.

"Do you know how I survived? I will tell you. I thought, it might be thirty years from now. It might be his granddaughter's wedding. A Fourth of July barbecue. A beach vacation. Wherever."

"Mister," Crowe began.

"I said to myself, I will get this man. I will find him and I will wait until he has the most to lose."

"I thought you were dead."

"Shut up." He went on, "I just pictured the day. That's how I survived. Pictured the day of torturing you."

"Goddamn it. This is crazy. You were already dead."

"You might believe that. Maybe it's been so long you believe that. So long you've deceived yourself. Because the opposite?"

"You want money?"

At this Catface laughed.

Then his face changed. He placed the forefinger of his free hand to his lips, circumspect, as if just remembering something he'd al-most forgotten. "Oh," he said. "Yes." He opened the top drawer of the bed stand. With both hands Catface presented the small box gift wrapped in silvery foil to Reed Crowe.

Crowe didn't move.

"A gift for you. For goo luck."

Crowe shook his head.

Catface placed the gift down on the nightstand. He watched Crowe for a moment. "Rude," he said. He *tsked*.

Crowe kept his eyes on the floor.

"Open it," Catface said. "Or I'll slice your throat. Believe it."

Crowe moved his eyes, but not his head. "What is it?"

"Open. Now."

Crowe reached slowly for the box, like a man about to defuse a bomb. He placed the box on his lap. He ripped the wrapping, lifted the lid. He gaped at what was inside. Something resembling a desiccated gray toadstool.

The odor, a foul sardine.

Crowe knew what it was. And for a moment he was strangely relieved. Because he'd expected worse. Beyond the powers of his imagination.

Crowe moved to set the box down on the nightstand. Catface snicked out his switchblade. Crowe froze.

Catface motioned with the blade. Crowe flinched. "Nothing stupid."

Crowe put the box down and returned his hands to his lap.

Catface said, "Guess what." Then he gaped his jaw as far as it would go. A grotesque pantomime of childish glee. He kept his face this way, leaning closer.

Crowe could smell beneath the catfaced man's cloying floral cologne, the sharp chemical stink of some mind-altering drug.

Crowe said, "I know what it is."

Catface watched Crowe for a reaction. "You don't like?" His face twisted now in clownish dejection. His version of it, what the scar tissue would allow.

"What do you want me to say?"

"Oh, oh, that's the wrong question. The question should be whose is it. Not what."

Crowe felt suddenly queasy. Eddie's? Why Eddie's? Yahchilane's? No sense.

"Wayne," Catface said. "Your friend."

Crowe retched. His gorge rose and it flew out before he could stop it. And before Catface could dodge the spate it spackled one of his loafers. His face twisted in fury. This time there was no clownishness.

He slashed out and sliced Crowe's left arm deep at the shoulder.

Crowe was vomiting and shrieking at once. He clutched at the gash.

Still pointing his blade Catface looked down at his shoe, all the while keeping one eye fixed on Crowe. His trouser cuff, soiled. Keeping his eyes on Crowe he jerked his leg, shaking off vomit.

Catface sat again. And his expression changed again, with switchblade swiftness. Clownish glee once more leapt to his face. "So you like it? Goo!"

Crowe sat there with his head hung like his neck was deboned. "So he's not dead," Crowe said. His voice was dry and tremulous, barely audible.

Catface's face changed quickly. Like a curtain dropped. The possibility had not occurred to him. Then his expression altered again, once more composed, a kind of bemused malicious serenity. "Wouldn't that be something. But no. He is dead."

Crowe said nothing.

Catface ticked his head back, a small incredulous rearing. His eyes narrowed. "Would you prefer him alive?"

"He's not dead."

"He's dead."

Crowe was quiet.

An angry spark leapt to Catface's eyes. "He es dead, cock. Truss me."

Crowe thought such a thing would make one of those headlines. Shit, too gruesome not to make the news. FLORIDA MAN GETS HIS DICK SLICED OFF IN PENSACOLA. Crowe didn't want to know and he didn't want to guess.

Catface's voice was harder now. He said, "Dead. And it was agony. Bloodbath. Not goo."

Catface watched Crowe for a moment.

Their breathing in the musty air-conditioned room. The crickets and frogs outside like shrieking detuned violins.

Finally Catface said, "You do not care."

"No."

"Disappointed I must admit."

Silence.

"I can do seventy-five grand," Crowe said. "Eighty maybe. It would take a few days."

"That's not even in the same universe of what you'd need."

"How much?"

"No earthly sum. It es no longer about money."

With this Catface stood. Crowe pulled away. Catface took out a wad of bills half as thick as a brick from his trouser pocket. He threw the money on the floor. With Crowe watching a few feet away, Catface unzipped his fly and took a minute-long piss on the cash.

When he was empty, Catface zipped up his fly, sat back on the edge of the bed. He looked at the floor. "Housekeeping?"

"Mister," Crowe said, weak-voiced.

Catface said, "I thought, He'll forget our paths ever crossed. He'll spend all that money and smoke all that grass and have a nice life and you did. Goo for you. It es over now. How I pictured this. The day I'd tap you on the back. The look on your face. It kept me alive in the swamp. The hospital."

Now Catface fell silent. He studied Crowe. The toothpick roiled ruminatively between his lips.

Meanwhile, Crowe kept glancing at the man with little side movements, infinitesimal, of his eyes.

He took the toothpick from his mouth and placed it in the glass ashtray on the nightstand. He stood and rummaged in the coat pocket. Almost debonair, this Catface, in his café-au-lait summer suit of Havana silk. A latter-day Bogart.

But the face. The face.

The pissed-on money on the carpet.

Catface withdrew his Mutiny Hotel lighter and crack pipe, lit a rock, inhaled.

He was not through exhaling his second lungful when Crowe sprang up from the bed and picked up the old-fashioned rotary phone one-handed and hurled it at his face. The cord snapped and the glass pipe shattered and Catface let out a sound that was part yell, part laugh.

Crowe sprang wildly at the door and opened it and went running as Catface cackled behind him.

"Goo," he said. "Goo. Run! Let's have some fun, conyo!"

WERE IT A DIFFERENT SEASON

IF THE SEASON WAS DIFFERENT THE old Conchs in the nearby beach houses might have spotted Catface from afar. Drawn by the headlights to their windows, they would have beheld a strange sight. A brand-new peach-colored Cadillac. Kind of a loud car around here.

Curious.

And pulled alongside the desolate beach road.

Emerald Island was a place of jalopies and trucks and vans and RVs.

Not brand-new peach-colored Cadillacs that looked just rolled off the lot.

This was a car of the sort you'd see around Miami.

No matter. There was no one around to witness.

The door of the Cadillac eased open without a sound. A slight man wearing an oatmeal-colored suit emerged. He clicked neatly in his burnt orange alligator shoes to the trunk. He popped it and took out what looked like a length of rope with a small anchor or grappling hook on each end.

No, a chain, a chain of spikes.

Stringer spikes.

The man in the suit pulled the stringer spikes across the tarmac. They raked like claws. Little blue-orange sparks spat up from the macadam. The heavens were massive above him, the sky a billion-stars strong.

Catface secured one anchor of the stringer spikes on one side of the road and then the other. Then he stood from his crouch and he smacked the sand off his hands fastidiously.

He got back into the champagne Cadillac and drove onward to set the next trap with like impunity.

A BLAST FROM THE PAST

JUST AS CATFACE KNEW HE WOULD, Crowe fled home. He fled home when he should have gotten into his hatchback car—the idiot, the conyo—and crossed the bridge and never looked back.

Instead, right into the trap. The game.

On the island side of the bridge Catface hotwired a skiff from the harbor. He motored the boat under the bridge, where high in the vaulted underbelly of the viaduct seagulls and pigeons settled in their night roosts. Wickery nests made of dried seaweed and marsh grass and soda straws.

The air was fuggy with the reek of guano and dirty wet feathers. The brackish smell of low tide.

In the sweep of his flashlight the water glowed murky emerald green. Twenty-odd yards underwater Catface could see three huge bull sharks patrolling among the pylons like submarines. Wondering what manner of life he was. Deeming him some species inedible and not worth their while.

Catface, Maglite clenched between his teeth, set an explosive at the foot of the pile. He fixed it to the barnacled post with ballistic clay. A makeshift bomb, fashioned from nitroglycerine and mercury fulminate and ammonium nitrate. The compound encased in a PVC pipe crucible and outfitted with a firing exciter and timed fuse.

Amazing what a gram of cocaine could get you in Miami. At the Mutiny Hotel especially. Some ex-con named Arana, "Oh, I could do that for you easy."

Now Catface boated to the other stanchion, set up a second explosive.

Hundreds of bird eyes, obsidian seeds, peered down as he worked.

Every now and then a feather drifted down in a somnolent spiral.

After he had the explosives placed he motored to the boat launch. At the dock he tied the motorboat to a cleat. Then he stood on the end of the pier with the remote detonator in hand. He reached into the front pocket of his silk shirt and he took out a toothpick and put it in his mouth. Mosquitoes and gnats swarmed at his face. He waved them off.

Catface pressed the detonator button.

Silence. The babble of waves. The hum of insects.

Then one explosive went off like a thunderclap. The sound echoed hugely over the bay.

Then another report blasted before the first was finished echoing.

Hundreds of birds flew panicked through the night, their cries querulous over the rumbling of the bridge.

A large chunk of concrete dropped. Another. Then another, one as big as a washing machine. It walloped the water massively, threw fish into the air. The silver of their scales caught the moonlight and firelight.

Decking collapsed. Girders toppled and splashed. Part of the parapet crumbled.

Catface stepped back before his shoes were soaked by the leaping waves.

The whole west side of the bridge started collapsing. Like a great dying beast losing its footing and sloughing on its haunches to rest.

Catface watched the avalanche. The rolling of rocks and rubble into the water.

Across the water was Emerald City, its warren of beach cottages and bungalows, the odd mission-style stucco manse with a cigar boat in the boatlift. The pier lights twinkling along the shore.

Maybe some of them had caught a glimpse of the explosion through their windows as it happened. Thought it the end of the world.

Catface imagined their vexed faces peering out at the blood-colored night. Faces washed orange by the light of the distant fire.

He laughed darkly.

Just the beginning.

Reed Crowe felt the island tremble beneath his feet.

Crowe was outside throwing another box of mementos and keep-sakes in the trunk of his car when he heard the concussion like a falling mortar.

Where the westward span of Emerald Island bridge met the island a huge column of smoke rose, lit within by a gyre of cobalt and copper-green flame.

Crowe went back into the house to the hallway closet. Rummaged among the shelves and the mementos, thinking, What the fuck are you doing. Go. Leave.

He had the wine crate full of mementos in his arms and was headed out when he saw one of the beach cats shoot through the front door pet pass.

A tortoiseshell.

She came up to him with her tail puffed and lowered. She stood gopher-like on her haunches and growled while peering through the back-facing windows of the house. Her mouth was ajar, tasting threat in the air.

Past his own reflection, past the lamplit room mirrored in the glass, he saw the wake of the vessel, a phantom thread stitching quickly across the water. A Jet Ski, he realized, from the small sound of motor. About a mile out someone was riding a Jet Ski straight east. Straight to shore, straight toward the beach house.

Straight toward him.

And he kept waiting for the Jet Ski to curve away, hook in another direction, but it was coming still and now a half mile out.

Crowe took the binoculars from next to the seashell lamp. He went to the sliding glass doors. He trained the binoculars. Through the glass he saw a man riding in hunch-shouldered silhouette.

Then he was gone.

Then Crowe saw him again. The madhouse grin slashed across the disfigured face.

The Jet Ski's white rooster tail kept coming, a fan of fast foam across the dark. Then the Jet Ski slowed. It slowed to a stop. The light went dark.

Crowe went outside.

Crowe's hands shook holding the binoculars and he swung the glass wildly left to right across the horizon.

Where the fuck was he?

What was he doing?

Where did he go?

Then the light snapped back on.

Crowe focused.

The Jet Ski grew closer. A searing meteorite flying shorebound across ocean. Yes, like a meteorite, but also like a skipping stone. A skipping meteorite coming closer and closer.

Crowe was sure the man would stop, at least slow. He did not. Full speed he reared ashore, cutting across the sand. Crowe glimpsed the scar-faced man trudging out of the surf. He staggered cackling across the beach.

Now he was about a hundred yards off, walking straight to Crowe's house. Crowe dropped the binoculars into the sand.

He ran inside the house.

He could hear the man calling behind him, but from his distance he only caught scraps. "Donde esta el niño?" he heard.

Then tittering.

Then something that sounded like, "Goo luck!"

THE CAT AND THE MOUSE AND THE LIGHTHOUSE

AS CROWE WENT THROUGH THE BEACH house he could see the man moving in the backyard. By the porch light he saw the catfaced man in the bespoke suit walk up to a chaise lounge and heave it above his head.

He hurled the chair at the sliding glass door. The chair flipped end over end and struck the door and the glass spiderwebbed for what seemed to Crowe an elongated moment before shards broke on the floor.

Catface stepped through the maw, one alligator-skin shoe after the other.

Crowe backed away. "I thought ya'll were dead. I'd never leave a dying man in the Everglades."

"Liar," Catface said. "Not goo."

In a few strides the man crossed the distance between them. He looked at the wine crate in Crowe's arms. The crate with memorabilia. Hanging out was a blanket with lavender elephants on it.

Otter's.

Crowe could see the man's face better now. Scars fanned outward from his mouth like whiskers. And in the hand of his dangling arm was a knife, a blade of exotic make. An assassin's knife.

Crowe turned and bolted for the door and Catface whipped his arm in a jackknife motion and the blade went whistling through the air. Crowe felt the hot small flare of pain in his leg.

He hobbled away.

Crowe got into the hatchback and he started it and just as the suited man with the deformed face came running out the front door, Crowe slammed his foot on the gas. For an instant the car went nowhere, spinning in place, bald tires spitting out gouts of limestone and powdered shell.

Then the hatchback shot backward.

Driving one-handed Crowe executed a wild five-point turn, tires screeching. Once on the main beach road he was speeding away, pulling the knife out of his leg. He let loose a sickly animal groan and wail. He tossed the knife on the passenger-side floor.

Crowe wasn't half a mile from the beach house and he was trying to staunch the gush of blood with his hand when there was a double detonation.

One explosion, then another a split second later.

Like two gunshots. That startling.

The hatchback tires, ripped to tatters by the stringer spikes.

The steering wheel leapt out of Crowe's hands like something alive. He tried to wrangle the wheel, couldn't. The car went careening and swerving. The rims scraped concrete, raising orange and blue sparks. Then the hatchback went off the road and beached itself into the sand.

Crowe got out of the car. He glanced over his shoulder. Still the catfaced man was approaching his own car, a Cadillac. Now he was getting into his car, climbing in slowly, almost leisurely, behind the wheel.

As if he had all the time in the world.

As if he were fucking with Reed Crowe.

Mocking him.

Crowe went hobbling down the limestone road toward the island lighthouse. He would not make it to the wharf, not in his state. Not in time to evade the scar-faced man.

The bridge was blasted.

Even if it wasn't, he could never cross what remained of it on foot. If enough of the bridge remained to cross.

Crowe limped onward.

Now halfway to the lighthouse.

Above him the heavens were enormous. Ursa Minor. The North Star. The Loon.

A meteorite slashed across the sky. The island night was so quiet Crowe could hear it sizzling as it split the atmosphere. Then the only sounds he heard were his own breathing, quick and raspy. The soft crashing surf beyond.

By the time Crowe reached the Emerald Island lighthouse he saw the headlights of the Cadillac approaching.

He went pounding up the steps, clutching the rail, gasping for air. He took the stairs two at a time. A trail of blood followed him, slicked the concrete. Crowe hardly felt the pain in his leg. Every nerve in him shrieked.

The keep's three portal windows overlooked the vast dunes.

Crowe moved from one to the other, squatting, clutching his gun, arms quaking.

Where Crowe's car was mired, the catfaced man now steered his car around the stringer spikes. But then the Cadillac got stuck in the sand on the other side of the road.

The engine sung higher, became a whine. Then the racket ceased.

Catface got out of the car cursing. Crowe could hear his voice coming from a distance. "Not goo," he shouted.

He started toward the lighthouse. He made like he was striding straight toward it. Then he dashed out of the road toward the water. Then he was gone, vanished amid the dunes.

Crowe went crouching from window to window with a Wesson .25 aimed into the dark. Its small parts rattled he was shaking so hard.

Still no sign.

For a wild instant Crowe considered sounding the lighthouse foghorn. Beaming the lighthouse light, sending out a signal. As if there were a superhero or a god to save him.

An old Conch.

Crowe knew they'd never make it in time. If they were stupid and intrepid enough to be so inclined.

The permanent visitors in the derelict Emerald Island Inn: shit.

And no tourists, this kind of weather.

Still he waited.

Waited.

A fucking exploded bridge, for crying out loud.

Crowe heard sirens, but they might as well have been on Mars. They came from a vast distance, from the wooded reaches of the mainland, and once they reached the bay, then what?

The ocean wind carried a cold iron tang. Crowe's cheeks stung. His leg ached. His back and his chest. The wind stung his eyes, a knifing silvery pain.

Then he saw the man appear again out of the dark. About a hundred yards away he dashed between the dunes, his light brown suit visible in the starlight.

Crowe fired the gun. The kick jolted him sideways. The tracer ripped a scar of light across the night.

Catface cackled, a fleet figure darting among dunes that stood as tall as slagheaps. Escarpments three, four hundred years old.

Closer, farther.

Ahead, behind.

The taunting voice and taunting laughter sounded as though it were coming from all points of the compass.

Disoriented and near delirious Crowe went from portal to portal.

He couldn't catch his breath.

He couldn't calm his heart. Its beating was crazed.

A hot coal of pain throbbed in his leg.

Behind this dune, behind that dune Catface went. As soon as Crowe thought he had a bead on the man, he was gone.

Jack be nimble, Jack be quick.

Now Catface was close enough that Crowe could see his grin.

Crowe fired again. Missed. A spit of sand went flying.

He heard the man's cracked-out woo-hoo laughter. "Not goo," the catfaced man said.

Then the man disappeared. A long minute ticked past. Another.

Nothing.

Around the lighthouse was a skirt of hard-packed sand. Now Catface was dashing across it toward the door.

Crowe squeezed off another shot. The bullet struck sand. A thin echo rolled across the beach.

"Uh-oh," the man, now out of sight, mocked. "One left. One bullet."

Crowe pounded down the spiral stairs. He stopped cold when he saw Catface walk through the lighthouse door. He looked up at Crowe, regarding him with a jagged grin in his vivisection of a face. "Goo evening!" he said.

He took his first step up the stairs.

Crowe, aiming the gun, went down the staircase.

Catface, wielding his dagger, went up.

When only a landing separated them, several stairs, Crowe fired at the man's head.

Missed.

The bullet bit out a divot in the wall. Pulverized plaster hazed the air.

Crowe kept coming down the stairs and when he was within spitting distance he threw the gun at the man's head. The barrel struck his forehead, bounced off, clattered on the permastone. Blood welled in the gouge, filled the assassin's eyes. The man's neat widow's-peak hair, raked vampirishly back, went flying, brilliantined licks of it falling into his gory face.

Crowe ran full force into him. The catfaced man, still shrieking, still clutching his head, slashed at him blindly with his free hand, slicing Crowe's arm with his blade.

Crowe ran on, away from the lighthouse, toward the wharf.

Every nerve in his body shrieked with pain, but it momentarily vanished with the exhilaration of escape as he headed for the wharf.

He ran into the boathouse. A big corrugated metal shed with a high peaked tin roof where twenty-five or thirty vessels bobbed in their slips. He went down the dock scanning the boats.

Most wore their names big on their butts. *Out Fishing, Yuck Foo, Old Feller.* Sloops and pontoons and catamarans. Most familiar to Crowe. At the far end of the wharf he spotted a small sherbet-lime motorboat. Red Hamilton's Chris-Craft. He ran to it. He knew Red Hamilton kept his keys in the center console because no one would ever want to steal the thing, was their joke.

Crowe was in the boat fumbling the mooring knot from the cleat when the headlights of the Cadillac fanned into the boathouse. The car came to a quick rocking halt. The door yawned open and a figure came running out with the car engine still going and the beams still spearing into the boathouse.

Crowe was still fumbling with the knot when he saw Catface striding down the dock.

Crowe ducked and stayed hunched.

Catface's eyes found Crowe. Their whites seared in the darkness. Even from so many paces away they glowed starkly white. They were latched onto Crowe with demonic intensity.

Catface stalked forward. "I see you. Comin' right at you."

The tin roof was so corroded there were holes in places. A spear of moonlight shot through one of them and lit the man's maimed face.

Crowe jerked the cord and the outboard motor coughed and spluttered. The Chris-Craft lurched away from the dock. Catface picked up his pace and lifted his arm to throw a knife. Crowe dodged sideways. He heard the lethal whistle of the blade passing through air.

Then the knife hit the water and flashed like a shiny mackerel showing its side before plunging down and disappearing.

Crowe watched Catface standing at the end of the dock ready to leap, his body poised as he gauged the distance.

No. Too far.

The boathouse fell back out of sight as Crowe motored out where the channel opened into the bay. The hot salt-smelling air battered his face as he sped. Gnats and beetles and mosquitoes pinged his skin.

A mile into the bay Crowe cut the motor and waited. And waited. Desolate this time of night. Oil riggers like spaceships far out in the Gulf. Freighters.

Satellites blinking and crossing the big starry Florida sky.

Crowe strained to hear any other boat and finally he heard the small whining engine coming from a distance. A Jet Ski.

Catface's shrieking laughter cut through the night. It came at him sourceless, echoing through the black veldt of the swamp.

Then Catface materialized from the night like a nightmare, his face crazed in the half-light. A dread comic book hobgoblin.

The Jet Ski was headed straight at the boat but about ten yards away it hit a sandbar and flew airborne. As the Jet Ski went soaring over the boat, Crowe could hear Catface's bellow above the motor.

The Jet Ski walloped back into the water like a meteor.

The catfaced man looped the Jet Ski around. He crouched and bent into the turn, ripping up a white spume. The Jet Ski skipped like a stone over the waves. It ramped up a bigger wave and then Catface slalomed and slewed.

The Jet Ski moved again toward Crowe.

Crowe had one hand on the tiller and the other in the stowage box. Crowe groped an emergency flare, jerked the string with his teeth, aimed, fired it at the Jet Ski. The tight bright ball of flame soared over the water. The fireball struck the catfaced man's arm. His sleeve caught fire. The catfaced man slapped at the flame and with both hands off the handles the Jet Ski wobbled and slewed and canted sideways.

Then the catfaced man was in the water bellowing and flailing as Reed Crowe motored away.

Finally Crowe aimed the boat toward Krait Isle. The tennis-court-sized barrier island teeming with snakes. Serpents with poison so virulent it could turn a man immobile in five minutes. Stop his heart and kill him in twenty.

On the lee side of Krait Isle Crowe cut the motor and got the flashlight out of the stowage box and beamed it through the mangroves.

So the catfaced man would see.

And he did.

Crowe could see the approaching gleam of the Jet Ski headlight. When it was about fifty yards away Crowe flung the flashlight into the thick black trees. It flipped and arced high over the catclaw branches. A branch snagged it before it hit the ground and the beam trembled and swung as if in a panicked man's clutch.

An egret winged huge into the night.

The flashlight trembled and wobbled.

"I see you," Catface said. "Stupid fuck!"

Crowe crouched in the dark, waiting.

The night was teeming with bug calls and frog calls.

On the other shore Crowe could hear Catface grounding the Jet Ski. He could make out the beam of his flashlight through the twisted mangroves. Crowe heard his wading through the water. His cursing. The snapping of twigs and the rustling of brush in the deeper reaches of the island.

Then there was a howl of agony.

Another scream as a third or fourth snake struck.

By now, Crowe knew, the venom was shuttling through the cat-faced man. Flooding his heart.

Finally the bobbling flashlight fell and came to rest. And then finally, too, the shouting and cursing on the island went silent.

Crowe hunkered in darkness on the skiff.

He waited for any sign that Catface was escaping the hammock.

The wash of waves rocked him. The mosquitoes and gnats buzzed bloodthirsty at his ears.

He watched the darkness of the hammocks, ink blots on the bigger darkness of the Everglades night.

No other boats out but pinpoint glimmers miles out past the dead coral reef, so far away they too looked like stars.

Minutes passed before Crowe thought he heard the voice of a motor. An angry wasp sound growing louder from some direction and distance Crowe couldn't determine.

No. Impossible.

Then came the human cackle, sickeningly familiar, over the din of the engine.

His ears had to be playing tricks.

It was panic. Exhaustion.

Then Crowe saw the white boiling wake like a white line in the water arrowed straight at him. The line growing longer, thirty feet away, now twenty.

Catface on his Jet Ski materialized specter-like out of the dark. He switched on his headlamp. The sudden gamma ray blinded Crowe as the Jet Ski came straight at him.

Catface overshot. Looped around in a wild gyre, cackling, the Jet Ski spinning like a haywire fairground ride.

He kept looping, spinning, churning up a wake.

Crowe sped shorebound. The skiff skipped over the pummeling waves.

Next time Crowe glanced behind his shoulder he saw Catface aimed again his way. Gaining. Reaching for something in his pant leg. Something strapped to his ankle.

The man was close enough now that Crowe could discern the man's face. The head, filled with poison, swollen grotesquely like a melon.

A kind of rabid foam dripped from Catface's lips.

Five feet away now and Catface had the blade in his hand. He coughed so hard he tightened his grip on the knife. He coughed again, so hard his body was wracked. The dagger dropped. Catface cursed.

Coughed, spat up blood, whipped his head sideways, hawked blood into the water.

He reached for his other ankle. The foam from his mouth started frothing out pink. Then pinker. Then red.

Now the stuff coming out of his mouth looked like melted red and purple candle wax mixed together.

He was gurgling, retching, screaming, reaching for the knife.

His body jerked with seizure and he pitched forward, draped over the steering bars.

The engine choke switched on and the Jet Ski fuel line was cut.

The Jet Ski sputtered and coasted to a stop, canting sideways. Catface slumped slack and lifeless as a feed-sack along with it.

Then the scar-faced man toppled into the water. The floating body receded, receded, vanished, as Crowe shot through the immensity of the Everglades.

His heart was galloping wildly.

He saw shooting stars. Fireflies. But no, they were in his head, floating little bright dots.

Oh, how had he gotten here?

How had he fucked up so much?

His wife, his girl.

Wayne.

Mariposa.

He thought of that night many years ago, the night the plane fell down from the sky, the men burning alive in the swamp. He remembered the smell of burning flesh. Remembered the eye of the man fixing on him, hexing him, through the dark.

So much strife, so much agony and horror since then.

The mother of all plants, one thing begetting another.

One error begetting the next. One fuckup.

If you believed in such things.

Reed Crowe never did, but on occasions such as these you had to wonder. You had to wonder because now, despite himself, he was praying. Praying not because he believed. He was praying because there was nothing else he could do.

And he didn't want to die. He wanted to live. Fiercely he wanted to live even as the night now seemed to grow darker.

WILD BLACK YONDER

(1986-1999)

MILD TO MEDIUM

HE WOKE UP TO INCANDESCENT LIGHTS glaring down on him. For a moment he wondered if he was on the verge of dying. One final big bang of blinding white light before he was flung into the wild black yonder.

But then a nurse's face entered his frame of vision. A woman of about sixty-five with curly gray hair and a dainty-featured cherub face. A beatific country aunt in a Norman Rockwell Christmas painting.

He tried to move and couldn't. Tubes were in his nostrils and mouth and arms. His breath scraped painfully in his throat.

"You've had a stroke, Mr. Crowe," said the nurse. "You're going to be okay. Everything will be fine. Don't panic. Oh, honey, let me get a doctor."

He tried to talk. Gobbledygook came out. As if someone shot his jaw through with Novocain.

He willed his arms to move. His legs. Like trying to move a cinderblock with his thoughts.

He whimpered, moaned.

He heard the nurse trotting away down the hall, her soft-soled shoes squeaking on linoleum.

In the empty room humming with machines and monitors Reed Crowe allowed himself to cry.

His tears felt strange.

Then he realized why. They'd shaved his beard. For the first time in decades his face was bare.

———

A stroke, according to Dr. Abramowitz. Mild to medium.

Was it permanent? Would he ever walk again? Talk? Would he be in a wheelchair? Reed Crowe's head flooded with such questions.

Would his dick ever work again?

How about the right side of his body?

So many questions. He was incapable of asking one.

Yahchilane had to ask questions on his behalf. For instance, how long his recovery would last.

They were outside the room standing in the hallway. They thought they were out of earshot, but Crowe could hear them.

The doctor told Yahchilane, "I've seen people fully recover in two months." He was an old man with a New Jersey accent. "It depends on the person. And it depends on how committed they are to rehabilitation. There's no question, it'll be difficult."

There was mention of forty percent chances, seventy percent chances.

Rehabilitation and neuroplasticity.

Recovery times of two months to ten years.

For a while after the bridge was blown away there was talk on the island and on the news of a federal investigation. Some pundits speculated that the demolishing was the work of environmental terrorists.

Yahchilane was called into questioning five times.

Crowe's interrogation would have to wait until his recovery.

It would probably become another one of those bits of local apocrypha. You remember the big storm of that year? Remember the year it snowed on the beach? Remember that year the goddamn Emerald Island bridge blew up?

Some Florida Man lost his shit that year, all right.

OTHER BREAKING NEWS

OF COURSE THERE WERE QUESTIONS FROM state and federal authorities. And even at an outpost such as this, a whole bridge exploding in the middle of nowhere? Well, holy shit. Prime-time news.

Another Florida story to cover.

Another freak show to add to the litany of tragedies and comedies and massacres. And so not five hours passed since the bridge's explosion before a convoy of news trucks migrated en masse from the violent streets of Miami, making its way through terra incognita to Emerald County, Florida.

A horde of locusts. Nineteen eighty-six, the dawn of round-the-clock news. A gold mine, this.

What could it be? Who? Was it a terrorist group? What kind? An environmental terrorist cell?

What could have been the motive? Drugs?

Satanists?

Nihilists? Anarchists?

Donahue, Morton Downey, Jr., Sally Jessy Raphael, all the talk show hosts had a field day.

Had the mayhem of Miami spread that far?

So many questions in the hive mind of the media, and so for an hour or two that late January 1986, when the first news crews arrived, a number of Emerald Island residents experienced their veritable fifteen minutes of fame.

Myrtle the mailwoman was unloading the empty satchels from her Toyota Celica when she heard a car cross the bridge.

"I knew somethin' was off. His face. I'm the postmaster here. Been for a while. You get to know the faces. And this face. I don't want to be mean or anything. I'm not talking homely. But you could tell he'd been in an accident. Bad, bad. But that's not what made him scary. I don't know how to describe it. He just comes speeding off the bridge, and I'm like? Because he gave me this cold weird smile. And maybe I would have forgotten it, but then, what happened. Anybody could have been on that bridge."

This was how she told it.

How she remembered it, a different story. So many details she wasn't able to put into words on the spot like that with the microphone in her face.

She would never forget it coming out of the quaking hot dusk as it evanesced. A sleek Cadillac quivering in the heat, mirages snaking off the road.

As it approached she heard a soukous beat. The syncopated rhythm over the keening insects.

The car was a convertible and the top was down and the music was coming out of the sound system. Horns and the guitar. The same Cuban rhythm. Not music you usually heard around here.

The late sun glared bronze on the windshield so she couldn't make out the driver's face at first. Then she saw a hand. The driver held it out of the car just as he was about to pass, flashed a peace symbol with two fingers, casually, the arm relaxed and loose. A round-faced golden ring.

Myrtle raised her hand. As the car passed she glimpsed the driver's face. He turned to look at her, the hand still hanging out of the car, flashing a peace symbol.

The face, it looked mangled, the smile warped.

Myrtle convinced herself it was an optical illusion.

Nonetheless dread settled in her stomach like a chunk of ice.

That face.

That day, the day of the bridge explosion, they also showed on cable via local affiliate the Big Gorilla Fireworks emporium engulfed in flame. A towering inferno, a boiling wicked column of fire and volcanic smoke. The whole sky, bruised and bloodshot. The camera shot was from at least two miles' distance, the heat and fire were so great.

They interviewed a deputy, haggard and harried, speculating that maybe faulty wiring was to blame. Ash was caught in his bushy eyebrows. Ash dusted his shoulders like epaulets. Ash was caught in the folds of his hat. "Best not to leap to any wild conclusions."

The newsperson was a young African American woman. Candy

Parker. A purple blazer with overlarge shoulder pads. Big faux-pearl earrings. "Wouldn't you agree, though, sir, that this is pretty wild?"

A pandemonium of fire trucks was in the background. Three different passels of men with fire hoses fought the conflagration.

"Well, you know what, ma'am? Best not leap to anything."

She waited.

"So yeah," said the deputy, "that's our policy."

He grinned an enigmatic hayseed grin at the newswoman.

With a small shake of her head she turned the microphone onto the fireworks kid.

"But you say there was a man in a suit? Mr. . . ."

The young man thought hard about this. "Well, I'd rather not say, Miss Parker."

"This is on live television, just so you know."

Barry Boone swallowed, a dry click. His face wrinkled like a baby's, turned pink, like he might cry. His face was very sweaty, despite the brisk day.

On the other hand, the heat from the inferno was that tremendous.

Finally Barry started, "This man, he just, just, just . . ."

"It's okay, young man. It's okay, take your time." Her face changed. She cocked her ear. She held up a finger to the camera.

She listened to a transmission in her headpiece. "Ladies, Gentlemen," she said.

Barry Boone stood there. His fifteen minutes of fame: thirty seconds.

"Ladies and Gentlemen," said Miss Candy Parker, plugging her one free ear against the racket of the distant helicopter, "we have other breaking news."

Eddie Maldonado too was on the television news. Albeit briefly. Fine by him.

Some underpaid intern was holding a boom mike aloft. It hovered above his head and bumped the crown every so often.

To anyone watching at home on television, Eddie Maldonado looked stricken, beyond traumatized. There was a twitch on one side of his mouth. Even his eyeballs were shaking. The anchor told the audience that maybe there was a language barrier. Eddie told her he spoke English. "I just cannot describe," he said.

Finally, after Eddie got knocked in the head four times, the newsman in the Band-Aid colored suit lost it. "Cut, cut, goddamn it, cut. Motherfucker! We'll do it live! On the count of motherfucking five, oh, this is bullshit out in the boondocks, one, two . . ."

"Wild West these days," the newsperson started over. He looked into the camera. Glossy helmet of black hair parted on one side, lemon-colored tie.

"You really don't remember anything about the man's face? Any little detail? Just keeping it real." This was the guy's catchphrase. Reilly "Keeping It Real" O'Connor.

Eddie nodded anemically. Because he was traumatized. Not only because of the cameras, but about the question about the catfaced man.

Never in his life would he tell another soul about Catface.

Which is why he was glad when the newsman held up a ruby-ringed finger. "Ladies and Gentlemen, we have other news to report."

WALL OF VOODOO (CATFACE REDUX)

THERE WAS A STORY EDDIE MALDONADO could have told, but he didn't.

Eddie Maldonado never told the story to a soul as long as he lived.

When Catface pulled the stolen Cadillac into the Mister Donut it was an hour until full dark. One of those long purple and red Florida twilights of late January.

Bats flitted above the spindly sand pines.

From behind the donut counter Eddie saw the car glide into the lot. A glycerin lozenge. The blood fruit light gleamed on the chrome rims and fenders and the polished paint job.

The man who stepped from the car wore tailored linen clothes, a panama hat angled, the brim tilted.

From his vantage Eddie couldn't make out the face. And once he did, he had a shock.

His face was mangled. Deformed. So scarred and roughly patched it looked made of bark.

"Evening," Eddie forced out.

The man gestured a greeting with his chin. "Café con leche?"

Eddie told him back next to the soda fountain.

The man held up a few fingers, gold wristwatch catching the harsh white incandescent light. He walked to the back.

Also in the donut shop were two Florida college kids. They'd heard the Spanish being spoken and looked at the man with the scarred face.

They chuckled low and dark. Joked in whispers.

The tinny music system played Wall of Voodoo. "Mexican Radio."

The man's alligator shoes clocked neatly on the floor.

"Ugly motherfucker," said one of the kids.

Laughter again.

Catface stepped up to them and stayed where he was even after they laughed nervously and looked away.

"What's up?" said one of the kids. This the kid with the diamond stud in his left ear. A camouflage cap.

Catface stayed where he was. His posture unchanged, hands in pockets, his shoulders easy.

"You looking before," Catface said.

"You in front of me," said the kid.

"Before. You said motherfucker. I fucked my mother?"

"Havin' private conversation." This the other kid with the pinched black eyes.

"Ugly motherfucker? Because my face?"

"Fuck off," said the kid with the cap. "Go back to Cuba, Mexico, whatever the fuck shit hole."

"Why you stare?" Catface asked.

"Maybe this is why," said the pinch-eyed kid. He reached into his pocket, drew out a butterfly knife. Flicked it open in an elaborate series of maneuvers.

Catface reached into his pocket and withdrew a knife and sheared off the kid's ear with a street criminal's greased swiftness.

For an instant the kid seemed unaware he was missing part of his head. He clutched at his ear. Glanced up with befuddled pique. He groped for his missing ear, confusion coming to his face when he found his fingers slicked with blood.

The next instant, the college kid regarded Catface's palm. A magician's coin trick, except with the young man's ear. Macabre legerdemain.

The young man grabbed the side of his head and wailed. He lashed out at Catface, tried to grab back his ear. Something in Catface's expression gave the kid pause.

The hard reptilian look of murder.

And then he saw the dagger in Catface's grip.

With a stricken face the kid backed up a few steps.

The kid's friend stood at a distance. Frozen still by this turn of events. Disbelieving.

Blithely Catface withdrew a cream silk handkerchief from his cappuccino summer suit and wrapped the ear. Pocketed it. Strode to the counter as the earless kid kept shrieking.

Eddie stood as far back from the counter as he could.

Catface, "Coffee. Just coffee. Por favor. And wet naps, por favor."

"Wet naps?"

"Si. Blood."

Eddie's face writhed. The small muscles around his eyes and mouth twitched. He gestured with his chin. His hands were held up half-mast, palms toward Catface.

Catface grabbed tissues and wet naps, went to the lavatory. Locked himself in. At the sink he scrubbed the spots of blood off his sleeves, his cuffs, his shirtfront.

He was lighting his butane torch and freebasing from the glass pipe when he heard the young men quarreling outside the door. Consorting among themselves in harsh urgent whispers about what to do. The cops, the hospital. Both were mentioned. Then a gun. A baseball bat.

"Good," Catface said through the door, breathing out crack smoke. "Call the cops. Goo. Go right ahead, conyo."

Silence.

Then, Catface sang from the bathroom, "Miami Dolphins, Miami Dolphins."

Catface could hear the other young man, self-appointed ambassador, step closer to the door. "Mister. We just want his ear, mister. We'll leave. We'll get right out of here, mister."

"You want this ear?" Catface asked through the door.

"Yes, mister."

"All needed was to ask," Catface said. He took the ear from his pocket. Unwrapped it from the bloody handkerchief. Slid the ear, speckled with lint and pubic hair, under the door.

The earless kid bawled anew. "Fucked!"

Catface stepped out of the bathroom. The college kids moved back. At the register Catface paid for the coffee. "Dos, por favor," he said, pointing at the coconut crumble donuts.

Eddie was looking at the man's necklace.

Catface asked him what the matter was.

"Your necklace."

"Tell."

"The face." Eddie pointed at the logo behind him, the sign hanging above the racks of donuts. "I thought it was Mister Donut."

Catface looked at his medallion. Then he looked at the donut shop's logo behind the counter. A baker in one of those old-fashioned baker hats jauntily tipped, the mustache, the wink.

It was true.

Few people, so struck by the spectacle of his face, mentioned Catface's necklace. No one had ever before remarked on the medallion's resemblance to the donut chain's logo. Catface himself had never discerned the resemblance.

"Hermanos," Catface said.

Eddie nodded.

"Ah!" Catface said. Pointed at Eddie. Wagged a scarred finger the color of a hot dog. "It's true. Observant, smart. Goo."

Eddie unfolded a donut box. Took the piece of wax paper to handle the coconut donuts.

Then Catface hopped a cracked-out hop, almost leprechaun like, an idea having just occurred to him. He clapped his hands, smacking them three times quickly in front of him, a giddy sprite.

"Hold on, amigo," he said. "Hold on, hermano."

Catface went outside. He popped his car's trunk and for an instant Catface was eclipsed. Eddie dared not move.

"Do something," wailed the one-eared kid.

Outside, "Miami Dolphins! Miami Dolphins!"

"You wanna die?" Eddie said.

"Call somebody."

Catface outside, "Greatest football team!"

"Marielito," Eddie said. "He'll fuckin' kill you."

Catface's head popped around the side of the trunk, vaudevillian theatricality. He held up a finger. Just a second.

"Jesus Christ," Eddie said. It came out in a shaky whisper.

At last Catface came dashing back into the shop. "Miami Dolphins! Miami Dolphins!" He was holding something that looked like a brick. He fetched to the counter. Smacked the brick-shaped parcel down on the glass.

Eddie was sure it was a test. And he had zero idea how to pass it.

A block of money. One-hundred-dollar bills.

Catface said, "For your problems. Pardon. Buenas noches, mi amigo. Goo luck, donut hermano!"

Then with his donuts and coffee Catface exited, got into his car, and wheeled off with shrilling tires into the night.

The television crews might have gone on about the Emerald Island bridge explosion had circumstances been different. They might have eventually interviewed Crowe were he not recovering from a stroke. Henry Yahchilane were he not visiting a woman friend in Boca Raton. They might have gone on to interview the whole island down to Sno-Ball Larry and Red Hamilton, but there was other news to report.

Tragic news.

It was January 28, almost 11:40 A.M. They saw the news in the sky. Due northeast, a contrail of smoke, a vertical scar of fire in the sky.

It was the space shuttle *Challenger*.

Then, all at once, like migratory birds switching direction on an ill-omened wind, the helicopters and vans lit from Emerald County due east toward Cape Canaveral, away from the Gulf Coast.

VISITING HOURS

THAT WINTER AND SPRING OF 1986, a train of visitors came through Crowe's hospital room. Yahchilane often came around. So did Eddie. Myrtle a few times, Red Hamilton once, Chill Norton once.

The men in particular seemed incapable of spending too much time with Crowe. They were at a loss for what to say. Avoided looking at him for too long. They tried sitting in the corner chair, but would stand again after a minute, pacing the room, probably wondering how much time qualified as a legitimate visit.

"Oh, this is bullshit, Reedy," Chill Norton told him. "You got this. Mild to medium? It's a pussy stroke. You got this. I know you got this."

Reed Crowe told no one about Catface. Not a soul. Twice Sheriff Schaffer came to visit Crowe asking about the exploded bridge, about his stroke the same night in the Everglades, but it seemed to Crowe he wanted the matter put behind him just as much as Crowe.

He had to relearn how to hold a spoon. His grip around the utensils was like a child's. Mutilating his food with his gawky knife, making scraping horrible sounds against the plate, the plate sliding on the table.

One morning Crowe was surprised when Mariposa visited with her mother, Nina. Surprised: He was gobsmacked. But his face, still palsied and lopsided, didn't show it. Immobile as stone.

Nina stood in her dark blouse and skirt at the foot of the bed. She looked over Crowe dispassionately. Keeping her distance, keeping her voice low and toneless, she wished Crowe a speedy recovery. She told him she would pray for him.

But that was the extent of her words. She then stood in the corner.

So the visit had been Mariposa's idea, Crowe realized. Not Nina's.

Or maybe the idea was Eddie's, though Crowe somehow doubted it. Yes, Eddie Maldonado had wed Nina Arango. A shotgun wedding. A sudden turn of events Crowe would never have expected. Mother of all plants, one thing begetting another. God bless the kid, Crowe thought. That time wherein he was smitten with the woman seemed incredibly long ago.

"I'm so sorry," Crowe wanted to say. "Look at you. Look at who you've become."

Yet she still had an air of a tomboy. Blue jogging shorts with white piping, a green polo shirt. Her hair was short and she was wearing a visor with a bill of translucent green celluloid, like a casino dealer's.

Unlike her mother Mariposa came to his bedside.

Crowe's arms were folded across his chest, his hands crisscrossed atop each other.

Mariposa reached for Reed Crowe, put her hand on his.

Nina cleared her throat. Nunnish. Peremptory.

Mariposa paid her no mind. She kept her hand where it was, tightened her grip. "You're gonna be okay, Uncle Reed."

Certain nights dreams harassed him. Nightmares.

In the dream there was a hand reaching out, reaching. Sometimes it was his daughter. Sometimes it was Heidi.

Almost always, though, it was his daughter.

Sometimes there were dreams about the catfaced man coming at him on a Jet Ski. On a giant anhinga. On a giant robotic bat. Out of the darkness.

Crowe would wake doused, as if he'd been swimming. The sweaty sheets tangled and thrown off the bed and to the corner of the room. His arms reaching and flailing, his hands clutching, in the dark.

April Fool's, no less.

Reed Crowe was released April Fool's Day, 1986.

Henry Yahchilane picked up Crowe from the hospital in his root-beer-colored van. He drove across the state, two hours through the Everglades on Alligator Alley, from the Atlantic Coast to the Gulf.

At the Emerald City wharf Yahchilane kept a small aluminum dinghy. It was early evening, two hours of sun left, the clouds like big pink frigates over the bay, when Yahchilane crossed the water to the island. A few tarpon the size of surfboards rolled in the glassy water, their big silver scales glinting.

They docked at Emerald Island wharf. Yahchilane strode up the embankment to the island-side of the bridge. Crowe crutched after him.

They crested the embankment.

"Holy shit," Crowe said when he saw the demolished bridge.

Yahchilane laughed his gruff short laughter.

Crowe asked Yahchilane what was so funny.

"That contractor," Yahchilane said, still laughing. By now his laughter had elongated to an old doggy wheeze. All those years of smoking.

Crowe stood there on his crutches gawking at the wreckage. The balmy bay wind was a bellows to his head after the sarcophagus of the hospital. He imagined a google-eyed Don Knotts as the contractor, the gadzooks! expression. The incredulous tremble of the lips and head.

And for the first time since Catface, since his stroke, since the beginning of this, Crowe laughed—or close to laughed, his stroke-victim version of it.

The matter was decided.

The contractor fucked off from whence he came.

For months Crowe pondered how the catfaced man found him. He suspected Schaffer might have played a part in spreading the word. Or Wayne. Or perhaps hearsay and rumor and backroom talk meandered up the coast, unfurling like the mother of all plants up the land of ten thousand islands, tendriling up the trellis of Florida. He kept vigilant for any sign that someone else was out to get him, but after a time he convinced himself that it was paranoia.

When she first saw Crowe, Heidi Karavas tried to hide her dismay. "Oh, Reed. Reed, what the fuck happened? I didn't know. I had no way of knowing."

"It's okay," he said. A heavy slur, like he was drunk.

She thought he was kidding. He was a kidder. But even this would be going too far for Reed Crowe.

She excused herself. She said she had to go to the bathroom. He could hear her soft sobs coming muffled through the door.

Oh, how he wished he was fucking joking.

She asked about the bridge. Of course she asked about the bridge. Everyone was asking everyone else about the bridge in Emerald City. Speculation ran amok about the culprit. Were his situation different, Crowe was sure Heidi would have asked if he was somehow responsible. If his stroke and the bridge explosion were connected.

Lord knew he'd gotten into trouble before.

After a lasagna dinner, Heidi Karavas delivered the news to Reed Crowe that she was leaving again, this time off to Italy for a three-year residency in Florence. She told him sheepishly, as if dreading his reaction.

He said nothing for a while. They were sitting on the sofa in the sunroom. They had a view of the dunes, the whispering sea oats. The big harvest moon over the dark Gulf.

They were into their second bottle of cabernet.

Crowe started railing about the time change. He'd gotten his voice back by now. He was a talker. Yahchilane liked pointing that out during the recovery lessons. "Yeah, yeah, egghead, I know you want to call your weed dealer, so you better start practicing quick. Because I can't read your fuckin' handwriting."

Yahchilane. God bless the man. His friend after all these years. Though Crowe considered him a complete island crank. As Yahchilane considered him, Crowe was sure.

And now that he had his mouth back, Crowe railed. "Complete idiocy." It sounded like "idioticity" but goddamn it if he wasn't getting there. "Dark at six stead'a nine. Saving time? For who? Who farms anymore, right? Right? Who saves time?"

Heidi set down her wine. "Every year the same rant." She took the white afghan throw draped on the back of the sofa and snugged it over her brown shoulders, bare in the orange sleeveless sundress.

She rested her hand on his forearm. He looked at her. "Three years," he said. A catch in his throat.

She drew in a long sharp breath, steeling herself. "You can visit."

"Come on."

"You come on."

Crowe said nothing. He sipped his wine.

"It works both ways. Once you're there, you're there."

"Three years."

He took two more quick sips of his wine. He was about to cry.

Heidi asked, "Don't you ever feel isolated?"

"No."

"Ever?"

"No."

"Come on."

"I got a car. I can leave when I want."

"You know what I mean."

"Well, it's getting late."

"Reed."

"No, that's okay. I got to go to bed."

He rose and picked up his glass and started walking to the kitchen.

"It wouldn't be a betrayal, you know."

Crowe halted. Half turned. He asked her what she meant.

"She's not here-here. You wouldn't be leaving her."

"I don't know what you're talking about."

"Yes, you do."

CALUSA CAUSEWAY

IT TOOK SEVERAL MONTHS TO REPAIR the bridge whole. And it was a month before the Emerald Island bridge was patched and buttressed enough to let through one car at a time.

But those several weeks before that ersatz route was constructed, the only way to and from the island was via boat.

Those fortnights the island was as desolate and quiet as it was in the pioneer days. Only the hale and hearty islanders stayed, the denizens with the old Conch blood.

In 1987 the visitors were few, the island preternaturally quiet. Even the Afro-Caribbean music every Friday and Saturday at the Rum Jungle, the steel drums and marimbas and scratchy Spanish guitar: silenced.

So Reed Crowe's daily walks were in solitude. At night, when the moon was new and not yet a crescent-waxed, the night sky was as he remembered it as a young boy. A planetarium of stars across deep Florida dark.

Meteor showers. Small weather satellites zipping along the sky-scape like misrouted comets. Lost UFOs.

Between the medical bills and the time he would have to spend convalescing, Crowe's stroke cost Reed Crowe his financial stability. He was faced with a choice. He could sell some of the land on Emerald Island, and that would no doubt cause a major rift within the community, because it would mean ceding the preserved land to commercial enterprise and development.

On the other hand, all his financial woes still tormented him, kept him awake.

Ultimately, after a hard few seasons, Crowe opted to put the Emerald Island Inn for sale. Someone else could take care of it, renovate it, because its heyday, for Reed Crowe, had long come and gone. The FOR SALE sign wasn't up a day before he received a call. From Eddie. He and his family wanted to buy the motel. It would have to be a handshake arrangement, for myriad reasons, and Crowe and Eddie had no choice but to trust each other, seeing that a laissez-faire principle prevailed on the island.

When the bridge was finally repaired in full Crowe in rare semi-formal attire—chinos and button-down white Oxford tucked in with a lizard-skin belt—attended the dedication ceremony.

And Yahchilane attended, in his denim on denim. His hair ocean-washed and in stiff curls. A cigarette smoking in the crease of his lips.

The benefactors dedicated the bridge to the Native American diaspora hailing from that area of Florida. Christened it the Calusa Causeway.

There was a ribbon-cutting with giant cartoon scissors. A retinue of old Conchs with houses on the island, snowbirds one and all, wearing their finest hot weather finery.

The women wore gold seashell jewelry. They were well-tanned and cap-toothed.

Their husbands were well-tanned and cap-toothed too. They clapped and whistled and bravo'ed. They shook hands and embraced and took pictures.

The benefactors made a short speech. The birdwatchers. The Emerald Island book club.

Then one of the snowbird biddies asked Yahchilane if he'd like to say a few words.

The group of two dozen people were beginning to sweat in the Florida heat.

Yahchilane was caught unawares when the silver-haired Conch women from Naples presented him with a green bottle.

Yahchilane looked at the bottle. "I don't drink champagne."

There was a smattering of laughter. It quickly ceased when the expression on Yahchilane's face didn't change.

"No, no, Mr. Yahchilane. To christen the bridge."

Yahchilane considered what the woman was asking. "I'm not doing that, lady," he said. "I'm sorry. Sure way to get cut and don't wanna go to the hospital."

He asked the lady to hold the bottle.

The woman's face ticked. Her eyes found her husband, a bow-tied man in a seersucker suit who shook his head in a quick and tight way. His face was constricted.

The nonplussed woman cradled the champagne to her heat-rashed bosom.

Finally Yahchilane looked up and down the length of the bridge. Took the cigarette from his mouth and held it smoldering between his big-knuckled hand. He said, "Looks like it'll work."

1988

THEN CAME DAYS REED CROWE WAS smote with self-pity. Days he was overcome with bewilderment. Days he felt like a cripple, like a eunuch. Days when he was full of fear that he would never be the same. That his life was over. Days when he was resigned to becoming a sot, a beach bum, a burnout.

More than he was, that is, before.

Everyday errands and chores were puzzles to solve. Communication, an Olympic feat. His tongue writhed like a clumsy slug in his mouth. The words came out marble-mouthed.

In those dark days of autumn after Heidi left for Europe, Eddie and Yahchilane were his most frequent visitors. He shunned others. Partly out of embarrassment and vanity. But it was also to spare others the awkwardness. He noticed their doleful piteous looks. He noticed how they struggled for words, always coming up with the same platitudes and sentiments.

Hey, he wouldn't know what to say either. He was sure whatever it was would be unadulterated bullshit.

So he stayed home. He stayed home even as people kept leaving messages on the answering machine.

Myrtle, Red Hamilton.

One day Chill Norton chastised him. "It's been a minute, Reedy. You want me to bring you over some oysters? Those'll go down easy."

Pause. "What're you doin' over there? Whacking off?" Another pause. "Is it true what they say?" Then there was a smile in his voice. "When your arm falls asleep, it's like getting a tug job from a stranger? Huh? Ah, fuck you, Reedy, come on."

Yahchilane would bring over conch and clam chowder from the Blue Parrot. From his home Eddie would bring picadillo, sopa de pollo, ropa vieja, leftovers in Tupperware.

And then one day Eddie brought over another surprise.

Mariposa.

Mariposa came on weekdays, every weekday aside from Friday, to help Crowe with his recuperation.

When before he embarked on his convalescence halfheartedly, now Crowe threw himself into the challenge fully.

He worked on his exercises with Mariposa. Knee extensions in the BarcaLounger. Wrist bends. Wrist extensions. Ball grips with a tennis ball.

At the kitchen table he laced his weak fingers together around a water bottle and tried to scoot it around in circles. He could not. He shook his head in anger and dejection.

"No woe-is-me shit, Uncle Reed."

Crowe sat there at the table with his head hung. The sea out there, so far away. The seagulls and sea oats. It would take him half a day to crutch that distance.

Across from him Mariposa, struck with a fresh idea, slapped her hands onto the table. "How about this," she said. "How about I make it your beer. How about I make it a bong. You got a bong in the house? Okay, we'll make it a beer."

"You don't have to come around here."

"I know."

"Your mother."

"Let me worry about my mother."

"If you say so."

And so he endured, he abided, one sunset and one sunrise at a time. He lived through his first time as a convalescent. Lived by looking forward to his visits from the girl. Hearing about her life as he worked on his repetitions.

Soon after Crowe was fully ambulatory Mariposa told Crowe that she had something to tell him. That maybe he should sit down.

"I been sitting for a goddamn year," he said.

It was a few weeks before Thanksgiving, nights getting darker earlier and earlier.

"Sit," Mariposa told him.

Crowe sat in his sunroom BarcaLounger.

And it was then when Mariposa told him that Wayne Wade was still alive.

Crowe was glad he'd sat, though he didn't believe what he heard.

"Sometimes I wonder," Crowe began. Then his throat caught. His voice. "Sometimes I wonder if I ruined your life."

Mariposa was taken aback. "My god, Uncle Reed. No. No." She leaned across the table and took his weather-beaten hands in hers.

Crowe sat there thunderstruck, disbelieving.

Mariposa wiped the tears off Crowe's cheeks with her knuckles.

Crowe was in denial. "He's been dead for years, honey."

"Coconut Grove. I'm positive."

"What were you doing all the way in Coconut Grove?"

"Field trip to Flagler."

"What was he doing?"

"He was at an ice cream shop. With a video camera. Sittin' there in a booth."

CRACKER LAZARUS

AND STILL TO THIS DAY CATFACE stalked Reed Crowe in dreams, tormented his imagination, hurtling out of nightmares on his Jet Ski, a cackling goblin caped with flame, veiled with fire.

Now it was Wayne Wade who came at him, sometimes on a Jet Ski, sometimes on his tricked-out bike, sometimes with Catface's face, sometimes with Wayne's face.

But he came always out of darkness, always yodeling his cracker laughter.

There was a part of Crowe that remained incredulous, in denial. He knew how your mind could play tricks on you. Jesus blue Christ, did he know. And say Catface hadn't slayed Wayne. That Wayne hadn't bled out and died an agonizing and humiliating death in some god-forsaken place. What would be the pervert's reason to live?

Perhaps he'd moved onto perversions even more sordid, twisted, unimaginable.

Shudder at the thought.

Once Crowe had his license reinstated and was recuperated enough to drive he rented a car at the Fort Lauderdale airport. Say Wayne Wade was still living like Mariposa said, he'd spot Crowe's hatchback at once. So in a gray Lincoln Town Car with tinted windows he cruised the streets of Coconut Grove, of Hialeah. He drove as far north as Boca Raton. Quickly dismissed the place. No, not Wayne Wade's style.

For weeks Crowe stuck to the beach strips, looking, looking, to no avail.

More each day he doubted poor Mariposa. And more each day he was relieved she might have been wrong.

It was finally by stroke of luck that Crowe learned of Wayne Wade's whereabouts. He was at Charley Alexoupobulos's hardware store buying lightbulbs.

"Some tan you got there, Mr. A," Crowe remarked at the register. "You dating again?"

It was true. The man with the fierce white hair and mustache looked like he was made of terra cotta.

"Trying out for *Sports Illustrated* swimsuit issue next year," Mr. A joked. Then his face changed. Circumspect wrinkles crimped his nut-brown forehead. "Speaking of tans. You never guess who I saw getting his skinny little ass kicked out of this hotel pool where my sis was staying."

PURPLE MARLIN HOTEL

THERE WERE MANY COMPLAINTS FROM THE visitors at the Purple Marlin Hotel about the carousing malingerer in the hotel pool. He loitered at the cabana bar, tried to engage young bikinied women in conversation. For the most part they ignored him.

He grew belligerent, leered.

He bought a new tropical drink. Umbrella, tiny plastic pirate saber speared through cherries and a big slice of pineapple. He went into the hotel pool in his beach trunks and sleeveless T-shirt and blue velour Kangol bucket hat. In his inner tube he drifted here and there among the groups of girls.

"Booger sugar?" Wayne sidemouthed, sipped from his curly straw.

A young Colombian woman in a coral two-piece told him, "From you? Get lost."

"Dykes," Wayne said under his breath.

He floated over to the next group, a Japanese trio standing around the artificial waterfall.

"What you girls into? 'Ludes? Uppers?"

"I'm into my husband. Over there. Ready to rip your dick off."

"You folks have a nice vacation."

Wayne floated on.

Finally someone from management came. A middle-aged man in an elegant butterscotch summer suit, designer shades. He was holding a leather-bound ledger. He told Wayne Wade he had to leave.

"Paying customer," Wayne said, still in the pool. "I'll have to talk to your manager, chief."

"I own the hotel."

"Wow, even worse. How you stay in business? You treat guests like this?"

"You're no guest."

"Whoa, wild accusation."

"Your room number?"

"Hell. My lawyers will make your head spin."

"Room."

"Hell."

"Room."

"Three oh eight."

Now two hulking security personnel stepped out of the wings and flanked the hotel owner. The owner consulted his book. "Your name is Moheem Kasaab?"

Wayne Wade frog-legged in his inner tube to the edge of the pool and as if beleaguered set down his drink on the epoxied Chattahoochee stone. He sighed and clambered the ladder. The swimmers and sunbathers watched.

Some of the girls in the pool clapped.

An old guy who looked like a mahogany Chef Boyardee, shirtless, said, "Adios, asshole."

Now people were catcalling and whistling.

Once out of the pool Wayne stepped out of the inner tube and he reached into his wakeboard shorts and rooted inside. But then he whirled around and ran, vaulting over someone's chaise, vaulting over the wrought-iron bars of the pool fencing before the security men could catch up.

GROUPER SANDWICH

AT THE BLUE PARROT DINER OVER his grouper sandwich Henry Yahchilane was incredulous. He was incredulous that Wayne Wade was still alive. Incredulous that Mariposa saw what she did. He shook his head. "Can't be. Somebody like that, never survive."

A windy night, twin red flags snapping on the public beach.

"I'm telling you, Yahchilane," said Crowe. "He's out there. Doin' god knows what down south. Mariposa saw him. Hardware Charley saw him."

There were some days he sounded as though a stroke had never befallen him. Especially when he was full of conviction, as he was now.

"The girl suffers from flights of the imagination," Yahchilane said. He put down his sandwich. With a napkin he wiped the crumbs from his mustache. Then he balled the napkin and tossed it atop his half-eaten meal. He shook his head. "Say he didn't bleed out. But I just don't see how. Think of who killed him. A man like that does not make mistakes."

"It sounds crazy. But I know she's right. Talk to her. You'll know. You'll know she's right. In a heartbeat. Her eyes. All you gotta do is talk to her."

"Last fuckin' thing I'm bringing up to that poor girl."

"Then go ask Charley."

For a moment they sat with the subject hanging between them, a change in the air. A dark charge.

They pulled from their beers.

There was no one else at the Blue Parrot except SnoBall Larry and Adele the honey girl at the cabana bar. Both of them were sloshed on Moscow mules. Talking about UFOs. Oblivious.

Crowe asked, "We have to assume it's true, right, Yahchilane?"

Yahchilane said nothing.

"What if?"

"Well, that changes everything."

A pause.

Then, Yahchilane, "He must be stopped."

They said nothing else. There was no reason. The dark notion had incubated in Crowe since Mariposa told him. He scratched his scruff, trouble lines creasing his forehead. "Isn't our place."

"Then whose is it?"

Crowe was silent.

"Some people the world is better without. Pure and simple."

At the Elbow Room on the Fort Lauderdale beach strip Crowe and Yahchilane sat at the cabana bar on barstools facing the Atlantic. A breezy calm night but still with the smell of the rainstorm the day previous, ocean wind stirring the palms ranged along the promenade. The neon-tinged air, the glimmer of bar and motel signs dancing on the black water.

They pulled from their beers, waited. There was no conversation.

From a nearby hotel pool came the sounds of revelry. Whooping, giggling. Radio music carried from passing convertibles. Trop rock carried from an oyster bar farther down the street. Smell of lobster rolls, Old Bay Seasoning. Someone's coconut suntan lotion.

Boom-boom-boom went the convertibles cruising past.

They were into their third beers when Crowe thought he saw him approaching from a distance. There he was, yes, his impish shape loping from afar on the sidewalk. His telltale walk with the hitch in it, though slower now, stiffer the gait. What with the snake bites, the infections, the beatings.

What with time.

He held a small camcorder by his side, gripped by its strap.

Crowe nudged Yahchilane. Yahchilane looked. Groaned.

"Goddamn it," he said.

They set down their beers. They angled their faces away, watched Wayne discreetly from a distance. Across the street, catty-corner, Wayne sat on the seawall facing the sidewalk, the pedestrians. For a while he'd stay where he was, casually smoking a Swisher Sweets cigar. The camera was set beside him on the seawall, positioned waist-level.

He watched the passersby. The thighs. The asses. The tits.

Once women and girls passed, he would nudge the camera so the lens pointed at their jiggling parts from behind. Women in their twenties, girls in their teens, girls hardly even yet budded.

Wayne Wade filmed them all.

They had no idea. Oblivious.

Crowe and Yahchilane watched Wayne for an hour and a half carrying on in this fashion before he went down the street and returned to his room in the Jolly Roger Hotel.

"You wait here," Yahchilane told Crowe. "Sit at the bar. Order something. Any kind of piss. Pay cash. Get the receipt. Keep it. Make sure you're seen."

"Let me," said Crowe.

Yahchilane looked at Crowe. Just with his look Yahchilane made words unnecessary. *You ever kill a man before?* his eyes asked. *You ever kill someone you know before?*

"There are other ways," said Crowe.

"Order your beer," Yahchilane said. "Tell some jokes. Ask for the time. Make sure you're seen."

Crowe watched Yahchilane walk to the convenience store down the street. After a minute Yahchilane exited the mini-mart with a plastic bag. He took a soda can out of the bag and popped it and drank it in three long pulls. He crushed the can and flung it into the trash. Then he pocketed the plastic bag and headed farther up the strip until he reached the JOLLY ROGER HOTEL sign.

Crowe waited for what seemed to him a very long time at the bar. He did exactly as Yahchilane told him. He ordered a Jameson shot with a beer chaser from the septuagenarian bartender, asked for the time.

Every atom of his body wanted to shoot up from the stool. Chase after Yahchilane before it was too late. He knew what was happening. Yet he stayed put.

He ordered another shot, downed it, tried to still his jangling nerves.

He wondered if now was the moment that Yahchilane, jack-of-all-trades, was jimmying the lock to Wayne's room. Wondered if now was the moment, now as he downed the first sip of his beer chaser, that Yahchilane slipped the plastic bag over Wayne's head as he slept. If this was the moment that he thrashed and kicked, held down until he drew his last desperate breath.

He waited, rubbing his sweating palms up and down on his wakeboard shorts, waiting for a subtle recalibration in the air, the earth sloughing off another soul he once new, but he felt nothing.

Nothing but nausea.

At last Yahchilane approached the Elbow Room from down the street, his pace casual. Once returned to the bar he sat down heavily next to Crowe.

"Yeah," was all he said. "I couldn't. Finish your beer. Let's go."

BLACK RUBBER BAG

BE BRAVE, REED CROWE WOULD REMIND himself, though he felt anything but. One hundred sixty-three mornings of protein shakes. One hundred sixty-three mornings of exercises with the physical therapist. One hundred and sixty-three lunches of fresh-caught fish and greens. One hundred and sixty-three afternoons, alternating days of lifting ankle and wrist weights and swimming in the Emerald City YMCA pool. One hundred and sixty-three evening walks along the shoreline, sometimes south, sometimes north, every time the drag marks left by his right foot growing fainter by the day. One hundred and sixty-three mornings and afternoons and nights thinking about Wayne Wade. Wondering, dreading, what he was up to down south. And on the hundred and sixty-fourth morning of his regimen he found himself able to make a fist with his right hand. A tight closed fist around his glass of freshly squeezed orange juice. His grip was firm, steady. His fingers did not tremble.

On that one hundred and sixty-fourth day he went to the bathroom and from the cupboard under the sink got out the electric clipper. In front of the sunny mirror with steady hand he started buzzing his shaggy gray beard, grown full again after the hospital.

"Pussy beard," he said as he trimmed first with the buzzer-clipper. "Pussy stroke," he said as he whisked the razor. Aiming for levity. Almost getting there.

It was true as people said. Once shorn of the beard he did look like a different man. Younger, though his vexed and bedraggled eyes gave away his age.

His history. Sad green eyes which made people think, "This guy's been through something. Something bad. I don't even want to know what the fuck."

1989

MANY NIGHTS CROWE WATCHED WAYNE WADE from afar, trying to work up the nerve.

A small obstinate part of him still didn't want to believe, refused to believe, though the rest of him knew it in brain, heart, blood, bone.

Crowe knew how to get into the room. That wasn't a matter. He used to own a goddamn motel. He could get into a room with a stick of gum and a match, *MacGyver*-style.

But he would have to get drunk to work up the nerve. But not so drunk he'd get sloppy and make a mistake.

If he botched the job? Crowe wasn't worried about the cops or legal repercussions. A man wanted by the cops wasn't going to the cops. No, Crowe was worried about Wayne, what he'd do, the lengths to which he'd resort, if he knew Crowe tried to murder him and failed.

Oh, Wayne would come after him, no doubt. Betrayed three times?

The key, the code, getting into the room, was no problem. A maid on her lunch break, a master key left on a hook in the break room, a thirty-minute trip to the locksmith around the corner from the motel, easy.

The rest? Killing Wayne?

Jesus Christ.

When Wayne Wade flipped on his motel room light switch and saw Reed Crowe sitting there on the edge of the bed you could see Wayne Wade's mind cartwheeling. His pinched eyes shunting underneath the grimy Dolphins cap.

He didn't recognize Crowe without the beard. So much time had passed since he'd seen Crowe without it. Since they were kids.

And quid pro quo Crowe hardly recognized Wayne, so derelict he'd become, so stooped, so wizened.

"Who the shit," Wayne said. He whirled and took the doorknob and yanked but it would not budge. He shouldered into it. Still it would not give. He cussed. Kept trying.

Finally Wayne Wade turned, showing his rotted teeth.

"Look," he began, assuming Crowe was a bookie, a goon, or worse. Someone after Mr. Video.

But then Wayne's face changed. He squinted and leaned and hunched in goober-toothed incredulity and saw that it was Reed Crowe.

"Hey, Reedy, whoa, scared the everliving shit."

Seeing the look on Crowe's face Wayne tried the door again. Useless.

Wayne shouted for help.

Also useless. A pool party outside. The girls shrieking laughter, the *huh-huh-huh* of the frat boys, guttural beery laughter.

Before he could change his mind Crowe sprang off the bed. He snared Wayne's head in the black triple-ply garbage bag. He cinched it around his neck, tightened his hold on the knot.

Wayne kicked and thrashed and his legs slewed and his checkered Van sneakers banged against the wall, leaving marks. Crowe threw Wayne onto the bed and tightened his hold on the bag. Wayne struggled and gasped and writhed.

Even with the curtains drawn the room was bathed in pink and blue neon, a sickly cough syrup hue. Wayne's legs scissored wildly. On the wall the shadows of his legs were also wild.

"Lily," Crowe said. "I know what you did."

Wayne grunted. Said something indecipherable.

"I know it," Crowe said. He could not believe what he was doing. He knew he would never believe it even after it was done.

Wayne's mouth gulped. It looked obscene. Like a hyperventilating sea anemone. An alien snuff film.

Then, as if attempting to provoke him, as if resorting to a last-second gambit to throw Crowe off guard, Wayne tittered. *Hehehehe,* like a comic book villain.

Crowe's hold remained obstinate.

Crowe's hold stayed true until the last seizure wracked Wayne's body and until the man he knew almost all of his life went dead still.

A VERY HENRY YAHCHILANE CHRISTMAS
(*CHATEAUNEUF-DU-PAPE*)

AROUND THIS TIME OF YEAR CROWE would think of his girl Lily.

The sound of her quick elfin laughter, its memory by the year was growing fainter, ghosting away inside his head.

How old would you be tonight, Otter? he'd think. How old would you be this Christmas?

Scratching his beach bum beard he scratched out the sad arithmetic in his head.

Would you be a little shit, Lily? Yeah, you probably would. Almost definitely.

He would tell her in his head, You were born on the night they said Hurricane Cleo was coming. And like Cleo you came howling into the world. You were just a natural-born hellion. I loved you at once. Right away. And the next day, I loved you more. I didn't think it possible, Otter.

I had no idea love could grow like that.

These days he was drinking too much. Alone. Staring at the wall, he could not banish from his mind the picture of Wayne Wade with the black bag over his head, his skinny legs kicking before going still.

Some nights he felt doomed. Occulted. He thought about those artifacts he dug up. The ones that used to be in the Florida Man Mystery House before Wayne stole and sold them.

The phone would ring at odd hours of the night, jarring him from a stupor, from nightmares where he had his hands wrapped around a catfaced man's throat. His hands wrapped around Wayne Wade's throat.

Other nights, he'd wake clutching air, groping for a girl's arm, trying to pull her out of the water.

Normally Crowe would ignore the ringing. But Heidi. He always hoped, though the hope winnowed by the day, that it was Heidi.

It wasn't.

"We are looking for Reed Crowe." Invariably some hotline operator from a far-flung Eastern province.

"It's pretty late. Senior or Junior."

"Senior."

"He's passed."

"There's still a score to settle."

"Pardon?"

"A balance."

"He's passed."

"Is this the junior?"

"Did you hear me? He's passed. He died years ago."

"May I have your Social Security number?"

"May you what? Shit. Look, who the hell is this? Are you even in this country?"

"Just the digits, please, sir."

"The digits like shit!"

On Christmas Eve shrieking black gales buffeted the island. Reed Crowe could not recall a winter this cold, not since January of 1977. The winter Heidi Karavas's new life started. The night the yachtsman bought one of her paintings, a painting he later hung up in his Manhattan living room. A few months later the *New York Times* critic saw it on the man's wall during a party.

Early in the night, as the wind cried in the cracks of the beach house, Crowe belted two fingers of Jameson to calm his nerves but it did no good.

If anything, a mistake.

He was too far gone in his own head. He felt claustrophobic. He paced the terrazzo back and forth the same he always did when he felt the past closing in on him. He paced so much he spooked the beach cats. From outside some of them stared like, *What the fuck?*

Finally Crowe got on his navy woolen peacoat and with a wine bottle in one hand and a Coleman lantern in the other journeyed to Yahchilane's house.

A small Christmas Eve party was under way. Crowe could see the people through the lit windows. Someone must have spotted Crowe and his lantern because after a little while a figure walked down the boardwalk and crossed the dunes and met him on the beach.

It was Yahchilane. He was in his denim and boots. But he also had on a corduroy jacket to ward off the unusual cold.

"I did a bad thing, Yahchilane," Crowe said.

"Come inside, warm up," Yahchilane said, as though he hadn't heard. He leaned his head, pointed his chin.

Crowe's face was raw from the cold wind. His lips were chapped and his nose was running. "I did a real bad thing."

"No."

"I gotta tell you."

"Don't tell me anything."

"You don't understand."

"I do. I do exactly."

The surf was crashing loudly behind them. The smell of cold seaweed was sharp in the air.

"I did a thing that's gonna send me to hell. I don't believe, but I don't know. I did a fucked thing."

With a sternness almost fatherly, Yahchilane said, "No, you did not, Crowe."

Enough of this, he meant.

Bury it, he meant.

"Listen to me," Yahchilane said, "you did not."

"I killed him. I killed somebody."

"That's enough."

"We were like brothers."

"Enough, Crowe."

They stood in the lamplit windy dark.

"Let's get out of the goddamn wind," Yahchilane said.

They started up the boardwalk that wound over the sand dunes. The sea oats thrashed and hissed. From the back veranda bamboo wind chimes clanged. Cocktail talk and cocktail laughter floated their way. The smells of a chimney fire burning, hickory wood, of roasted turkey, mulled cider.

A fifteen-foot Christmas tree stood in the barrel-shaped house's grand room, its big-bulbed lights shining colorful through the windows. The old-fashioned parti-colored bulbs Crowe remembered as a kid. Otter liked the little ones, probably because he called them fairy lights and pixie lights.

A sudden pang of nostalgia swept through Crowe like a mistral wind.

"I'm starting to forget her face, Yahchilane." It just came out of Crowe, the confession.

Yahchilane didn't break his stride. But there was a ruminative set in his shoulders. And something, Crowe couldn't quite peg it—relieved. Relieved, probably because Crowe had dropped the subject of Wayne Wade.

He'd never get over it.

Yahchilane offered, "Well, you haven't. You haven't forgotten her. That's what's important."

No more was said. Such was their rapport at this late stage. And for the time being, for at least this very moment, this sufficed.

As an added consolation, Yahchilane threw a glance over his shoulder and said, "You still a wino, egghead? I bet you are. Let's get you some good wine, besides that shipwreck shit you've been drinking. You ever hear of Chateauneuf-du-Pape, you philistine?"

Together they walked toward the shaggy-shingled barrel-shaped house, toward the cocktail laughter, the yuletide light.

A NEW YEAR

IT WAS THE DAWN OF A new decade, years into Crowe's recovery.

The New Year came and Heidi throughout the winter sent him postcards from Paris. From Berlin. From Oslo. From Rome.

They used to come a few times a month.

Then one every other month.

Little pedestrian details that could have come from anyone.

Heidi Karavas, after living all this life, was becoming with each passing year more of a mystery to him. Stranger.

Absence, in Crowe's experience, did make the heart grow fonder. But it also made the heart forget.

It made the heart stronger, harder.

———

He remembered Heidi now in fragments. But fragments so tangible and corporeal they might as well have been slides in a picture-show carousel. The images fossilized in the amber of memory.

He remembered her hair. How he'd loved that wild curly hair. How it hung slicked back from her brown forehead and her green-hazel eyes when she emerged from the Gulf after a swim. He loved the way her hair dried in wild sea-smelling curls.

How her head smelled like the sea that night.

He remembered how he could spot her figure a mile distant on the beach. Her gait. Even in a crowd he could spot her figure. The curve and sway of her hips. Her low-slung buxom body, short and round and warm and tan throughout the year.

Her tan lines. Like being clothed and nude at the same time.

He remembered all the days she spent under the beach umbrella with her sketchpad. He remembered how the pictures changed almost as quickly as she changed. The strokes and lines of her watercolors becoming confident. Quick, assured.

He remembered her laughter. Loud and long and hearty. She was quick to laugh at his silliness. One thing he could say about her big Greek family, they were good laughers.

Good drinkers, good laughers, good cooks.

Maybe that's why they lived so long.

Maybe their longevity had something to do with living near the water.

Crowe knew his did. Without the water he probably would have been dead years ago. Some trouble or another.

KRAKEN

THE CALENDAR OVERHANGING THE CARPORT WORKSTATION still said February, but on a springish day Crowe was slouched back with his legs stretched in his beach bum chair close to the surf, his first sip of the first beer of the day not yet swallowed, when he sensed a presence behind him.

He looked over his shoulder.

Yahchilane.

Yahchilane strode long and easy, in his gangly well-oiled way, toward him. A gait Crowe would have recognized from a distance even if it weren't for the vulpine carriage of the man.

Crowe swallowed his beer. Winced against the cold sting in his teeth. The cold burn in his chest. He put the can in the holder and stood. Waved and watched Yahchilane in his jeans and sleeveless denim shirt cross the distance.

They shook hands.

It was almost noon.

"What's the chisme, man?" Crowe was in an expansive mood, the sun on his face and in his hair.

Yahchilane, "Say what?"

"The chisme," said Crowe, behind his big green Polaroid sunglasses.

"I have no idea, the chisme," said Yahchilane.

"The gossip."

"Gossip. I have no gossip."

Sometimes Crowe wondered if Yahchilane were from a different planet.

"How're you doin', Yahchilane?" Crowe scratched his white beach bum beard.

"Fine."

They stood there looking at the sea. A trio of pelicans in chevron formation flew past, gliding inches above the water with wings outstretched to pocket the sea breeze.

Finally Yahchilane told Crowe that there was something Crowe needed to see.

Crowe asked what.

"You have to see it."

"Just as mysterious as ever, Yahchilane."

They walked up the beach and got into Crowe's hatchback.

With Yahchilane inside the car seemed a toy. His knees poked up gangly and gigantic, his legs shoved up against the dash.

Yahchilane fumbled for the seat lever and fooled with it.

"Far as it goes back," Crowe said. "Don't bother."

They were quiet as the road unspooled and took them to the

southern tip of the island. On the right side of them, a beachfront property rearing every now and then on the horizon. On the left, the bay-facing houses behind skeleton-skinny sand pines.

At Yahchilane's barrel house something had washed ashore.

Some kind of kraken or sea monster. A giant squid, a goliath cephalopod. Like something from a mythological lithograph. As long as a bus, maybe longer. It was sheened like a porpoise, a graphite silver shot through with purple and green.

"Holy shit, man," said Crowe. He moved forward for a closer look. The stench was incredible. He gagged, retched.

Yahchilane stepped aside. "Not on my boots," he said.

Crowe blocked his mouth and nose with his forearm. "Oh god, this motherfucker stinks."

The creature's tentacles were enormous, covered in suckers. Its snout protuberant. Its teeth donkey-like. Its eyes goat-like. Flatulent pustules squirted a stinking cheese. Hundreds of jewel-shiny bottle flies swarmed.

"What is this?" Crowe asked Yahchilane.

"No clue," Yahchilane said. "Ever see anything like it?"

"Shit no."

They studied the kraken.

"Jules Verne shit," Crowe said.

Yahchilane asked Crowe if he wanted a beer.

Crowe told him he wouldn't mind a beer.

Yahchilane trudged up to the shaggy-shingled barrel house and when he returned with the icy cans Crowe was prodding the creature with a length of driftwood he'd found on the beach. Flies buzzed in a frenzy, like angry television static.

They popped the cans, drank.

Crowe said, "We gotta call somebody."

Yahchilane shook his head.

Crowe coughed again at the stench. Turned his head away and tucked his nose into his shoulder. He picked up an end of his Guy Harvey T-shirt and covered his face with it like a mask. His eyes were asking why not.

"Imagine all the assholes. Like them flies."

Crowe knew Henry Yahchilane was right. A circus. A media frenzy for a week. And on Henry Yahchilane's land. Then what? Their privacy invaded. Their anonymity forfeited.

All their secrets revealed.

Some people wanted to remain anonymous.

Shit, just about everybody on Emerald Island.

Why they'd sought refuge here in the first place.

Crowe and Yahchilane were in the beeswax orange hatchback again, headed outside the city limits of Emerald City toward the fireworks emporium. Yahchilane said there was no firework in the world that would blow up the decomposing kraken. Crowe told Yahchilane that he was going to make a big firework out of little fireworks. "Trust me," said Crowe.

Yahchilane, "You some kind of pyro?"

Crowe considered this. "Maybe." He chuckled behind his big green aviator sunglasses. Scratched his beach bum beard. "I'll tell you what, no bigger pyros than this family running the fireworks shop. Their place blows up, everybody almost dies? Fuck it, open up another place."

Yahchilane grunted cryptically.

Crowe turned on the radio. Buffett. He switched the radio off. "Fuckin' Buffett."

For a few minutes the tires sang on the mirage-bright tarmac.

Crowe finally broke the silence. "What percentage they say? The ocean? What they discovered, Yahchilane?"

"What?"

"In the ocean. What they discovered. Creatures."

"No idea."

"Something like ninety?"

Yahchilane moved his eyebrows.

"Ninety percent of shit, man, they got no idea."

They went through Emerald City. A four-way intersection with a stoplight, a non-denominational church, a small post office no bigger than a snow cone stand.

Out of Emerald City he turned on a narrow two-lane that cut straight through pine flats. Stunted swamp scrub, hammocks of bog cabbage and saw palmetto. The occasional lagoon where carpets of swamp lilies blazed white under the radioactive eye of the sun.

They passed a man in a Panama Jack shirt and olive galoshes fishing with a cane pole in an irrigation ditch, his cranberry Tercel backed up to the levee with the doors flung open and the car stereo playing Creedence Clearwater. Reared behind him were the remnants of the old Dinosaurium, another forsaken attraction from the fifties tourism boom. Big Cat Gas.

Now the gas station was closed and concrete dinosaurs stood abandoned and neglected, grown over with ivy.

Crowe, "I keep a crab trap, man, over by the dock? I checked it, crab had teeth. Fucking human. No kidding. Fucking human teeth."

"Strange," said Yahchilane.

"No shit, man," said Crowe. "Strange, you said it. No shit."

"You think you're paranoid, Crowe?" Yahchilane said.

"Why you ask?"

"The pot."

"I'm not paranoid."

"You think you're a pyro?"

"I don't think so. No."

"Sometimes, the things you deny the most are the truest."

Crowe considered this. Said, "I'm not hung like a Tasmanian donkey."

Crowe stopped the hatchback to let a gopher turtle cross the road. About a minute passed before another vehicle appeared. A service truck for a brick and tire company. It slowed and inched to a stop until it was almost bumper to bumper with Crowe's car.

The driver slammed the horn.

"Jesus fucking Christ, this guy," Crowe said. He rolled down the window. He gestured with his arm, pointing at the road. "There's a turtle here, man," he yelled at the driver.

He looked middle-aged, a man who wore his hair in a highly sheened Afro.

He too rolled down his window to shout at Crowe. "Fuck him."

"You want me to run over a turtle? Serious road rage, man."

For a moment the driver stared blankly, eerily, at Crowe from behind mirrored shades. Crowe could even see a tiny version of himself reflected, his head jutting out of the open window, his hand aloft in a vexed gesture.

"Jerry Garcia–looking, tomato-ass-looking motherfucker!"

"Holy shit, man, you need to chill."

"Hijo de puta!"

Then Crowe saw also reflected in the shades the passenger-side door of his car open. He saw Yahchilane emerge, a giant rising slow and easy from a clownishly picayune car.

He stared down the driver.

"I got a family to feed," the man said.

Yahchilane, arms akimbo, stood there.

The driver cranked his window up angrily.

Yahchilane stepped over to the front of the hatchback, where the gopher turtle was still waddling across the road. At Yahchilane's approach the turtle darted its head and legs into its shell. Yahchilane picked up the shell, carried it over to the saw grass, set it down gently.

At last Yahchilane got back into the hatchback and they were on the move again, the truck following a few car lengths behind. Cautiously.

At the fireworks emporium, Big Gorilla Fireworks, Barry the red-headed manager greeted them with near exultation. "Far out, man," he said when he saw Crowe.

"Barry Boone, there he is!" Crowe remembered the kid's name. He always thought when he saw the kid: There goes Barry Boone, Daniel's redheaded stepbrother. Not in a bad way.

They high-fived. Executed an elaborate jive handshake.

"When's this new place gonna blow up?" Crowe asked.

"Today, I hope."

"Help me out, man," Crowe told him. "Fixin' to blow up another wedding. Ex-wife number two."

"Far out, man." Barry chuckled, his teeth perfectly straight now from his orthodontia.

Yahchilane and Crowe went down the high, brightly colored aisles, Crowe clutching a shopping basket and throwing in the most lethal fireworks his eyes lit on.

"Tell me why I had to come," Yahchilane said. He was walking with his thumbs tucked into his jean pockets.

"You're paying for this shit, Yahchilane. You think I'm Goodwill?"

Yahchilane, grim-lipped, seemed none too pleased by this development, but nonetheless the men strolled along, Crowe every so often rubbing his thumb and forefinger together in delectation. Shades half-perched on his nose.

Yahchilane remarked that all the fireworks were the same.

"You want that rot off your property, don't you?"

"Look at you. You're a pyro."

"I didn't have this planned today," Crowe said. "I'm trying to help you out."

Yahchilane paid for the fireworks, cash. One hundred and eighty dollars.

"Gonna have to ask you to sign, sir," said the young man to Henry Yahchilane.

Yahchilane hesitated, lifted an eyebrow.

Crowe took the pen from Yahchilane. Signed a name.

Jebediah Marmalade Johansson III.

Around sunset Crowe returned to Henry Yahchilane with his jury-rigged stick of dynamite.

Yahchilane eyed the duct-taped PVC pipe with the long green fuse. Like something out of a Wile E. Coyote cartoon.

Crowe, his voice aquiver with boyish excitement, said, "Just get behind the dune. Enjoy the show."

"Gonna blow yourself up."

"Get behind the dune."

Watching Crowe, Yahchilane smoked a cigarette behind the dune. Crowe ranged stork-like down the beach with his hands on his hips. After a distance he spotted something and picked it up. A large pin seashell. With the seashell he scooped a divot out of the rotted flesh of the kraken. Retching at the stink. Blocking his face every now and then with his forearm.

Then he shoved the explosive into the squid's body.

It took a few flicks of his BIC with Daisy from *Dukes of Hazzard* emblazoned on the side to get the fuse burning. Then Crowe scampered away in a low crouch, coughing, almost barfing. "Oh, shit, motherfucker stinks," he said, shielding his face with his forearm.

Behind the dune they watched the bright yellow sparks of the burning fuse. And in the distance now, about a mile down the beach, appeared the minuscule figures of a couple on an evening beach stroll. They were holding hands.

The explosion went off like a claymore mine. The kraken blew apart, chunks hailing down onto the beach. Gobbets thudded in the sand and smacked the water. A flock of shrieking seagulls started to descend and baitfish thrashed in the shallows.

The couple froze in the distance.

It was one of the first and last times Crowe heard Henry Yahchilane laugh. A gruff short laugh like clearing the throat.

That evening they laughed hard and long.

MR. WHY

CROWE WAS SURE THEY WERE A different breed these days, kids. He remembered when they had their Spider-Mans and Supermans. Smurfs and Strawberry Shortcakes. There were lost blankies and teddy bears he used to have to fetch. He-Man figures lost in the bog.

Rubik's Cubes. Plastic light sabers.

How quaint, all of that now.

Now half the kids were on glorified methamphetamines. Adderall. They were hopped up on the stuff. Ten-year-old tweakers.

Yet with Yahchilane their interest was piqued. Something about his gravelly stentorian voice.

Dude might be an old fuck, you could see them thinking, but dude isn't fucking around.

"The Everglades," Yahchilane told them, "is no longer really the Everglades. That's just a name people have for it. A baloney name." Yahchilane went on. "See the quote unquote real Florida. You see those signs? Miss Tonya, you ever see those signs?"

"Yes, I have."

Yahchilane explained how the Everglades had been rerouted and dredged, gouged away and parceled out, the original landscape so butchered by development and agriculture and pollution it no longer resembled the swampy wild of his youth.

The sky looked different.

The clouds hung lower, dirtier.

The water was darker, a boggy molasses. Some years brushfires burned throughout the summer.

On these trips Yahchilane spotted oddities he scarcely believed. He saw insects he'd only seen in documentaries about Tanzania, New Guinea. He saw poison spiders and giant purple grasshoppers and salamanders mottled to look like lichen.

Ersatz herpetologist that he was, he knew the insects and reptiles didn't belong here.

They weren't native.

They were invasive.

The strange snakes and the reptiles, Yahchilane knew they were exotic pets escaped from their owners. Run amok in the Florida wild. Or, somehow, one way or another, they'd found their meandering way here from an improbable distance. By stream and canal, by shipwreck and by storm. By hook, by crook. By fin, wing, tail.

"See that right there?" Yahchilane would point out. "Karum tree. We never saw these three years ago. This year I've counted twenty."

"Are you very interested in trees, Mr. Why?" That's what the kids called him. Mr. Why. Easier than Yahchilane, which they had a hard time getting their mouths around.

"Not more than most people," he'd tell them.

"You seem to know a lot about trees."

"You know how old I am?"

"No."

"I'm so old our television was trees."

HIS TOURS CHANGED

ON OCCASION, IF THERE WAS A big field trip from a middle school in a neighboring county, Reed Crowe would take the *Merman* out for a boat tour. But his swamp tours changed. He told the tourists and kids the truth instead of what they wanted to hear.

Whether Yahchilane or Crowe, they told them wild tales about Okeechobee. The mammoth lake that took up a huge swath of central Florida, how sheer limestone bluffs over one hundred feet tall bracketed the water. How these bluffs were riddled with innumerable caves. And how these caves housed monkeys—face-eating monkeys!—and spiders the size of a man's head, spiders that spun webs that could ensnare a man whole.

And there were Native ambushes. Developers and surveyors attacked from all sides in a terra incognita they could not fathom, let alone map. There was no charting these territories.

But the swamp boomers and swamp barons forged on undeterred. They thought they could grow plums, pineapples, sugarcane, coffee, tobacco, bananas, all kinds of tropical fruits. And they thought settlers would come later, drawn by this land of opportunity. They brought their rollers and their riggers and shovels and tractors and dredgers. They braved fevers. They were slashed by saw palmettos and saw grass. No-see-ums and mosquitoes sapped their blood. The sun sapped their strength. Hurricanes and tropical storms killed half of them off. Crowe knew himself too soft a man to have made it through half the ordeals.

Crowe told them about how the swamp magnates set about building a railroad and for every mile the new Florida tycoons built the federal government gave them a parcel of land. Nobody wanted the tractless waste. A quagmire of saw grass and water cabbage and water hyacinths. An outpost run amok. Mile long hammocks of sable palms and coconut palms. Innumerable beasts and reptiles and insects, bloodthirsty enough to eat a man whole. Alligators and bobcats and bears and jaguars and panthers. Mosquitoes thick as smoke. The smudgepots and palmetto fans were useless dispelling them.

All the work that went into trying to tame this outpost, the Natives no doubt played a big part. Digging postholes under water, logging and clearing the way for massive steamboats that tore through the lettuce bogs.

Sometimes Crowe wondered about the skeletons he found all those years ago with Yahchilane. Who knew. Yellow fever might have done those people in. Maybe they perished in a storm.

Worst-case scenario, Reed Crowe supposed, was that white men murdered them after services were rendered. White men who reneged on their bill.

Crowe thought of his great-grandfathers and sundry kin from days of yore. He wondered if they played any part in dirty business, to what degree. You had to wonder. He'd heard rumors over the years. On the other hand, this part of Florida, the town so small and sequestered, so much of its history was based on folklore and hearsay and Florida cracker bullshit.

That stuff about Al Capone, for instance. All those bootleggers and trappers. During Prohibition Al Capone was rumored to have run a distillery in the swamp.

Every so often a tourist would ask a question about Capone if Crowe didn't work a mention of him in that day's spiel.

And every so often, rarer, but it happened, a tourist would ask about Krait Isle.

"It true there's an island out there with hundreds of deadly poison snakes?"

Crowe would think of Catface and that night and splinters of ice would shuttle through his veins.

"Only two kinds of snakes my dad used to say," Crowe would say, keeping it short. "A live one and a dead one."

And that was about as much as Crowe wanted to talk about Krait Isle.

BUTTERFLY

LAST THURSDAY EVERY MONTH REED CROWE would meet Mariposa for a late lunch at the Blue Parrot diner. One Thursday, the last Thursday of winter, on the cusp of spring, a friend accompanied her. A girl with long hair dyed scarlet. Her skull was shaved on one side and the hair drawn back in a ponytail so it jutted out like a kind of tail.

Her name was Tonya. But she went by Tee. Tee took in the musty ambience of the place. "Michelin-rated?"

"It's seen better days," Crowe said. He was sitting across at the booth and glanced from behind his menu.

Tee said, "When? Ponce de Leon?"

"Interesting fact about Ponce. He took his prom date here. It's true. Didn't tip the waiter or anything. Real asshole."

Crowe excused himself to the bathroom. Sliding out of the booth he said to Mariposa, "Order me a conch chowder, kid?"

"Hold the pubic hair," Tee said.

The girls giggled.

After his piss when Crowe exited the bathroom he had a shock. Thankfully the girls had their heads turned. They were leaning close to each other. They were kissing on the lips.

After what seemed a long moment to Reed the girls parted.

Crowe quickly composed his face and coughed loudly into his fist. He slid back into the booth. He took a napkin from the dispenser, wiped his mouth.

The girls were looking at him. He was looking at the girls.

Crowe looked around for a place to put the napkin, finally put it in the pocket of his safari shorts. "Order that chowder?"

"Yeah."

"With the pubes?"

THIRTY

ONE DAY EDDIE CONFIDED IN CROWE as they cleaned the charter boat that he could stand life with Nina no longer.

About matters large and small, Crowe observed over the years, she had proven relentless.

He didn't think there was any residual ill will about this sentiment.

"I don't know how much longer I can take it, Reed," Eddie told him. Finally, after all these years, Eddie was calling him by his first name.

Maybe something about Eddie turning thirty.

"Eddie," Crowe told the young man, "look at me. I'm the last guy you should be asking for advice. I'm a beach bum."

Buddha-eyed Eddie, "You've been with many women."

"Nah."

"How many?"

Crowe waggled his hand. "Not so many."

"You've been married."

"Yeah, and look at me."

"You seem okay."

Crowe shrugged: *I'm okay.*

"Do you get lonely?"

"I was more lonely with her. We both were. We made each other lonely."

Grief, Crowe came to learn belatedly, could draw people closer just as easily as it could cleave them apart. Grief could keep them together. And Reed Crowe and Heidi Karavas stayed together longer when they might not have had the girl lived. They loved each other but they were also tired of each other. Sickly tired. The way she put ice cubes in the glass from his beloved icemaker, tossing them in there to make a point. The way he would leave sand and grit in the bed from his beach bum feet.

Then she'd go abroad for months at a time, longer and longer these days, and when she returned she had that girlish glow about her again. He saw her with eyes anew.

"Look at you," he'd tell her. "You're something else."

He'd try to rekindle a dalliance for a few months when she visited, but more often than not these days, she'd accuse him of nostalgia. Of sentimentality.

"Well. Yeah. I suppose so."

MARIPOSA, SURFER ROSA

THERE WERE OTHER DAYS WHEN EDDIE accompanied him that Crowe could just tell things were wrong. Something amiss once again in the casa de Maldonado. The heaviness of the poor kid's face. Kid. He was a man now. Crowe had to remind himself, even though Eddie looked so much older than that skinny whippet of a teenager, that kid with the black fuzz on his upper lip, who started selling Coca-Colas on the *Merman* so many years ago.

Now, he had his own daughter with Nina, Maribelle. His hair was a steely gray and worry lines were graven around his eyes and mouth, across his forehead.

Life with Nina and the girls had taken its toll on Eddie, especially since Mariposa's quinceañera. Shrieking fights every other night, schisms worthy of a telenovela.

After the melees Nina would stay holed up for days in her room.

When Eddie accompanied him on the fishing charters he'd relate a lot of this to Reed Crowe.

To Crowe it all sounded to him like standard kid shit. Black lights, magic mushrooms, weed.

Then he'd remind himself he was responsible for the girl's distress. Partly, at very least. And that was a generous perspective.

Other times during these talks Crowe would feel a pang of bereavement. Less keen these days, but he had to wonder what would have become of Lily. His Otter. He had to wonder if they would have experienced similar troubles. With him as a father? Shit.

Lily would have been a full adult now. And if their situations were reversed, if it were Lily they were talking about instead of Mariposa, would he have been as flip?

Dinners were wars, Eddie hunkered down like a soldier in a foxhole half-chewing, half-swallowing his meal. Maribelle, the quiet one, had her eyes someplace else, her mind far away, tuning them out. His girl almost seemed not to hear any of it. On her face she wore an improbable look of serenity. An introspective child, quiet. A reader. First in her class, always.

Mariposa was very different. Eddie loved the girl like his own—he considered her his own—but she was so very different. And so very much like her mother.

Just one night's peace, Eddie told Crowe. That's all that Eddie wanted at this point. Just one night's silence.

His poor daughter Maribelle would sit there every meal, her eyes somewhere else, an expression of near serenity on her face. She seemed barely listening to the idiotic arguments over their oxtail soup on Sundays, the albondigas soup on Wednesdays.

"What's this?" Nina would say at the table, her eyes full of ridicule. "Who's this ghoul sitting at the table tonight? You look like devil-worshipper."

"I have," Mariposa said. "I've started to worship the devil. I'm afraid I won't be able to make it on Sunday."

"What? What? Oh Jesucristo. Oh god."

Eddie pinching the bridge of his nose. "Please, Butterfly? Why? Why poke the bear? I beg of you."

Nina whipped her face toward him. "I'm an animal now? I belong in zoo?"

"Dad," Mariposa said, "I was just sitting here drinking my Tab. Thinking about what the devil and I are gonna do Saturday night."

Nina threw her silverware onto the plate and shot up from the chair and fixed her daughter with a look of ire. Then she went down the hall and slammed her bedroom door so hard the framed family portraits in the hallway trembled.

Another day, after a Saturday afternoon in the Galleria mall, Mariposa came home with purple streaks in her black hair, safety pins rowed along the rim of her ear.

Nina told her daughter she looked like a circus freak. A ghoul. "You show yourself in church like this? Like a clown?"

"Why not? Church is a joke."

The mother seared the daughter with a look. Asked her to repeat herself. When Mariposa said nothing, Nina demanded.

Eddie had to come between them.

Nina followed her daughter down the hall. "What's the smell? Cigarettes? Come here. Let me smell you."

Mariposa kept moving, blocking herself with her forearm.

"I want to see. Open your mouth."

"I've been smoking crack with el diablo."

"Open your mouth, you monster."

"Crazy, crazy. I'm not letting you stick your nose in my mouth. So crazy."

Mariposa slammed her door so hard one of the framed portraits in the hall fell to the floor. The glass shattered.

Nina flung the door open and barged into the room.

"You look like a ghoul. Someone should tell you."

"Get out of my room. Get out!"

Eddie came to the threshold. "That's enough."

Mariposa and Nina were inches apart. Nina looked at Eddie. "Pardon me? I don't get to tell my daughter she looks like some freak?"

"No."

Nina was livid, incredulous, that Eddie had voiced even this little.

He spoke again. "I said no. Enough. Enough of this. It's like living with lunatics."

Nina launched into a tirade. "I came here for this shit. I sailed across the sea for this shit. Your grandfather sailed across the sea for this shit. He died. For this shit. And for you. You. You, to be like this."

"Say it," Mariposa said.

"I did."

"Say what you really want to say," Mariposa said.

Nina's wide angry eyes toured the room. The punk rock posters. The cassette tapes stacked on the bed stand and the bureau, the spines showing bubbly handwriting, little colorful doodles. Mix tapes from one of her girlfriends.

Finally Mariposa's mother went to one of the posters on the wall. She glared at it, shot a spiteful breath through her nose. On the poster was a photograph that appeared so old it might have been a tintype. A flamenco dancer caught mid-pose. She was topless, her fulsome breasts in plain view. Behind her, a crucifix on a stucco wall.

PIXIES, said the poster. SURFER ROSA.

"Sick, so sick, mierda," Mariposa's mother said. Then Nina let loose a litany of curses under her breath. They grew louder and angrier until she launched herself at the wall with her fingers curled like claws and started ripping the poster off the wall.

Mariposa grabbed her mother by the shoulders, pulled her away.

Eddie ran so he was between them and it was only when he said he could stand it no longer, that Maribelle could stand it no longer, that Nina left the room and shut herself into her own.

The strife, the discord, the madness, escalated by the day. There were moments Eddie considered divorcing Nina. That time she waited up until one A.M. after the junior prom, sitting in the dark in the kitchen with an air horn because Mariposa had missed her eleven o'clock curfew, blasting it the moment Mariposa snuck in late through the house's side door and flipped the light.

This is it, Eddie would think.

Divorce.

But there were the repercussions to reconsider. Nina would lose her citizenship. And the girls. What would happen to the girls? And if he so much as brought up the possibility of a divorce, Nina was Catholic to the bone. She'd butcher him in his sleep sooner than sign divorce papers. She'd somehow get Pope John Paul II involved. Shit, that guy would throw up his hands. I give up. Show me the door to hell.

One morning not long after Eddie stepped sullenly on the boat with his regular good morning grunt. Crowe volleyed back with his usual, "Hey, man."

A cloudless October day, an early north wind.

Crowe prepped the lines and tackle and leaders. Eddie stocked the icebox.

The thing Reed Crowe most appreciated about Eddie, he was quiet. Comfortable with silence.

But today as they prepped the lines and the tackle and they baited the hooks Crowe knew something was different but couldn't figure out.

Then, "Your mustache. Why'd you shave, Eddie?"

"I look estranged?"

Eddie years ago told Crowe to always correct his English when he was wrong. Which he hardly ever was these days, but now, "Strange."

"Strange."

"Always, Eddie. You've always been strange."

"Serious. I hate it." His fingers kept returning to the bald patch above his lip.

"Why?"

"Nina said I looked stupid."

"Nah."

"You're smiling."

"Takes getting used to."

"You're smiling."

"You look twelve."

Eddie kept brooding.

A trio of pelicans waited in the water, brown wings tucked close to their body. Crowe threw them the chum scraps. They yawned their gigantic beaks wide and swallowed the mullet pieces whole, heads tipped back, flappy throats working.

Finally the pelicans winged off.

Crowe spray-hosed the bait cutting board. "Maybe stand up for yourself, Eddie. You wanna mustache, grow the mustache. Take a stand."

"Stand."

"Yeah."

"Hit her?"

Crowe stopped spraying. "Jesus Christ, no."

Eddie was looking at him.

Crowe put down the spray nozzle. He fingered up his green aviators so the lenses were nested in his beach bum cedar and gray hair. He put his hands on his hips. "You think I'd suggest that? Goddamn, Eddie. First, she'd rip your head off and use it as a bowling ball."

"This is true," Eddie said.

Crowe remembered his father. How he used to backhand his mother. Several times Crowe saw this happen in his boyhood. He had no idea if such a thing was common back then. He had no other boyhood to compare it to.

His old man. He wanted to hate him, couldn't. He loved him.

But he sure as hell didn't like him.

That one Christmas, when the old man was bourbon-and-eggnog drunk. He backhanded Crowe's mother and she cried and Reed, nine years old, jumped on his father's back and tried to fend him off.

And his father's history, there was a lot he didn't know and could never know. All those old Conchs were dead now.

His father, dead. Crowe remembered when he was a teenage boy, looking through the kitchen window above the sink, his father climbing into the black sedan for another weeklong business trip. He had a red McIntosh apple in his hand and it fell. The apple rolled in the driveway. He collapsed to his knees. Through the kitchen window he saw his father buckle, clutching his chest. He fell and then was still.

A heart attack, fifty-five.

His father's voice. Once in a while he'd hear it still. Clear.

Get out in the sun, son.

Go on and have a glass of cold water and go run in the sun.

Now he told Eddie, "I don't know shit about life, Eddie. But the second you lay a hand on that woman, it's over."

Eddie nodded. "My father. Not nice to my mother."

"I understand," Crowe said. And he did. Yes, he did. He told the young man, "Try to be friends with her, Eddie. Be honest. Kindly honest. That's all I know about women."

HURRICANE ANDREW

BY 1992 THE SHAGGY-SHINGLED BARREL HOUSE needed serious renovation. As much as it pained Henry Yahchilane to admit, the house had fallen into disrepair. Much to his chagrin. He had always prided himself a fastidious man. A man who took care of his own property and maintained it and did all the work with his own hands.

But that year in June, Yahchilane fell off the ladder while cleaning leaves out of the gutter pipes of the barrel house. He dropped five feet before striking the cedar porch board smack on his side.

Yahchilane was well into his sixties.

He went to Dr. Vu, who told him he was lucky he didn't break his hip.

Her eyes were scolding above the rims of her round glasses. "What are you doing on a ladder?"

"Cleaning gutters."

"Lucky you're not paralyzed."

Later that year, when his son, Seymour, came for a visit in August before his classes at Tulane began, he said nothing about the blight, which was somehow worse, because usually such a sorry sight would have occasioned some ball breaking.

Instead, Seymour only said, "We gotta get somebody out here, Pop."

"It's fine."

"What's that, you're limping? Something happen?"

"No."

"What happened?"

"I got old. Nothing. Leave me alone."

That summer the blossoms fell early from the trees and bushes. A bright confetti of jacaranda and bougainvillea petals gyred on summer scorched winds.

In the kitchen of the barrel house the speck-tiny sugar ants filed in quick black lines up a groove in the grout and into a pinprick hole. As if intuiting something beyond his comprehension.

A few days before the storm they were calling Andrew made landfall, Yahchilane began patching some of the storm windows, the splintering boards, the warped and weatherworn places, but too little too late and by the time he drove out to Charley Alexoupobulos's hardware store the place was all but ransacked.

Rumor was, Andrew was going to be a big one.

It was just when the first bands were whipping the island, the barrel house beginning to moan and creak and groan, some of the siding flying wild into the night, when Yahchilane braved the sojourn to Reed Crowe's house. He brandished a tin garbage can lid as a makeshift shield, a colander as a makeshift helmet.

If the direst of the predictions proved true, Andrew would blast Yahchilane's house into tinder sticks.

Crowe had decided to ride out the storm. And when Yahchilane came out of the night with his shield in one hand and the flashlight in the other, Crowe at first jerked in shock. Then he seemed temporarily heartened by the new company.

"Jesus, this is a lot worse than I thought," Crowe joked. "The storm too."

Crowe had the bathtub full and he had the patio furniture in the house. The electricity was out but the kerosene lamps were burning inside. And Crowe had a small generator running. He had a big cooler full of ice and water and beer. He had sterno burners and canned goods.

Remarkably, Yahchilane made another grudging admission to himself, the egghead was more prepared than he for the storm.

On the dawn of August 24, 1992, Hurricane Andrew cut through the state like the grim reaper's scythe.

Like many old Conchs, most of the Emerald Islanders decided to stick it out.

Crowe hadn't expected the storm to hit as hard as it did.

All was blindness for the next day. Dark rain raking away shutters and shingles and road signs. Coconuts flew off the palms. Gales tossed them like bocce balls across the land.

The sand blew like snow.

The flags snapped against their poles, machine gun fire.

Homestead, devastated.

Southern Miami, leveled.

On the southwest coast, boats in the wharf had smashed together, broken apart like tinker toys. Mobile homes were ripped asunder. The energy was out for three days. But for the most part, the island and its homes and buildings were spared the full brunt.

The Florida Man Mystery House, ramshackle and rickety as it was: pilloried.

So in this manner the matter was decided.

A storm named Andrew made the decision for him.

THIS IS IT, EDDIE

ONE EVENING THEY WERE DRINKING BEERS at the Rum Jungle and Crowe told Eddie, "This is it. The boat tour. I don't want to deal with the stuff anymore. I'm getting tired. I think I'm just fishing from now on."

His hearing in particular had been giving him problems of late on the tours. Some tourist would introduce themselves as Senelarium or Orbadelia and Crowe was left wondering what the hell he'd heard or if such names really existed.

Crowe was closing in on fifty.

"I understand," Eddie said.

Crowe asked the young man, "You gonna be okay on your own?"

Eddie laughed.

Crowe asked what was so funny.

Eddie shook his head. "It's okay, Reed."

It was a mellow evening, the September sun setting bronze and peach, a flame-colored swath as wide as a highway in the Gulf.

"Was it that bad?"

"No. No. You're happy."

Crowe shook his head. He did not consider himself so. Nor did he consider himself unhappy. "I'm fine, yeah," he said.

There was still a smile in Eddie's voice. "You're okay."

"Yes. I'm okay. Eddie? What're we talking here?"

"You're okay now. We worried about you. Even Nina."

Crowe didn't know whether to be touched or insulted. "What! Jesus."

"No, I worried. Worried. No longer."

"Did you? Shit. Don't worry about me."

"I won't."

"Just ask me."

"I don't have to."

"I don't get you, Eddie."

"You're good."

They drank the beers with the lime wedges squeezed into the necks for a quiet minute. The crashing Gulf murmured, a distant susurrus. There was slow lazy conversation between two old rummies at the other end of the bar. One of the old rummies would not stop referring to Don Shula as "the brainstem." The other kept calling Dan Marino "the statue of liberty." "No maneuverability in the pocket," was a frequent refrain.

Two bar dogs, Labrador and hound mixes, barked at each other, fighting playfully under the big-bulbed Christmas lights. Then one of the beach dogs went over to the four-foot glowing plastic Santa Claus and lifted its leg and pissed.

Eddie and Crowe themselves got to talking about the Dolphins and their season when a commercial for soda came on CNN.

"Remember that time I asked you about the stolen Cokes?" Crowe asked Eddie.

Eddie nodded, gave him a side eye with his elbows cocked on the bar. He was looking out at the water, the sea birds diving after baitfish, their caws carrying from about a quarter mile off.

"What did you think? How angry were you?"

"I wanted to knock someone's block off."

"Mine?"

"Anyone's."

Crowe stroked his beard. "You were so quiet. You still are. But then? The shit you took."

"I had no choice."

———

The Florida Man Mystery House, whole weeks went by when he didn't give the place a thought.

And now, good for him, Crowe thought, Eddie Maldonado and his brothers and cousins were making money hand over fist, the need for builders in south Florida was such after the clobbering of Hurricane Andrew.

The Florida Man Mystery House stuff, all the bric-a-brac and hokey junk, languished in storage.

Reed Crowe bought a forty-foot catamaran. A few times a week, several if it was peak fishing season, he chartered the boat.

He rediscovered his boyhood love for fishing. He'd grown bored with shore fishing. He always ended up catching the same kinds of fish. Whiting and sail cats and stingrays. Hardly worth the time or bait. And their razor-sharp dorsal fin sand-whipping rapier tails could rip right through your skin. And red drum, he wasn't a fan, too fishy for his palate. He was a catch and release guy unless it was pompano, which he caught less and less often these days. Maybe he'd lost his touch. Or maybe there were just fewer in the Gulf.

The deeper waters of the Gulf, though, where the shelf fell and the ocean deepened to dark blue, hosted species stranger.

When fishing season arrived, a few times a week Crowe took out charters, rough-hewn Florida types, jolly, always mildly beer-drunk. DUI on Wednesdays every so often was the extent of his trouble. A little too loud at the rodeo, but in a "Hey, buddy!" kind of way.

Good old boys.

One day Crowe had a guy from Bacon County, Georgia, named Buddy Bigalow and his brother, Bobby Bigalow.

The fish was like nothing Crowe ever saw.

It was three feet long and shaped like a whipping paddle and had green-purple scales and a flesh-colored head. It also had a foot-long thing, flesh-colored, that looked exactly like a human cock.

"What in sweet baby Jesus Christ is that," Buddy said, his meaty bulldog face sweaty and red.

For a second Crowe was going to pretend he knew what species it was. He was going to make up a name. Lavender cockfish, but he just shook his head.

"Holy shit, man. I have no idea."

Buddy said, "Thing's got a bigger dick than you do, Bobby."

The brothers, laughing, took pictures with the fish.

Sometimes, if the anglers were capable enough, he went it alone without other crew. Sometimes Eddie accompanied him. On rare occasions, about a few times a year, Henry Yahchilane, and then only to dip his own line in the water for a big fish that would feed him for a while.

Grouper.

Tuna.

Swordfish.

All fewer these days.

Mangrove snapper. Red snapper. Yellowtail. Fewer too.

Still, they had their lucky days out in the Gulf Stream.

He'd forgotten. He'd forgotten how much he missed these days out in the sun, out in the water, on the boat far away from his problems and anxieties. How much he missed fishing those long peaceful blue hours out at sea, a line with bait sunk fathoms deep. Never knowing what he'd catch. What amazing oddity.

The grouper as big as dune buggies out of the shipwreck depths. The amberjack, the wahoo, the cobia, the red snapper, the mangrove snapper, the yellow tail snapper. The African pompano. The triggerfish.

DEEP SEA FISHING

CROWE AND YAHCHILANE WOULD SPOT EACH other on the island and sometimes across the bridge and they'd tender a cursory wave or nod of the chin. And then when they did finally speak after a spell, Crowe was always taken by surprise how much time had passed since their last encounter. Several months, a year. The time, both men agreed, was sneaking up on them, all the more so with Crowe, so undifferentiated and foggy-headed were his days. When Yahchilane visited Crowe's beach house, it was to cadge a quarter or a half of ganja, which would tide him over for a year.

Some years, Yahchilane would bring over some oddity or another in a mason jar with holes knifed out of the screw top lid. *Look what turned up in my garden. Look what washed ashore. You ever seen anything like this?*

A kiwi-sized beetle, fever-hued, fluorescent pink with black speckled wings and a horn crowning its head.

Never, Crowe would tell him. Not in his nature guides and illustrated books, not on his boat tours, which he was making less and less often these days.

Or once it was a translucent squid the size of a pickle which, when it got dark or when you turned off the lights, pulsated with a soft lavender bioluminescence.

Crowe would ask Yahchilane, "Ever tell you that time I saw a crab with, like, human teeth, man?"

"Yeah. At least a dozen."

"Bullshit."

"A dozen."

On such occasions Crowe would worry that his memory was failing him, like what happened to his mother. Hard to tell how much was hereditary, how much was a result of his bad habits.

MEET ME AT THE BEACH HOUSE

A NURSE FROM THE POINCIANA NURSING Home called Crowe one blazing hot February morning. The nurse told him of his mother's recent episodes. One, a stroke so small a few days ago that they were unsure if it was a stroke at all. Then another spell in the night.

Spells. Episodes.

Crowe didn't have to ask questions. He knew from the faltering, soft-voiced way the woman was delivering the news.

It was time, he knew.

Time to bring his mother home to the beach house.

Transporting her in the orange hatchback wasn't an option. He went to Henry Yahchilane to borrow his van. Yahchilane told him he wasn't about to let an egghead drive his van off the bridge and into the ocean. But he also said he was willing to drive. "Got errands to run down there anyway," Yahchilane told him.

En route to the nursing home they passed one of the old Florida Man Mystery House billboards. The sign was sun-beaten and peeling in swaths and beneath the strips in palimpsest you could see one of those old Coppertone suntan lotion ads, the one with the little pigtailed toddler girl getting her bottoms yanked off by the rambunctious dog, her tan-lined butt showing.

Yahchilane saw the sign. He was looking straight at it. Smoking his cigarette, his mouth slightly ironic and bitter.

Crowe felt slovenly, derelict. He had no idea why he gave a fuck. "Yeah, gonna have to give that one up," he heard himself saying.

Yahchilane still said nothing. He tapped the ash off his cigarette. He took another deep drag and exhaled and flicked the butt into the saw grass blurring past, a vast track like a serrated savannah.

A sudden silence filled the car. The air-conditioning blasted on high but still they were sweating in the miserable Florida heat.

Crowe cleared his throat, ran his fingers through his crinkly beach bum beard, drove on.

At the Poinciana they threw an early birthday party for Crowe's mother. There was a Carvel ice cream cake shaped like a whale. Fried chicken from Fran's off Federal Highway in Boca Raton. A resident's false teeth fell out and there was laughter over this. Then a man named Mr. Brewster pissed his pants and the nurses said it was time to bring the party to a close. Crowe and Yahchilane helped pick up the paper plates and Dixie cups.

Crowe's mother thought Henry Yahchilane was someone called Larry.

"Larry, oh my god, how long has it been?"

Yahchilane took Crowe aside and asked what to do.

"Easier just to go along."

Henry Yahchilane said to Crowe's mother, "It's been a hot minute. How are you, ma'am?"

"Oh, Reedy's just bringing me home for Otter's graduation. Is that why you're in town?"

There was so much he'd still meant to ask her, especially recently, and now it was too late. Later on in life, perhaps as a result of curbing his vices, Crowe started remembering more by the year instead of less. Maybe something had been knocked loose in his brain. A passage unblocked, like the skull so many years ago rolling into the grotto.

Memories from when he was five or six came to him.

He remembered for the first time since perhaps he'd experienced it, his father screaming. He was screaming *life, underground, money, over, away, future*. Then he heard his mother say *Reedy will hear, you'll scar him for life acting like this*.

Then Crowe remembered the hallway light was on and his red Mickey Mouse suitcase sat beside the door. He glanced at the night-stand clock: one in the morning. He heard a car grumbling outside. He cracked open the drapes and saw an old Buick in the driveway. Behind the windshield his grandparents sat, tired lined faces eerily lit in the streetlight and dashboard glow.

This was when Crowe heard his father say, "I might as well just blow my head off."

Crowe went down the hallway to his parents' room, creeping so he wouldn't make a noise. Then he saw his mother standing at the foot of the bed, dressed like she would be during the day, in black pants and an angora sweater. His father sat at the foot of the bed, his face red and tired in the lamplight.

He saw Crowe. Then Crowe's mother noticed him too.

A gun lay in his lap, a .38 special.

His mother said, "Reedy, go sit in your father's lap. Don't be scared. Go sit in your father's lap and tell him you love him."

Crowe went over and his father placed the gun aside on the bedspread. He climbed clumsily onto his lap.

"Son," his father said, holding him close, his sobbing voice full of abject animal grief. "My son."

What else was going on around this time?

Did it very much matter now?

At any rate, there was now no way of knowing. His mother was gone. The disease had eroded her memory bit by bit, until now only a loose scattering of flotsam and jetsam like sea wrack remained.

They loaded her Airhawk reclining gerichair into the back of the van, Yahchilane taking the highway slow as Crowe's mother dozed. The Florida wilderness scrolled by. A bright haze of green spattered with bright flowers. A Monet gauziness from the heat. Dragonflies hovering everywhere.

She was asleep when Crowe and Yahchilane carried the chair up the steps and into the house where Crowe put her up in the guest room bed. A palliative care nurse would visit in the morning from Emerald City to discuss home visitation plans.

But sometime in early evening his mother awoke with a cry. Crowe, sitting in the solarium, set down his glass of wine and half-trotted into the room. His mother was propped up in the bed and looked at him with foggy eyes that didn't know who he was. That didn't know where she was. Or maybe who she was.

"It's okay, Mama, it's Reedy," he told her. "You're in the beach house."

If you're in trouble, go to the beach house, that used to be the refrain when Crowe was a kid. If you ever get lost, or if you're ever in trouble, go to the beach house.

Now, realizing where she was, Crowe's mother at first seemed disbelieving, even incredulous. Her breath was a labored moan. "I need some sea air."

"Then let's get you some air, Mama."

"I think I had an accident."

"Don't you worry about it. Happens to me all the time."

He changed her. He lifted her out of bed, so fragile, no more than eighty pounds, and he set her carefully down into her gerichair and wheeled it out into the sunroom and opened the sliding glass doors. He bumped the chair over the transom.

"Get me a blanket, Reedy. Some water?"

"Yes, Mama, of course. You comfortable?"

A feeble nod. A cough that wracked her skinny shoulders. His mother, shrunk to the size of a girl. An old girl.

He kissed her on her wrinkled, soap-smelling cheek.

She clasped his hand, a bird-boned papery grasp. "It's a beautiful night, isn't it?"

The wind chimes hung on the porch clanged mellowly. The distant surf broke, a soft murmur.

"It is, Mama. I'll be right back."

He went inside and got the blanket and the glass of ice water but by then she was already gone.

WALK IT OFF

THE LONG BLACK LONELINESS WEIGHED HIM down like a vulture squatting on his shoulders.

Mama, Crowe would think.

He was the oldest Crowe left on earth.

What were the words? It saddened him that there would be no one left alive who remembered her face.

His face.

Lily's face. Otter's laugh.

Who would Lily be now? He wondered if she would be more like him, or like her mother. He wondered if she'd find him the kind of father she'd like. The kind of person.

He walked it off. He walked in the morning and the night. He walked so much that season that the backs of his knees got sunburned, even before spring.

A VERY HENRY YAHCHILANE THANKSGIVING

TRY AS CROWE MIGHT, THERE WAS no avoiding the holidays and their monsoon of sentimentality. Everywhere you turned: colored bulbs and tinsel and fake snow. The glowing red life-sized plastic Santa under the cabana at the Rum Jungle. The weird junky crèches over in Emerald City.

There was no escape. The saccharine jingles played in the gas stations, the bait shop, on every commercial during football.

This holiday season especially, with Heidi gone, there seemed no escape.

His daughter gone longer than she was alive. *Otter, Otter, my god Otter, how could you be gone so long?*

And with his dreaded birthday on the horizon.

There were the nights he missed Heidi acutely. A crack gaped wide in his heart. He wanted very much that night to put his nose in her hair. He wanted to feel her hot sticky skin against his. He missed her breath, her accent.

Sometimes he lost himself in other women, it was true.

There was a marmalade maker over in Naples, Penny.

A few days before Thanksgiving, Crowe spent the night at her house.

The whole night after they fucked, the woman's cats wouldn't stop making a racket. The cats loathed Crowe. They smelled Emerald Island cats on him.

Penny would chuck a doily into the dark. "Stop it, kitties. Stop it. Quit it." She fussed at them more. She explained to Crowe, "They're battin' around the broken angel head. The cats got the damn ornament. They're battin' around the damn broken angel head. Hey, kitties. No, kitties. No."

It was some wee hour of morning. The two cats, executing acrobatic twists in the air, were flipping the grape-sized porcelain head soccer-like with their hind legs.

Every so often the head would crash against something in the dark and startle Crowe awake.

"Godfuckingdamnit."

The woman would snap her fingers and fuss again. "Kitties, no, kitties."

Finally Crowe sat up to the edge of the bed. The sandy ache of insomnia smarted his eyes. He pulled on his jeans. Porcelain doll faces peered down from the shelves. Some fucked-up spooky demondoll jury.

"I gotta go."

"But it's the holidays."

"I gotta go."

"No, kitties, no."

Let's beat this motherfucker. So was Reed Crowe's resolution the night before Thanksgiving.

He drove over to the Hoggly Woggly and bought all of the traditional holiday fixings. A twelve-pound turkey. New potatoes. String beans. Pecan pie. Cranberry sauce. Yams.

A few magnums of wine.

So Crowe the night before got crocked. He cut up celery and chunks of bread and he made homemade stuffing. He peeled the beans. He boiled and mashed the potatoes.

Before bed, shitfaced, he went outside and told the cats, "Tomorrow, we're gonna have us a turkey. How's that sound? Ha. All right. Merry fuckin' Christmas, man! That's right. High five? No? Okay, let's see tomorrow."

But in the morning he discovered that he had not taken the turkey out to thaw. All that preparation, and he had not taken the motherfucking turkey out of the fridge in time. The thing, still frozen solid. A bowling ball.

He made an animal sound of dismay and picked up the frozen plastic-wrapped bird and it fell to the kitchen floor.

Barefoot he kicked the frozen bird. His toe bones crunched. He wailed and hobbled.

He called Heidi. She did not answer.

He drank a few glasses of wine.

He called Heidi again. She did not answer.

Crowe drank another glass of wine. Remembered all the old Conchs and rummies who used to live on the island, dead for several Christmases.

This time of year, Good Old Mac, the long-dead bartender of the Rum Jungle, used to have a special fancy drink for him. The Green Eyed Loco Man.

One day, "There he is, in trouble again, Green Eyed Loco Man." And without Crowe's asking, without Mac's announcing, unbidden, the old man made an elaborate impromptu concoction.

Aperol, St-Germain, Angostura bitters, chartreuse, spiced rum, Pimm's, orange zest, cinnamon, mole.

And it was delicious.

Refreshing, not too sweet, like a hitherto undiscovered fruit, mellow in the mouth as watermelon, he was the first man to taste.

A few times a year when he was down in the mouth, stormy-eyed and gloomy—shit, these days few was on the verge of becoming several—Mac would make the drink for him. Again unbidden. And miraculously he replicated it exactly from memory every time.

Some other classic drink given another name, Crowe was sure.

But no, the old-timers at the Rum Jungle, inveterate drinkers one and all, vouched for Mac. Swore on their mothers. Swore on their drinks.

From their earnest oystery eyes Crowe knew they spoke the truth.

Crowe remembered Old Mac's last Christmas presiding over the cutting of the turkey, the Santa cap on his head, the apron, beach shorts, flip-flops. The big-bulbed Christmas lights glowing on the wind-bent coconut palms. A soft December wind rustling in the fronds.

Get out of the house, Crowe told himself. Clear your head.

So that's what he did.

———

At twilight, Reed Crowe in his longshoreman sweater and cargo shorts and moccasins went down the tideline of Emerald Island beach with a bottle of shipwreck wine tucked under his arm.

He was headed toward Henry Yahchilane's house.

At very least the hike would kill an hour. Clear his head.

He pictured Yahchilane answering the door. His bark-like face. His inscrutable squint. He imagined what he'd say to the man. "Hey, Yahchilane, man, remember that time we almost died? In the cave?"

Henry Yahchilane would blink his slow turtle-like blinks. Henry Yahchilane would invite him in for a drink. To shoot the shit for a while.

"Don't mind if I do, if it's no inconvenience. Hey, man. Remember the squid, Yahchilane?"

When Reed Crowe reached Henry Yahchilane's shaggy-shingled barrel house he saw that all the windows were lit. And through the sea-facing windows he could see the high-ceilinged main room lit and full of people. A Christmas tree decorated with ornaments and bulbs and garlanded with tinsel, a hearty monster towering to the ceiling.

Reed Crowe stood watching the house and was turning away when he saw a tall man coming down the length of the pier.

Henry Yahchilane.

"Crowe," said Yahchilane.

"Yahchilane," said Crowe.

The two old men faced each other on the beach in the waning daylight.

"You act as if surprised to find me here. This is my house."

"Yeah, man, I know."

"Are you lit?"

"Of course."

Yahchilane stood there, hands shoved in his jeans, thumbs hooked.

"Just taking a walk. Happy Thanksgiving and shit, Yahchilane. Though I don't know how you feel about all that nonsense."

"Hey."

Crowe still walking away, said, "Yeah."

"Come on in."

"No, it's all right."

"Come on in."

"Just taking a walk. Thanks."

"Come on in, egghead."

Crowe was so overtaken by the man's hospitality that he broke down weeping with gratitude.

"What the fuck," Yahchilane said. "Get yourself together, man."

Crowe pinched the bridge of his nose.

"Hey, man," Yahchilane said. "It's okay, come on in, egghead." He whacked Crowe's shoulder hard and chummy, cupped his hand there. "The turkey isn't that bad. Give yourself a minute and let's get your fish stick–looking ass into the house."

Inside Yahchilane's big barrel house were about twenty people, and before Henry could make introductions, Crowe right away excused himself to the bathroom.

He was afraid he reeked of pot and wine.

He was also afraid that he looked deranged, swollen-eyed from crying, snot in his beard.

He was not expecting this many people, this kind of scene.

In the bathroom medicine cabinet he found a travel-sized tube of toothpaste. He squeezed a pellet onto his finger, ran it across his teeth and gums. He looked in the mirror. "Jesus." He smelled his hands. He washed them. Smelled them again. He rubbed potpourri on his fingers. Then he scooped up a big handful, ran the shavings through his beard.

Crowe met the relatives. There were grandchildren. There were a few far-flung cousins and a few friends who'd driven the distance.

Good smells wafted from the kitchen. Turkey and cranberry and mulled cider.

A big fire crackled in the stone fireplace.

If they noticed anything strange about Crowe in appearance or behavior they didn't let on. They welcomed him heartily.

"I'm Reed Crowe," Crowe said. "Your all's dad calls me egghead."

One of Yahchilane's brood, a very tall black-haired, sharp-smiled woman with cat-like eyes, seemed mortified by this bit of information. "Oh no."

"Yep," Crowe said, "but I've been called much worse."

"Daddy," she said. Her name was Natasha, and she was dark-haired with Yahchilane's same cheekbones. His same nose. But her eyes, they were large and black and long-lashed and caught the amber light in the room.

Yahchilane waved her off. "Oh, come on, I call everybody that."

"I'm comfortable with it," Crowe said. "It fits."

The big dining room table was long and teak and manmade, Viking sturdy. Over it was the most elaborate stained glass chandelier Crowe ever saw in his life. The walls, the floors, most of it good solid wood.

Crowe knew he'd be dead within two weeks of living in such a place. He'd burn himself alive. Between the bongs and the joints and the candles and the pyro explosives, a powder keg.

There were several stocked bookshelves. The leather-bound books of the autodidact. Crowe was surprised to see, among them, the Golden Guides he grew up with. No, not surprised that Yahchilane had grown up, like him, with the books. Every boy had them. Books of the stars, books of the animals, books of the fish. But Yahchilane's collection still retained the brassy luster of a prize-winning ticket.

Crowe, a tumbler of hot buttered rum in hand, surveyed the hundreds of hardback spines peering augustly down from the walls.

There was a big *Oxford English Dictionary* on the pedestal. The pages were onion-skin thin and slick to the touch. The kind of book you found yourself wiping your fingers on your pants before touching. An august tome, big as a gravestone, as imposing.

In it was a rawhide bookmark that said CATAWBA. His eye skimmed and lit upon a word.

"'Haecceity'—the quality that makes a person, being or thing describable as 'this'; its 'thisness,' the property that declares an entity's singularity, performs its individuation."

———

For the meal Yahchilane sat at the head of the big Viking table under the stained glass chandelier the size of a lemon tree. Across from him was Natasha. Catty-corner from Natasha, Crowe. He tried not to stare at the woman. Her pretty eyes.

Natasha must have caught a whiff of potpourri because she eyed him. "Why do you smell like frankincense?" she asked.

"Say what now?" Crowe said.

Natasha smiled a small knowing smile. Her black hair spilled down her back lustrous as a raven wing. Crowe tried not to think of Nina's black hair. Every so often he still felt a heartsick pang for the woman. Then he'd feel foolish. Maybe he more missed that time in his life, so unlike the eras before and after.

The waning evening showed through the big beach-facing windows. A few ruby fingers of daylight left. A melancholy lavender settling over the sea.

The glass threw back their reflections. The lot of them sitting at the long Viking table under the brassy light of the chandelier. The fire crackling in the big coral-rock fireplace.

He held up his fork, heaping with the gravy-soaked mashed potatoes. So warm steam was still wafting off. The comforting warmth of the food in his stomach. Piano, Professor Longhair, played softly on the stereo. Notes quick and rippling soft like the burble of a water fountain.

Crowe could not recall food this delicious. His standard meals were austere. Fish and chicken, peppers from the garden because he liked his food spicy. The rare concession to green vegetable matter.

But this food. The almond haricot beans. The cranberry sauce that tasted faintly of orange zest. The stuffing with bourbon-soaked pecans dusted with brown sugar. The buttered biscuits that he used to sop up the peppery gravy.

"God, this is great. Thanks, folks."

"Daddy cooked it. Not me."

"Yahchilane. A cook."

Natasha said, "A curmudgeon."

"Haecceity," said Reed Crowe. "Ha."

"Here we go with the nonsense," said Yahchilane.

There was a man at the table, Seacoffee, who said he could trace his heritage back to twelve hundred AD. Timucuan Indians. He told the table that his ancestors lived in a small village built atop a shell mound. Oyster shells, left over from what they ate to survive.

Seacoffee asked them, "You ever notice those hill-like things when you're driving through Florida? Easy to spot, 'cause the state's so damn flat. I seen one as far north as Paines Prairie one time. Just south of Gainesville. Still got buffalo there. And still got some mounds. Couple'a stories, wouldn't you say, Yah?"

Yahchilane finished chewing his food. Swallowed. Wiped his mouth with his napkin. "Sometimes, I've seen some as tall as sixty feet."

"Well, my relatives come from one of those mounds you seen. Not the sixty-foot. My Uncle Bert was afraid of heights."

"Bert?"

"It was a joke, Crowe," Yahchilane said.

Crowe stroked his beard. He looked at Seacoffee. "You know, I've found these things. Maybe you ought to take a look."

Crowe explained the artifacts to Seacoffee and to the rest of the table. About half a minute into his spiel he regretted the impulse. Ill-begotten at best. He worried that he sounded like a blathering drunk.

"And one time Yahchilane said it looked like the guy was smoking," Crowe heard himself saying. He could feel his face redden, the scorch of embarrassment in his cheeks. He was thankful for the concealment of his beach bum beard.

He went on, "I said it looked more like a snake. Like maybe he had snakes coming out of his head, you know? But maybe smoke makes sense. Did they smoke back then? Tobacco, I mean? Or anything? Snakes, I thought snakes because it looks like a crown, you know?"

Seacoffee said to Crowe, "Well, I wouldn't go having a mudpull over them."

"Yeah. No. Of course not."

Yahchilane told his friend Seacoffee that Crowe had been in touch with some academics from the state universities, which seemed to satisfy Seacoffee.

Seacoffee told Crowe, "I don't know what that cult-ass stuff is you're talking about, but I can tell you it's not my tribe."

The badinage grew drowsy. The firelight waned.

Crowe cleared his throat. He proposed a toast. Cleared his throat again. He started to stand, knees knocking the underside of the table. But the table was so imposing and sturdy no one took notice. Crowe sat back down. Everyone at the table watched. Waited. An expectant air presided over the table.

He cleared his throat again. Then he hoisted his glass. "I want to drink to Yahchilane calling me an egghead. I don't mind it."

"All right, cool it, Christmas Eyes."

The grandchildren, four kids middle-school-aged, sat on the other end of the table, talking about something called Super Mario Bros.

"I know nothing of your father," Crowe said to Yahchilane's kids. "He's a complete enigma."

Henry Yahchilane sat there stoically chewing his bread.

The clink and clatter of forks and knives on plates.

A friend of Yahchilane's, a black man named Tyrone who'd served with Yahchilane in the war, said, "We called him the Enigma, the platoon."

"No kidding?"

Tyrone nodded, laughed, sipped his wine.

"He hates talking about himself," said the daughter, Natasha.

"He hates talking, period," said the son, Seymour.

"There's nothing to talk about."

"He's the worst conversationalist," said the son.

"It drove our mom crazy," said Natasha.

"You gotta pick your battles," said Yahchilane. "The woman's a motormouth."

"Let's watch it," said Seymour.

"I couldn't hear any more. It was just another noise in the room."

There was a four-foot-and-a-half nut-brown woman with snow-white hair, a cousin of Yahchilane's, next to Crowe. So far quiet, now she said, "We always thought he was mysterious. All my girlfriends had a crush on Hank."

Natasha, "But he always says he loves us."

Crowe, again, "He calls me egghead."

Now Yahchilane's kids were laughing.

Crowe, "This is delicious. Thanks, folks, for having me."

They were finished with dinner and everyone was still drinking wine when Natasha and Seymour shared humorous stories about Yahchilane's childhood.

Crowe egged the kids on. Everybody started getting a little tipsy. Tyrone said he'd chip in money. Crowe got his red-wine face. His coarse-grained Scots-Irish teeth showing purple as he threw his head back with laughter.

"Go on, go on, more, man, you're makin' my night, man." Crowe pouring wine for everybody as Yahchilane chewed stolid, turtle-like. "I'll pay you for more stories. Five bucks a story. Ten bucks a story."

Crowe lifted a buttock, groped for an imaginary wallet.

"Keep on smoking dope, Christmas Eyes," said Yahchilane.

"Daddy," said Natasha.

"It was a joke. You guys joke. I can joke."

"You're so deadpan, Daddy, maybe he doesn't know," said Natasha.

"The deadpan enigma," said Tyrone.

Crowe, "I'll agree with you except the pan part, Natasha."

Yahchilane chewed on his bread.

"Okay, I got one for you," Natasha said. "My daddy worked for Burdines Department Store. It's true. A model. That's how he met our mother."

"They gotta have separate Christmases," Yahchilane's son said. "Because they act like infants. They can't act like adults. So they split Christmases up."

"I won't say a bad word about your mother."

"You've been sayin' bad about her all night," said Seymour.

"Oh, I mean it affectionately."

"Motormouth, a term of endearment?"

"Oh, enough horseplay," said Natasha.

"I'm sure I deserve it. I'm difficult to live with. Which is why I live alone."

"All this makes him sound so bad," Natasha told Crowe. "Daddy always told us he loved us. Every night."

ZEST

REED CROWE REMARKED THAT YAHCHILANE'S CRANBERRY sauce was probably the best he'd ever tasted. He lifted a hand, showing a palm. As if swearing on a courtroom Bible.

"Wow, you really dig the cranberry sauce," said Tyrone, Henry's war friend.

"Never cared for it. But this? Love it."

"Cranberry sauce man," said Tyrone.

"I'm a convert. Full-blown." Crowe asked what the secret was.

Yahchilane, a brow cocked, tearing off a hunk of his biscuit, said, "Secret?"

"The cranberry sauce. The secret ingredient. Because I'm getting something."

"Orange zest," Yahchilane said. He chewed the chunk of his biscuit.

"Orange zest," Crowe mused. "I would have never guessed."

"Orange zest man," said Tyrone. "The man digs zest."

"I've never seen anybody so excited over zest." Natasha laughed. "You sound like you're about to break into song."

"The zest man," said Tyrone.

Over the course of the evening, Crowe had learned that Natasha worked at an investment firm in New York, inside the Twin Towers. Crowe was unsettled by how attractive he found Yahchilane's daughter. Because she was Yahchilane's daughter.

Natasha had her father Henry's same sharp cheekbones. But her eyes were very large, big indigo eyes. Her laughter was earnest and full-bodied, smoky and quick. Not like Yahchilane's gruff bark. Which Crowe had heard all of how many times? Seven, eight? Surely he could count on both hands.

Her brother, Seymour, who was an adjunct professor, art therapy, seemed more like his father. Dour.

Over the course of the evening Crowe had been aware, peripherally, of Seymour's mounting ire. Truth of the matter, his attention was fixed on Natasha. But at one point he overheard Seymour mention Rodney King. Another time it was the misallocation of Florida Lottery funds.

Now it was on to Thanksgiving. Which, according to Seymour, was complete bullshit.

"You see me in a damn pilgrim outfit?" Yahchilane asked his son.

Sitting catty-corner to Crowe, Tyrone shot Crowe a covert look of supreme wariness from across the table. He mouthed quickly, very distinctly, "Every year."

"I'm just saying, here we are. Thanksgiving."

Yahchilane told his son that his broadsides were sophomoric. "I like turkey. You see me with a musket and a powder horn?"

"You two cool it," said Natasha.

"How are those Seminoles this year?" Yahchilane asked. He made a tomahawk gesture with his arms.

Tyrone hummed the Florida State Seminoles war chant.

Seymour was looking down at his plate, chewing small quick bites of his food.

"What an evening," Crowe said, to break the tension.

Seymour turned to Crowe and asked what he meant.

Crowe stroked his beard. He gestured vaguely.

In the great coral stone fireplace a log crumbled. Embers helixed up, blue and orange sparks. There was a soft tumbling ashy sound. Charles Mingus, *Pithecanthropus Erectus*, played faintly on the stereo speakers.

It was a beautiful evening, Crowe remarked. He looked around the table. And meant what he'd said. The pastel gradients of the Gulf dusk laddering down into the horizon. The fire cracking, and in the huge glass windows facing the sea the room was full of mellow honey light, reflected and superimposed over the panorama of the beach.

"What's your last name again?" Seymour asked Crowe.

"Crowe."

He leaned forward, one forearm on the great Viking table. "Why are you laughing? I'm asking a serious question."

"Would you like more cranberry sauce, Reed?" Natasha asked.

Natasha passed the blue china tureen. Crowe helped himself to a few dollops while Seymour brooded. He had his elbows on the table and his hands stitched together over the plate.

Seymour asked about Crowe's family history in the area. His ancestry.

Crowe cleared his throat. "A lot of that stuff, lost in hurricanes. Ledgers, records, yeah."

"Convenient," Seymour said.

"Seymour," Natasha said.

Crowe went on. "A little bit of everything. Scots-Irish on my mother's side. My father's side, all mixed up." He continued, almost involuntarily, so unnerved he was by Seymour's interrogator's gaze. "My grandfather was a rum runner. That I know. I know he worked with Capone. That's fact. I have the pictures somewhere. I'll show you sometime. If you like."

Truth was, Crowe couldn't help but wonder if they were somehow culpable, his relatives, in the abuse of the Natives. He supposed they were. No doubt they had to employ some Seminoles and Calusa Indians. He thought of the Seminoles digging postholes under water. How they labored and cleared the way, backbreaking work in the hammering Florida sun, all for pennies, so the massive steamboats could lumber and tear like beasts through the lettuce bogs.

Finally, nodding, as though agreeing with himself, Crowe said, "So, a lot of stuff in the bloodline."

Seymour said, "You can take tests these days."

"Genetic you mean?" Crowe said. "Do they extract your zest?"

"Zest man," said Tyrone.

Natasha laughed.

Even Yahchilane's Fu Manchu mustache moved a little.

"You think it's a joke," Seymour said.

"I'm sorry. Just trying to liven things up."

The small nut-brown woman with cotton-white hair who'd said nothing all night put a hand on the sleeve of Seymour's brown corduroy suit. "You're beginning to sound like one of those crazies."

"Come on, Aunt Georgette."

Yahchilane, looking levelly at his son, said, "He gets mixed up in these political causes and he's getting scammed. Oh, oh, blood quantum this, blood quantum that. That whole fucked-up political world."

"It's important."

"Yeah, yeah, it's important. But don't try to be something you aren't. You ate Cheerios like everybody else. Acting like you were born in a wigwam."

"You did. You grew up in a village."

"So what? That makes you more authentic? You? I was forced to do that."

The kids went back to gabbing about Nintendo. The bamboo wind chimes clanged mellowly.

After dinner, Yahchilane stepped up to Crowe in the kitchen. "Hey, man."

"What's that?"

"You look at my daughter, I'll cut off your dick."

Crowe was shocked. "What?"

Tyrone stepped up to Crowe. "Relax, brother. He's fooling with you. Have a beer."

Crowe sipped the fresh beer. He asked, "What's that mean, Christmas eyes, Yahchilane?"

At the big Viking table, the kids were now playing Uno, arguing about who'd bent one of the cards in the corner. "I'll whip your face, motherfucker," said one.

"Cool it," said the small nut-brown woman. Her voice was surprisingly large and commanding.

The kids settled.

Yahchilane told him, "Christmas eyes. Your eyes. Red, green, and white."

"In that order?"

The last time Crowe heard Henry Yahchilane laugh was later that night. The party sputtered out and Crowe knew it was time to leave after the card game though he would have happily stayed. Wanted to stay. But he told everyone good night and they rose from their chairs and shook his hand and asked him if he was sure he didn't want a nightcap.

Bushed, Crowe told them.

Yahchilane and Natasha walked Crowe down to the beach. It was almost eleven. A light winter-kissed breeze. Sweater weather.

"Sure you don't want a ride?" Natasha asked.

"He's fine," Yahchilane said.

"I'm good," Crowe said. And he was. He started walking home. Waved over his shoulder.

The clouds were gone and the moon was late and small, a sharp pewter dime high in the sky. The yuletide stars many.

"Hey, egghead," Yahchilane called. "Just remember, go straight. Left, that's the ocean."

"Daddy," Natasha said, mock-scolding.

About forty-five minutes later, Crowe had his clothes off and was in his robe when there was a soft inquisitive rapping at his front door.

"Hello?" Crowe called.

"Reed," a woman said.

"Natasha?" Reed said.

"Hey, you still awake?"

Crowe went to the door. Locked, and with the burglar chain clasped, a precaution he never observed before Catface.

"Hey," Crowe said.

Beautiful Natasha, her long black hair shining in the porch light, asked Crowe if she woke him.

"Course not. You?"

"Did you wake me?"

"What? No. Is everything okay?"

"I'm horny."

Crowe stood there mistrusting what he'd heard. His hearing, dodgier and dodgier these days.

He cleared his throat, scratched the crown of his head.

"I'm horny," Natasha said again. Matter-of-factly, with no bashfulness. "It's cold outside. Won't you let me in?" Her dark winesleepy eyes full of light, her dramatic nose. A simper on her lips.

Crowe recalled what Yahchilane told him in the kitchen between coffee and the brandy. "Keep your dick away from my daughter or I'll cut it off."

Crowe was opening the door wider to let Natasha into the house when Yahchilane leapt out of the hedges flanking the walk. He was brandishing giant garden shears over his head, a handle in each hand.

"I warned you, you son of a bitch!" he shouted.

Crowe reared back, forearm raised as if to block a blow.

Then Yahchilane stopped and lowered the shears and laughed his panting dog laughter.

His daughter joined in, a feminine version of the same laughter.

For an instant Crowe was pissed. But almost as suddenly he was laughing with them.

"We couldn't take my big mouth son anymore," Yahchilane explained. "A hardcore Christian conservative. My own son. Can you believe it?"

"He got started on politics and now he and Tyrone are at it. We needed a break and snuck out," said Natasha.

"Your face, the shears," Yahchilane said.

That night they laughed and joked and listened to records, drank a few bottles of Crowe's shipwreck wine until the wee hours of morning.

EBENEZER MCFORNICATION

SOME NIGHTS, WHEN HE WAS HELPING Eddie out with the Emerald Island Inn for extra cash and for something to keep him out of trouble and get him out of the house, Crowe night-managed the old motel. One night a woman complained about someone's wee-hour debauch. There were, according to the woman, sounds of fornication coming from one of the rooms. Her words. The right side of her face was puffy and pink, somehow babyish, as if she'd just woken. It was past two in the morning and she wore a moss-green anorak rain jacket over her bedclothes. Crowe would have put her in her late fifties. She was tan and had a mole above her lip and her bottle-blond hair was clasped back with a hasp.

"There's got to be some decency," she said. Crowe reckoned her accent from Alabama.

Crowe, helping out like he did on occasion for Eddie, was in no mood. He asked the woman what room she was in.

She told him.

Honeymooners, Crowe explained. This was true. A check-in, earlier that day.

"It sounds like a porn shoot."

"Who knows," Crowe said. "Maybe it is." Deliberately flip. *This isn't the Cincinnati HoJo, lady,* he wanted to say. With her hand—without a wedding band, Crowe noticed—she clutched the collar of her coat together. He had in all his years of terminal bachelorhood and tomcatting made it a habit of looking there first.

"What's your name, sir?"

"Ebenezer."

A tight quick shake of the head. "What?"

"Ebenezer McFornication."

"Goddamn you," the woman said.

Crowe knew he was being an asshole. It was his girl's birthday. His girl Otter's birthday. Were she alive today she would have been thirty. It didn't seem real to Crowe.

The woman demanded the manager.

Crowe bowed like a butler, flourish of the arms and all.

The woman eyed something on the side of his head. The joint tucked behind his ear. Half-finished and forgotten before now. Crowe, defiantly, made no gesture to remove it.

"You know what, I don't like your attitude."

He pointed to the complaint box, marked as such in handwritten Sharpie, standing atop the pamphlet rack. A repurposed orange crate from Webster Brothers Co. St. Cloud, Florida.

Shocking, how many people fell for this con over the years. Marching over there like they were going to save the world. Like they were amending the Constitution.

The Alabama woman spent a surreal three minutes writing on a complaint card. She slipped it in the box. She glared over her shoulder on the way out.

She was halfway across the lot going to her room when Crowe came out with the woman's complaint card, lit it with his plastic lighter, and used the flame from the complaint card to ignite his joint.

She might not have noticed his presence if it weren't for the flick of his BIC.

The woman in the overcoat turned. He'd not exhaled his first puff when she began to cry.

"Well, Jesus Christ, lady." Suddenly Crowe felt awful. Like a cretin. "It's just a joke. I'm the manager."

There she stood in the crushed shell parking lot near the sizzling pink and turquoise neon of the sign. She put her face in her hands and kept crying.

Crowe stepped half the distance.

"Lady, I'm so sorry. Don't cry now. I was just bein' a jackass. I'm the manager. I'm the owner. Used to be. I was demoted. I was just joking."

"Why would you do that?" she asked.

Her face was stricken with so much grief Crowe was at a loss. He flicked his joint, which now seemed doubly inappropriate, like a party hat at a funeral, into the crushed shell.

He heeled it out with his zorie.

The woman said, "I just got back from my ex-husband's funeral."

"Gosh, I'm sorry, lady. I was just having a bad day."

It was a sticky windswept night, a taste of rain in the air. Thunder voicing out of the Gulf. Soon there would be one of those predawn downpours.

The woman stood in the light of the Emerald Island Inn sign, pretty in the pink and turquoise neon. Distressed, but pretty.

"Oh," someone cried in one of the rooms. The apish grunt of a man deep in the throes of eros.

"Oh god, fuck me, daddy," cried a woman.

"Oh, shit, baby," said the man.

Even with their door closed and the curtains drawn, even from this distance, even with the first storm winds rattling the banyans and palms, they could hear the couple.

"Good god," Crowe told the woman. "You weren't kidding."

She had her key fob in her hand. Her face was writhing with small tics, as if she didn't know whether to laugh or cry or shout.

"I'm sorry. So sorry. The room's on the house."

"No need."

"Please, I insist."

"We both had bad days."

There they stood apart from each other, some emotional stand-off, ten paces away.

The woman knuckled sudden tears from her cheeks. "Oh god, here I am. Crying in front of a perfect stranger. I mean, here I am. This is life."

"I cry in front of strangers all the time."

The man hollered again from the neighbor's room. "Good god-damn fuck."

"Serious fornication," Crowe said.

The woman let out a little snort.

"I'm sorry for your husband. Wanna know something? Let me tell you something."

"Tell me."

"I was sad about my little girl tonight. Gone too. I took it out on the wrong person. That's the truth. That's it. As much as I under-stand myself."

"I'm sorry for your girl."

"It's okay. It's fine. It's been a long time."

"I'm sorry."

"Thank you, ma'am. I'm sorry. Good night."

She was at her door and Crowe was watching her key into her room when she said without turning, "Maybe we should try being nicer to one another, you know?"

"Yes," he said, "I think you're right. Truce."

They approached each other with arms held out. They hugged a friendly hug. Crowe patted her on the back. He started to pry away but she held on. She drew him closer. She put her face into his T-shirt.

Later, he was on top of her and inside of her and she was clutch-ing him and trying to pull him closer and deeper.

"How about the people next door?"

"Nobody there."

"Over there?"

"Yeah."

"Nobody. Positive."

And he was positive. Next door was Wayne Wade's old room.

Crowe said into the woman's ear, "God, you smell good."

"Sh."

"Are you sure this is okay?"

"Sh."

"Goddamn, woman," Crowe said as he thrust. "Yes."

They lost themselves in each other as only people who would never see each other again could. They went at it like kids and every so often they laughed at themselves. They laughed into each other's mouths. They were still at it when the first fits of the deluge fell.

And when the phone rang at the Emerald Island Inn reception desk, a complaint about a banging headboard, it went unheeded.

HER NAME WAS GABBY

HEIDI STILL CALLED ON OCCASION, TO check in, to ask about life on Emerald Island. She asked about Yahchilane. Nina and Eddie and their kids. Usually she could not disclose her whereabouts. She was in charge of ferrying works of art across countries, across continents, and there were always art thieves looking to hijack their vans and trucks in transit.

Sometimes she asked if he'd seen the doctor.

At her insistence he did, and this time, in his middle fifties, Dr. Vu surprised Crowe at the end of her visit by finally saying yes to one of his jokey advances.

"Really?" Crowe said, buttoning up his shirt on the paper-lined examination table.

The woman was an inscrutable imp to him.

Her answer was, "I don't like your triglycerides. And I heard a heart murmur."

"Do you like Italian?" Crowe asked her.

Her name was Gabby. He made lame jokes about her name. The gist being that she hardly spoke at all. Instead, Crowe was the gabby one. He found himself apologizing. "I like your voice," she told him flatly, on one of their first dinner dates, perhaps the first compliment she'd tendered him.

"What is this?" he asked her.

"Does it have to be anything?"

The woman had a point. It was what it was.

"I think that's the first compliment you've given me."

"I like your general air of dishevelment," she said, spearing a gnocchi with her fork and munching it.

"You think I'm disheveled."

"It's endearing."

"I never considered myself disheveled."

They saw each other once or twice a week, for dinner, a movie.

He caught her stealing occasional affectionate looks. Her small hands. Her smell, sandalwood and pomegranate shampoo. They spent many wordless evenings in the kitchen with Crowe's stereo playing softly, she acting a line cook to his chef. Sometimes as he stirred the garlic sautéing in the skillet with a wooden spoon she would sneak up from behind and plant a kiss on the back of his neck.

Sometimes she'd spend the night. She was quiet but ferocious in bed. She liked being on top.

It was what it was.

One night he asked her what changed her mind about him. "Out of curiosity," he said.

They were at his place in the sunroom, sitting on the reclining BarcaLoungers and watching the purpling sky above the Gulf. She curled her forefinger. She was mid-bite, her gnocchi. She finished chewing, not quickly, but at the same pace. The forefinger still curled before her cherub lips.

One of her little quirks that Crowe liked.

Finally she said, "I used to think you were silly."

"I am."

"Yes. Sometimes. But I used to think you were ridiculous."

"A girl used to call me silly a lot."

"Your daughter?"

"No, no."

"I'm sorry."

"No, it's okay." And it was.

Crowe thought of Otter less often. Until at last he thought of her only a few times a week. Around the holidays, around the girl's birthday.

So much time had passed.

He supposed he'd forgiven himself.

And even when Crowe did remember her now, it wasn't with the heartsick knife-through-the-ribs feeling of regret, but instead with a throb of melancholy nostalgia.

Gone so long, that sweet girl. Sometimes when school let out for the summer and the families came down from up north he would swear he heard amid the chatter of the crowd her laughter pealing.

And he was again reminded of her voice for a spell.

But the pain was gone.

He'd changed.

Or time had changed him.

"It's okay to be silly sometimes," Gabby told him finally.

"I think so."

"I wish I were more silly sometimes," Gabby confessed.

"Well, I find you very, very silly, for what it's worth."

"Do you, now?"

"That's my official diagnosis, yes."

WHOMP

ONE SUMMER SUNSET HE WAS IN a wine-buzzed mellow mood, Charles Mingus's *Pithecanthropus Erectus* playing low on the record player. He was sitting in his cream leather BarcaLounger chair in the sunroom with the lights turned low. He had just had lunch with Gabby at the Blue Parrot diner.

That evening through the big Gulf-facing windows Crowe could see past the dunes, the late low sun making a wide copper swath on the dusk-calmed sea. A golden bridge.

A speckled trout fillet was thawing on the kitchen cutting board. He was drinking a glass of red wine. He lifted one of the wine corks out of the bowl beside the chair and held it to his nose. Wondering if he was smelling its scent or just his memory of it.

It was then that a huge pain like a hurled bowling ball struck him square in the chest. He dropped the cork. He dropped the wineglass and it shattered on the terrazzo. He grabbed at his chest and said, "Oh, man."

Blood whomped in his ears.

There was a roar as if he were falling through a black void, the tear of wind ripping past his ears, and then Reed Crowe was dead.

SUGAR CUBES

THERE WAS NO FUNERAL. AS REED Crowe would have preferred. And the wake was a modest affair held on the beach behind Crowe's home on a blustery gray day in September. Many of the old islanders were in attendance, a passel of people from up and down the coast who'd heard the news. SnoBall Larry and Adele the clover honey girl. Eddie with his wife, Nina, and their daughters, Mariposa and Maribelle. An archeologist named Baxter PhD from Gainesville, Florida. Myrtle and Moe with their shaggy beach dogs. Some old Florida Conchs from the Keys who'd heard the news from other old salts in the Panhandle. Chill Norton from the Pervy Mermaid. A few of Reed Crowe's woman friends from over the years. Dr. Vu.

And among the mourners was Marlon Arango, now a citizen, now married to a Lebanese-American phlebotomist. Marlon himself worked on the docks of Port Everglades in Fort Lauderdale as a yacht mechanic. He owned a shop near Bahia Mar within sight of the Pier Sixty-Six Hotel, the one with the giant crown on top of it. Henry Yahchilane knew it well, passing it before taking the Las Olas Bridge over the Intracoastal on the way to the Swap Shop and old Thunderbird Drive-In.

"I bet you got stories," Yahchilane said, and he meant it. Those huge gleaming mansions on the sea, lined up and down the canals below the drawbridge. Vessels worthy of kings and queens. Who the fuck knew went down on them.

"Oh, you'd be shocked. Even you, Mr. Yahchilane. Best saved for another day."

"Well, I'm glad you're all set."

"Thank you, Mr. Yahchilane. I'm sorry for your loss."

The remark took Yahchilane by surprise. "Oh. Yes. Well. Thank you."

The mourners were still crowded on the beach when Henry Yahchilane waded out to his knees wearing his brown corduroy suit, the first time anyone on the island could recall seeing him in attire aside from jeans and denim. He opened the plastic bag of cremains and cast Crowe's ashes into the water where blue-silver fingerling baitfish rose to the surface with nipping mouths.

Almost certainly illegal.

Fuck it.

It's where he belonged.

After the eulogy they shared memories and anecdotes about Crowe.

Myrtle and Moe talked about Crowe's deathly fear of the U.S. mail and post. "He'd think he was invisible in that orange car of his. The beard. The green shades. Like I didn't see him. Like he was going incognito for the FBI. I've never seen a man with such aversion to U.S. mail."

Everyone seemed surprised when Dr. Gabby Vu cleared her throat softly and spoke. "One time Reed, I guess you all called him Crowe, invited me to dinner," she said. "I asked him what he was having. Reed said chicken potpie. Would you like to come? And I said sure."

It was Dr. Vu who found him the day after his death, 1999. A few months before the Columbine shooting. They'd made plans to go to the Salvador Dalí museum, a day trip to St. Petersburg. She rang the bell. Tried the door. Locked, since all those problems years ago, since the bridge explosion. She tried his landline on her cellphone. No answer. She circumnavigated the house, the feral cats darting among the bamboo stalks and the crocus plants and the beach scrub. In the backyard she saw him. She saw him through the sliding glass door. It was partially ajar. Some of the cats were at his feet. One was in his lap. He was sprawled on the BarcaLounger in the sunroom. A glass of wine, half-finished, on the end table. His hand dangling, a wine cork on the terrazzo as if just fallen out of his clutch.

People waited. Dr. Vu licked her wind-chapped lips with the tip of her tongue. She pushed up her round-framed glasses with her forefinger. Her bobbed black hair whipped in the wind. "So I come over. No dinner. Well, no chicken potpie. There's chicken. A few pieces, fried, mini-mart chicken. Gas station chicken. And there's pie. A frozen apple pie. And there's pot."

An uncertain chuckle passed among the mourners.

"He was high as a kite."

Then everyone joined, grateful for the opportunity to laugh.

A windy beat of silence passed. People were waiting for someone else to speak. Somehow most of the glances fell upon Yahchilane.

He wasn't expecting to speak.

Yahchilane could have many stories. A treasure trove. You live so long in Florida, even on a remote island, especially on a remote island, you were bound to have stories.

To live them.

An island itself was a story, when you thought about it. As was Florida. But imagine saying this at someone's funeral. They'd throw the big butterfly net over you and haul you off in a white van.

Henry Yahchilane did not tell the story about the time of the assassin, or the time of the refugees, or the time of Wayne Wade, or the time of getting stuck in that grotto for days on end.

Once upon a time there were two eggheads. One egghead was named Reed Crowe. The other egghead was named Henry Yahchilane. Two Florida men. Two Florida eggheads.

Two Florida eggheads who braved out Hurricane Andrew in 1992.

Yahchilane told the story about the sugar cubes.

Yahchilane went to Crowe's for shelter when the first bands of the storm lashed the island. Yahchilane was afraid how the old shaggy-shingled barrel-shaped house would fare. More than half a century old, hewn of weather-cured wood, some of the lathing giving way in places.

He drove the van through tempest winds and airborne debris like buckshot to Crowe's.

Crowe, "Oh, it'll take a last-minute turn. Like it always do."

Wrong.

It was late at night, into the early morning, when the storm scythed across the state. Yahchilane and Crowe drank beers and watched the news and when the reception of every television station fizzled, they played Neil Young records. Loud.

Sometime in the evening Yahchilane, poker-faced as always, had told Crowe he was on LSD. At first Crowe didn't believe it.

Crowe told him, "I can't picture you on LSD."

Yahchilane kept mum.

"I mean, no offense? You're so fuckin' serious."

"I prefer not to make a fool of myself."

"What's the implication?"

"It wasn't an implication."

"An outright insult?"

To this Yahchilane offered no reply.

"Strong stuff?" Crowe asked.

"It works," Yahchilane said with a shrug in his voice.

"Let me buy some?"

"No. I'll give you some."

Crowe was immediately animated. "Am I going to see bats with my mother's face and shit, Yahchilane? What should I expect?"

"It works differently for people."

"Let's do this."

They popped the sugar cubes and let them dissolve on their tongues. They played records on Crowe's stereo.

"Oh man, I can taste these sounds," Crowe said. This confession as John Coltrane's "Bakai" was blaring on the hi-fi stereo speakers.

"You ramblin' about, egghead?"

"It's incredible, Yahchilane. I can't describe it."

Thirty minutes later Crowe started wigging out, thinking maybe they'd made a huge mistake, not fleeing the storm. The hurricane blew demonic over the island.

The island was by then a mess of downed utility poles, power lines ripped apart and tangled. Other power lines still live and whipping like hell-bent electric eels. Trees had boards and shards of glass driven straight through them. Palm trees were felled atop roofs and cars. Boats in the bay capsized and half-sunk. Others knocked together and busted apart like Tinkertoys. Cottages and bungalows wiped away.

Now Yahchilane told the people at the funeral what he finally told Crowe once he started panicking. Crowe was telling Yahchilane, "Oh god, I think I'm losing my mind, Yahchilane. Do you feel him outside? The grim reaper?" when finally Yahchilane put the poor guy out of his misery and told him.

Just sugar cubes.

Of course, reticent and taciturn speaker that he was, Yahchilane related the anecdote in a version greatly abridged. The whole time he stood with his head hung down and his eyes on the ground, calloused fingers folded, working, as if they were kneading a hat he'd removed out of respect.

People tightened their collars and bunched their shoulders against the gusts. They remained silent for a minute in the dove-gray afternoon, the chevrons of whitecaps arrowing toward shore, spangles of sand sidewinding down the desolate expanse of the beach.

APHRA AKA LANDFALL IMMINENT

(2008–2019)

IN THE BEGINNING OF AUTUMN 2008, Yahchilane was besieged with a two-week cough that wouldn't go away. In the mornings, his hacking was so loud and constant the blackbirds were scared out of the pines surrounding his house. The coughing got so bad he couldn't hide it from his kids when they were on the phone. At their behest, expecting the worst, he went to see Dr. Vu.

She took blood tests and X-rays. Lung cancer, aggressive. Dr. Vu told him his only chance was removing the lung, excising it entire from his body like a pea from a pod.

In the small windowless examination room, Yahchilane absorbed this information without change of expression. His mouth stayed set as concrete. He nodded.

Finally Yahchilane rose from the examination table and thanked the doctor. As if the doctor had merely given him directions to the highway.

"Thank you? Henry, you heard me, right?"

"Yeah, yes."

She asked if there was anything he wanted. A drink of water. Anti-anxiety meds.

Yahchilane told her he was fine.

Dr. Vu asked, "Henry, what can I do for you right now?"

Yahchilane said he wanted a cigarette.

Dr. Vu went outside with Yahchilane. A muggy day, the big clown grasshoppers rattling from deep within the croton bushes, mating.

Yahchilane and Dr. Vu stood under the awning of the medical office, ninety-five degrees in the shade.

As Yahchilane smoked, Dr. Vu referred him to an oncologist in Fort Lauderdale. Her cousin, a specialist.

"Will you see him, Henry?" she asked.

He said he'd consider it.

"Don't be an asshole, Henry," said Dr. Vu. "It'll be ugly. You'll need chemo. But we caught it in time."

"No chemo."

"You say that now. Try telling your family."

Yahchilane said nothing.

"There's counseling."

"Okay, Dr. Vu."

"Don't write it off. Don't be an asshole."

Yahchilane thanked the doctor. He wished her a good day, stubbed out his cigarette in the gravel of the standing ashtray. He got into his van and gripped the wheel and exhaled a long shuddering breath before falling into a fit of coughs.

COFFEE BEAN

HENRY YAHCHILANE SURVIVED THE SURGERY, EMERGED from the procedure one-lunged and twenty pounds lighter, a gaunt, sharp-featured old man with a huge scar on his body that made one side of his torso look like a coffee bean shell.

He got along fairly well considering he was a walking dead man. A cat with his tenth life.

He felt like shit. Sure. Shit on a shoeheel. But he felt like shit before.

When during a follow-up visit a few months later Dr. Vu told him she'd witnessed a miracle, that he was cancer-free, Henry Yahchilane accepted the good news much the same as he did the bad.

"All right," he told Dr. Vu.

"Don't be an asshole, Henry," she told him. "You're gonna be around for a while longer."

It was only a one-minute walk across the lot to his van, but even that short a distance left him gasping, the back of his denim shirt sweated through.

He lit a cigarette.

Took a puff, retched, rolled down the window, flicked the cigarette out.

In the rearview mirror he saw his face, wan and yellow and exhausted.

"Well, here we go," Yahchilane said. "Whoopdy-fuckin'-do."

STRANGE WEATHER

THE NEXT DECADE THERE WERE DAYS Henry Yahchilane had trouble keeping up with the days. There were years he had trouble keeping up with the years. He used to keep track by the change of the seasons, but that was no longer a reliable measure. The weather was getting weird, unpredictable. Irate.

The people, too: strange.

He suspected the economy was to blame. The dearth of jobs. The oil in the water. The tainted oysters and lobsters and shrimp and fish.

The heat. It got to people's heads.

Plus, all the newfangled drugs popping up around this part of the panhandle. Like the mother of a thousand plants.

One night at the Rum Jungle, some guy started pushing around another guy just because he looked at his lady friend the wrong way. The bartender told them to take their bullshit outside. They did. They brawled behind a midden of oyster shells. They threw wild drunken punches and pounded and walloped each other into minced meat and every time Yahchilane thought someone was about to go down the man recovered his sea legs and brawled anew.

All the while the seagulls flew circles above the hill of shells, shrieked their witchy shrieks into the night.

A cop finally arrived and broke up the fight. But by that time both guys were so mutilated and concussed they were ambulanced to the emergency room fifty miles away in Cooper City.

Those guys, who knew what the hell drugs they were on. Surely on some heavy-duty shit, Yahchilane surmised.

One of the new drugs, the little foil packages looked like condom wrappers. You could buy the stuff at sketchy mini-marts and gas stations. How it was legal, anybody's guess.

A kid in Miami snorted the stuff. Two hours later, he was eating off a guy's face in Coconut Grove Mall. Just tackled the poor old janitor down in the food court and gnawed off his nose.

Finally the cops arrived and told the kid they'd shoot if he didn't stop. The kid looked over his shoulder and growled, the man's eyeball hanging out of his mouth.

The police shot him dead in front of all of those families.

Scarred for goddamn life, those kids.

One year, 2019, a four-day fog fell over the island. Fog so thick that walking through it left Yahchilane's denim clothes soaked. Fog so thick the bridge appeared swallowed in the distance, bifurcated. Yahchilane had never seen such fog on the island, could not recall such strange weather.

The fog collected in Yahchilane's black hair like jewels.

A hundred yards out all was lost in an opaque pearlescent curtain. A ghost world. The purse seiners and sardine boats were dark lurking shapes that might as well have been phantom galleons risen from the depths, summoned by the occulted weather.

As Henry Yahchilane's cancer remained in remission he noticed big changes in the weather. On the television news. Right on Emerald Island, at his doorstep.

The flash floods were fiercer now, the droughts drier and longer, the summers so brutally hot that breathing the air felt like sucking gelatin into your lungs. Your mind swam. You saw mirages in the distance, summer specters evanescing and shimmering, as if beheld through the warp of melting glass. The tar roads turned gummy under the gamma ray sun. Yahchilane thought of the La Brea Tar

Pits. A woolly mammoth and sabre-toothed tiger bones mired in sludge.

One day Yahchilane saw a group of eight or ten turkey vultures swarm upon a live raccoon. The animal was tottering alongside the road nosing through the wickery wildflowers for grub and then suddenly, all at once, the birds swooped upon him.

A horrifying spectacle. Like a gang rape. They didn't even wait for the raccoon to die. The evil black wings flapped up a tempest.

Yahchilane caught a glimpse of the animal's face, the pure abject terror, its fangs bared in a shocked rictus, its yellow eyes rolling wide, as the birds ripped it apart, guts stretching like pink taffy.

Holy Mary Mother of god, Yahchilane thought.

Some years there were no winters at all. No denying, water was encroaching toward the shaggy-shingled barrel-shaped house, a few feet every year. Numbers and figures on the news: bullshit. It was worse than anybody speculated. Ancient though he was, Yahchilane knew damn well what he saw.

Worse. Far worse.

Across the bridge, on the mainland? These midsummer tempests, only a matter of time before the dilapidated remains of the Florida Man Mystery House were swept away and swallowed under.

Some summers the heat lingered unabated into Christmas. If it weren't for the decorations in town, the lights and tinsel and grubby plastic Santas and reindeer bedecking the storefronts and the pastel cracker cottages, Yahchilane would have no idea it was the holidays.

If it weren't for the kids, he wouldn't give a shit.

He saw them less often these days. They were the matriarchs and patriarchs of their own big families and clans now. They were scattered and busy. Emerald Island was very far away.

"If only you'd get your stubborn ass to Tallahassee and take a plane," his kids and grandkids would gripe and wheedle over the phone.

"Okay, honey, next year," he'd tell them.

Yahchilane never put much stock in his age. Only now he felt har-
bingers of death in his bones. Aches and pains beset his body. Not
the sharp stomach-swooning agonies of his surgery and recovery so
many years ago, but a constant minor-key fugue. And fogginess
clouded his brain. Sometimes he'd find himself in front of the open
refrigerator with no idea what brought him there.

His lady friends came around less. That's how he thought of
them. Lady friends. And in turn, many of them would call him boyfriend, others man friend, and one woman named Janey the psychic
called him a fuck buddy. But now, many of them were too old to
drive. Or fuck, for that matter. Join the club, Yahchilane thought.
One was blind. Another, she took a cab all the way from outside
Emerald City to see him, the sweetheart, but that was the last time
he saw her and that was going on three years now. He figured her
dead.

His walks around the island grew shorter. Some days he was so
sapped he could only manage dragging the cheap aluminum chair to
the edge of the sea and sitting with his face in the sun.

At night there was still so little light pollution on the island that
to look up into the sky was to fall into it.

Galaxies upon galaxies.

The mother of a thousand plants.

The mother to a thousand galaxies.

The spectacle made him acutely aware of his insignificance.

The vastness of what he didn't know and couldn't imagine was a
cold comfort.

Some nights Henry Yahchilane would stand in front of the television
and clutch the remote as if he was wringing a chicken's neck, flicking through the channels, mashing the buttons with his knobby callused fingers.

Always bad news.

Bad news, pill commercials. More bad news.

The news seemed to get worse and worse. He was old enough to know it wasn't just his imagination. Stabbings in airports. School massacres with assault rifles.

As he watched the footage a look would siege Yahchilane's face as if he'd bit into a rancid apple.

Florida Man this, Florida Man that. Florida Man at large.

It wasn't really funny anymore, the Florida Man thing.

FLORIDA MAN BOMBS SCHOOL. FLORIDA MAN IN KKK OUTFIT KILLS BLACK TEEN WITH PITCHFORK. FLORIDA MAN BULLDOZES MOSQUE.

The biggest news these days: The current president, who Yahchilane only deigned to call President Shit-for-Brains, suffered from early onset of dementia, Alzheimer's.

People were already on edge. Earthquake weather. Wildfires swallowed swaths of the California coast. Fifty mile infernos. Tornado cells decimated Birmingham and Jackson and Mobile. Floods submerged New Orleans and New York City. A sinister brown fog blanketed Peshawar like atomized rust. A floating island of plastic blazed off the coast of Honduras. The raging conflagration, viewed from a space satellite, looked like a marooned island aflame in a sea of darkness.

During the hurricane season one year, a series of demonic storms churned up in the Caribbean. Category five storms. Such storms the forecasters and scientists had never seen. Storms without precedent, though doomsayers among the meteorologists for decades had predicted the day.

Now here it was.

The time of reckoning.

And they delivered this news with a kind of grim vindicated aplomb. *Like I've been saying for years, folks. Here we go.*

Polar vortexes and frostquakes and fire tornados.

They gave the storms human names, the names of boys and girls, men and women.

Yahchilane remembered many of the big Florida storms. Donna. Camille. Carla. Andrew. Irma.

He thought of Crowe the egghead and how he used to give all those cats names. His plants, his car, his snakes and frogs and lizards in his yard.

Gone for a while.

Just bones, powdered bones indistinguishable from all the grit of the Gulf.

Just bones, just sand.

As the summer wore on that year so did the heat. And so did the storms. Tropical squalls. Five or ten minute fits of rain, gushing tantrums, then over. Then the radioactive sun searing down again. The rain steaming off the tarmac and the car hoods and the tin roofs of the canneries.

Late in the summer bees started dropping from the sky like a strange flurry. Their dead bodies choked the gutters and clogged the drainage ditches. They covered mailboxes and cars and floated by the thousands in backyard swimming pools. They blanketed front yards and houses, macabre tapestries. Meteorologists attributed the phenomenon to a freak occurrence, a temporary vagary of weather. Others, scientists, voiced bleaker forecasts.

Slashing veils of rain washed dead bee bodies into the ocean so all you saw of the sea was a veldt of yellow fuzzy carcasses, a freak algae.

APHRA

APHRA THEY WERE CALLING THE STORM that October.

Hurricane Aphra.

Aphra, Yahchilane marveled. Giving such a thing as this storm a name like that.

On television meteorologists stood in front of the map of Florida. The whole state looked ensnared in the tentacles of a black octopus.

The epicenter, ground zero: Emerald Island.

This was after Hurricane Katrina, all those people crammed in the Superdome. After Hurricane Sandy. After people, thousands, were left for dead in Puerto Rico, no food or water or electricity for months. After volcanic eruptions on Hawaii. After the wildfires as big as Emerald Island that blazed up and down the California coast and turned whole vineyards and valleys to cinder.

Sirens blared and wailed. Evacuation orders were decreed. Too late for sandbagging and plywood and putting up storm shutters if they weren't already in place.

Still, some of the old Conchs stayed.

Including Henry Yahchilane.

At the Rum Jungle and at the Blue Parrot diner the patrons watched the televisions with mounting dread. People were closing their shops and stores.

The storefronts and restaurant windows were covered over with plywood. On the wood were messages spray-painted red.

SHELTER AT SEMINOLE HIGH SCHOOL. SHELTER AT CORAL REEF EL-EMENTARY (PET FRIENDLY). PRAY FOR EMERALD ISLAND AND EMERALD CITY! GOD BLESS YOU AND YOUR FAMILIES AND YOUR HOMES. GET OUT NOW! EVACUATE! IT'S ALMOST TOO LATE.

At the Hoggly Woggly grocery, the scene was pandemonium. Aisles were littered with manhandled goods. Plastic bags were ripped apart and eviscerated. Bread everywhere. Hotdog buns, cereal pellets, crackers.

Two men threw blows over the last pallet of drinking water. Yahchilane could hear the meaty thwacks.

One guy's tooth flew out of his mouth and skidded on the linoleum, leaving a squiggly bloody trail.

In the parking lot people were backing cars out of spaces and hitting grocery carts. "Hey, hey, you fuck, my daughter," some guy screamed. A pack of ripped-open saltines was spilled on the tarmac. Seagulls lunged with their beaks, battling for the shattered crackers.

The manager blurted over the intercom, "People, people. Panic idn't gonna help and fighting idn't gonna help."

Lightning flashed somewhere nearby. Thunder went off like dynamite.

As he loaded his beer and canned goods into the van, Yahchilane felt the boom in his heart.

"Aw, Jesus," a woman cried.

Sparks flew from a transformer. People's shocked faces incandesced.

Over the intercom, the store manager pleaded, "People, people, rippin' the bread idn't gonna help."

Someone in the haste of evacuation had left the Sea Cave Arcade open.

Just as well, Henry Yahchilane surmised, since most of the games were long out of commission and now it was more of a crack and weed connection among the local under-the-bridge types.

The television mounted on the concession stand was on the local news and they were showing the spaghetti models of the hurricane track. Every one showed the state in the storm's path.

Then they showed scenes of wreckage and chaos in Puerto Rico. Storm-blasted bridges, boats capsized and battered, the sea spuming in a white fury over brick walls and docks, swallowing beachside roads. Thousands of people awaited rescue, marooned on rooftops. Others navigating lagoons choked with wreckage in puny dinghies.

Yahchilane played pool alone in the empty arcade. Every so often someone would dash past on the sidewalk. Men carrying plywood. Other men toting sandbags and lumber and sheets of corrugated metal.

One of the volunteers, a woman wearing two fanny packs and a Tampa Bay Buccaneers jersey, glimpsed Yahchilane through the front window of the Sea Cave.

She doubled back and stepped inside, eyed him with a mixture of incredulity and contempt. Waited for him to make a remark. He did not. She waited another moment, asked, "Just gonna stand there?"

Yahchilane, cue in his hands, looked at his boots. Looked at the cue again, glanced around at the old arcade games. The red-knobbed joysticks balky and stuck.

"Do something," the woman said.

"I'm doing it."

Sarcastically the woman told him, "Thoughts and prayers."

"Thoughts and prayers," Yahchilane finally spoke, because he'd had enough of her megachurch-attending-ass, "I hear that said a lot."

Another man, an old Conch, passed with a wheelbarrow heaped with bricks. The sky behind him was a dark cinder.

The woman told Yahchilane, "Well, you can use some thinking. And praying."

He asked, "What're you thinking?"

"What?"

"I said what are you thinking."

"Mister, you need mental help."

"When you say thoughts and prayers what are you thinking?"

"The victims, mister."

"But thinking what? What are you praying? Specific."

"Mister, standing here suckin' down sodas and playing tiddledywinks. I ain't sharing philosophy lessons with you."

Yahchilane wanted to say, "Thoughts and prayers. This island doesn't give a shit. It'll shake you off like the last drops off a pissing dick."

Instead he said, "Thoughts and prayers."

"Go fuck yourself, mister," said the woman.

The cars and trucks headed away from the Gulf Coast in a long slow exodus, like those shambolic gypsy caravans of yore. Except now instead of revelers harried fathers and mothers helmed the wheels. Their faces were wretched, vexed. All they could cram of their earthly possessions, everything that was precious to them, filling their beat-up vehicles.

Just beginning, this shit.

This ordeal.

This clusterfuck.

He was on his way home, almost to the Emerald Island bridge, when he saw a phalanx of cars and trucks pulled over in the turnaround.

Yahchilane eased over to the shoulder and nosed into the scrum. He stepped out and joined the band of spectators. They were looking out at the bay, drained so thoroughly and quickly it was as though a dam had broke.

He remembered the long baths he used to take as a boy in the outdoor galvanized tub. The pulled plug, the water gushing out. God, so long ago. He remembered his mother telling him, "Time to get out, butterbean, before you turn into a prune."

Now, the bay was sinking lower and lower. The pilings showed. The marks the water and the storms had left over the years.

And the water sank lower still, lower and lower, until the harbor was a vast tundra of sulfur-stinking mud, the barnacled boats marooned and mired.

Fish were sucked up into the sky along with the water. Yahchilane spotted a few bull sharks in the mud. A porpoise. Rusted anchors. The carapace of a two-prop aircraft. An automobile of seventies vintage. A horse or mule skeleton. A refrigerator.

Artifacts dropped upon an apocalyptic waste.

By the time Henry Yahchilane got home, the clouds far out above the ocean were mottled green mackerel gray. Waterspouts tendriled out of them, delicate fingers touching the Gulf.

Yahchilane counted three, four. Then, incredibly, two more struck the rain-hazed ocean horizon.

Six waterspouts. The most he'd ever seen at once.

The last people on the island were evacuating. The old beach bums in their Jeeps and trucks with their luggage strapped to the roofs and their dogs crammed into backseats and truck beds. Their old jury-rigged trailers would be blown to scrap with the first stiff gusts, so they were wise to leave.

An old bohemian ornithologist couple braked their VW van in the street before Henry Yahchilane's house.

The old gray-haired woman shouted against the wind, "You live in that barrel house."

Yahchilane had to step closer to the van to hear. He was moving lawn ornaments from the outside to the inside, had the top of a birdbath in his arms. He set it down on the ground.

"The barrel house?" she repeated. "You don't plan on staying there."

"I live there."

"We know, Mr. Yahchilane. But you're staying there for the storm."

Yahchilane said he was.

Only now did the hippyish man at the wheel finally speak. Regarding Yahchilane he said, "Well, good luck, dude."

Yahchilane gave him a thumbs-up. "You too."

More cars gunned past, honking short inquisitive honks. What the fuck? The drivers meant with their little dipshit horns.

Yahchilane waved. Meaning: *Yeah, yeah, get outta here.*

As the last stragglers fled, the honking turned reprimanding. *Are you drunk? Are you senile? Are you crazy? Are you stupid?*

Probably, Yahchilane thought.

SOS (THE PHONE, THE PHONE)

EVERY OTHER MINUTE THE PHONE RANG and he stopped in the middle of what he was doing and cussed and went to the kitchen. "Who the fuck now?" He'd swipe the phone off the wall and then, mild-voiced, calm, answer, "Hello" or "Yes" or "Yahchilane residence."

"Are you staying?" was everyone's question.

At first he told them yes.

They tried to change his mind.

His mind was made.

Finally he started lying to people. Easier that way. "Yeah," he told Dr. Gabby Vu, now retired in Vermont, "getting out. About to leave. Packing. Took a swerve, didn't it."

It was Dr. Vu who told Yahchilane years ago around Crowe's funeral that he should go visit Crowe's beach house, now collapsing into the earth, the island, the sand.

Though they'd had relations, there was a lot of stuff she wasn't comfortable with going through, so the task was up to Yahchilane.

Going through the mess of Reed Crowe's house, amid the other paperwork, Yahchilane found a provisional will.

Provisional, of course.

Oh, you fuckin' egghead, he thought.

He would have to go see some people over at Big Cypress, get the papers certified.

Instead of feeling honored Yahchilane felt burdened. He would let his son, Seymour, take care of it. He loved to get tangled in such business, Seymour. Like his uncle Cy in that way. Ten years gone now.

Anyway, Seymour had been in touch with some egghead in Gainesville working on his dissertation called "The Eldritch." An archeology student, very eager to take a look at what Crowe had accumulated over the years.

Yahchilane continued looking the will over. His cash and savings to Eddie's daughters, $8,435.62. Prepaid savings plan, so it would appreciate.

Mostly Yahchilane spotted liens and warnings and final-chance bills. Jury summons completely ignored.

Much of the mail was addressed to Crowe's father. He'd heard rumors over the years, nothing that he ever prodded Crowe about because he figured Crowe liked his father just as much as he liked his, which is to say not at all.

Mostly though, the cubbyholes of his escritoire in the sunroom were filled with bright postcards.

Netherlands, Oslo, Luxembourg, Rome, Tokyo, Egypt.

Here was the atlas of Heidi's life so far.

Yahchilane tried to imagine Reed Crowe getting on an airplane headed to Tokyo. He couldn't. Beyond the powers of imagination. The man would have to be zip-tied, hog-tied, a restraining mask yanked over his mouth.

All of these places, and where had Reed Crowe gone?

The toilet.

Compared to Heidi Karavas, Crowe might as well have been a barnacle clinging onto a piling.

That, in essence, was the story of Reed Crowe's life in Henry Yahchilane's surmise, his biography writ on a scrap of fortune cookie paper, and there was nothing wrong with it at all. It was what it was. And he also surmised that what was true of Crowe was true of many men.

Yahchilane? What would his story be? "He wanted to be left the fuck alone."

An epitaph shorter than Crowe's.

Before the storm, Yahchilane's phone kept ringing.

It was usually his daughter, Natasha, or his son, Seymour. What choice did they leave him, all the pestering? "Yeah, going to a friend's," he'd tell them.

More pestering.

"No, I'm not smoking. Look, I got shit to do. Love you."

Two minutes later the phone rang again. "The phone, the phone, this fucking phone's gonna kill me."

One time it was his goddamn ex-wife of all people. "I'm good. I appreciate the gesture. Yeah, I'm smoking. I won't lie. Not too smart, you're right. Yeah, yeah, goin' to that shelter."

Sweet of her to call, he had to admit. Funny, how the grudges sloughed away over the years. Penelope, his ex, told him she was going up to Spokane to be with her sisters. He wished her well, knowing it was probably the last time he'd hear her voice unless something awful happened to one of the kids.

Eddie called from North Carolina, where he and Nina now lived. Mariposa was in New York City, Maribelle in Tibet.

Other people on the island were long gone. Chill was dead, stroke. Mr. Charley the hardware owner, long gone too, a slip in the tub, a crack of the skull against porcelain. Krumpp, may he rest in peace and also go fuck himself, met his end in a half-assed shootout. A holdup at his liquor store. Another gun casualty, another

Florida Man who tried to go out in a blaze of glory but ended up with his dick in the dirt and his ass in the headlines, the butt of a joke, $11.68 in the register.

GET OUT NOW

THE STORM WINDS STRENGTHENED. THE CLOUDS lit up like a stoked furnace. The bamboo wind chimes banged together dementedly. The wind tangled them up and the bunch of them slammed the side of the house. Yahchilane got up on a footstool, took the chimes down. Far down on the beach, miles distant, red warning flags snapped in the dark afternoon.

The seabirds watched Yahchilane as he scoped the beach from his porch. Anhingas and seagulls and pelicans winged against the stiffening gales, making little headway. They regarded him while flapping in place, a quality almost plaintive and accusatory in the beadlet eyes.

The feral beach cats were already hiding in their crannies under the house.

On the television the European models showed a last-minute strengthening and surge and had the hurricane aimed straight at the southwest Gulf Coast. Emerald City had hoped a last-minute jog of the storm. Prayed for a winnowing of its winds, a fraying of its fury.

No such luck.

Nope.

And anyways Yahchilane had always found this a strange sentiment. Say the hurricane was to strike somewhere else. Well, it was hitting somewhere else. With people. Who were also praying.

Thoughts and prayers.

In the hours before the first bands made landfall a strange calm befell the island. The coconut palms stood windless, the fronds like shaggy hula skirts.

But by afternoon the black thunderheads mounted and brought a blinding wall of water.

Yahchilane loved a good storm. Savored them more than he really should. Primal, this craving for biblical drama.

It stirred some caveman energy in his heart.

But this storm, Aphra, seemed another beast entirely.

On the local channels, old fat-faced Sheriff Schaffer held a news conference.

"Look at this egghead," Yahchilane said, standing before the television with his thumbs in his jeans pockets.

There would be no water, the supply cut off by the county, Schaffer said. No rescue. No service. All federal personnel were ordered away from the path of the storm. Should the power go out, which was an ironclad certainty given how fragile the infrastructure this deep and far-flung into the state, there was no telling when it would be restored.

Weeks, months.

"I know you guys been through ten of these. Some of you old Conchs been through fifteen, twenty. Believe me, you've never been through anything like this and all you folks thinking yeah, yeah, yeah, I heard it before, I promise you, you're wrong. You've never been through anything like this before. She's out to get us."

Then the weatherman came on. "Get outta Dodge!" he said with Pentecostal aplomb. "FEMA says this is gonna be a doozie!"

Before the bitch named Aphra made landfall, Henry Yahchilane hustled. He lugged the potted plants from the back porch to the garage. But soon the garage was full and he had to start hauling the plants inside the house.

He moved over five dozen bushes and small trees. He carried cacti and succulents and myriad tropical flowers and what spices and herbs would grow in the fierce Florida climate. The bigger plants Yahchilane had to haul with a wheelbarrow. The potted fig tree. The pepper tree.

By the time he had them all inside the house, it looked like some atrium. A jungle sprouted indoors.

Yahchilane's back was on fire with knots of pain. His knuckles and joints felt like there was sandy glass in them.

He thought of himself as a living fossil. Winnowed down to a flint knapping. One damn lung. He belonged in one of the Florida Man Mystery House exhibits.

Gone to jungle and rot long ago, that place. Another relic. Weeds standing two or three stories tall out of the cracked concrete. Plywood. NO TRESPASSING signs. As if anyone would have the desire.

THE SERPENTARIUM

HENRY YAHCHILANE HAD MOST OF THE storm shutters rolled down and all the plants and bushes of his garden sheltered and he was about to hunker down and wait out the storm when something occurred to him.

It occurred to him when he overheard a public service announcement on the radio about remembering to take care of the animals, the pets.

The zoo. The shitty three-acre zoo in Emerald City. A moribund place that should have been shut down and condemned long ago. Why anyone would want to pay good money to see these miserable half-dead creatures so estranged from their natural habitats had been beyond him.

Hard to believe that was more than half a century ago, working at the serpentarium. And hard to believe he still had his key, but he never handed it in and he had no reason to think that they'd changed the locks in the time since.

And, knowing the locals, Yahchilane had no reason to believe anyone in their haste to leave had given thought to the animals.

Yahchilane got on his poncho and got out his Coleman lantern and he plodded from the house against stinging needles of rain. He got into his van and drove across the deserted bridge. Waves broke, exploding foam over the sides. It was early evening but dark as night. He flicked the headlights on. In the beams he saw small silver catfish flopping in the road.

Henry Yahchilane watched through the rain-blinded windshield, waiting for a break in the storm. The serpentarium key was already picked out of the ring and gripped in his aching pruned fingers. He was sopping and shivering and short of breath and what he was about to do hadn't even started.

In the first hurricane winds, palm trees and banyans and jacarandas thrashed, branch shadows jigging in the sodium arc lights.

When there was a lull between gusts Yahchilane hobbled from the van across the empty lot. His ill-fitting poncho was ripped at the shoulders. Rain ran down his collar and down his back. It collected in his lung scar.

His galoshes crashed through muddy limestone puddles. "This is bullshit," he said into the chain-mail rain. "Those guys just leaving, assholes, pure bullshit."

Inside the serpentarium, the electricity was out. The emergency exit signs glowed red. Lightning flared in the windows and filled the cypress-paneled main room with phosphor light.

Glass dioramas the size of shoeshine boxes hung on the walls. In the lightning flashes, the taxidermied snakes and scorpions and tarantulas were imbued with sudden fleeting life. Their shadows stretched, quivered, recoiled, darted back to their cages.

In the reptile room the lights that usually glowed above the terrariums were dark. But Yahchilane could see in the red strain of the emergency lights and in the glow of his lantern the many lizards and toads and snakes. The skinks and geckos. Every time the thunder rumbled, the shelves trembled. The cages and terrariums shook. The reptiles darted into tiny plastic human skulls. Lizards retreated into small clay caves. Toads reared against the glass. Snakes tightened their coils and tasted the air with their dancing tongues.

Hunched and wincing from the volcanic pain in his back Yahchilane carried the reptile cages one by one and set them on the back porch under the awning. After twenty minutes he had all the terrariums and aquariums outside. His knees and his arms and his shoulders were on fire with pain. But Yahchilane kept moving. He unscrewed the lids, tipped the open cages sideways, away from the building.

He stood back and watched as the snakes and toads and lizards crept warily, almost reluctantly, into freedom.

Afterward Yahchilane went down the zoo's main concourse, his lantern swinging by its handle, its light feeble and wobbly, a measly island of illumination.

Ripping gales made his progress halting.

Cold rain bulleted his face.

Styrofoam cups and beer cans and potato chip wrappers flew in dervishes through the dark.

From their pens, their wigwams, their jungle gyms and concrete grottos, the spooked animals watched him. Their eyes were forsaken, accusatory. As if he were their jailer, the engineer of this pandemonium.

He went down the main thoroughfare and opened the cages one by one, fumbling through the beehive-sized wad of keys. "Motherfuckin' eggheads," Yahchilane spat into the pissing rain.

He went along opening gates, leaving them partially ajar, wary of what the animals might do with their perceived jailer. But the animals were just as wary of him.

They took a tentative step, froze, another tentative step, sniffing the air for danger.

A grim gray-faced chimp with cataracts frowned in the rain.

Onward.

An orangutan stared blearily, like a philosopher, at the dark weeping sky.

Onward.

A goat with a tumor-riddled back screamed in the downpour.

Onward.

Every so often Yahchilane would turn to see a head hung out indecisively. Inquisitively. It was hard at first to make out the kind of animal. Then he saw the stripe on the fur, the yellow eyes, the hunch of the hackled back.

A hyena, peering at him from down the lane.

"Get," he said.

The hyena growled. Advanced a step. Then it froze in a pouncing stance.

"Get lost," Yahchilane said. "Fuck you."

The hyena whimpered. But then its muscles relaxed, its tensed haunches loosened. By slow degrees it turned, casting a final backward look, baleful, at Yahchilane before loping away.

Yahchilane moved along the zoo's main concourse.

Toucan. Bobcat. Gray fox. Weasels and minks. Nutria. Two black bears and their cub. Rabbits.

Flamingos.

Then Henry Yahchilane became aware of an animal behind him. A smell, a huge lurking presence.

The hyena returned, he reckoned.

No.

Holy shit, no.

A jaguar. A gray female jaguar fully grown.

The animal looked at him. He looked at the animal.

The distance between them nothing for the animal to breach.

Yahchilane stood defiantly, his mouth a tight slash. His black hair whipped in corkscrew tendrils around his face. The bitter slantwise rain bulleted down.

The creature charged full bore.

Yahchilane yelled out a garbled curse—*gawfuckshi!*—crossed his arms as if to fend off a curse. Futile. He was knocked hard and windless to the ground. The creature was on top of him, Yahchilane's body trapped between the huge straddling legs. His face was smashed into the dirt and there was the taste of mud and blood in his mouth.

Fireflies flew figure eights inside his head.

The jaguar's massive animal stink was enough to make him gag. Musk and hay and the fetid meat stewed in the acid of its belly.

The jaguar lowered its face and breathed hotly on the back of Yahchilane's skull.

This is it, Yahchilane thought. Some way to go.

Those zoo motherfuckers.

The giant cat opened its mouth and swiped its sandpaper tongue down his neck.

Then, purring, the jaguar stepped away and strolled into the night.

Yahchilane struggled up. Shaking, nearly palsied, with adrenaline.

At the end of the zoo's main thoroughfare the animals were filing out.

Donkey, goat, hyena.

In the weird light they looked like the last creatures hoping to reach the ark before its departure.

The last stragglers, belated and bedraggled and beset.

THE TERRARIUM

A FEW HOURS LATER THE FIRST hard ragged bands of the hurricane were flaying the island when an SUV came jouncing up the drive of Henry Yahchilane's shaggy-shingled barrel-shaped house.

A figure emerged. A woman in a ragged poncho hunched and running through the gray tumult of rain. Late seventies, maybe somewhere in her eighties. Acajou skin, dark hair turned lavender gray. The hoodie of the olive drab poncho was cinched tight around her face.

Heidi. It took a moment for Yahchilane to recognize her, the rain was so blinding.

It had been so many years. How many? The last time he'd seen her, it was to deliver the news of Reed Crowe's passing. She had no idea of it because of the nature of her art-transporting job. Yahchilane had met her at a brasserie in the shadow of the Centre Pompidou. It was a gray day late in October, a bite of autumn in the air, the city trees turning to rust.

As soon as she sat across from him, she knew from his face, from his dour mien, that he was the bearer of bad tidings. "Is he gone?"

She'd expected this, Yahchilane realized.

And now her worst suspicion was proven true.

Smally, soberly, with closed eyes and lowered head, he nodded.

She asked how Crowe died. If he was in pain.

"Heart gave. He felt nothing."

She closed her eyes. As if trying to memorize a word. Or remember one. She inhaled a long quivering breath. Exhaled. "Oh god," she said. She pinched the bridge of her nose with shaking fingers. Then she opened her eyes and asked for a cigarette.

Yahchilane fished out his pack and shook it so a cigarette tip stuck out. She reached for it. Then Yahchilane reached across their tiny outdoor table and lit the cigarette with his sterling silver flip-top lighter. A raw wind was rising. Heidi's cheeks were rosing up.

"Was he alone? In general."

"He was dating a woman. Dr. Vu?"

Maybe the cigarette, something in Heidi's eyes snapped and they found their focus. "What're you doing here, Henry?"

He lit a cigarette for himself. "Just smoking."

"Come on."

"Never been. Getting old."

"Getting?"

"Yeah."

Her smile was sad and small and jittery, her eyes shiny with tears, but none spilled. "I hope you didn't come all this way to tell me."

Yahchilane said he was meeting his daughter in Amsterdam. A wedding gift.

Heidi raised her eyebrows. *On the honeymoon?* she meant.

"Her other wish was getting me out of the house and on a plane. So." He explained that they were a month into their honeymoon already, and it was a lifetime dream of hers, to see the Van Gogh Museum with her father.

"Nice guy?"

"Van Gogh?"

"I see Reed had an unfortunate influence on you."

"Pretty awful," Yahchilane joked. "A huge asshole, actually."

Not true at all. The young man, Torrie, was a math professor from George Washington University. The first African American math professor of the institution. Yahchilane called him Bo Paradiddly because the kid could play the drums like a red-hot mother-fucker. Krupa, Rich. James Brown shit.

"The only way drums should be recorded is mono," the kid told Yahchilane.

Yahchilane couldn't agree more.

In this manner the young man endeared himself at once to Yahchilane. He'd expected to be wary of the kid. Because he was wary of most people. And this was his daughter the man was marrying. Yahchilane could not imagine a better husband or son-or-law and considered himself lucky in this regard.

Yahchilane had also visited Heidi to deliver a letter. He'd discovered it in Crowe's sunroom, atop the scroll-top armoire. *Dear Heidi*, it began. Yahchilane glimpsed through several pages. Not out of nosiness. The last thing Yahchilane had wanted to know about was any kink or strangeness or secrets now that Crowe was dead. They already had too many fucking secrets. But no, this was a love letter, Yahchilane could tell from just a cursory glance.

Love. Sorry. Lily. Otter. Mistake. Love. Mistake. Otter.

These words leapt at him.

And, though the letter was unfinished, perhaps owing to the fact of Reed Crowe's pathological aversion of the mail, or owing to the fact of his habit of seldom finishing what he started, he saw a few lines that stayed with him.

For what it's worth, the only time I felt kiddish in my heart was with you, Heidi. I love you, Heidi Crowe. I love you, Heidi Karavas. I always will.

And now, here was Heidi Karavas, all this time later.

Yahchilane threw back the hood of his poncho just to make sure. The wet tendrils of his black hair snapped at his skin. Heidi looked up at him. Gaunt and sun-beaten, cheekbones that knifed through his face. His clothes were still muddy from the zoo. Bits of chaff and bark and leaf litter stuck to him.

"The hell happen to you, Henry? You get trapped in a tornado?"

Yahchilane leaned closer, cupped his ear. The storm was so loud he couldn't hear.

Heidi tried again, "Tornado pick up your ass?"

"Jaguar attacked me."

"Communication issues. This dang wind. Jeez Louise."

So her hearing was going too, like his. Hard to believe she was an old woman. Well, an older woman. Still youthful, especially compared with Henry Yahchilane's old Jurassic ass.

"Come inside," he told her.

"Henry, this place'll be blown off the map."

"Your poncho is ruined," Yahchilane told her. And it was, the plastic beneath the armpit ripped, the sleeve ragged and torn, a flap snapping in the wind.

"Henry, you're crazy staying."

"Yeah, lady, I know."

Far off in the foggy distance, gray and ghostlike, the ocean raged. Waves five, six men high. Tall as the masts of ships. Thirty-foot waves crested and toppled, erupting with volcanic explosions of foam.

"Let's go inside and get you a new poncho. One minute."

"One minute," Heidi said.

Inside the shaggy-shingled barrel-shaped house the porch plants and citrus trees and pepperbushes crowded the rooms with their leaves. Heidi laughed. An indoor jungle. And scattered here and there in the big main room were pots and pans pinging with rainwater. Small tinny plinks sounded all around them, some fey miniature tune from a broken music box.

"Welcome to the jungle," Yahchilane said.

"You're the only one left," Heidi said. "Besides the crazies. The druggies. The alkies."

"My people."

"I gotta go, Henry. Let's stop bullshitting. Come."

"I know, I know, boss." Henry Yahchilane motioned with his head, started walking to the hallway closet. "Get you sorted first." He opened the closet and pulled the cord and the bare bulb lit. Arranged neatly upon the shelves were flashlights and hurricane lamps and candles and sundry other storm supplies. Canned goods. A first aid kit.

And a stack of several ponchos, new and still wrapped in their cellophane bags.

Yahchilane handed her one. "Not gonna do anyone any good with pneumonia."

Heidi took the poncho. "Are you okay? Your health?" Heidi asked.

Yahchilane nodded. Waggled his hand. "Old as shit."

"Lovely. I wish we had more time to catch up."

Now Yahchilane asked Heidi where she was going.

"Colombia."

"In this weather?"

She told him she would return to Colombia, Bogotá, after the storm. Now, she was staying in Tarpon Springs. Volunteering, the evacuation effort.

"Hell getting to Tarpon now," Yahchilane told her.

"Tarpon'll be fine. This part, though."

"I've heard it before."

"But this time."

She was right, he knew. He lifted his eyebrows wearily. "Yeah, looks that way."

They were quiet for a moment. The storm raging like a kraken, bellowing into every crack and corner of the house. The wind shrieking like a mob of aggrieved ghosts in the eaves and flues.

The kitchen phone rang. Heidi asked Yahchilane if he was going to get it. He told her no.

"Probably Seymour. Five times today. Five times I told him I'm staying. Natasha got the hint after the second try."

"I'm wasting my breath, but here I go. Come and stay in Tarpon Springs. Family's got a place. Hurricane shelter."

"Tarpon, you better get going."

"I know the back roads."

"And the side ways. And the byways. The down roads, the up roads. Florida lady. Florida woman."

"I'd beg you to leave," Heidi said. "I guess I already did."

Yahchilane was looking at Heidi.

"What's this look?" she asked.

He shook his head. "I just remember you walking on the island. When you were a little girl. I guess you were almost a teenager. I was already a geezer. Used to see you and Reed walking on the island."

"We used to see you too."

"I used to think, Wow, those two sure look happy."

"We were. For a while."

"Yeah, yeah, I know that story all right."

Heidi's look changed. "I used to have a crush on you."

"Bullshit."

"It's true. I thought you were very mysterious. God, I was a baby."

"I know. You still are."

"You're so full of shit. Henry, it's the end of the world. What're we doing?"

"Coffee to go?"

"Stop it," Heidi said.

"Florida woman," Yahchilane said.

"Florida broad," Heidi Karavas said.

"Florida dame."

"Florida bitch."

"Come on, now, young lady."

"I bet Reed called me that all the time. Bitch."

"Never ever once and I'll swear on it."

"I trust you, Henry."

"Few plants? I got succulents. Cacti. Going cheap."

"Stop it, you."

"Yeah, you'll be driving in rivers. Go, go."

They embraced. Awkwardly at first, but then they loosened and hugged like old familiars. As if the same realization struck them both at once.

This was it. Never again would they see each other.

"Okay, man," said Henry Yahchilane to Heidi Karavas's back as she went into the slate gray ripping curtains of rain, her yellow poncho blowing and snapping.

"Okay, man," she said. Yahchilane couldn't tell from her strained voice if she was crying or laughing or both.

And then she was in her car, taillights fading and finally vanishing in the howling rain.

BUTTERBEAN

LATER THAT EVENING HE WAS LOOKING out at the gray bluster when he sighted the silhouette of a stout man staggering near the waves. He appeared to be sweeping with a broom. Then Yahchilane realized: metal detecting.

Lunatic, Yahchilane thought.

FLORIDA MAN METAL DETECTS DURING THE END OF THE WORLD.

Perhaps it was an old man escaped from the nursing home in Emerald City. One of those old time Elks or Kiwanis, a World War II vet, thinking he was minesweeping before the cavalry stormed the beach.

"Hey, mister," Yahchilane called, yelling as loud as he could. Yelling as loud as a one-lunged man could.

Futile. Like shouting into a typhoon.

Yahchilane went into the house to fetch the flashlight and binoculars. Outside he beamed a signal with the flashlight. Then he peered through the binoculars, glassed the horizon.

The man, whoever he was, gone.

Vanished in the tempest haze.

But then Yahchilane spotted something else. What appeared to be a huge moving sand dune.

He wondered if he was hallucinating, in the grip of some wild fantasia. A stroke.

But he saw the shape move again. Then a neck emerged, a head.

A gargantuan turtle.

He wondered if it was Bogart, Crowe's old turtle from the Florida Man Mystery House, but if he recalled correctly that was a freshwater.

This one, just as big, though.

It waddled slowly, stolidly, into the raging surf, the pounding waves.

Yahchilane set down the flashlight and binoculars.

He groaned and reached and yanked down the last storm shutter, the rusted bearings crying as it jerked down.

The electricity went out after midnight. In the dark Yahchilane flicked his cigarette lighter and went up the stairs.

And as the storm grew louder and darkness grew darker, into greater darkness he went, retreating into the bedroom of his shaggy-thatched barrel-shaped house. Not the thinnest tracery of outside light showed. Dark as death.

But he knew the way blind. These steps to his bed taken so many times through the years that a path was worn in the floor, a sickle-shaped trail grooved into the wood.

He sat on the edge of the bed and he unlaced his boots. He took them off and set them neatly side by side on the floor. Then he took off his socks and he rolled them up and shoved them in the throats of his boots. Wearing his jeans and denim shirt he lay flat on his back above the covers. Just as he used to when he was a baby when his mother found him quietly awake in the middle of the night. His brothers and sisters were colicky and loud and quarrelsome and would cry over anything.

But not Yahchilane.

His mother would find him awake and above the covers in the dark, "Everybody always fussing, but you little butterbean, why don't you cry, Mr. Little Butterbean?"

Now the wind cried in the cracks of the house. The storm wept in the timbers. All around him the tempest raged like a curse finally arrived. A cosmic comeuppance. The leviathan, the kraken, coming to suck him and everyone and everything left on Emerald Island into the black drink.

But it was a good house. Looking back Yahchilane surmised them the best years of his life, sleeping on the beach in the tent, building the house.

How deeply he slept those nights, under the stars. How careless were his dreams then. The bark flakes in his hair and the good smell of fresh-cut wood still on his hands in the mornings.

And now Henry Yahchilane lay back easy. He lived this long and he'd gone this far, he'd done and seen so much, he could think of nothing else left to do, and where else would he do it but here, right here?

He was a Florida man.

It's where he belonged.

Few dead men have such good fortune.

ACKNOWLEDGMENTS

My mother, Lynn Elizabeth McIlvaine, above all. I love you, Mom, and if it wasn't for you I'd surely be a devious drug-addicted con-artist. Well, it's not too late! Let's see how this book fares.

My brother, Mike Cooper, one of my most perspicacious and generous early readers.

My long-suffering partner, Kathy Conner, the same.

Old chums Richard Pearlman and Claudia Sanchez.

My mother's fiancé, Greg Smith, for being a good sport for more than a decade. I'm glad I got to spend time with your brother and thanks for telling me your stories.

Josh Joseph, Jesus Christ, brother, the pep talks. And the loans!

To the memory of Lily and Cleo, two great cats who died in my arms, a year apart, during the writing of this book. You were my little gremlins and I don't give a shit about how much "cat lady" ribbing I get.

To the memory of all the dear idols we've lost in the last five years. It's been a slaughterhouse. I can name the names. You know them. But for me, my "idols"—as close as I have to any—died when I was writing this. I thought of them and how much they inspired me over the years, and that's the only way I could really wrap my head around the loss. Right now. RIP, David Berman, David Bowie, and Mark E. Smith.

I also wish to thank the independent booksellers throughout America and Europe who championed *The Marauders* and gave it a second life. I wish I was the kind of person who wrote thank-you notes. But once that Hallmark shit gets started, there's no end. This is not a slippery-slope fallacy. Send one, then everybody wants a card. So I can never just send one. You understand. Big prize people, well, that's different and you just have to because otherwise you seem like a barnyard animal.

But I digress.

I thank Forrest Anderson and the people at Catawba College for being such generous and gracious hosts. The same for the people behind Festival America, in Vincennes, especially my editors Francis Geffard and Carol Menville. Also, thank you to all the staff at one of the best bookstores in France, Millepages, for taking care of me when I was writing a terrible second novel. I didn't know it. You didn't know it. But here we are and I'm happy that you finally have a second book to sell. Ha!

The same for the folks involved with the Crooks' Corner Prize in Chapel Hill. The same for my sponsors and friends at La Marelle, Marseille, where a good portion of *Florida Man* was written. Thank you for your hospitality. It's because of generosity like yours I was impelled to slog forward when I wanted to forgo the damn thing.

The kindness of strangers. We can use a little more of that these days, eh? Well, you showered it upon me. Thank you.

Apropos, thanks as well to all the good people in Switzerland who work at the Librairie du Midi, especially Marie Musy, who brought me an audience I might not have otherwise enjoyed.

Thank you to Germany's internationales literaturfestival for its hospitality when I began this book in the autumn of 2017 in Berlin.

Thank you to Lee Ofman for letting me use his "Miami Dolphins Fight Song."

I'd be remiss if I didn't thank some other people. The krewe at New York Pizza, Magazine Street, New Orleans. You encouraged me through periods of doubt and hardship.

Thank you to my New Orleans friends who did the same. You know who you are. It's been a tough few years. On all of us. But we're getting through.

Thank you to my agents and editors who work so hard on my behalf—in America, in particular Duvall Osteen, Ben Greenberg,

Clio Seraphim, and Dennis Ambrose. Thanks for believing in me. This book was a real goddamn mess.

Thanks to the libraries and book clubs.

Thank you, reader.

Best,

TC

FLORIDA MAN

9-6-17

to

8-21-19

WORKS CONSULTED

The Enduring Seminoles: From Alligator Wrestling to Casino Gaming, by Patsy West, 1998.

Weird Florida, by Charlie Carlson, 2005.

National Audubon Society Field Guide to the Southeastern States, by Peter Alden and Gil Nelson, 1999.

Cryptozoology A to Z: The Encyclopedia of Loch Monsters, Sasquatch, Chupacabras, and Other Authentic Mysteries of Nature, by Loren Coleman and Jerome Clark, 1999.

Totch: A Life in the Everglades, by Loren G. "Totch" Brown, 1993.

Pulphead: Essays, by John Jeremiah Sullivan, 2011.

Hotel Scarface: Where Cocaine Cowboys Partied and Plotted to Control Miami, by Roben Farzad, 2011.

Histories of Southeastern Archeology, edited by Shannon Tushingham, Jane Hill, and Charles H. McNutt, 2002.

Southeastern Ceremonial Complex: Chronology, Content, Context, edited by Adam King, 2007.

The Story of the Chokoloskee Bay Country, by Charlton W. Tebeau (with the reminiscences of pioneer C. S. "Ted" Smallwood), 1976.

Death in the Everglades: The Murder of Guy Bradley, America's First Martyr to Environmentalism, by Stuart B. McIver, 2003.

Ill Nature: Rants and Reflections on Humanity and Other Animals, by Joy Williams, 2001.

The Florida Keys: A History & Guide, by Joy Williams, 2003.

A New Deal for Southeastern Archaeology, by Edwin A. Lyon, 1996.

ABOUT THE AUTHOR

Tom Cooper was born in Fort Lauderdale, Florida. He now lives in New Orleans. *The Marauders* was his first book and *Florida Man* is his second.

ABOUT THE TYPE

This book was set in Fairfield, the first typeface from the hand of the distinguished American artist and engraver Rudolph Ruzicka (1883–1978). Ruzicka was born in Bohemia (in the present-day Czech Republic) and came to America in 1894. He set up his own shop, devoted to wood engraving and printing, in New York in 1913 after a varied career working as a wood engraver, in photoengraving and banknote printing plants, and as an art director and freelance artist. He designed and illustrated many books, and was the creator of a considerable list of individual prints—wood engravings, line engravings on copper, and aquatints.